THE CHAOS AGENT

THE CHAOS AGENT

MARK GREANEY

BERKLEY
NEW YORK

BERKLEY
An imprint of Penguin Random House LLC
penguinrandomhouse.com

Copyright © 2024 by MarkGreaneyBooks LLC
Penguin Random House supports copyright. Copyright fuels creativity, encourages diverse voices, promotes free speech, and creates a vibrant culture. Thank you for buying an authorized edition of this book and for complying with copyright laws by not reproducing, scanning, or distributing any part of it in any form without permission. You are supporting writers and allowing Penguin Random House to continue to publish books for every reader.

BERKLEY and the BERKLEY & B colophon are registered trademarks of
Penguin Random House LLC.

Library of Congress Cataloging-in-Publication Data

Names: Greaney, Mark, author.
Title: The chaos agent / Mark Greaney.
Description: New York : Berkley, 2024. | Series: The Gray Man ; 13
Identifiers: LCCN 2023040199 (print) | LCCN 2023040200 (ebook) |
ISBN 9780593548141 (hardcover) | ISBN 9780593548158 (e-book)
Subjects: LCSH: Assassins—Fiction. | Artificial intelligence—Fiction. |
LCGFT: Thrillers (Fiction) | Spy fiction. | Novels.
Classification: LCC PS3607.R4285 C47 2024 (print) |
LCC PS3607.R4285 (ebook) | DDC 813/.6—dc23/eng/20230911
LC record available at https://lccn.loc.gov/2023040199
LC ebook record available at https://lccn.loc.gov/2023040200

Printed in the United States of America
1st Printing

Interior art: Black-and-white Paris map © Nicola Renna / Shutterstock.com
Book design by Kelly Lipovich

For Scott Miller. A great agent, and
an even better friend.

It has become appallingly obvious that our technology has exceeded our humanity.

—ALBERT EINSTEIN

CHARACTERS

COURTLAND GENTRY: former CIA Special Activities Division paramilitary operations officer; former CIA Directorate of Operations singleton operator

ZOYA ZAKHAROVA: former SVR (Russian foreign intelligence) officer

ZACK HIGHTOWER: former CIA Special Activities Division paramilitary operations officer/team leader

MATT HANLEY: CIA deputy chief of station, Bogotá, Colombia

SIR DONALD FITZROY: former MI5 (British domestic intelligence) officer; former owner of Cheltenham Security Services

CHRIS TRAVERS (VICTOR ONE): CIA Special Activities Center paramilitary operations officer/team leader

JOE "HASH" TAKAHASHI (VICTOR TWO): CIA Special Activities Center paramilitary operations officer

JACK TUDOR: owner of Lighthouse Risk Control Ltd.; former MI5 (British domestic intelligence) officer

ANGELA LACY: CIA senior operations officer

ANTON HINTON: entrepreneur, software developer, inventor, futurist, owner of Hinton Lab Group

GARETH WREN: vice president (operations) for Hinton Lab Group; former warrant officer 1, SAS (Special Air Service)

XINYUE "KIMMIE" LIN: personal assistant to Anton Hinton, Hinton Lab Group

KOTANA ISHIKAWA: doctor of information science, Osaka University, Japan

TOMER BASCH: lethal autonomous weapons (LAW) and artificial intelligence (AI) expert

JU-AH PARK: doctor of electrical and computer engineering, Yonsei University, Korea

RICHARD WATT: director of the Defense Innovation Unit, U.S. Department of Defense

LARS HALVERSON: chief technology officer, Massachusetts Automation Endeavors, Inc.

DR. VERA RYDER: artificial intelligence ethicist

WILLIAM "TREY" WATKINS: deputy director for operations, CIA

CARLOS CONTRERAS: Mexican intelligence, surveillance, and reconnaissance (ISR) technician

MARTINA SOMMER: former German Federal Police communications specialist

THE CHAOS AGENT

ONE

Morning sun warmed the rain-slick tin roofs, forming blankets of steam that rose in perceptible waves as they buffeted the sixteen-ounce quadcopter drone buzzing over the little town. Panajachel, Guatemala, stood at 5,200 feet of elevation, so the four tiny plastic rotors spun furiously in thin, moist air, the machine moving southeast at a steady pace, its camera taking in everything below.

The town lies on the northern shore of Lake Atitlán, a fifty-square-mile body of water in an immense volcanic crater in the Guatemalan Highlands. A strikingly beautiful place in the middle of a bitterly impoverished country, the town is a *way*-off-the-beaten-path tourist attraction for budget travelers from all over the globe. Cool in the mornings this time of year, even despite the sunshine, its air is many orders of magnitude cleaner and clearer than smoggy Guatemala City, a three-hour drive to the east.

Few people walked the cobblestone streets at seven in the morning on a Saturday—most visitors were sleeping off Friday night's bar bill—but the drone's camera locked on to a trio of young women pounding thick tortillas by a smoky kettle fire next to a tienda, registering their faces in a fraction of a second and then dismissing them as non-targets in a fraction more.

An old man pushing a vending cart took longer to evaluate, his cowboy hat obstructing the periocular region of his face where most biometric identification data was acquired, but in under a second and a half the man turned his head and then his features were registered by the eye in the sky. Almost instantly the drone's onboard artificial intelligence image classifiers told the machine that he was not the subject it was hunting for.

The device then whirred over a small two-story red apartment building on Callejon Santa Elena, and here a blond woman in a green tank top and jean shorts stepped out onto a balcony and began hanging laundry over a clothesline.

The camera caught the movement, but it did not have the right angle to scan the face because the wet towels she hung to dry were in the way.

Drone Reconnaissance Nineteen, or RC19, kept going; there was no need for it to stop, because five identical airships crisscrossed the sky above Panajachel in search of their collective target, each on a coverage route determined by a pilot working in the back of a rented van below, and augmented by artificial intelligence. Sooner or later, RC23, RC29, or one of the others would pass by this street from a different trajectory and assess the face of the blond woman, just as they had been doing with everyone else in town this morning.

The target was here, the pilot knew it; it was just a matter of pinning down the target's location.

RC19 flew on down Callejon Santa Elena, heading off in the direction of Calle Principal and the center of town, systematically scrutinizing unsuspecting faces from three hundred feet in the air.

The blonde on the balcony never saw or heard the copter. She finished hanging her towels and then took a moment more to look out over the town and sniff the fresh air. The smell of cooking fires, baking bread, and wet jungle flora were all pleasantly jumbled together.

She closed her eyes and turned her face to the sun. A cooler breeze drifting up from the lake caused goose bumps to form on her bare arms. She smiled a little. She liked it here. No, she loved it here. She could see herself staying a few weeks or more, although she knew that wasn't the plan.

The plan was to keep moving. She didn't like the plan, but the plan had kept her alive for four months, so she guessed she'd stick to it.

With a wistful sigh, Russian national Zoya Fyodorova Zakharova stepped back inside the second-story apartment, walking on bare feet through a small bedroom, past a pair of messy twin beds, each set up with blankets and backpacks under the covers to give the appearance of bodies at rest.

She stopped at the open closet door.

A dark-complected bearded man with tousled brown hair lay on the floor under a well-worn but still colorful poncho. He opened his eyes and looked up at her, his legs slightly bent to fit in the small space they both had shared the night before.

Zoya lowered herself down and lay with him, curling up to fit in the closet, tucking herself under the poncho. She rested her head on a pillow taken from one of the beds and faced the man lying there.

"Sleeping in?" she asked, sounding like an American from the Midwest, with no hint of Russia in her voice.

The man rubbed his bleary eyes before speaking. "What time is it?"

"Seven fifteen."

"I was up for a . . . couple hours in the night."

"Again?" The woman propped her head up on an elbow as she looked at him, no attempt to hide her concern. "How many is 'a couple'?"

"Two a.m. till five."

"Shit, Court."

Courtland Gentry rubbed his eyes again. "I'm fine."

"The insomnia is getting worse, isn't it?"

"It's not insomnia. Just having some trouble sleeping."

"That's literally the definition of insomnia. The last couple of months . . . it's more and more."

Still smiling, but more emphatically than before, he said, "I'm okay. Really. Just need some coffee."

Zoya held his gaze. "What's going on?"

Court sat up now, and she did the same. They put their backs to the wall of the otherwise empty closet, their feet sticking out into the bedroom. He said, "I don't know. It's just . . . everything's great . . ."

"But?"

"But . . . doesn't it kind of feel like the clock is running out on all this?"

"All what?"

"Peace and quiet. The walls are closing in. I can feel it."

While Court seemed unsure, Zoya was resolute. "Well, *I* can't. We've been smart. We've kept mobile. We've stayed off the radar." Pointing a finger towards the balcony and the town beyond, she said, "We hunker down here a few more days, then we move on. Same as before. I was thinking we could head overland towards Honduras next. We'll stay lost."

Court nodded a little, but he seemed unconvinced.

"No?" she asked.

"Yeah, sure. But . . . but the enemy gets a vote, too. I'm not worried about *our* strategy, I'm worried about the adaptability of our adversaries."

"Christ," Zoya said with a little laugh. "You just woke up two minutes ago and you're already talking about the adaptability of our adversaries. You remain one dialed-in son of a bitch."

"It kind of seemed like *you* started this conversation."

She put a hand on the side of his face. "We're solid. We're running non-stop countersurveillance, and we've had no problems. Not here, not in Bolivia, not in Ecuador. In Peru we spooked, we'll never know if we were being overly cautious or not, but we got out of there, and since then we haven't sensed anything. We've got nothing to worry about."

"We have *everything* to worry about."

She ignored the comment. "We'll keep up the vigil, and if we *do* smell anything we don't like, anything at *all*, even if the hairs on the back of one of our necks stand up like they did in Cusco . . . then we bolt." She added, "What else can we do?"

Court nodded. "Okay."

She eyed him another long moment. "There's something else going on with you, isn't there?" she asked.

His eyebrows furrowed. "No. Nothing." He brightened suddenly and looked into her eyes. "I love you."

She didn't return the smile. Still, she replied, "I love you."

They kissed, and then he asked, "What's on the agenda?"

"There's an agenda?" She said it jokingly, but she knew when Court was trying to change the subject. After a moment she let it go. "I have to run to the market. We should grab lunch after at that place by the lake we saw yesterday." When he didn't reply, she said, "It's fine. They have a courtyard, masonry construction. We put our backs to the wall facing the entrance, we scan for trouble, we eat our lunch and enjoy our day."

"Backs to the wall. Sounds like a plan."

"Enjoying our day is the plan. 'Backs to the wall' is just a tactic."

Court climbed to his feet, helped Zoya up, and kissed her again. His right hand brushed her left forearm, and she felt him run his fingers over a ragged gunshot wound there. He traced his fingers up to another scar on her arm and then felt around to two more small scars on the left side of her back.

"Four months ago tomorrow," he said softly.

"Still get that nerve tingle in my elbow every now and then, but that's to be expected. Doesn't hurt. When I caught an AK round to my hip a few years ago, that sucked much worse."

"Yeah." He raised her forearm and looked at the wound there, then kissed it. "You really need to stop getting shot."

She shrugged. "I've made it four months in a row. Shooting for five."

"As long as no one is shooting back." He brushed her hair back behind her left ear. Holding a strand and looking at it, he said, "I'm still not used to you as a blonde."

"I'll dye it purple next. See how that strikes you."

Court smiled as he headed for the bathroom. He was shirtless and Zoya registered his lean but muscular back and arms, well pocked with scars— he had more blemishes than she did, but the way things had been going in the past couple of years, she wondered if she'd someday catch up.

He flashed a look back her way, gave a last little smile, then stepped into the bathroom. As he disappeared behind the closing door, the smile on Zoya's face faded.

She felt absolutely certain he was keeping something from her, and almost certain that she knew what it was.

TWO

Between them, the foursome preparing to tee off at the eighth hole of Baylands Golf Links had a combined net worth of over six billion dollars, which necessitated the presence of three of the five bodyguards in the two carts parked near the eighth tee.

The other pair of bodyguards were Department of Defense employees, and while their protectee was a pauper when compared to the rest of the foursome, a meager government employee on a meager government salary, he was no less worthy of protection.

The weather in Palo Alto this May Saturday morning was characteristically exquisite, and the players had enjoyed nearly an hour of golf and conversation on the course within sight of the South Bay without any business creeping in.

And this was exactly the way Rick Watt liked it. The oldest of the players by nearly two decades, he'd invited the other three out for a relaxing morning, free of business. After golf, all four, plus their security, would head back to his office for a Saturday afternoon of meetings, and only *then* would he get down to the reasons he'd asked for this get-together.

And after work, the men and their wives would go to dinner at Taurus Steakhouse on the taxpayers' dime, and here, again, no business would be discussed.

Richard Watt served as the director of the Defense Innovation Unit, a DOD initiative charged with obtaining and optimizing existing commercial technology for use by the military. Reporting directly to the Secretary of Defense, Watt had offices at the Pentagon, in Boston, in Austin, and here in Silicon Valley, and he had built a reputation in his tenure for being anywhere he needed to be to achieve the stated aims of his organization.

Today he found himself jovially golfing with the three young businessmen, not one of them yet forty, and all with advanced engineering or computer information degrees. The three also shared another trait: they ran companies racing up the ranks in the high-tech sector, specializing in the fields of automation, digital mapping, and videoconferencing.

And the director of the Defense Innovation Unit wanted their collaboration on multiple projects the DOD was undertaking.

But again, work would be this afternoon. Now it was play.

Rick Watt stepped up to the teeing area and placed his ball, and then he laughed off the digital mapping mogul when he asked if he wanted to put a grand on whether or not he'd keep it out of the nearby South Bay a few hundred yards away.

Everyone laughed, the security officers on the cart path included, and then Rick cleared his mind, took a moment to settle his stance, and raised into his backswing. At the apex he paused a moment, and then the club began arcing back down towards the ball.

The face of the driver made contact with a satisfying crack, the ball rocketed high and straight, and then Rick Watt's golf club left his hands, spinning off to his left. The digital mapping mogul leapt to the side to avoid being struck by the twirling driver, and then Watt himself spun around in the same direction as his club.

He dropped hard to his knees, and then his body slammed face-first into the tee box.

"What the fuck?" the videoconferencing CEO shouted in surprise.

A low report broke the still air over the golf course. None of the three men in the tee box understood what was happening, but all five security men on the cart path did, and they raced onto the green, handguns drawn and sweeping all around.

Three of them shuffled their principals back to two of the golf carts and sped off.

The pair of security officers left behind were the DOD men charged with protecting Watt, so they were now committed to covering the lifeless man with their bodies as they searched for the origin of fire.

A suburban neighborhood sat to the west, office buildings behind it; shimmering San Francisco Bay was to the north, and Palo Alto airport to the east and south. Neither of the men saw any boats on the water, so they concentrated on the other compass points, but only for a moment, because then they saw what looked like a fat exit wound on their protectee's back. They rolled Watt over and saw a small entry wound right in the center of his chest.

He'd been facing west as he teed off, so the shot had come from that direction.

The two security men were young and fit, but hefting the obviously dead protectee and moving him off the greens and back to a golf cart, all while potentially under the gun of a skilled assassin, proved to be an exceptionally stressful chore.

"Director Watt? Director Watt? Sir?" the man holding Watt's arms called to him over and over as they lumbered back to the path, though he had the medical training and the common sense to clearly determine that the director was wholly incapable of responding.

At the cart the men lowered to their knees, hopefully moving themselves out of the line of fire, and they rolled the body onto a seat. One crawled behind the wheel as the other climbed onto the back, holding Rick Watt's body in place.

They launched forward towards the clubhouse as the passenger pulled out his phone and hit a button.

Before bringing it to his ear, he said, "Had to have been five hundred yards."

The driver said, "Twice that. There was a good two seconds from impact to the sound reaching us. That's a thousand yards. The shot must have come from one of the high buildings behind."

"Jesus Christ," the driver added. "A sniper? Here? In Palo Alto?"

"That's the Gray Man, dude."

"You don't know if—"

"The fucking Gray Man!" the man in back shouted this time, and they rolled on, back to their Suburban in the clubhouse lot, as the man in back spoke to the 911 operator.

The driver stayed vigilant now, concentrating on his and his partner's *own* survival, because they'd failed at the task of keeping their principal alive.

The assassination of Richard Watt had not, in fact, been carried out by the Gray Man.

Seven hundred twelve meters away, forty-seven-year-old Scott Patrick Kincaid folded the stock on his Ruger Precision Rifle and slipped it into a white laundry bag half filled with towels that he shouldered as he ran in a low crouch back towards the door to the emergency stairwell of the hospital.

Dressed in the uniform of Environmental Services—hospital-speak for sanitation—he wore a badge and key cards around his neck, a blue uniform, and an N95 mask over his face, all following the protocol of the facility.

He'd killed a man this morning to obtain the disguise, a worker in the hospital who, Kincaid had been told by the person controlling him, looked the most like him from internal hospital records.

Not that the person running the assassin knew what Kincaid looked like. His controller was a French woman who worked at an operations center, he did not know where, and she did not know his name. She called him Lancer and he had provided her with a general description, trusting himself to make any changes to his person necessary to resemble the face and build of the man behind the identity he would steal.

Once he had an address, he'd simply rung the Environmental Services employee's front door, dealt with the person who answered it, and then found the orderly taking a shower. A bullet in the forehead, fired from a massive and suppressed 10-millimeter pistol, dispatched the hospital employee quickly and cleanly.

He'd dressed in the work clothes he found in the closet, and then, on his way through the apartment, he grabbed the dead man's keys off the kitchen peninsula and headed for the door. Just before leaving, he stepped carefully over the body of a dead woman, herself dressed in hospital attire.

The orderly had a girlfriend; Kincaid had not been briefed on that, but she'd not put up a fight, and collateral damage was just one of those things that happened in Kincaid's line of work.

Now, just two hours after the double homicide in Cupertino and ten minutes after the homicide in Palo Alto, Kincaid tossed his bag containing the rifle in the back of the stolen Nissan Murano parked in the covered hospital parking lot, climbed behind the wheel, and left the area.

Kincaid had to be on a private plane in forty-five minutes, and then he would have a few hours to clean up in flight and prepare for another time-sensitive operation, this time in Mexico City.

Kincaid was never late, and he never made mistakes. This he told himself with the utter unwaveringness employed by all true narcissists.

He'd been in the military, in an elite special operations force, and there he'd learned skills, yes, but more importantly, he'd learned the discipline he needed to do what he did, and to do it as well as he did it.

Scott Kincaid, known the world over as Lancer, one of the most infamous killers for hire on the planet, felt supreme satisfaction as he sipped a Diet Coke behind the wheel of the Murano. He'd had a tough few years, back when he got out of the military, dealing with the bullshit and the accusations and the backstabbing that was just the price a true American patriot had to pay for doing the right thing.

But since his trial ended, since his acquittal, and since he'd slipped out of the public eye and into the dark shadows of the contract killer lifestyle, everything, *every thing*, had been going his way.

He had no idea who he'd killed that morning on the golf course. He'd been given the GPS coordinates for a particular tee box in Palo Alto along with a description of the target and a general time of arrival, and disambiguation information—pictures of the others who would be in his foursome so that he didn't accidentally put a .308 round through the chest of the wrong man.

It had all worked to plan. He was proud of and cocky about his success, and then he thought a moment as he pulled up to a light just before merging onto the highway.

All to plan, except for that dumb bitch who opened the orderly's door. *Her fault, not mine*, he told himself.

Lancer gave a little smile as the light turned red; he lowered his N95 again for another sip of Diet Coke, wholly unaware that a traffic camera caught a reasonable image of his face in the process.

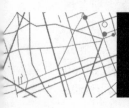

THREE

Court Gentry and Zoya Zakharova stepped off the bustling Guatemalan lakeside street and into the quiet courtyard restaurant at eleven fifteen a.m., took a table facing the open entrance of the restaurant, and put their backs to a wall covered in red bougainvillea, surrounded by other colorful plants spilling out of pots and garden beds throughout the space.

They had a view to the entrance of the building, beyond which was the street and then beyond that the lake, placid and crystalline in the midday sun.

After they ordered coffee and juice, Court looked at the rooftops of the two buildings in sight over the courtyard walls, then up at the sky. Softly, almost to himself, he said, "The rains won't start till midafternoon today."

Zoya perused the menu as she spoke, a little giggle in her voice. "There's my Central American meteorologist. I've been anxiously awaiting for your daily weather report."

"Rainy season," he said. "Get used to it, because it's every damn day."

"Just like your forecasts since the middle of May."

When their drinks came they ordered their meals, pork tostadas for Court and jocón de pollo—green chicken stew—for Zoya. When the waiter left them, they sat in silence, still taking in their surroundings. Court was armed with a SIG Sauer P365XL that he'd purchased on the black market in Lima almost four months earlier. It was a small weapon, but it carried thirteen rounds of hollow-point ammunition, and on the slide it wore a red dot optic for faster target acquisition than iron sights.

The gun and a couple of spare magazines were tucked into his brown denim pants and hidden by his plain light gray T-shirt.

Zoya had a steel-framed Jericho 941 9-millimeter in the little daypack at her feet, purchased in Guadalajara and no doubt originally stolen from a Mexican police weapons locker, as it was the duty pistol of the state cops there. Her weapon carried seventeen rounds, and she had two extra sixteen-round mags of hollow-points.

A few more tables filled with lunch guests, and together Zoya and Court evaluated the new patrons. A group of three young hippies—they sounded American—sat by a fountain in the middle of the courtyard and chatted amiably. An older couple, well into their fifties and speaking German, sat a little closer.

A silver-haired woman was seated at a table by the ivy-covered masonry wall well to their left, and she immediately opened her laptop and then, in Dutch-accented Spanish, ordered a cup of coffee.

Court was in a contemplative mood and would have been fine sitting in silence, watching the comings and goings in the restaurant, but soon Zoya leaned closer to him.

"I'm worried about you."

Here we go again, he thought. "Because of the insomnia?"

She shook her head. "I'm worried that you're bored."

Court looked at her quizzically. "Bored?"

"Four months without work. You're more withdrawn, not sleeping. I think you miss it."

He sipped his juice, saying nothing as his pork tostadas were placed in front of him. Once Zoya had her stew, he turned and leaned closer to her. "These have been the best four months of my life."

Zoya did not smile. "But?"

With an exasperated look, he said, "There's no 'but,' Carrie."

In public she was Carrie and he was Sean, the names on their passports, created for them in Ottawa at great expense and declaring them to be Mr. and Mrs. Busby, a husband and wife from Hamilton, Ontario.

She shook her head. Speaking softly, she said, "You miss the work. You miss making an impact. It's not a bad thing. You do it because you're honorable." She shook her head. "No. You're a hero. But . . . I'm like most people. I'm not drawn to danger like you are. Not anymore. I just want to survive."

"I'm not a hero, and you are, in no way, like most people." Court took a bite of his tostada, a swig of juice, and then he asked, "Where's all this coming from?"

"It's coming from the fact that you're growing more restless every day, and you can't hide it from me."

Court ate while he tried to think of something to say. Nothing came at first, but soon enough he looked back to Zoya. "Trouble finds *us*, we don't have to go looking for it. There will come a time when we *need* to get back to work, and you know that as well as I do. And you can say all you want that you aren't interested, but I've seen you motivated by causes before."

"When my back is against the wall, yes, I'm motivated."

"Well . . . half the planet wants me dead. And at least one country wants you dead. Don't worry. We'll find our backs to the wall sooner rather than later, then we can worry about getting back in the game."

She said nothing, and then Court added, "I feel it, Carrie. Something's coming. It's closer every day."

"When it comes . . . will you be happy or sad?"

He deflected a little. "All that matters is that we're both ready. My brain is tuning up for it, that's all you're seeing."

Zoya took a bite of the hot stew, and she focused on something out in the courtyard now. "Let's talk about it more later."

Court took this to mean she wanted privacy before they got deeper into the topic of the worldwide manhunt against them, and he was all too happy to table the conversation for now, here in a public place.

He followed her eyes and saw the hostess escorting an older man in a linen suit and a fedora through the space to a table by the fountain, seating him two tables from the three young Americans. The man spoke softly and was out of earshot, so Court couldn't hear him, and then the man lifted his menu and put on reading glasses.

Zoya had already returned her attention to her lunch.

They ate, more or less in silence now, and then they paid, rose, and headed back through the courtyard. Past the Dutch woman with the laptop and the older couple and the hippie kids and the man in the linen suit and the fedora, who now sipped a margarita alone, although a second salt-rimmed margarita sat untouched across from him, as if he were waiting for a lunch companion who was running late.

Back on the street bordering the lake, Zoya took Court's hand, pulled him to her, and kissed him. "If something *is* coming for us, like you say, I want you to know that these have been the best days of my life, too."

Court softened, hugged her. He smiled. "Maybe I'm wrong. But if I'm not, we can only get through it if we work together."

She nodded, a solemn expression on her face, and then they began walking back to their rented apartment. After less than a block, however, Zoya stopped and looked through her backpack. Retrieving her wallet, she said, "I have to go buy a sundress. Any chance you'll come along with me?"

"Only at gunpoint."

She lightened a little. "I won't subject you to the horrors of shopping. I'll meet you back at the flat."

They kissed again and headed off in opposite directions.

The older man in the tropical beige linen suit sat alone in the courtyard of the café, sipping his margarita and pretending to take in the flowing bougainvillea, the heliconia, and the bird of paradise that grew all around the open space. He snatched his napkin from the table, pulled off his fedora, and wiped perspiration from his face and head.

A nervous glance at his watch added to the impression that he was agitated, but he sipped his drink and sat there, shifting a little in his chair.

As he began to look back towards the rear of the courtyard, he caught movement out of the corner of his eye. Someone had slipped in behind him and was now sitting down at his little table.

The man turned back, watching the beautiful blonde in the green tank top as she pulled the metal chair forward, and his eyes met hers.

The woman glared back at him. They sat in silence for some time, and then she spoke first.

In Russian.

"How much trouble am I in?"

The older man smiled wistfully now, and he answered back in Russian. "Surely, Zoyusha . . . you knew you could not hide forever."

Zoya Zakharova made no reaction to the man using the diminutive of her name. Instead, she gave a little nod, took the margarita that had been sitting there waiting for her, and looked at it.

"Poison?"

"Seriously?"

She held it out for him.

"That hurts my feelings," he said, and then, without breaking eye contact, he took the drink and downed a long sip.

She took the glass back but did not drink from it. "I knew I'd be found eventually, but I couldn't have imagined in a million years it would be by you."

The man gave a genuine smile now. "I didn't find you, dear. But someone from the embassy in the capital saw you get on a bus to Panajachel. I learned about it through the grapevine, and then I rushed down to talk to you."

"And now somebody is up in the hills with a rifle optic centered on my forehead?"

The man's smile gave way slowly, and his face turned grave. "Would that keep you rooted in that seat long enough for me to tell you what I have to tell you?"

"Most likely, yeah."

"Fine. There's a rifle aimed at your head."

Zoya shot the remnants of the margarita in one gulp, maintaining eye contact as she did so. "All right, then, Uncle Slava, what's this all about?"

Three hundred twenty feet directly above the two Russians sitting at the table by the fountain in the restaurant courtyard within sight of Lake Atitlán, quadcopter RC25 hovered, its lens focused on the man's face.

One and a half seconds later and nearly eleven thousand miles away, the images recorded were broadcast on a large wall monitor in an auditorium-style room on the top floor of Building Five, a glass-and-steel structure at the Singapore Science Park in Queenstown, Singapore.

It was past two thirty a.m. here, but looking at the image in the office were a team of nineteen men and women, assembled from around the world, most sitting at computer workstations and all with their eyes locked on the wall monitor and another large screen next to it.

This office had been designated Tactical Operations Center Gama; it had been acquired just six days earlier, and five days ago the team occupying the desks in the dark room had met, everyone's first day on this job.

An instant after the image of the older man in the linen suit seated in the courtyard froze on the screen, a red bounding box superimposed around his face, and the deputy operations chief read information off the monitor in front of her.

With excitement in her voice, the middle-aged American said, "ID confirmed. Borislava Genrich."

Clapping and cheering commenced in the auditorium.

The director of the operations center was a thirty-six-year-old Norwegian, and he kept his eyes on the image as he rose from his chair. Instead of celebrating with the others, he spoke over them. "Who's the woman?"

The American quickly looked down at her monitor. "Scan is running now." Two seconds later she answered his question. "ID coming in. Zakharova, Zoya F. Russian national. Thirty-four years old. Former officer in SVR. Spetsnaz trained. Currently wanted by the Russian government."

"Wanted for *what*?"

"No information other than that there is a Russian national intelligence directive to capture or kill. Odessa code, their highest-level sanction." She paused, then said, "The Kremlin *really* wants this chick."

The director cocked his head. "So, Genrich flew to this little town in Guatemala last night to meet with a wanted Russian fugitive."

"Why would he do that?" a Moroccan asked from his desk high at the rear of the room.

The Norwegian director shrugged. "Don't know, don't care. We'll just wait on instructions from Cyrus."

"Bet Cyrus has us call in hitters," chimed in a young South African man near the front.

In the back row, a French woman said, "I bet Cyrus tasks Lancer. He's in the air now, just leaving California, headed to Mexico City. If they reroute him, he could be in Panajachel by late afternoon."

The director said, "Everyone stop speculating. Cyrus will make the determination." He turned to a German woman in the back row of the auditorium. "Fourteen, contact the on-scene wrangler in Panajachel, make sure he has another platform overhead so we can trail them both if they split up."

She replied quickly. "Yes, sir."

A forty-year-old male analyst from Holland called out now. "Sir. Recon 29 passed over this restaurant thirty-two minutes ago on its AI pattern, well before Genrich arrived. I went back over its data and . . . and Zakharova was already there, having lunch with a Caucasian male."

"Did the bot run an iden check on him?"

"It got nothing. I just manually input his image through the system to make sure. Still nothing. We're designating him Unsub One."

The director's eyebrows furrowed. "Low-quality image or an invisible man?"

"The pic looks sharp enough, sir."

After a moment, he waved a hand at the analyst. "Forget the unsub. If he links back up with these Russians, then we'll give him some attention. If he doesn't, then he's not important to us."

"Understood. The woman?"

"We stay on her."

Fourteen spoke up again from the back row, her German accent strong, but her English flawless. "I'll have Wrangler Zero One assign RC20 to the woman. It's on a full charge."

"Good." The man from Norway running the OC in Singapore, staffed by men and women from around the world, looked at the wall monitor a second more. Softly to himself and inaudibly to the others in the room, he said, "What the *hell* are we even doing?"

They were going to be ordered to kill the Russian man and, quite possibly, the Russian woman. He was certain of that much, because they'd been killing people around the world for the last eight hours.

But the operations director in the office at Singapore Science Park had not the faintest clue as to why.

He cleared his head of his uncertainty; he was in charge here. "Okay, the rest of you, concentrate on Israel. We might not have movement till tomorrow morning there, but if our target flushes in the night, we'll take him then."

When eyes remained on him a moment more, he said, "That means now!"

FOUR

Court Gentry sat alone at the little table on the balcony of his rented flat in Panajachel, nursing a beer and looking out over the rooftops in the direction of the lake. He didn't have a view of the water from here, but he didn't care because he wasn't looking at anything. His mind was lost in thought, and his eyes just gazed vacantly as distant thunder rumbled softly in the sunny afternoon sky.

He heard the main door to the flat open and someone enter, but he didn't stand, and he didn't reach for the pistol in his waistband. He knew Zoya from the sound and cadence of her footfalls, so he just sat there, his face all but expressionless.

Eventually she stepped out onto the balcony, kissed him on the cheek, then looked out at the buildings and the surrounding hills for a moment. She sat down across from him and slid her little daypack off her shoulder.

Zoya pulled out a light green sundress as she let her bag drop to the ground. "What do you think?"

Court glanced at it, then looked her in the eyes. "That's a sundress, all right."

She cocked her head, sensing something, but she said nothing.

He took a sip of his Gallo beer and put it back on the table in front of him.

"Drinking at one thirty? That's not like you. That's like *me*."

"Safer than the water."

"You're right," she replied, and then she went back inside, headed to the kitchen, and retrieved a Gallo for herself. She was back at the table in thirty seconds.

"Anything else happen while you were out?" he asked, his voice emotionless.

She looked him in the eyes for a moment, then said, "There was a band playing in a bar down on Rancho Grande, you could hear the music from the street. It was that song by that group you like . . . the old one."

Court said nothing.

She remembered. "'Have You Ever Seen the Rain?'"

"CCR."

"Right. But these guys were playing it really fast, and singing it in Spanish. It was beautiful, actually." When he made no comment, she added, "You would have loved it."

"That *and* a sundress? Quite an eventful afternoon."

A staring contest lasted twenty seconds.

A rooster crowed, and a poorly tuned bus engine backfired in the street below. Passing merchants hawked their wares loudly in the distance. A propane vendor in a truck spoke through a microphone, his voice amplified through a large speaker on the roof. "Zeta Gas! Zeta Gas!"

"What's going on?" she finally asked.

"You tell me."

Zoya slowly turned away from him and looked out over the street.

"You tell me . . ." Court repeated, then added, "while you are looking me in the face."

Her eyes flitted back over to his. "Something . . . something else happened."

"Huh," he muttered, taking another sip of his beer. "Obviously something less important than buying a dress or hearing a cover band butcher a classic, or else you would have led with it."

Zoya stiffened, fixed her gaze on his. "I'm not loving your tone right now."

"What happened today?"

She looked away. "It sounds like you somehow already know what happened." When he did not reply, she spoke with a touch of outrage in her voice, but it sounded forced. She wasn't mad; she was defensive. "Have you been spying on me?"

"It's kind of my thing . . . so."

"You're *not* a spy. You're Sean Busby, from Hamilton, Ontario."

"You lied to me, and I want to know why."

Now Zoya's jaw tensed, and the rippling muscles in her fit neck and shoulders twitched. "Don't act tough with me. I don't believe it, so I don't feel the threat you're implying."

"There's no threat implied other than the threat that I get up from this table, grab my bug-out bag, and bug the fuck out of here. Right now."

She reached across the table, grabbed the wrist of the hand holding the beer. Softly, she said, "No. I can explain."

Court went silent. His face was stone, but hers reddened, her eyes misted. "I hate that you don't trust me," she finally said.

He pulled his hand back to his lap. "And *I* hate that not trusting you turns out to have been the prudent thing to do. If we're going to live this life together, we have to be open and honest with one another. If you have a good reason you lied, then I'd like to hear it, because right now I don't have any idea what is going on."

"You saw me in the café."

"I did."

In the near distance, the gas truck had moved on, but the speaker on the roof continued squawking from a distance. "Zeta Gas! Zeta Gas!"

Zoya could almost see the walls going up around Court; he was angry and hurt and confused, and it uneased her more than she was letting on. She was ashamed. Court was not a trusting person; she might have been the only one on earth he really put his trust in, and she'd violated it. Her voice quivered when she said, "I was going to tell you. I was just trying to figure out what to say."

"Maybe try the facts on, see how they feel. What happened?"

"What you already know. At lunch today I saw a man that I recognized."

"Linen suit, hat. Sixty-five?"

"He's not sixty-five. He's a healthy seventy or so. His name is Borislava Genrich."

"A Russian. Wow. This day keeps gettin' better."

Zoya heaved her shoulders a little, and then they sagged. "My brother and I called him Dyadya Slava."

Court bolted upright now. "*Dyadya?* He's your fucking *uncle?*"

She shook her head. "A friend of my father's. He was always around growing up, he was just Dyadya Slava, his wife we called Tetya Olga. I haven't spoken to him in over a decade."

"Why is he in Guatemala, and why was he three tables away from us at lunch?"

"I didn't say anything to you at the time because I wanted to handle it. To see what was going on. I didn't think it was a coincid—"

"Of *course* it wasn't a coincidence."

"That's what I *just* said! *Jesus!* This doesn't have to be an interrogation. I'm going to tell you everything."

Court's fight-or-flight reflexes were amping him up. She understood. She took a sip of cold beer, wished like hell she had a shot of tequila in front of her instead, and then she began talking.

In the café courtyard, Zoya Zakharova shot the remnants of her margarita in one gulp, thankful for the tequila right now as she maintained eye contact with the older man across the table. "All right, then, Uncle Slava, what's this all about?"

Borislava Genrich leaned closer and spoke slowly, his voice masked by the gentle bustle from the other patrons, the sounds from the street behind them, the chirping and singing of birds in the foliage of the courtyard. "You and I have always had a good relationship. Since you were a child. Your brother, too."

Zoya did not disagree.

"I knew the charges against you were fabricated. I knew you wouldn't turn on your nation."

To this, she said, "I *did* turn on my nation, Dyadya."

He looked at her a moment. "Extenuating circumstances, I'm sure."

Zoya had been framed to take the fall for an operation gone wrong, and a kill order had been placed on her head by the Russian government. She then shot a senior Russian foreign intelligence operative who'd tried to kill her, and she defected to the Americans.

"All sorts of extenuating circumstances," she said softly, thinking about everything that had happened to her in the past few years.

The older man in the fedora said, "That's not why I'm here. *No one* is here but me. You have my word . . . over the grave of your dear father who, as you know, I loved like my own brother." Zoya's father had been head of the GRU, Russian military intelligence, and Borislava Genrich's close friend.

Zoya looked around again. "If Moscow knows where I am, why aren't they here?"

"I'm sure you watch television. Russian foreign intelligence operations have been crippled by the release of financial records from a Swiss bank. Everything is a shambles now for Moscow."

Zoya didn't have to watch TV to know something about this, because she had been one of the people who had safeguarded the information so that it could see the light of day to damage Russian intelligence.

But she made no mention of her involvement. Instead she said, "If foreign ops are crippled, then why are you here?"

"Because I'm not from the intelligence services. I was army: plain, vanilla, army. Not like your father. I retired, then started a private company. I've been working on certain . . . commercial endeavors."

"Meaning?"

"Meaning I work in the private sector, helping acquire technology."

"Military technology?"

"Not necessarily . . . but sometimes."

"And you sell it to Russia?"

"Not necessarily . . . but sometimes."

Zoya gave him an icy stare. "And you live with yourself? What does

Olga think·about what you are doing?" She ordered another margarita from a passing server, then looked back to the Russian man.

Calmly, he said, "Olga died nine years ago. Cancer of the liver."

Zoya exhaled a little. "I'm sorry. She was . . . she was always nice to me. You both were."

Slava shrugged. "And as to my sleep . . . my sleep is troubled, but it is troubled from what I did in Afghanistan, in Chechnya, in Dagestan. Not for what's happening now. I did no fighting in Ukraine. I did no planning for this terrible war. I live in the West. I find out what new tech is being developed by private industry all over the world, and then I find ways to get the plans, the blueprints . . . sometimes even the brainpower itself, and I sell it to other companies, occasionally to private concerns in Russia, but often to other third parties."

She rolled her eyes. "Look, you might not be in the intelligence services, but what you're doing sounds a lot like espionage."

"Industrial espionage," he corrected with a wave of his hand.

"And this brings us to what you want from me."

"It does."

FIVE

Borislava Genrich leaned forward even closer, his linen suit straining with the movement, and he spoke so softly Zoya could barely hear him.

"A Russian computer software engineer is holed up in an apartment in Mexico City. He claims to have information about a new artificial intelligence weapon that's about to go live."

"What kind of artificial intelligence weapon?"

"He only knows coding. He's a software guy, as I said. He doesn't know the platform the software is going to be used on. It could be a pilotless aircraft, a missile with the capability to learn about its target's defenses while in flight, a robotic tank. Whatever it is, he's stolen a portion of the code, and he's certain the weapon is just weeks, or maybe days, away from going online."

"So . . . what's the problem? Go to Mexico. Bring him in. Ask him what he knows."

Genrich shook his head. "He's being watched. He doesn't know who they are. They've pinned him down, or at least they know the neighborhood he's in. Surveillance is all over the place; he's spotted men in the street who don't belong; he thinks he heard a drone fly overhead. He's terrified, and he's got every right to be. He wants SVR or GRU to personally retrieve him and get him out of the country, but I can't get SVR or GRU there to do it, because Russia doesn't have intelligence officers who can travel without being uncovered thanks to the revelations from Switzerland about the Kremlin's ops."

"A Russian intelligence officer saw me down here, or so you said."

"A Russian who was aware of the Odessa order saw you. An intelligence operative, but one tied to the embassy here, known by the local government. A pencil pusher, I'm sure. Not someone who could pose any threat to you. And not someone who could extract a man out from under a kill team in Mexico City and bring him to safety."

Zoya sipped her drink. "Then it sounds like your engineer is fucked."

Genrich shook his head. "Not if *you* go, Zoyusha. I will tell him I'll have the best operator in Russian foreign intelligence spirit him out of the city. He'll comply. You can do it, too. Slip in, disguise yourself and him, and then get out. There's an airport fifty kilometers outside the capital, Felipe Ángeles International. I'll have a private jet there waiting for you both."

"I'm no longer a Russian intelligence officer."

"Yes, well, we won't be mentioning that to him, will we?" He paused, then said, "Name your price."

"You're going to give this stolen code to Russia?"

Genrich did not respond, but Zoya took that as an answer.

She leaned back, spoke a little louder now. "You can't pay me enough to help Russia. Not after what's happened in the past two years."

Genrich kept his voice low. "Don't think of it as helping Russia. You are stopping, slowing down, at least, the development of a revolutionary weapon."

"So says this nameless, faceless *Russian* engineer."

"If it weren't true, why would there be a kill team after him?"

Zoya still didn't get the urgency. "Artificial intelligence . . . some new tech. I'm sure there are developments all the time. What's so special about—"

He barked out a quick whisper. "Because what the engineer is describing is a lethal autonomous weapon that can operate at machine speed."

"What does that mean?"

"The human is totally taken out of the process. The weapon, whatever it is, works on its own. It can destroy anything in its path because its algorithm takes nanoseconds to decide who or what to attack. It would be almost impossible to defeat. The technology itself, no matter the platform it's applied to, will make war infinitely more deadly, and humans, *all* humans, unable to combat it."

Zoya wasn't buying it. "Russia doesn't want this guy so they can make the technology disappear. They want this guy so they can have it for themselves."

To this Genrich nodded, almost apologetically. "That is true, of course. But if both sides have the same technology, the technology won't be employed. The West loses its advantage. The world is made a safer place. You *do* remember that the U.S. and the Soviets both having a nuclear arsenal ensured the state of mutually assured destruction, so that neither dared use their weapons, don't you?"

"You can do some good. We all can."

Sarcastically, Zoya replied, "Right. This is just one big humanitarian operation. A peace mission. For the Kremlin. I wasn't stupid twenty years ago when you knew me, and I'm not stupid now."

Genrich put his palms on the table. "I don't have time to explain the specific dangers of this technology. I only understand how destabilizing it will be in a general sense. Once you get the engineer, he'll tell you everything on your drive to the airport, and then you will see what I *already* see. The act of leveling the playing field by obtaining what he knows will be a net benefit for everyone on the planet."

"The engineer is in Mexico because . . ."

"Because he slipped out of a nearby country and went there to hide. Somehow he was found."

"*A nearby country?* You obviously mean the USA."

"Look. There are details . . . matters that don't pertain to your operational exigencies, that I'm not at liberty to discuss. On top of that, there are things the engineer has not yet revealed, even to me. He knows his information is valuable, and he's using it to buy his way to safety."

Zoya was neither surprised nor annoyed. All operations worked thusly. "What do you know about the people after him?"

"Some local hit men, plus the surveillance detected near the safe house. We've picked up information that a well-known American asset code-named Lancer is involved, as well, but he hasn't been spotted in the area."

"Never heard of him."

"You know his work. He's one of the most sought-after killers for hire in the world, perhaps second only to the one they call the Gray Man."

Zoya didn't miss a beat. "You buy into the Gray Man story? Sorry, Dyadya Slava, but I don't believe in ghosts."

The man smiled. "I know people. In Moscow, in Murmansk, in Kiev. People who believe, because they were there when he was there, and they saw his wrath. Lancer is not the Gray Man, but he is a capable operator. He was responsible for the events in Utrecht last year. The killings in Bucharest a few years back."

Zoya raised an eyebrow. She knew the incidents he was referring to. "You're *really* not selling me on this mission by telling me that."

He smiled a tired smile. "I'm torn being here. I love you, Zoyusha, always have, and I worry about sending you into this." He finished the remainder of the drink he'd been ignoring for the past ten minutes. "But this is too important. Forget about Russia. *I* need you. The world needs you."

She looked away for a moment, lost in thought.

Genrich used the opportunity to ask her a question. "Who was the man with the beard?"

Zoya took another sip and looked his way. "Just some guy I met down in Honduras. We're traveling together." She shrugged. "For a while. We'll grow bored of each other soon enough."

"You could be back with him the day after tomorrow. One day for threat assessment, to plan the exfiltration, and then a few hours operational." He added, "You are the most beautiful woman in the world. This man will wait for you, I promise."

Zoya drank in silence a moment, then asked, "How can I reach you?"

"*Reach* me? You have to *go* with me to Mexico. Now. I don't have time for you to think—"

"Tonight. I'll call you back tonight. If I go, I'll be there before dawn to work up a threat assessment and an operational plan."

Reluctantly, Genrich reached into his pocket. "I'm heading back to

Mexico City immediately. I'll fly commercial, leave my aircraft here at the capital for you." Pushing a business card across the table, he said, "If you turn me down tonight, I'm going to have to try to do it myself."

"Slava, that's nuts. You're seventy years old."

"I can't hire anyone the man will trust, not in the time frame I have. Lancer and his colleagues will have him before I can put anything together. You, down here, a two-hour flight from Mexico City . . . *you're* my only hope."

Zoya pocketed the business card, stood, leaned over, and kissed the man on the cheek. "Tonight. I'll call. I promise."

She left the café as the man at the table reached back into his pocket and pulled out his phone.

Thick, low clouds had formed over the apartment balcony in the ten minutes Zoya had been talking. Court looked up at them for the first time as she finished her story.

"Rain," he said. "Any minute."

On cue, a low clap of thunder rolled in over the lake, momentarily drowning out the din from the streets of the little town.

Zoya said, "I couldn't have told you in the restaurant that we'd been blown. You'd have grabbed my arm and walked me out through the kitchen, and we'd be out of town in fifteen minutes."

"You say that like it's a bad thing."

"There was no way I could assure you, not right then and there, that Slava coming to Panajachel like that, waiting patiently for me, was no threat to us. I know him, I trust him. I had to find out for myself what he wanted."

Court did not respond to this. Instead, as another rumble of thunder filled the air, he said, "I'm not going to Mexico City."

"But . . . what if what he said was true?"

"That Russia wants to steal American technology? Whose fucking side are you on?"

The conversation was going downhill, Court knew, and he also sensed that he was the one causing it. Still, he was furious, hurt, destabilized by her deception, no matter her justifications for it.

She repeated herself from earlier. "I trust Slava. He is a kind man. If I can protect him from harm, then I think I should."

"You don't even know what this weapon he's talking about is, and you're smarter than me, so I *sure* as hell don't understand it. We can't just go to Mexico to help the Russian government take possession of something we can't even comprehend."

Zoya looked away without responding.

"Two hours ago you were telling me you were scared that I was bored and wanted to get back into the field. You said it like it could ruin us. Now you've done a one-eighty, and *you're* the one that wants to go back out."

"I . . . If it were anyone else asking . . ."

"My answer is no, Zoya, and I really hope yours is, too. I know Lancer. I worked with him. I've really got no desire to get on the man's bad side. If you haven't noticed, we aren't exactly in the best operational shape of our lives. *Either* of us."

She cocked her head. "You worked *with* the assassin?"

"Years ago. Trust me . . . Lancer sucks." Court added, "To him, collateral damage is a *feature* of his work, not a glitch."

"So I just let this guy find and kill Uncle Slava?"

Court leaned back in his chair. "He's not your uncle! And he's not mine, either." He stood up suddenly. "We should have bugged out two hours ago. I'm leaving town as soon as I have the cover of darkness. You need to figure out what *you* want to do."

As he headed off the balcony and into the flat, Zoya called out for him. "I love you."

"Then you will listen to me. If just this once. Let's just keep running."

The sky opened up, Court went inside, and Zoya just sat there looking up into the black clouds as it rained down, unaware of the unblinking eye above looking right back at her.

SIX

At Tactical Operations Center Gama in Singapore, the Norwegian director turned away from the large monitor showing the apartment balcony from above, and towards a technician from South Africa. "Still nothing on the male?"

"He's a ghost, sir."

Martina Sommer, the forty-three-year-old German communications specialist known here in the room as "Fourteen," called out, "Sir, the weather has started. Forecast says four or five hours of gusting winds and precipitation. Suggest we contact the on-scene wrangler and have him pull aerial coverage."

Before he could acknowledge her request, the director heard a beep on his laptop, and he looked down at it. "It's the boss. Stand by."

Words popped up in the instant message box soon after.

This is Cyrus. Be advised, the Mexico City tasking is on hold. Cyrus is now designating Genrich, Borislava I, as target Gama 17, and Zakharova, Zoya F, as target Gama 18. Tasking asset "Lancer" into AO. Local support en route.

Lars typed a response quickly on his keyboard.

Understood. Be advised; halting ISR mission over Panajachel until weather clears.

ISR was intelligence, surveillance, and reconnaissance, the quadcopters beaming images of the area. The expected afternoon rains and wind could easily send the devices crashing to the ground, so an immediate recall was warranted.

Cyrus replied.

Unfortunate, but understand conditions not conducive to ISR at this time. Resume coverage at earliest possible opportunity.

The director finished his instant message conversation, then stood up and addressed his team. "Physical assets are moving in." He turned to Martina. "Fourteen. Contact the wrangler in Panajachel and have him recall all drones. I want them charged and ready for when Lancer and his team arrive. We *will* be providing eyes for the assault force."

"Yes, sir," the woman replied.

Just after relaying the order to the drone pilot in Guatemala, Martina Sommer took off her headset, dropped it onto the desk in front of her, and ran her fingers through her thick copper red hair. She rubbed the dark circles under her eyes, closed her eyes a moment, and wondered how the fuck her life had managed to come to this.

What was she doing here?

A wanted Russian spy is a target, a Russian businessman is a target, a Russian engineer is a target. Fine. Someone is killing Russians. But what about the American Defense Department employee in California or the Japanese artificial intelligence expert in Osaka? And what about the hits in Sydney and Bangkok, and the other assassinations they had planned? None of these targets are, or were, Russian.

Martina Sommer had worked for the Bundespolizei, Germany's federal police, as a communications officer after serving ten years in military counterintelligence. She'd lost her job the year prior because of a drinking habit that seemed to grow more serious the older she got, and then her husband had been removed from his senior position at a Berlin bank after a series of loans he made went bad.

The couple's life had been in a shambles for the past six months; they'd moved with their two small children back to her little hometown outside

Bonn to live with her aging parents in their small cottage, and neither she nor her husband had been able to secure gainful employment. He *had* managed to find an assistant manager position at a local hardware store, but he spent his nights in fits of depression while Martina had resorted to delivering groceries when she was sober enough to do so.

And then one morning while she was searching her family's cramped room for her car keys, the pounding headache that came with last night's vodka and schnapps doing nothing for her mood, the email had arrived in her inbox.

A man named Jack Tudor ran a company called Lighthouse Risk Control Ltd., and he reached out to her about a job. She'd known him for nearly two decades; they'd even dated for a short while when she was young. She'd appealed to him for work in the security industry, and now he was coming through.

The message was cryptic in many ways, offering a temporary position using her skills in communications and intelligence to work for a private concern in Asia.

Soon she entered into a text conversation with Tudor, and he told her she would be supporting an intelligence operation that would lead to the deaths of several "terrorists" around the world for the benefit of an undisclosed national actor and humankind itself.

Martina Sommer didn't really believe she'd be doing good with all this; she assumed this was some sort of sub rosa proxy mission being run by Russia, China, Israel, or some other nation. But she *did* believe she had to save her family from the downward spiral they were in, so after only a few clarifications as to what her role would be, and after the assurances from Jack Tudor that she would sit at a desk thousands of miles from danger and only be part of the surveillance arm of the operation, she had accepted the position.

She felt like shit for doing so, but to Tudor she had portrayed her mood as utterly enthusiastic.

Now she lived and worked in some office complex in Singapore, she hadn't left the building since she'd arrived five days earlier, and the killing that seemed so remote a few days ago had now begun in earnest.

The building was crawling with security—locals, as far as she knew—

and they seemed to be as interested in keeping the nineteen in as they were in keeping anyone else out.

Martina knew she couldn't get up and leave, even if she wanted to, and this kept her at her desk and focused on her assignment, but her feelings of regret and remorse also made stomach acid tear up her insides.

She was supporting the murder of civilians around the world on behalf of some bad actor, and she saw no way out.

Slowly, reluctantly, she shook away the welling panic and reached again for her headset because she had work to do. A mission was under way in Guatemala, and it was her job to coordinate the on-site surveillance.

She told herself not to think about the work but to think about the money, about moving back to Berlin, about saving her husband from his depression and the children from sharing a bed at their grandparents' house, and these images served to get her back on task.

For now, anyway.

The whirr of jet engines grew softly, the sound emanating from the southwest, steadily rising over the insistent noise of the bustling city of Quetzaltenango, Guatemala. Impossibly low gray clouds hid the origin of the noise until a sleek white Embraer Legacy 500 private jet appeared in the sky just a quarter mile from the airport, emerging from the vapor just four hundred feet above the Earth on short final. The landing gear had already lowered, and the aircraft, sleek and shiny-slick after passing through wet blankets of cloud cover, lined up its nose on runway 05, and then it flared before touching down, a spray of water kicking up from the tires as it did so.

The Legacy taxied to the terminal of Aeropuerto Internacional de los Altos, then parked on the tarmac a few dozen yards away. As the door opened, a single black Chevy Tahoe SUV pulled up next to it, and a door opened.

A man climbed out of the back seat and, ignoring the heavy drizzle, walked towards the Legacy just as the hatch opened and a single passenger emerged.

The man from the Chevy was local, but the new arrival appeared to be a typical gringo: a white male wearing a denim shirt and khakis, a bald head contrasting with a thick brown beard. He looked out at the airfield, then up at the sky.

The foreigner appeared to be in his forties; his only luggage was a large black backpack, and Tom Ford sunglasses hung from his open collar, unnecessary in the gray Central American afternoon.

The gringo stepped down the jet stairs, shook hands perfunctorily with the local, and then they both walked back to the Chevy without exchanging a single word.

Once in the back of the SUV, the traveler spoke English. "I'm Lancer." His accent was American, the local immediately discerned.

"Bernadino." The local then motioned to the driver and the front passenger. "Chico and Alfredo."

All three locals were in their twenties or thirties; they were short but hard-edged, dressed in casual civilian attire, with rain ponchos crammed into the door pockets next to them.

The man called Lancer looked over the locals carefully, and he made a few deductions because this wasn't his first rodeo. The Hispanic men's names began with the letters A, B, and C, so they were likely as made up as Lancer's code name was, but he saw this as prudent tradecraft and therefore a positive sign.

They were all former military, he could tell. They'd all killed before. He could tell this, too.

"What training do you have?" he asked Bernadino.

"Kaibiles," came the reply, and then the Guatemalan looked deep into the man's face to see if there was any sign of recognition of the word.

The American knew the Kaibiles were the Guatemalan Armed Forces special operations wing, and he confirmed his understanding by asking, "How long since active duty?"

Bernadino spoke in Spanish to the pair up front, and after they answered him, he said, "I've been out a year. Chico, the driver, four years. Alfredo has been out about two years."

"You've all been working since?"

To this Bernadino flashed a smile. "Every day, señor."

The American didn't ask what they'd been doing. He could deduce they worked for organized crime, most likely in Guatemala City.

"Weapons?" Lancer next asked.

Bernadino said something else in Spanish, and the man in the front passenger seat reached into a duffel between his feet and pulled out a squat Heckler & Koch MP5 9-millimeter submachine gun with a collapsed stock. He handed it back to the foreigner, and Lancer looked it over. It had simple iron sights instead of a more advanced red dot optic, but the weapon appeared to be in decent condition.

Bernadino said, "We each have one of these. We were told you'd have your own gun."

"I do," Lancer said as he continued inspecting the HK in his hand. He ejected the magazine, looked over the ammo. It was full metal jacket, a relatively cheap brand, but the gun would fire and the bullets would kill, so he handed the weapon back up front to Antonio before looking again at Bernadino.

"You three are my ground support element. We'll have ISR support, as well." With a hard look, he said, "I will prosecute the assassinations of Zakharova and Genrich myself."

The Guatemalan relayed this to the others, and the Tahoe drove through the rain, closing steadily on their target.

SEVEN

Shvedya Street snakes through the posh Denia neighborhood in the northern Israeli city of Haifa, a hilly and high-dollar area three miles inland from the Mediterranean. The homes were ornate, the lawns and gardens well kept, and the cars winding through the tree-lined streets were Mercedes, BMWs, Maseratis, and Range Rovers.

A modern split-level home rested on a hill on Shvedya, its front garden walled and dotted with eucalyptus, juniper, and palm trees growing out of the ground between tiers of ornamental stone. Belying the placid landscaping in the front yard, however, inside the home was the hustle and bustle of a family of four cleaning up after dinner on a Saturday evening.

This family was wealthy, even for Denia, but otherwise typical. Tomer Basch was forty-six years old, a former Israeli Defense Force captain in the Intelligence Corps before moving to the United States, where he attended MIT to obtain a master's of science in intelligent information systems.

After college he'd been immediately snatched up by the robotics division of Boston Dynamics, and he eventually started his own lab with partners back in Tel Aviv. Specializing in military robotics software, Basch and his team of coders and engineers were considered pioneers in the field of creating artificial intelligence for prototype military combat platforms.

After more than a decade, Basch sold his company, and he now worked as the director of intelligent systems at the Israel Institute of Technology here in Haifa, where he continued to advance programs involving artificial intelligence to be used in all types of military equipment, from armed drones to autonomous sentry guns.

Tomer sipped a glass of Netofa Tel Qasser, a crisp white from a popular Israeli winery, and he poured another glass for his wife before they both headed out of the kitchen and into the den to turn on a movie with the kids.

Halfway to his sofa, however, Tomer's cell phone vibrated in his pocket.

He put the bottle down on the coffee table, then checked the phone. It was a name he recognized, but someone who never called on a Saturday night, so Tomer quickly excused himself and stepped back into the kitchen.

"Evening, Ami. Everything okay?"

Ami Madar was the director of security at the Israel Institute of Technology, a former Mossad officer, and a good friend of Basch's, because the work Basch and his team did at the institute was government classified, and therefore Ami was intimately involved with the lab's security.

Ami was always serious, but he seemed even more urgently so this evening. "Everything okay with you, Tomer? No issues?"

"Everything's fine. What's going on?"

"Richard Watt was killed this morning in America. Murdered."

Tomer put his wineglass down on the kitchen island. "Rick? My *God*. By who?"

"Unknown. A sniper got him on a golf course. The shooter got away."

Tomer Basch cocked his head now. He knew Watt, but not closely, so he didn't understand what this had to do with him. "And you think . . . you think *what*?"

"Dr. Kotana Ishikawa was killed six hours ago in Osaka. She was run over in a parking lot after leaving her mother's retirement home. A witness said it was no accident."

"That's terrible."

"Ethan Edgar's car ran off the road in Sydney this morning, and Montri Churat was shot dead in his home in Bangkok. All four of them died in the past twelve hours."

Now the Israeli understood. Kotana Ishikawa was, like Tomer Basch himself, one of the top two dozen or so pioneers of weaponized AI in the entire world. And Rick Watt, while not a developer himself, had been at the very forefront of acquisition of the technology that Ishikawa and Tomer had created. He knew as much as if not more than they did about which research labs in which countries were developing which AI initiatives, at least as far as military applications were concerned.

Ethan Edgar and Montri Churat were also leading AI pioneers and acquaintances of Tomer Basch.

"Are you saying I might be in danger?" Basch asked, but this was Ami, the security chief and a very serious man, so Tomer knew that was *exactly* what he was saying.

"Your officers are in place?"

Basch looked out the window over his kitchen sink. A private security car sat parked in the driveway. Two men armed with rifles leaned against it, their eyes out to the street ahead.

"Yeah. I'm looking at them now. No issues."

Even though this entire community was regularly patrolled, covered with cameras, and as safe a neighborhood as one could find in all of northern Israel, he always had guards on his property during the nighttime hours, just to ensure his family's safety.

Ami said, "Okay. I'm sending an extra team of our guys from the institute, just to watch over you."

Basch thought a moment. "Okay, get them here for my family, but I'm coming in to work."

"On a Saturday night?"

"If someone *is* targeting me, I'm going to figure out who it is. I can't do that from home. I *have* to get to the office."

Ami protested. "Tomer, we don't have to figure out who's doing this because we know. It's the Chinese, obviously. They've been amping up their efforts to win the AI arms race. This could just be the next phase. Killing their competition."

Basch said, "You may be right, but there might be something else going on here. I need to get in there and make some calls."

Ami Madar breathed into the phone a moment. "All right. I'll meet you there. Take your weapon with you for the drive."

Tomer's heart was pounding in his chest. He suddenly felt like he was back in the IDF, a young man facing the threat of death every day.

He turned away from his kitchen, looked back into his den at his family. "Ami, I'm not going to say anything to Lior about this. She'd just get upset. But get your guys here as soon as possible."

Ten minutes later he climbed into his blue Mercedes AMG E63, fired the throaty engine, and pulled out onto Shvedya Street.

As his AMG wound through the beautiful neighborhood for a few blocks, he turned to a classical station on his satellite radio to calm himself, then made a left turn onto Abba Khoushy Avenue.

Basch had helped design both hardware and software for many different autonomous platforms, including drones, and he therefore had the ability to recognize the distinctive buzzing of a UAV, even a small one, when he heard it. But his brain's total absorption on getting to the office while thinking about the puzzle he was facing, plus the powerful strings and horns of Rachmaninoff's Second Symphony's Allegro molto coming from his Bowers & Wilkins speakers, made it impossible for him to detect the tiny quadcopter following his every move from above.

Not long after the turn onto Abba Khoushy he did notice, however, a black cargo van ahead of him in traffic. It bore the emblem of a local heating and air conditioning service, and didn't seem in any way out of place, but it slowed in his lane, so he flipped his blinker to pass it on the right, then waited a moment because a scooter with both a rider and a passenger was coming up the lane quickly.

The forty-six-year-old waited for the scooter to pass him by, but once it came level with him on the right, it slowed to match his speed. He saw two helmeted figures on board; neither was paying any attention to him, but he was stuck there until they moved on.

At forty kilometers an hour he waited for either the van to turn off or change lanes, or for the little bike on his right to get out of his way, but as he listened to Rachmaninoff, he noticed movement from the man on the back of the scooter.

Basch looked back to the van in front of him; it had slowed further, but when he shifted to his right again, he saw the scooter still there, keeping level with his rear passenger door.

"Son of a bitch," he muttered. Basch didn't have a perfect angle looking through the mirror, so he turned and glanced back through the window, and just as he did so, he saw the passenger on the bike swing something, a rope with a large pack on the end of it, over his head and down towards the Mercedes. Before he could react, he heard a loud impact on the roof of his vehicle, just above and behind the driver's seat, and then the scooter peeled off abruptly to the right.

The passenger no longer had the pack in his hand.

Tomer shouted in surprise, and then he slammed on his brakes, desperate to get out of his sedan because he knew what was happening.

The scooter passenger had just affixed explosives to the roof of his car.

The van revved off, Tomer Basch threw open the door of his now stopped AMG E63, and he unfastened his seat belt as fast as he could.

He was not fast enough. The bomb on the roof detonated, sending shrapnel and flame through the vehicle; the gas tank erupted, and Tomer Basch's body was ripped to shreds in a ball of fire.

Operations Center Gama in Singapore tracked the images from the recon drone high over Haifa Street on a large wall monitor.

The American woman who served as second-in-command spoke loud enough to be heard around the room. "That's a kill."

Men and women high-fived, bumped fists, and shook hands.

In the back of the room, however, Martina Sommer rubbed her temples with her fingers, a show of stress she hid from the others by leaning down behind her monitor.

After the rest of the group spent a few seconds of rapt fascination watching the wreckage on the street in far-off Haifa, the Norwegian director turned to a Dutch technician who sat two cubes down from Martina. "Number Nine, stand down the assets in Tel Aviv; I'll have Cyrus wire them the rest of the money."

"Yes, sir."

He turned to an Indian woman seated to Martina's right. "Thirteen, contact the on-scene wrangler. Have him recall the drone and report in when he is clear."

"Yes, sir." She tapped the talk button on her headset and spoke directly with the person on the ground in Haifa working the aerial surveillance coverage mission.

Martina thought she was going to be sick.

The director sat down at his own workstation, positioned behind a glass partition at the front of the small theater, then opened a chat window with the title **Cyrus** on the top bar.

He began typing. **This is Gama Leader. The elimination of target Gama Five is confirmed.**

In under one second a reply window opened, and after a few more seconds a response came. **Message received by Cyrus. Excellent news. You have forty-five hours to prosecute the remaining thirteen targets.**

The Norwegian smiled as he typed. **We will complete our directives. Don't worry.**

I don't worry. Good job today. Cyrus out.

He sat back in his chair a moment, running his hands through his brown hair. The job in Israel was done, but that only meant it was time to set up for the next one. To the room the operations chief said, "We begin coverage in the United Kingdom in one hour."

A British woman spoke up now. "Wrangler Zero Three is on station near the target and awaiting our launch order."

"Very well." The director looked at the clock on the wall. Thirteen people left to eliminate. A professional challenge, to be sure, but he told himself that it was nothing he couldn't handle.

He had assets all over the world, he had an employer who was always available and more than willing to throw massive amounts of money at any problem, and the hits were all taking place so quickly that he and his team retained the element of surprise, though with every death and with every hour, that would slip away more and more.

He had nothing against his targets, but what he did have was both a drug addiction and a gambling addiction, and overseeing operations against several people in other countries he didn't even know, operations that involved murder, but murders committed by others, was a small price to pay for him to reboot his life and try to get himself sorted out.

If people had to die to make this happen, the director reasoned, then so be it.

He assumed that his unique lack of empathy was shared by everyone else here in Operations Center Gama, and he was right, for the most part.

But, unbeknownst to him, German national Martina Sommer was now on her knees in the bathroom, vomiting into a toilet.

EIGHT

The Chevy Tahoe carrying the American assassin and his three Guatemalan support assets rolled into Panajachel a few minutes after six under heavy rain showers, persistent thunder, and lightning. The streets were mostly empty because of the weather; locals and experienced tourists knew to wait out the evening Central American storms and resume any outdoor activities once they passed.

But the men were on a schedule, so they pulled into a graveled parking lot surrounded by a rusted tin wall on Calle de los Arboles, then began walking to the southwest, all four now wearing ponchos to ward off the rain.

They made it to within three blocks of their target location, and then Lancer put an earpiece in his right ear and tapped it with a fingertip. "Control, Lancer. I'm on sight."

"Lancer, Control. Be advised. Genrich has returned to the capitol. We think he is going to the airport to return to Mexico. Zakharova is your target in Panajachel."

"Roger that. Update on the weather and ISR."

The woman with the French accent said, "Overhead ISR will resume as soon as able. Recommend you hold position until coverage returns."

Lancer made his decision quickly. "Negative. Moving to location now and will act at first opportunity. I'm on scene and the weather is breaking. Find a way to get me overhead eyes."

He again tapped the earpiece, this time ending the call, and then he and the three locals headed out through the storm.

Five minutes later they stood in sight of the apartment building. Lancer put his hand on Bernadino's shoulder and turned him into a little cobblestone driveway that led to a small hotel, and the other two shuffled quickly behind.

Here they were out of view of the target location, hidden by a stone wall and thick foliage, even though they were only thirty yards away from the front of the two-story apartment building.

A corrugated tin roof hung over part of the drive, apparently to provide shelter for a security guard at the gate, but the gate was open and there was no guard. Lancer led the others under it. The wind had picked up just in the few minutes they'd been out of the vehicle, and light rain pelted their faces, even here under the roof. Lancer said, "Chico will get the SUV and bring it one block to the south. Tell him to park on the street in front of the post office, facing away from the target location."

Bernadino translated and Chico acknowledged.

Lancer continued. "Alfredo will go around back, cut off any escape route. Find some good cover and be ready." This was also acknowledged after the translation. To Bernadino he said, "You will go into the lobby and take the stairs. Get in the hallway outside their door and cover. I'll make entry through the balcony." He reached into his raincoat and pulled his pistol, holding it up in front of his face.

"I'm suppressed and the ammunition is subsonic, but it's still going to sound like someone slamming a car door."

From the gawking expressions, it was clear none of the Guatemalans had ever seen anything like the weapon in the American's hand. It appeared to be a very large Colt 1911 but was in fact a Republic Forge Longslide in the relatively unique 10-millimeter caliber. It wore a large, boxy, Aimpoint optic on a mount on the top of the slide, and its six-inch barrel was affixed with a stubby suppressor, elongating the weapon even further. The pistol's magazine extended several inches out of the mag well, and the grip's texture was deeply knurled.

The handgun was one hundred percent custom-made to Lancer's specifications. Big, bulky, and hard to conceal, but a powerful battle weapon in the hands of an expert.

Lancer, the expert, reholstered under his rain poncho, then drew a knife from a sheath at the small of his back. "If you don't hear anything, this is why."

He popped open the stiletto, its blade coated in black.

The men separated at six thirty p.m., but Lancer didn't go far. He crossed the street in the diminishing rain, then stood in an alcove in front of a language school, giving Chico a few minutes to get to the SUV and Alfredo time to find a hiding place around back.

Eight blocks from the target location, twenty-five-year-old Carlos Contreras sat in the rear of a white Ford Econoline van, his hands laced behind his head and his feet resting on the swivel chair next to him. This chair, like the one he now sat in, was bungee-corded to a hook in the wall behind him so it wouldn't slide away while the van was moving.

In front of him was a table that folded down from the wall, and on the table a pair of closed laptop computers sat, placed in slight recesses so they would remain in place even if the vehicle was on the move. Also in the van with him was a bungeed-together stack of hardshell cases, closer to the driver's and front passenger seats.

Each case contained a small quadcopter, and all the cases were filled, because the weather presently made operating a drone over Panajachel a risky endeavor for the devices.

Light showers and strong winds continued to buffet the vehicle, and although it seemed the rain was definitely letting up, the wind was definitely not.

Contreras was code-named Wrangler Zero One for this operation, and drones were his life. A hobbyist since he was a boy in Monterrey, Mexico, he'd taken a job at fifteen flying for a photographic mapping company in Houston, and then he was headhunted by a drug cartel in Jalisco. Still officially in the employ of the cartel, he was known as their best operator and even one of the best pilots in the industry, but a brutal cartel war had made his job with Jalisco less enticing than it once had been, so when he received a message in his inbox inquiring about his services for an operation in the capital hunting a Russian engineer, he took the job immediately.

After a couple of days in Mexico City he was told he was being replaced by another wrangler there, and he needed to get down to a small lakeside village in Guatemala and locate a Russian businessman on an urgent mission.

Hispanic and only five foot six, Contreras could pass as a local, so he blended in well here in Guatemala, as long as he didn't have to talk, because he was Mexican and his accent would be instantly identifiable to a local as such.

After he rubbed his tired eyes, then glanced at his watch, a voice entered his right ear. It was the German woman at the TOC he'd been speaking with since he'd arrived here late last night. "Wrangler Zero One, this is Control. I'm showing the weather at the target location has passed. How long till ISR is back online?"

Contreras looked out the window of the van. A palm tree in the courtyard of a tiny vacation rental whipped around wildly. "Too much wind."

"Wait one," came the reply.

Contreras opened a can of mango juice that he'd pulled from a little cooler, then looked down at his watch. He didn't think he'd get any of his copters back in the air tonight, rain or no rain.

The German woman spoke again; her voice sounded a little meek and unsure. "We need eyes, Wrangler. The operation is about to begin. Can you get one platform on station over the target location in the next five minutes?"

Contreras sighed. He'd already told them he couldn't do it. "Not without risking losing equipment."

Suddenly, a new voice spoke in his ear, this time in a European accent, a man who sounded at once authoritative and angry. "Risk it, then! Get a drone overhead to watch for anyone trying to squirt. This target must be prosecuted tonight!"

The man was well educated, in charge, and pissed off; all of this Contreras could instantly discern.

Still, he was the wrangler in the field, not this asshole European. "Who is this?"

"This is Gama director. I'm giving you an order."

"But the wind—"

"You were sent because you are supposedly the best drone operator in the Americas. Now is your chance to prove it."

Carlos Contreras looked out the front window; foliage rising over the wall of an automotive engine repair training center thrashed as a gust blasted up the street from the lake. He said, "It is my professional opinion that any attempt to fly right now at this altitude and in this weather will result in the crash of the platform."

"Those aren't *your* platforms, Zero One. Those aren't my platforms, either. If it crashes, it crashes, but I need to tell the assets we at least tried to get eyes on. They are demanding it."

Contreras's jaw fixed in anger. "I don't tell the assets how to do their jobs, and they probably shouldn't tell me how—"

The European interrupted again. "I expect coverage over the target within five minutes. Gama out." The transmission ended.

He sighed loudly, almost a groan, then put down his juice and scooted over to the cases. All his units had been recharged in the four-and-a-half-hour halt of flight ops, so he grabbed the top case and popped it open, then removed a dark gray rectangular device only four inches by eight inches. He extended four arms, spun the propellers on the top of each one to make sure they hadn't been damaged in the case, then turned the device on by holding down a button on its belly with his right hand, just aft of the bulbous camera lens shield.

With his left hand he opened the laptop in front of him and tapped a few keys, and a soft blue light flickered on the roof of the device.

Another series of inputs and the propellers began to spin.

Contreras rose to a crouch, made his way past the cases to the back door of the van, and looked out through the smoked-glass windows. Seeing no one around in the little parking lot, he opened the door and stepped out.

The wind had lessened for the time being, but he wasn't hopeful about any of this.

The Mexican said a quick little prayer as he always did when he sent one of his devices on a mission, then gently tossed it into the air.

Instantly the quadcopter rose and disappeared over the top of the van into the night, its buzzing rotor noise fading in no more than three or four seconds.

Contreras ducked back into the van and closed the door. Still praying the wind didn't gust too hard, he opened his other laptop and put his hands on the pair of joysticks in front of it.

The quadcopter was on autopilot, racing to the target location, but he knew that if enough wind hit it to where it spun out of control, then the autopilot might disengage automatically and he'd have to try to recover it himself before it crashed.

He concentrated on the feed in front of him, willing the device onwards towards the action that was about to start one quarter mile to the northwest.

NINE

Court Gentry looked out the window next to the balcony door, his eyes on the darkened street below. The precipitation had mostly stopped, but he could tell there were occasional blasts of wind from the off-and-on-again buffeting of the window glass, and rainwater ran deep in the gullies below him. TukTuks and small vehicles passed by from time to time, moving down the middle of the two-lane street to avoid being caught up in the small rivers on each side of the road heading down towards the lake.

But he saw no one on foot at all.

He wore a black hooded raincoat and his backpack; his SIG pistol was jammed into his belt in the small of his back, with extra mags in his pocket, positioned for quick reloads.

As he continued looking at the scene outside, he heard Zoya step up behind him.

"He's not answering his phone."

"Genrich?"

"Yes. He could be in the air. Flying back to Mexico City. He had to go commercial."

Court turned to her. "Yeah, he could be a lot of things." Looking her up and down, he saw she wore a raincoat, and her large gray backpack was over a shoulder, with her smaller daypack on her chest. "You going some-where?"

She looked sad and, for the first time today, he felt for her. He was mad and hurt that she'd kept Genrich's appearance a secret from him, but he could now plainly see this man meant something to her.

She sniffed a little, holding back tears. "I am coming with you."

His heart lifted, but he tried to remain stone-faced. "You sure?"

"I guess the question is, do you *want* me to come with you?"

"I do. But I want you to do it because you know it's the right thing."

She looked down. He could see the confliction on her face. "I would help Uncle Slava if he was working for another cause, but I can't support Russia. Not now." She looked back up at him. "Just answer me this. How did you know I went back to the café?"

"Microexpressions."

"When I saw him?"

"Your face transmitted the fact that you knew him. You covered it so fast I was certain this was important. I waited for some sign from you . . . but nothing came."

Zoya finished the explanation for him. "So when I left you on the street, you doubled back to the café because you knew where I was going."

"Went through the kitchen. Watched you through a window. You couldn't see me because of the reflection."

Zoya nodded. "What now?"

"We take a bus to Guatemala City. We stay there tonight and leave for Belize in the morning via private car."

She nodded. "I know you think we might be under surveillance, but I swear to you, Dyadya Slava would not lie to me."

Court just looked back out the window. His silence spoke volumes.

After a time she said, "There's no one out there."

Turning to head for the door, Court passed her by. Without looking at her, he said, "Humor me while we run an SDR anyway."

A surveillance detection route was tradecraft-speak for moving in ir-regular patterns around an area to identify anyone who might be follow-ing. Both Zoya and Court had conducted thousands of these in their years of work in the shadows, and tonight would be . . . *should* be . . . no different.

Zoya didn't respond to the American's curt comment; she just followed him out the door.

They stepped into the hallway, then stopped next to a window overlooking the small rear parking court.

Court knelt down next to it. Carefully peering around the side, he saw that a milky white mist now hung in the cool highland air.

He scanned left to right over the space, taking in shapes, hunting for movement. The idling engine of a parked car, the glint of light from a flashlight, even an illuminated watch face, anything that stood out.

He saw nothing at first, but then he began to rise, revealing more of his body to the window, and suddenly he detected a shift in the darkness, possibly the wind but possibly something else.

Softly, he said, "Hold."

Zoya reached into the daypack on her chest, put her right hand around the grip of the 9-millimeter Jericho she'd packed there. Court held a hand out to calm her, but his eyes remained focused on the rear parking area. A row of colorful bushes hung over a tin fence, casting shadows from the light on the pole above it. Finally, he said, "Got a figure in a black poncho back here. He's mostly behind a tree, under the bushes by the fence. Can't tell if he's armed."

Zoya hesitated, then asked, "A Guatemalan?"

"I don't know."

"Uncle Slava wouldn't turn on me."

Court said nothing to this. After a moment he said, "If this guy is a rear blocking force, that means others will be coming up the stairs, or via the balcony back in the room."

She shook her head. "Or maybe he's just a security guard, or a guy talking on his cell phone to his girlfriend outside his flat so his wife doesn't hear."

"Maybe," he said softly.

He dropped low, took off his backpack, and scooted under the window. As Zoya did the same, Court pulled out his lock pick set and began working on the door to the apartment there. He'd noticed that the place was unoccupied when they arrived the other day, and he'd neither heard movement nor seen anyone coming or going since then.

In seconds he had the door open.

The unit was dark and empty—good news—and he quickly moved across to the balcony there. Looking out over the little buildings on the opposite side of Callejon Santa Elena, he went outside, then peered down to the street.

Zoya appeared behind him. "There's movement in the stairwell, one pax, heading up. Probably just a neighbor," she added.

It was *not* a neighbor, Court was certain, and he wondered if Zoya even believed what she was saying, or if she was simply trying to manifest the fact that nothing was amiss, because if something *was* amiss, then it likely meant Genrich had double-crossed her.

Without a word he rose and moved to the northern corner of the balcony; there was no lighting here, either from the building or on the street below. He kicked a leg over the low iron railing, then hung down. Dropping the last three feet to the sidewalk, he collapsed his body as he landed, then rolled onto his backpack to blunt the impact.

Court pulled his weapon and kept it down behind his leg as he stood up, looking around.

Quickly he clocked a black SUV parked a couple blocks down the street in front of a post office; its engine was off, its lights off, as well, its grille facing in the opposite direction.

But steam rose from the hood, as if the engine was warm.

The SUV must have just arrived.

It wasn't far away, but it wasn't right up on the apartment building, either. It was, in Court's estimation, exactly where the wheelman for an assassination force might park his ride.

He whistled softly, his way of telling Zoya, still on the balcony, to look around. The wind swirled in the street, then blew hard; torn-away palm fronds skittered past, along with water picked up from the gutters.

Twenty seconds later Zoya dropped down next to him in the near pitch-black night, and then she rose and leaned into his ear. "The Tahoe?"

"Yeah. Not close enough to be part of the assault, but close enough for the exfil."

Zoya said, "We're getting ahead of ourselves. We don't know—"

Court turned to her. Angrily, he said, "We *don't* know, that's the problem."

Zoya sighed audibly. "Okay. Bus depot still?"

He shook his head. "Let's go to the dock, get a boat to San Juan la Laguna, across the lake. The village is tiny, just one hotel. If anyone is after us we'll know it instantly, and tomorrow we can get on a chicken bus to the capital."

"The lake is that way." She nodded towards the Tahoe. "You want to bypass the vehicle?"

Court said, "No. We're running an SDR. Let's see if the Tahoe is here for us. We move past it with our hoods over our heads. If they're a bad actor, they won't know it's us, but they also won't be able to rule out the possibility. They'll have to follow. If they do, we slip away."

The two of them began walking through the darkness as another gust of wind blew hard into their faces, causing them to hold on to their hoods.

Carlos Contreras sat in the back of his Econoline, eyes riveted to the monitor in front of him that showed the image from his UAV, just now arriving over the target building. The feed wasn't clear at all, this he saw instantly, so he switched to infrared.

He didn't love his view. Between the water vapor gathering around the lens of the camera and the buffeting air at three hundred feet, the image from the drone was little more than a blur.

Still, he was up, and every few seconds the picture would focus for an instant and he could see the area below with some clarity.

Seconds later Contreras peered closer to the screen. He tapped a button on his keyboard, and the drone began broadcasting thermal images. He said, "Control, Zero One. I have two subjects moving southwest. Can't fix facial recog on them because I'm on infrared. Plus, they're wearing hooded raincoats."

"On Callejon Santa Elena?"

"Affirmative."

"Yes, we see them. One of our assets is in the SUV they're about to pass. Stand by."

Contreras waited several seconds, watching the pair of pedestrians, both wearing backpacks, as they moved down the street past an SUV. A moment later the German lady spoke again, her voice filling his earpiece.

"Zero One, Control. Our asset relays that's two males. Negative ID on Zakharova. Stay over the target location."

"Understood. No other movement out of area."

"Keep monitoring."

Contreras hung up, then spoke softly to himself in Spanish. "I know how to do my job."

Just then, the van rocked on its chassis as a strong gust of wind came from the direction of the nearby lake. Contreras quickly looked to his monitor and saw the real-time thermal image captured by the drone move; the clarity of the image lessened for a moment, and then it sharpened again. A quick scan of data on his other laptop showed him that everything on board the unit was working fine, but seconds later the image blurred once more, green data points on his second laptop flashed red, and when the picture cleared again, he could see that the UAV was literally tumbling through the air.

Contreras grabbed the controls. The autopilot had shut off, and he struggled to right the device plummeting through the sky nearly one hundred yards above and a quarter mile to the northeast of him.

The battle for control continued, and while it did, the German woman came back into his ear. "Wrangler, Control. We've lost the image—"

He shouted back as he furiously worked one of the joysticks. "Yeah, and I'm about to lose the entire platform! Leave me alone!"

Another blast came in, RC19 spun again, and a quick glance at his data screen showed Contreras that the tiny aircraft was only seventy feet above the ground and still losing altitude.

He realized his only chance to save the device was to forget about trying to fly it back to the van and land it right where it was. He kept up the descent while simultaneously looking for a flat piece of ground somewhere below.

At forty feet and falling he decided on a crash-landing attempt on the flat roof of a long, low building two thirds of the way back to his van from the target location. He maneuvered the joystick expertly, zeroing in on the corrugated metal surface, and pulled back on the power when it was only a few feet above it.

RC19 bounced to a hard and likely noisy landing, finally coming to rest upside down just inches from the two-story roof's edge.

Contreras took a long breath to relax, and then he tapped his earpiece. "Control, Wrangler Zero One. RC19 crash-landed on a rooftop four blocks from me." He added, "In this weather, nobody could have done better than that. I'm going on foot to retrieve it."

He climbed out of the van, leaned into the wind, and began heading to the northeast, cussing under his breath because this screwup was not his fault.

TEN

Court and Zoya had passed the SUV and the lone man sitting inside it thirty seconds earlier, but so far there was no indication the man had entered into either a vehicle or a foot follow.

Zoya said, "I think we're fine."

Court shook his head. "He might not have pinged us for some reason, but he could still be a bad actor."

"Hey, it was *your* plan."

Court shoved his hands into his pockets and trudged on through the night. Zoya walked along next to him, occasionally holding her hood forward and down to keep the wind from blowing it back.

She said, "You really think we're going to find a launch or a boat that will take us over the lake in these conditions?"

"If not, then we're stealing one."

Since the rain had stopped fully now, there were more people out on the street by the minute. It was a Saturday night; men and women filed into and out of restaurants and bars in this tourist town, and locals headed to tiendas and bus stops.

Zoya and Court eyed everyone they saw, surreptitiously, of course, and Court looked in every reflective surface he could find, hunting for an indication they were being followed.

But so far, anyway, Zoya's insistence that they had not been compromised seemed to be holding up.

With the strong wind to his back, Contreras arrived at the building where he'd crash-landed the drone minutes earlier. It was a long and simple two-story structure with a corrugated metal roof, festooned with signage. On the first floor, a small grocery and an arts and crafts shop were closed for the evening, and the second floor housed an optician and a dentist, also apparently dark and empty.

A kiosk that normally sold T-shirts was boarded up in front of the building, and its little roof was exactly half the height to the second-floor wrap-around balcony. Contreras was no gymnast, but he'd had to climb up many trees, buildings, boulders, and the like to retrieve his wayward equipment in the past, so he figured he could get himself up there to his device without any trouble.

A bus passed, spraying water from its tires onto the Mexican. He cussed loudly, then snatched a five-gallon bucket off the sidewalk and took it over to the kiosk. Climbing onto this, he grabbed hold of the metal roof and, with some effort, pulled himself up.

From here he jumped across to the balcony, grabbed on to the wet railing, and then climbed up onto the roof.

Soon he was on his knees in the dark, folding up his white quadcopter and placing it into his backpack. Two of the propellers had snapped, but he had dozens of spares back in the van, so he just detached them and left them there.

A fresh gust of wind came from the southwest; he turned away from it and, as soon as he did so, noticed a pair of individuals appear out of a street running off to the east and then begin moving his way.

Instantly he thought these might be the pair he'd seen with his drone coverage earlier, the ones eliminated by the ground assets as being targets.

As the two approached, not more than twenty meters distant and two stories below him, another gale roared in from behind Contreras, and the hood of one of the passersby blew back.

Contreras saw the blond hair, then recognized the face of the target tasked as Gama 18, and he was certain neither she nor the man with her had seen him, as he was in pitch-black darkness up on the rooftop.

Still, he froze, did not move a muscle till they had continued down the street for half a minute.

Then he tapped his earpiece.

"Gama Control, Zero One."

The response was quick from the German at Gama. "Go for Control."

"I have the two targets moving southwest."

There was a pause, and then the woman replied, "We aren't receiving any images. How do you—"

"I *saw* them. I physically saw them. I'm at 595 Calle Santander, and they passed my position thirty seconds ago. Looks like they're heading towards the lake."

"Roger. Control out."

Contreras waited a little longer, then began climbing down to the balcony. He wasn't putting another copter in the air, no matter what Gama or the assets wanted, but he did need to get himself, his van, and his suspicious-looking equipment out of here before it all went loud. Which, judging by the urgent, almost panicked voice of the German woman on the other end of the line, would probably not be very long at all.

The assassin known as Lancer holstered his massive pistol in the middle of the dark and empty apartment. He'd checked every room, every closet. He opened the door to the hall, saw Bernadino standing there, and the young Guatemalan just shook his head.

He was just about to notify his controller that they'd hit a dry hole when the French woman broadcast into his earpiece.

"Lancer, Control."

"Go."

"Zakharova and her male associate are six blocks to your southwest, on foot, heading in the direction of the lake."

The American was moving in an instant. To Bernadino he said, "Get Chico up here to pick us all up. Target acquired."

. . .

Court and Zoya approached the water's edge and passed a red-roofed restaurant that—through the windows, anyway—seemed reasonably full despite the bad weather. The Porta Hotel del Lago lay on their left as they faced the water, and in front of them they saw a row of simple wooden piers jutting out into Lake Atitlán, and more than a dozen boats of various sizes bobbing close together.

Court knew Zoya was right; there probably wouldn't be any captains out and about at the moment because the lake was whitewater rough.

"Let's take one of those small launches," he said as they walked past a low stone wall separating the dock area from the roads and buildings higher on the hill. "It's not going to be a fun crossing, but it will be easier to fire an outboard motor than to boost one of those engines on the bigger watercraft."

Zoya responded dubiously, her eyes on the choppy conditions. "Are you a good enough captain to get us across?"

They began walking down one of the piers towards a pair of wooden launches. "It's still just a lake. I've made it over a lot stormier seas than that."

Zoya said nothing.

They arrived at the end of the wooden pier, where Court eyed a pair of two twenty-five-foot boats, both with low covered wheelhouse areas and bench seating in the back.

"Which one?" Zoya asked, but before Court answered, he looked back up towards the town.

A young Guatemalan man on a bicycle turned off the road and came down the boat ramp, then bumped his bike's wheels up onto the pier. He didn't appear to be a threat, but both Court's and Zoya's hands hovered close to their weapons: his on his hip, and hers in the outer compartment of the pack on her chest.

The man rolled under the little light at the end of the pier and stopped his bike just twenty feet or so from the pair standing by the launches. He wore a raincoat and a ball cap, and he appeared to be no more than twenty years old.

In English, he said, "My boat." He nodded to the one on Court and Zoya's right.

Court answered him in Spanish. "We need to go to San Juan."

The young man said, "En serio?" *Seriously?*

"En serio," Court responded. In Spanish he said, "One thousand quetzales." This was over 120 U.S. dollars, and easily four or five times what the young man would normally make taking passengers a couple miles away to another village.

The Guatemalan's eyebrows rose. "Muestra me." *Show me.*

Court pulled a wallet out of his front pants pocket, then from it retrieved a fold of bills. "We leave now," he said.

The man looked up at the sky, then shrugged. "Hay viento." *It's windy,* he said, but then he climbed off his bike, hefted it onto his shoulder, and boarded the little boat. He put the bike down on the small deck.

Zoya leaned closer to Court and spoke softly. "This kid looks sixteen."

"He's been boating on this lake longer than I have."

"Five minutes boating on this lake is longer than you have."

"Exactly my point."

Zoya climbed aboard, and Court prepared to do the same, but a vehicle's lights appeared on the road, and then they shut off before the car stopped some fifty yards away.

Court immediately recognized the vehicle as the black Tahoe he and Zoya had passed several minutes earlier.

The four doors on the vehicle opened in unison, four men climbed out, and Court saw a black short-barreled weapon in the hands of the driver.

None of the men seemed to notice him yet, but they all scanned the area.

"Fuck."

Zoya stood there on the deck, just now pulling off her packs to put them on the little gunwale bench. Court leapt into the air, landed next to her and the bicycle, and pushed her down to the deck. An instant later he rose back up, grabbed the confused Guatemalan launch captain by the arm, and swung him up and over the gunwale and out into the water, where he crashed below the surface between his boat and the one bobbing five feet away from it. This put the noncombatant out of any line of fire, but it also drew more attention to this boat and this pier.

Court drew his pistol and turned to find Zoya staring at him just as the first gunshot snapped in the dark night. The wooden launch they stood on splintered up at the bow.

More gunfire kicked up, boards on the dock next to them cracked, and it was clear the enemy had fixed their position.

Court rose to look over the helm, then squatted back down. To Zoya he said, "Four hostiles. Subguns. They've split up and are in cover behind the rock wall."

Zoya knelt there on the deck, unmoving, her eyes wide in disbelief. She hadn't even drawn her gun.

"Hey!" Court shouted. "Snap the fuck out of it!"

"Whoever this is . . . this isn't Uncle—"

"I don't give a shit who it is! We've gotta move."

To her credit, Zoya Zakharova did, in fact, snap the fuck out of it. She reached into her chest pack and pulled her pistol, then lowered herself behind her main pack, now on the deck.

The engine had already fired on the launch, but it remained tied to the pier by the bowline, and Court didn't want to crawl up to where he'd be in direct line of sight of the men behind the wall. Even trying to shoot the line meant exposing his body to withering fire around the side of the helm. He holstered quickly, pulled his own pack off, then hefted it up on his shoulder.

To Zoya he said, "Next boat."

"Got it."

A thirty-foot launch with a covered helm and a pair of outboards was tied down just five feet away on the adjacent pier. Court heaved his pack over to it and slammed it down onto the deck, and then Zoya called to him over the sound of incoming gunfire.

"Suppressing! Get to the next one and find cover!"

Zoya opened fire in the direction of the men at the rock wall while Court rose and took two steps across the little deck, then put his foot up on the gunwale and sprang up and over. He flew above the black water and landed on the deck of the next vessel. Zoya kept up the steady fire at the four shooters, who were now separating even farther behind the wall.

As soon as he rose into a crouch on the next boat, Court pulled his weapon and aimed in on the man closest to him. He fired a half-dozen rounds in rapid succession; the first few hit the wall, but at least one seemed to find the upper torso or head of the man, because he fell back away from the wall and did not reappear.

As Court kept up the fire, Zoya's backpack crashed down next to him, and then she came leaping over, landing on the wet deck and slipping onto her back.

Court finished his twelve-round magazine, then knelt low to reload just as Zoya came up behind him and began firing over his head.

This assassination was turning into a shit show, and Lancer knew who was to blame. He had been first out of the vehicle, and he'd almost immediately spied a man standing on the pier near a boat, an odd enough sight in thirty-mile-per-hour wind gusts, but he knew he needed to get closer to look for Zakharova. He'd only taken a couple of steps away from the Tahoe, however, when Chico climbed out from behind the wheel, his weapon in plain view.

The man on the pier jumped into the boat behind the helm, a loud splash followed, and suddenly both Chico and Bernadino opened fire at the source of the noise.

Lancer knew his prudent course of action was getting to cover, because if the Russian and her friend were armed, they'd be shooting back in moments, and he didn't want to be standing out on a lighted street when the exchange of bullets began in earnest.

He'd made it to the wall, where he drew his heavy pistol just as the return rounds began snapping over his head.

Lancer held his fire as the three Guatemalans arrived at the wall and passed behind him; they then separated behind the cover, giving the enemy a more complex puzzle to solve.

Lancer had yet to see Zakharova, but after a moment he realized someone had jumped onto the next boat, this one tied at the adjacent pier.

He realized they were trying to move laterally, possibly to find a boat they could use to speed out of the area.

He ran in a crouch towards Chico now, but when he was still five yards away from the man firing his MP5 over the wall, the Guatemalan tumbled back and away, dropping his weapon in the process.

Lancer continued running in a low crouch, bypassing the injured Chico without so much as a glance—the idiot had earned that gunshot, he reasoned—and then he ran on towards Bernadino. Here he crouched just as the man began reloading his HK.

The American leaned into the Guatemalan's ear to be heard over Alfredo's shooting. "You two stay here and keep their heads down, I'll flank from the east. When you see me get on a boat, cease fire, go back to the vehicle, and get the hell out of here before the cops come. Don't you fucking shoot at me, or I'll kill your fucking families."

Bernadino slammed the bolt closed on his weapon and then looked his way. "You're getting on a boat?"

The American did not respond; he just rose again and resumed running low along the wall. As he did so he tore off his poncho and his shirt and drew his stiletto, while behind him Bernadino began firing again.

ELEVEN

Court leapt across five feet of water and landed on the rocking deck of yet another vessel, this one a small fishing trawler nearly a foot higher than the one he'd just hurdled from. Zoya, her pack, and Court's pack were already aboard, and he scrambled up behind the little wheelhouse, then fired around the left side at muzzle flashes forty yards away.

This wasn't working from a tactical standpoint. They couldn't continue bounding from deck to deck. The men on the road had superior numbers, superior firepower, and the high ground. Court had no doubt the enemy would eventually pick Zoya and him off unless they changed tactics quickly.

He knew they could jump into the water, but then they'd lose their heavy packs with all their possessions, and the currents in the lake would push them straight to shore, as they no doubt had already done to the young boat captain he'd tossed in forty-five seconds earlier.

No, he needed to untie one of these vessels, hot-wire the engine, and get the fuck out of here.

Looking to his right at the next boat over, he saw it was exactly what he needed. A forty-foot touring boat with a covered deck and windows at the front, it had an open deck with bench seating at the rear and, most importantly, a pair of powerful but older-model Yamaha outboard motors that Court knew he'd be able to start up, even without a key.

Court shouted to Zoya as she fired. "We're taking that one! I'm going to boost it. I'll need about a minute and you'll have to cover me."

They made yet another leap, Court first while Zoya remained on the fishing boat firing the pistol at a pair of targets intermittently popping their heads and arms over the impenetrable rock wall. She wasn't getting hits, but she was keeping the shooters from sending accurate fire her way.

Court called her over and began firing himself. She changed magazines, slung her backpack five feet to the deck of the tourist boat, then jumped, landing just behind the covered portion of the deck on a wooden bench. Quickly she dropped to her knees to make herself a smaller target, then raised her pistol back towards the town. As she did this she shouted, "Last mag!"

Court slid Zoya his weapon, which she stopped with her knee, and then she hefted it and forced it into the back pocket of her jeans, barrel down. "Full mag," he said. He pulled another magazine from his pocket and slid it to her. "That's my last."

She snatched it up and shoved it into her other back pocket, moved forward under the deck roof now, then began slowly firing through the front window of the boat.

Court reached into his pack and pulled out a multitool and a tiny flashlight, both of which he crammed into his jeans pockets. He then crawled up toward Zoya but stopped before he got to her, focusing his attention instead on the helm console. Here he needed just seconds to remove a plate next to the marine switch panel with a screwdriver on his multitool, and he felt his way along a series of wires. Popping two out, he twisted them together, and the control panel instantly lit up.

The battery meter came alive, showing a full charge.

With the electrical power on at the helm, he flipped the trim switch down, and this lowered the two outboard motors into the water behind him.

Still, he didn't have a fast way to turn the engines on without a key, so he found a small wire under the control panel, this one going to the boat's cabin lighting, and he freed it from its soldering with a hard yank.

He placed this eight-inch coated copper wire in his mouth, and then on his hands and knees he scampered back to the pair of engines at the stern. He ignored the port-side Yamaha and concentrated on the starboard one.

He popped the cowling off, pulling the big plastic shroud off the engine, exposing the mechanics inside, and dropped the cowling onto the deck next to him.

Just then, a round cracked past him on the right and kicked up foamy water ten feet away.

"Keep 'em down, Carrie!"

Zoya returned fire behind him, then shouted, "I think the cops are here. Flashing lights up on the hill."

"Make that ammo last until the shooters have bigger problems than us."

He turned on his flashlight and put it in his mouth, then leaned over the stern to the back of the engine. Quickly he found a small black relay box zip-tied to some wires near the starter and pulled it free. Holding it close to his face and inspecting all the wires protruding from it for a moment, he identified a red wire and a purple wire. As with all the other wires, there was a corresponding plug on the other side. He pulled the wire from the control panel out of his mouth and carefully placed one copper end inside to touch the red wire, then bent his cabin lighting wire and slid the other end into the relay box against the purple wire.

The big Yamaha coughed to life.

Over the roar he shouted up to Zoya. "Shoot the bowline!"

"Half a mag left!" she said, and then, "What?"

"You have to shoot the bowline from where you are, otherwise we're not getting out of here!"

"I'll try!"

He didn't want Zoya up on the bow untying the line; she'd be in full view of the assassins and shot dead in an instant, so the only solution remaining was a very precise 9-millimeter round cutting the line in the dim light.

As Court untied the line at the stern, he heard a succession of outgoing gunshots from closer to the bow; Zoya needed four or five rounds to hit the line, but soon enough she shouted back to him.

"Bowline is free! I'm dry." She was now completely out of ammunition.

The boat began to bob and shift even more than it had been, the waves rocking it forward, closer to the shore, just twenty yards or so away. Court had to get the cowling back on the engine so water wouldn't short out the wiring, and Zoya was much closer to the helm, so he shouted, "Put the transmission in reverse and give it full power!"

He finished clamping the cowling over the powerhead just as he heard the engine he'd hot-wired rise in pitch and felt the boat surge backwards, out towards the lake.

At the same time, the slow but steady gunfire from the shore stopped abruptly.

Court thought the enemy might be bugging out with the arrival of the police. He put his multitool and his light back into his pocket, and he began moving forward towards the controls, under the roof and halfway up the length of the boat. He could see Zoya kneeling at the helm, a hand on the wheel but trying to stay out of any line of fire, and she was all but gunning the single engine in reverse.

As he advanced on the helm through the open back seating area of the tourist boat, Court felt a slight rocking that was out of rhythm with the wind, and he looked to his right just as a bald-headed and bearded man, soaked to the bone and his tattooed chest bare, kicked himself adroitly over the gunwale less than five feet away.

The man had a long-bladed knife in his teeth; to Court he looked like a pirate.

Court reached for his multitool, the closest weapon to his grasp, but before he could wield it, he had to back away from the charging attacker.

He shouted up to Zoya, but at the same moment she powered up the engine in reverse even more, and her eyes and attention were focused, quite reasonably, on the shoreline.

Court saw the pirate take his knife in his right hand and then slash it forward. Court avoided the swing and then charged, spearing the man in the chest with his shoulder, but there wasn't a lot to his blow, so his enemy did not fall to the deck. The movement of the tourist boat sent both men stumbling, but even off-balance, Court controlled the knife arm with both his hands, then shifted around, backing into the man and shoving him with his powerful legs.

Court drove backwards again, slamming the attacker against the side of the boat. He heard a grunt of pain, and then the knife fell from the man's hands and clanked to the deck, which Court originally took as good news.

But when the man broke away, stood up, reached behind his back, and drew an improbably large pistol, Court realized he'd much preferred his chances with the knife.

He could do nothing but try to close the distance. He ducked low and left and charged again, and the gun went off; the round missed Court's face by inches, but the flash out of the suppressor on the end of the barrel of the massive weapon all but blinded him. Court spun around quickly as he closed even more and came out of his turn at the attacker's gun hand, grabbing the arm with both hands.

He couldn't wrench the weapon free; his opponent was at least his equal strengthwise.

Suddenly, the man's grip relaxed a bit; Court tried again to pull the pistol out of his clutches, but the man instead ripped it out of Court's hands, then spun to aim it at another target, just behind Court on the boat.

This could only mean Zoya was standing behind him, and she was about to be shot dead.

Before Court could even react to throw himself in front of the weapon, a pair of gunshots barked from the lakeshore; the man on the boat with Court stumbled back a little and, using the same motion, he turned away, leaping over the side, splashing into the black water, and disappearing below the choppy waves.

Court turned around to see Zoya standing there at the entrance to the covered deck, a pistol in her hands aimed at where the bearded man had just been standing.

The launch continued moving quickly in reverse, now nearly fifty yards from shore, but Court made no attempt to take control of the craft.

Instead, he just kept staring at Zoya.

Stunned, he said, "You . . . you told me you were out of ammo."

"I am. I was trying to distract him."

Another gunshot from the shore sent them both to their knees for cover. Court looked and saw two Guatemalan police officers at the water's edge, sixty yards away now. They both held Uzi submachine guns, and they aimed them at the boat.

Court and Zoya ducked down farther just as the cops fired again.

Zoya said, "Why are they shooting at us?"

"Let's not stick around to ask."

He crawled to the helm, spun the wheel to the left, pulled out of the reverse, and shoved the transmission forward. Once they began moving he applied full power again, and soon the single Yamaha outboard behind him began racing them away from the area.

They stayed low, the police stopped shooting, and within half a minute they were out of range. Court hugged the coastline with the wooden boat, but this took all his attention because the lake felt like a roiling sea.

After two minutes the lights of the city disappeared behind them.

He knew the police wouldn't be able to fly a helicopter in this weather, even if they had one standing by near sleepy Panajachel, but he imagined they'd be climbing into boats that moved a lot faster than his little tourist craft with one working engine, so his plan was to beach at the first opportunity.

Zoya came up behind him as he looked at the coastline to his left, hunting for a place to go ashore.

She put her hand on his back, saying nothing.

"You okay?" he asked after a moment.

"Fine. You?"

"Yeah. That was Lancer," Court said flatly.

Zoya seemed surprised. "Are you sure? It was pretty dark."

"When I knew him he didn't have the beard, so I couldn't really make out his face. But the dude's got a very distinct choice in firearms. A big ten-millimeter suppressed hand cannon. Some custom-made piece, subsonic ammo. As soon as he drew his gun I knew it was him." He shrugged. "Plus the fact that he had some kind of Nazi tattoo on his chest. That's also part of his brand. A big gun and membership in a club of dickheads."

Zoya said, "Did he recognize you?"

"I don't know. Probably not. We didn't know each other well."

"You think he's dead?"

Court shook his head. "Not a chance. He jumped over the side, he didn't fall in. They might have grazed him. No more than that."

Zoya took a moment, then spoke, her voice full of emotion. "Listen, Court, you *have* to believe me. This wasn't Slava Genrich. You see that. *Right?*"

Court was already thinking about who was responsible, and he agreed with Zoya. "Genrich said Lancer was after the engineer, right?"

"That's right."

"The people running Lancer must have known Genrich was down here trying to recruit an asset to save the engineer. They saw you, maybe they saw me, and they sent a team in to stop us before we became a problem."

Zoya nodded, obviously relieved she wasn't going to have to continue trying to convince her partner. "Which means we're being watched down here in the middle of nowhere, and somebody's going to incredible lengths to silence this engineer."

Court looked to the sky, to the rough water around him. "We'd have spotted a foot follow. They must be using ISR, and there's no way they're running ISR in this weather. We're clear . . . for now."

Court saw a small beachside villa up ahead, lights on the shoreline and twinkling up a jungled hill.

Zoya said, "Santa Catarina Palopó. It's a little nothing town, but they'll have transpo out of here."

He turned the wheel and cut his power a little. "We'll land, find a chicken bus going anywhere, then make our way back to Guatemala City."

As they neared the shore, Zoya squeezed his shoulder. "I'm sorry I put us in danger."

But Court shook his head, his eyes still looking out beyond the bow. "We've talked about this before. Who we are . . . what we've done. By being together, we both put each other in danger, and we agreed to accept the risks."

He added, "Just promise me next time you will tell me what's going on, whatever the fallout."

She nodded adamantly. "I promise. Again . . . I'm sorry."

"And I promise not to be such an ass." The adrenaline was leaving Court's body, as was his half-day-long tension with Zoya.

He turned back to her. With an incredulous look on his face, he said, "You pointed an empty gun to draw fire away from me."

She looked into his eyes but said nothing.

"I just want you to know . . . and I mean this from the bottom of my heart. *That* was stupid as shit."

Zoya laughed now, the tension finally cut.

Court smiled, too. "You can officially stop apologizing and start gloating on what a badass you are."

She smiled wider, but the stress remained evident on her face.

She kissed him, and he kissed her back, and then he focused his attention on beaching the boat while Zoya went to the rear deck to put her backpack on.

TWELVE

The Victorian gothic façade of the Randolph Hotel in the city of Oxford, England, loomed large over Beaumont Street and reflected against the crystal black surface of the massive Mercedes Sprinter van as it pulled up to the portico in front of the door. The vehicle came to rest and a driver in a gray flannel suit climbed out and stepped around the van to the sliding door, which had already begun opening on its own with a gentle hiss. A side step extended out from just below the body of the vehicle, reaching out to the sidewalk, and the driver glanced inside to make sure everything was ready for the VIP and his entourage.

This Sprinter model was called Jet on Road, and it was no mystery as to why. Four leather cabin chairs in the front, a three-seat leather sofa in the rear, flat-screen TVs, tray tables, even champagne flutes hanging in a small wet bar area.

The driver's and front passenger seats were shielded from the cabin by a partition with a window, its plastic shade drawn. The entire ceiling of the Sprinter was a grid of LCD panels, now giving off a soft blue light, and alpha wave music swept softly through the cabin like a breeze.

Everything appeared to be in order, so the driver turned back towards the portico and spoke into his cuff mic.

"We're clear."

Seconds later a small crowd emerged on the red-carpeted steps under the portico, and they moved with purpose towards the van, less than ten meters away.

There were nine in the entourage in all—one woman, eight men—and one of the men walked in the center of the cluster, while two men in black suits holding what appeared to be briefcases flanked him at his shoulders.

Another individual in black walked just ahead of him, and two more just behind, and it was clear to all that these five members of the entourage were the detail protecting a principal.

Two other men walked ahead of this scrum, one in a dapper gray suit and the second in a rumpled brown suit.

The lone woman in the group, an Asian in her thirties, lagged behind the rest, pulling a rolling duffel and slinging both a purse and a leather folio. She seemed all but forgotten by the men, and she appeared somewhat flustered and rushed.

Unlike the others, who were dressed in business attire, the man in the center of the group most assuredly was not. He wore loose gray cotton yoga pants, a red tracksuit top zipped up to his neck, and Nike Air Force 1 Louis Vuitton shoes that sold for upwards of one hundred thousand dollars.

A red backpack slung over a shoulder shifted with his urgent stride, and massive over-the-ear headphones hung around his neck.

The driver returned to the wheel, and as soon as the group climbed inside the plush interior of the Sprinter, the door began to shut with a hiss, the side step retracted, and the vehicle began to move.

With the automatic shades drawn, as they were now, it was almost impossible to distinguish the cabin from the interior of a private jet.

Four of the five bodyguards in the entourage sat in the four cabin chairs, with the other riding shotgun up front, while the principal—the man with the Nikes and the track top—sat in the middle of the sofa in the back, flanked by the Asian female and the man in gray.

The man in brown sat stiffly on a small folding jump seat up by the bulkhead.

The VIP with the hyper-relaxed dress code was named Anton Hinton. He was an oddly boyish forty-six-year-old, with short brown hair cut into a fade, the sides shaved down to nothing and the top longer, adorned with hair product for lift and volume.

Hinton was a billionaire, dozens of times over. Originally from Wellington, New Zealand, he'd lived in Silicon Valley, Boston, here in the UK, and in other places, spending decades of his life, ever since he could remember, playing with, learning about, and then developing computer software. A gamer, then a student, then a programmer, then an entrepreneur, Hinton was a pioneer and a self-made man.

And with his wealth and his success and his decidedly high-profile lifestyle, he had become an international celebrity.

Hinton's specialty was the expanding realm of intelligent design, and a decade earlier he'd cofounded an electric car company called Adamas that, at its peak, boasted annual revenues of over ten billion U.S. dollars.

Two years ago he sold Adamas to an international consortium centered in Ningbo, China, and since then he'd focused on his dozens of other companies, all working on developing AI applications for industry and the home. He had also become known for giving speeches around the world on the future of intelligent design, both its wonders and its dangers.

One of his primary concerns was the jeopardy of adopting artificial intelligence in the defense industries of the world, and this had made him unpopular with many in his field, because there was an incredible amount of money in R&D from defense contractors.

But Anton Hinton's company, Hinton Lab Group, had a motto, a mission statement: "A bold, secure future for all."

And Anton claimed it as his own personal mission to do nothing less than revolutionize life on planet Earth for the good of humankind.

Now Hinton looked around the van's interior at those with him, his right knee bobbing up and down with nervous energy. Soon his eyes focused on the woman to his right.

"Kimmie," he said, his New Zealand accent strong. "What time's the charity dinner tonight?"

The woman didn't need to consult the iPad she'd pulled from her purse as soon as the van began moving. Her attractive face displayed her Chinese heritage, but her accent revealed her London private school upbringing. "The event is at seven p.m., but Gareth said you would not be attending. I was just about to send contrite regrets to—"

"I'll make a game-time decision," Hinton replied. "The kids need support."

The man on his left was the oldest person in the vehicle, at fifty-seven, though his weathered face and close-cropped gray hair made him, from the neck up anyway, appear to be in his sixties.

From the neck down, however, it was a different story. He was lean, exactly six feet, with broad shoulders and a posture that gave off an air of supreme formidableness. Under his suit he appeared carved in stone, possessing not an ounce of surplus body weight, and he carried himself as if he were a twenty-five-year-old professional athlete.

It was only eight a.m. now, and Gareth Wren had already spent a grueling hour and fifteen minutes this morning in the gym at the Randolph.

Upon hearing his boss's declaration that he might, in fact, attend the charity dinner that evening, he spoke up. Wren was English, from Nottingham in the East Midlands, and his own dialect was distinct from but as strong as Hinton's.

"We've been through this already, Anton. Need to avoid high-profile scheduled events, at least for a few days while this all gets sorted, yeah?"

Hinton leaned his head back and listened to the alpha waves to focus his thoughts and calm himself. Then, after a moment of contemplation, he said, "Fine, then." He turned to the woman. "Kimmie, along with . . . what did you call it? 'Contrite regrets'? Let's increase tonight's donation to the children's hospital by . . . a third."

"Very generous, Anton. I'll take care of it." She'd just finished saying this when her phone buzzed. She touched the AirPod in her right ear and answered softly.

Hinton turned back to Gareth Wren now. "They need my money more than they need my face, anyway. All right, now, mate. What's the plan for this morning's appointment?"

"*My* plan, if you recall, was to *cancel* this morning's appointment."

Hinton made a face of annoyance but said nothing. He then turned to look straight ahead. There, one of the security detail had swiveled his cabin chair around to face the group.

Hinton said, "Emilio? You and your men are ready for this?"

Emilio was Chilean, but his English was excellent. "Yes, Anton. Everything is under control at the university. I've already been in touch with security there."

Gareth Wren protested immediately. "Whatever is going on, we need to keep you away from crowds and open spaces where—"

Kimmie ended her call. "Anton?" Her voice sounded grave enough for everyone in earshot to stop and look to her. "I just heard from Bucharest. Bogdan Kantor was found dead in his yacht earlier today in the Black Sea. There's no cause of death yet."

Hinton, Wren, and Kimmie all knew the Romanian businessman; he'd worked for over a decade at Hinton Lab Group, rising to the rank of director of operations, the position Gareth Wren now held. He'd left two years earlier to start his own artificial intelligence research firm, and Wren, Hinton's former bodyguard, was promoted into the position.

Anton rubbed his face in his hands. Softly, he said, "When's it going to stop?"

Wren, however, remained upright and engaged, taking this as an opportunity. "Trust me, Anton. It's just begun. Bogdan's death is just another reason you need to cancel today's event."

Hinton shook his head, still looking down at the floor between his knees. "Bogdan didn't have security."

Gareth replied calmly. "The others did. Bodyguards can stop *some* threats, but not all."

Hinton looked back to Wren. Softly, he said, "And this chap from the *Economist*. What's his name?" Both men looked to the man in the brown suit sitting uncomfortably up front and looking at his phone.

Wren said, "David something. I forget."

"I can't let the bloody *Economist* see that I'm running scared. I've got to keep up appearances."

The small man from the *Economist* suddenly shuffled to the back of the van, holding on to the cabin chair occupied by Emilio for balance. "Have you heard the news about Kantor?"

Anton nodded, his eyes welling up with tears.

"I'm very sorry, but could I ask for a comment for the online—"

Wren waved an angry hand. "Bloody hell, David. Give him a few minutes."

Chastened, the small man returned to his seat.

Emilio waved at his four other men as he addressed the powerfully built Brit. "Trust me and my colleagues to do their jobs. Anton will be safe for the meeting. Me and my men will guard him with our lives."

Wren began to press. "I just don't think today's meeting warrants the—"

Again, Hinton chimed in, but first he patted a hand on Wren's leg in a calming and friendly gesture. "Look, mate. I'm scared. I get it. Somebody's murdering my friends and former business partners. The threat, whatever it is, is real. I don't deny it. But I absolutely *need* to be here for this demonstration today, and you are my chief of operations. *Emilio* is the head of my security detail."

When Wren said nothing, Anton Hinton sighed. "I'll give you the charity dinner, you give me this demo at Oxford."

Gareth Wren emitted a little sigh, sounding like a man who knew he'd just lost an argument, and then he reached inside his coat with his right hand, placing it on the grip of the pistol in his shoulder holster on his left side.

Hinton noticed the action. "You've armed yourself, have you?"

"Thought I'd bring hardware until the killers are found, done, and dusted." He forced a little smile. "I'm scared, too, mate."

Hinton said, "To be honest, that's a relief. Look at that . . . now I don't only have Emilio and his four well-trained former cops protecting me, but I also have a former SAS soldier watching my back. I'm surrounded by a proper team of bastards. If I can't get into a school building safely, then *no one* can get into a school building safely."

The driver came over the intercom. "We're a minute away."

Soon the van slowed to a stop and the door began to open. Two security men, the pair with the black briefcases, leapt out before the side step had even deployed, finding themselves on a pavement to the left of the front doors of Oxford University's Saïd Business School. It was a straight shot ahead to the entrance, with a large bike rack area filled with dozens and dozens of bicycles on the right, and Hythe Bridge Street on the left.

The pair of officers scanned all sectors as Gareth Wren emerged, and then he stepped a few feet away from the van and began his own overwatch of the area.

It was a typical gray morning at Oxford University. A few people milled about on the sidewalk; they appeared to be students going about their day. A trio of women in their twenties all looked at something on the same phone by the corner of the building, a biker began pedaling away from the large stand, and another pair of young men calmly climbed off their racing bikes on Rewley Road and walked them over towards the stand.

Soon Emilio stepped out; Hinton followed and then was instantly flanked by the men with the briefcases.

As Wren walked for the doors, he saw four uniformed university security officers step out of the building and take up positions, effectively covering the entire street in front of them with their eyes, then heard a quick shuffling behind him. He spun around to make sure everything was okay, but in so doing he saw the Chilean security officer on Hinton's right turn quickly in the direction of the bike racks, holding the black case with one hand and reaching into his coat with the other.

He was going for his weapon.

"Gun!" the security man shouted, and with his right hand he swung the briefcase out in front of him.

The case seemed to elongate with the force of the movement, and instantly it extended into a large black mat, some five feet in length. It was a Kevlar ballistic shield, and the man had just held it up as Emilio got his gun out and began shifting to face the bike racks.

Wren stood ten feet in front of him; he expertly drew from his shoulder holster and swung his Beretta pistol as he swiveled his head back in the direction of the bikes.

Gunfire boomed on the pavement before he found a target; Wren knelt to make his body smaller, but he kept on mission. Scanning with his weapon, Wren saw the two bikers who had just arrived aiming stainless steel semiautomatic pistols, both dumping rounds at the entourage.

The gunman on the right seemed to twitch as if he'd been hit, but he re-aimed his pistol just as Wren got his own handgun up and into the fight. Wren centered on the target's chest and pressed the trigger, and his Beretta snapped in his hand. Firing a second and then a third time, he saw the young attacker whipping back over a bicycle and falling to the ground.

The other man got a second shot off just as Wren began to shift to him. He fired a third time, focused on his target and not looking in Wren's direction. The former SAS man fired once into the side of the man's chest, dropping him to the ground ten feet from his compatriot.

The gunfire ceased instantly, but Wren now heard shouting. He turned for his principal and saw one of the men with a ballistic shield covering Anton Hinton as they ran back towards the van, its door already reopened as the driver prepared to get them out of the area.

Anton appeared unhurt.

Two other security men ran with them, their guns out and sweeping, and Wren could see that Kimmie was already back in the vehicle.

Gareth Wren had only taken a single step back in the direction of the van when he saw Emilio lying facedown on the pavement in front of him, blood pouring from an exit wound at the back of his head.

Wren raced toward the man, his pistol still up in front of him, but then he leapt over Emilio and kept running.

A university security officer wailed in pain on Wren's right, but he didn't even stop to look in the man's direction, so focused was he on getting his employer out of the line of any more fire.

The door to the van was wide open as it sped off up Hythe Bridge Street; one of the bodyguards had draped his heavy ballistic shield over Hinton on the sofa, and Kimmie lay on the floor, tucked in a ball so that the others could have some space.

As the door shut, Wren tapped the intercom button to reach the driver up front. "Back to the Randolph! Call an ambulance for Emilio and at least one other wounded back at the scene, and then call Dr. Patel and have him ready to check Anton out when we get to the hotel."

"Yes, sir."

Now the fifty-seven-year-old former warrant officer looked over to Hinton; he could barely make him out from around the side of the shield, and instantly he worried that the man had, in fact, been shot. His face was white, his eyes wide but unfixed, and he lay on the sofa while his protector all but sat on him, the shield sandwiched between the two bodies.

Gareth moved to Hinton quickly, pushed away the shield and the security officer, and ran his hands all over his employer's body. Soon he realized Anton was only suffering from shock.

Kimmie crawled on her hands and knees to the front of the cabin and sat in one of the chairs next to the reporter, whose face was as white as Hinton's. Wren saw Kimmie and David and recognized the distress. "Are either of you hit?" he shouted at them, hoping to break them out of any shock they might have been experiencing.

The reporter for the *Economist* said, "I . . . I'm all right."

Kimmie pushed long black hair away from her eyes. "Emi . . . I think he's hurt."

He's more than hurt, Wren thought. He said, "An ambulance is on the way."

"Shit!" Hinton shouted suddenly, his first real sign of life since being shuffled out of the gunfight, and Wren looked back to see what was going on. The New Zealander sat up on the sofa next to two bodyguards. His head dropped into his hands, and he looked utterly distraught.

Wren knelt on the floor in front of the sofa. "You're okay, Anton."

"Emilio. Is he . . ."

"I don't know."

"Oh, God! I made us go today. I made us go!"

"Listen to me, Anton. Emilio was doing his job, you were doing *your* job. You're not at fault for this. The shooters . . ." He hesitated, then said, "The people who ordered this . . . this is on them. *Only* them. You've got to get your head right, because this shit is going to happen again."

Hinton cocked his head a little. "Again?"

"You're still alive! Whatever this is all about, it's bloody apparent somebody needs you dead. As long as they're out there, you are in danger!"

Hinton stared off into space as the Sprinter van raced through morning Oxford traffic.

THIRTEEN

Scott Kincaid looked into the grimy mirror of the communal bathroom of the backpacker hostel and examined the bruised and abraded right side of his rib cage, and then he twisted around, looking back over his shoulder. Even in the piss-poor light from the dull bare bulb above him, he was able to see injury there. Just to the right of a full back tat of a front-on skull with colorful flames emerging from its mouth over the words "BREATHE FIRE," he saw the ugly gash from a bullet's graze on his right latissimus dorsi. It wasn't deep, it wasn't deadly, but he knew the pain from it would get worse before it got better.

Not that he minded the discomfort. The assassin known as Lancer found focus in pain; he'd been injured countless times in his forty-seven years on this planet, first by the hands of his father, who beat the living shit out of him back home in Seattle. And then during the arduous training he'd endured at BUD/S, the U.S. Navy's Basic Underwater Demolition/ SEAL assessment course.

He'd suffered further pain from three IED blasts in Afghanistan, and he was once hit in the back with a ricochet from an AK round in Syria.

Pain was Kincaid's companion. It was a salve that cleansed him, let him know he was really alive.

Inflicting pain let him know he was alive, as well. He'd left the Navy under a cloud, charges he knew to be bullshit, accusations from other SEALs who were jealous of him, threatened by him, and then he'd gone into private contracting so he could continue to deal pain to blunt his own.

A short stint in Nigeria and another in Mali had been without incident and without enjoyment, but then he was contacted by a man who asked him if he was interested in real work.

Quickly Kincaid knew he'd been headhunted because of what had happened with the SEALs in Syria, or what he'd been accused of, anyway.

Soon he found himself plotting an assassination on the streets of Fez, Morocco.

He did the job, did it well, and then his employer told him there was more work out there if he wanted it.

Scott Kincaid wanted it very much, but he didn't want a boss; he wanted to remain a free agent.

He worked on a contract basis for a fixer named Sir Donald Fitzroy for a short time, doing jobs in Europe, and he worked with a man in Dubai and another in Dallas.

Now he worked for a new handler, a Welshman named Jack Tudor, whose security company, Lighthouse Risk Control Ltd., was essentially a front to run covert operations personnel and contract killers. Lancer had performed over thirty contract jobs in his years in this line of work. They weren't all killings, but many were, and they had all been successful.

Kincaid considered himself an undefeated prizefighter. The heavyweight champion of the world when it came to murder.

And then . . . last night in some little nothing village in Guatemala, he'd almost bought the farm.

He shook his head in disbelief, and then he touched the wound on his right lat, still sighting it through the mirror.

He winced, but the pain was there to refocus him. He remembered he was a killer, a hunter, and through the discomfort he longed to get back into the hunt.

It had been five hours since he'd dived into the water to duck the police shooting at him, and he thought about everything that had happened since. He'd lost the Tahoe; it would have been crawling with cops by the time he got out of the water, so he'd waited till he'd dried off, then hired a taxi to take him all the way back to Quetzaltenango. He'd not gone straight to the airport; the driver would eventually be found by the authorities and questioned about the bearded American fare, so instead he had the taxi drop him off at the Alamo Bus Terminal.

Lancer had wandered into this backpacker's hostel, sat at the nearly empty twenty-four-hour bar, and downed a couple of shots of Johnnie Walker, then he'd come back here to the bathroom next to the dormitory-style rooms, no doubt full of stoned or drunk American and European kids.

Once he'd evaluated his injury, he put his shirt back on and left the bathroom, the bar, and the hostel, and turned up the street to the north.

He walked thirty minutes through the windy cool night, his rib cage complaining about each and every footfall, until he arrived at the airport. Here his torso protested even more when he climbed a corrugated metal fence.

A lone Embraer Phenom light jet waited on the tarmac, its jet stairs down, and Kincaid stepped up to it.

The pilots were on board, both sleeping on cabin chairs with their feet up, and Lancer kicked one man's foot and then the other, rousing them.

They hadn't been expecting him, but he didn't blame them for that. He could have called, but he'd wanted to wait, to let his employers sweat it out a bit, a penalty for sending him straight into a fucking buzz saw.

"Sir?" the American pilot said as he quickly sat up.

"Preflight the aircraft."

Both men scrambled to their feet and headed for the cockpit. The pilot spoke as he moved. "You could have let us know, we'd have been ready."

"We might not be going anywhere," Lancer replied. "The job here isn't finished yet. But I want you ready if we need to relocate to the capital."

A minute later he had his shirt off and the aircraft's first-aid pack in his lap as he sat in one of the recently vacated cabin chairs.

He sprayed antiseptic on the injury, popped a couple of cold packs, then placed them over his ribs and wrapped them tightly with a compression bandage.

He then pulled his pistol out of its holster, unloaded it, and disassembled it. As he cleaned the parts of the weapon with a cleaning kit he retrieved out of his spare rucksack, he turned his phone back on, slipped in an earpiece, and placed a call.

He knew his controller would have been trying to contact him for the past several hours, but Lancer had needed to think about what went wrong.

His mind settled, he waited for someone to answer on the other end.

"Hello?"

It was the same French woman from earlier. She sounded exhausted. He didn't know where the operations center for this mission was located, so he had no idea what time it was where he was calling. "Relay status."

"I'll *tell* you my fucking status. The three locals are either dead or arrested by the cops, I'm wounded, and the target escaped."

There was no emotion in the French woman's voice. "All three assets are dead."

He sniffed angrily. "They weren't assets, they were liabilities. And you lost Zakharova?"

"The only eyes we had were the UAV, which crashed before you acted."

He sighed. "They escaped in a boat, long gone from Panajachel. Could be anywhere."

"Understood. Where have you been the past six hours?"

"Thinking over my career plans."

"What does that mean?"

"This job . . . when I agreed, was four targets, perhaps some security. Now I'm up against multiple tier-one operatives. I think it's time we renegotiate."

"I'm not in a position to—"

"Of course you're not. Connect me with someone who is."

There was a pause, then the woman said, "I will. But first, what went wrong?"

"One of those fools you hired revealed himself to the oppo before we had time to set up. We were on the back foot from the start, and it went downhill from there. Zakharova's associate is a highly skilled operative."

"We have been unable to identify him."

"I'll help you out, though it isn't my fucking job to ID personalities for your organization. His name is Gentry. He's American. Former CIA. Worked in the private sector for a handler named Fitzroy several years ago."

"How do you know this?"

"Hey, that's my intel, take it or leave it." Lancer finished cleaning the barrel of his big pistol, and now he pulled out a bottle of lubricant/protectant and began oiling the gun's internal mechanics. He then said, "Put me on with the boss or I'm hanging up."

A man came on the line instantly; Kincaid detected a northern European accent.

"Lancer?"

"What do I call you?"

"Call me Director."

"Okay. Two point five million U.S. a hit. Starting yesterday, continuing as long as this op lasts."

"I'm not the one who pays you."

Kincaid was surprised. "You're not the one who contracted me through my handler?"

"Absolutely not. I don't know you, and I don't know your handler. If you want more money, you have to talk directly to Cyrus. We all work for him."

"Who the fuck is Cyrus?"

There was a long pause. "The code name of the person who employed you. Employed me. Employed all of us here." Quickly the man said, "If you have a handler dealing with your contracts, contact them; they will know how to reach Cyrus."

Kincaid thought it over. So the director of the operations center didn't know who he was working for, either. Interesting.

"I will," he said, momentarily taken aback.

"In the meantime," the director continued, "Borislava Genrich is back in Mexico City. We need you to prosecute him there tomorrow morning."

"I'm not doing anything until I get my—"

"Talk to your handler, get your money, but you need to keep working in the meantime."

"Why would I—"

"Because this is a fast-moving operation. I'll hire someone else if you can't make the operational window in Mexico City, and if that person does a good job, I'll send them to Boston, and then to Toronto from there. Not you. Your two million will turn into nothing if you don't get yourself to Mexico City."

Lancer felt his sore ribs through the cold packs and the bandaging. The thought of flying hours through the morning to Mexico, and then taking up a position in order to kill a man there, was anything but appealing, but he knew the pain would fuel him.

The director said, "We have targets Gama Seventeen and Gama Eight fixed in Mexico and will continue surveillance. You will act against them as soon as you arrive."

Lancer reassembled his pistol, flipped up the takedown lever, and dropped the slide, making a loud click in the otherwise empty cabin. "Roger. Lancer out." He tapped the earpiece, reloaded his weapon, and reholstered.

Five minutes later he was texting with his handler on this operation, the Welshman named Jack Tudor, and ten minutes after that, Tudor confirmed that Cyrus had agreed to the raise to two point five million per job, beginning with Palo Alto.

Kincaid began to stand up to go to the cabin to let the pilots know they were heading to Mexico City, but then he thought better of it. OC Gama would be communicating with them now; he didn't have to do a thing.

He looked out the window, and in moments the aircraft began to move.

Tomorrow in Mexico City, two jobs. Then the next day in Boston, one job. And then up into Canada for another, and then he'd be done.

Or would he?

He wondered if someone else would be sent after Zakharova, or if he'd be facing her and Gentry again before this work was done.

He'd like another crack at both of them. A mission on his own terms.

But for now he made his way into the galley, yanked a full-sized bottle of Johnnie Walker Black from a tiny bar, and filled a plastic cup with ice.

Pain was his friend, this was true. But he had other things to focus on, so this was no time for friends.

. . .

At Tactical Operations Center Gama in the Singapore Industrial Park, the director listened as one of his techs informed him that Lancer was in the air and on the way, and then he walked back over to his workstation in the spartan office suite, sat down, and typed a message on his computer.

Cyrus. Gama Actual. Asset Lancer identifies associate of target Gama 18 as "Gentry," former CIA, currently a freelance contract agent.

There was a significant pause, and through it, the Norwegian rubbed his eyes, ran his fingers through his dark hair, then took a sip of now-lukewarm tea.

Eventually, a reply came.

The Gray Man. Interesting.

He cocked his head, eyes on the words in front of him. Of course he had heard of the Gray Man, a legendary assassin without peer, but even when he'd worked for Norwegian intelligence, he never found out if the Gray Man was real.

Rumors and speculation. Massive operations in Europe, in Africa, in North America, in Asia. The Gray Man was, as far as he could tell, like the bogeyman. Blamed for anything that happened that couldn't be easily explained.

He typed an interrogative. **You are saying Gentry is the Gray Man?**

The response came almost instantly. **That is the intelligence I have received. Moderate confidence.**

Moderate confidence, in the intelligence realm, meant the analysis was likely to be accurate. If Cyrus was right, then that meant the Gray Man was no myth, and it also meant that Lancer had faced off with him the night before.

"Incredible," he muttered aloud as an icy chill went up his spine, and he couldn't help but look back over his shoulder.

But why the hell would the Gray Man be in some sleepy Guatemalan hamlet with a former Russian spy?

When Cyrus wrote nothing more, he responded, **We can avoid Gentry. Avoid Zakharova. We assume Genrich went to Guatemala to recruit them to help him get target Gama 8 out of Mexico City. They didn't go** back with him, and Lancer is already on the way up there to do the jobs tomorrow. I don't think either of the targets we went after in Panajachel remain priorities to our mission.

The reply came quickly. I designate mission priorities. Not you.

The director sighed, then typed, Of course, but I am suggesting with our workload for the next three days we need to—

A bubble appeared on the screen, and then it was filled with text, as if Cyrus were writing at very high speed. Locate Zakharova and Gentry. They remain a high priority to the mission.

The director replied quickly. Acknowledged. We will use facial recognition on all cameras we can access in Central America. If the targets show up anywhere, we will know.

FOURTEEN

Zack Hightower tossed his bag in the back of his Ford F-150, waved good-bye to a couple of old-timers at the gun range, and then unslung the hunting rifle from his shoulder and slid behind the wheel with it. From the front passenger seat he picked up a softshell case for the bolt-action Nosler 21 in his hand and slid it in the lambswool interior of the case.

With the gun resting on the seat and the floorboard next to him, he opened a bottle of tepid water and looked out the dusty windshield of his truck at the flat, hardscrabble land in front of him.

This gun range was on five hundred acres of land just south of Hondo, Texas, which itself was just west of San Antonio. He'd spent the past three hours here shooting a variety of weapons at a variety of distances, but mostly defensive pistols and bolt-action hunting rifles.

Today had been a diversion. Zack worked as a hunting guide here at a ranch outside San Antonio, but he didn't have any clients booked for the next three weeks, so he was spending his downtime honing skills he'd first learned as a young boy, hunting here in Texas with his dad.

These skills had been honed to a higher level when he became a Navy SEAL, even further when he was brought into the elite SEAL Team 6, and further still when he left the military and joined the CIA as a paramilitary operations officer.

He'd eventually left the Agency to become a hunting guide, though he'd been called back on a few ad hoc missions over the years.

But now, well into his fifties, he was pretty sure he'd spend the rest of his days helping rich men and women track and kill trophy whitetail, blackbuck, and wild boar.

As he fired the engine of his truck and turned the AC vents so that they'd blow cold air hard in his face, his phone began buzzing in his pocket.

He yanked it out while taking a sip of water. "Yeah?"

"Is that Zack Hightower?" It was a man with a gravelly voice and a British accent. Instantly Zack assumed the caller would be seeking a hunting guide.

"It is. Who's asking?"

"It's Gareth Wren. Ring any bells?"

Zack sat up straighter and his face lightened instantly. "Wren? Holy shit, man. That name's a blast from the past."

"Was hoping you'd remember."

"All those joint ops in the sandbox? How could I forget?"

"Might try gin. Does the trick. For some, anyway. Not me."

Zack sniffed out a laugh at the gallows humor. "How'd you get my number?"

"Mutual friends, from back in the day. Need I elaborate?"

"Negative."

Wren had been SAS, and Hightower had worked with him multiple times in Afghanistan, Iraq, and Libya, both when he was a Navy SEAL and then as a paramilitary for the CIA. He hadn't thought about Gareth Wren, or any of the Brits he'd run with back then, in a very long time.

"Good to hear from you, man. But why am I sensing this is not a social call?"

"Probably because I've never rung up anyone for a bloody 'social call' in my life."

The American grinned, happy for this diversion right now. "What's up, man?" He took a long sip of water, again looking out the dirty windshield of his Ford.

"Cuttin' right to the chase, mate. I work for an extremely well-known businessman who had an attempt on his life yesterday. A bit of a mess, and yes, I'm applying typical English understatement. Anyway, we need a new director of security, and I reached out to some chaps from your old shop— the Company, not the Teams—and they said you might be sort of . . . under-utilized at the moment."

"Those *mates* of yours are too kind. I haven't been utilized in years."

Wren laughed. "I was applying some English understatement there, as well. Honestly, they told me your prime days were being misspent running hunting trips for wealthy people you can't stand."

"When I can get work, yeah. Having a dry spell at the moment."

Wren barked into the phone now. "Well then, it's settled, isn't it? You're coming to work for us. Proper good pay. Plus full hazard duty now, after the attempt yesterday."

"Who's the famous client?"

Wren paused, then said, "Does it matter?"

Zack cocked his head. "Shit. That bad?"

"No, didn't mean that. It's just that people have a strong opinion of him, one way or the other. It's Anton Hinton."

"Shit," Zack muttered again, then, "Damn." The man was a household name. He blew out a sigh. "Somebody took a swing at him?"

"In the UK, just yesterday, as I said. It's all over the bloody news. You living under a rock?"

"I try to, anyway."

"Right. Yeah, well, Hinton wasn't hurt, but his security chief took a bullet. Didn't make it."

"Sorry."

"Chilean chap. Caught a nine-mil through the jaw. Madness."

"Who were the shooters?"

"Contract boys from Bulgaria, haven't a clue who hired them, but there've now been six killings of high-tech experts in the same general field as Anton, all over the world, and all in the past day and a half. Surely it's all related. We can do a proper threat assessment when you sign on. Look . . . I can charter a plane at whichever airport is closest to you right now and bring you out to London straightaway, yeah? I'll fill you in in person, you can meet Anton, see what you think."

Wren spoke up again. "Look, mate. This job is for you." He paused, "Unless you know something I don't."

"Meaning?"

"Meaning the old Hightower, the one I worked with all those years back, he could do this work. I just don't know if you're still up for it."

It was a little psychology Wren was employing on Zack—a challenge, and it was a challenge Zack accepted.

"Charter a plane in San Antonio."

He could hear the relief in the voice of the man on the other end of the line. "I'll call you with the time and location."

"I will travel with my own gun. Can you get it into the UK?"

"No need to bring any kit. We'll get you sorted straightaway."

Zack reached down to his appendix area and put his hand on the butt of the big Staccato XC pistol, still warm from use this afternoon. He said, "Nonnegotiable, Wren."

"Americans," the Englishman muttered, and then he took a moment before saying, "Yeah. We'll work something out. I'll have men meet you at the aircraft to carry your things. They're licensed, they'll take your weapon through the customs process as if it's theirs, give it back to you once you're clear."

"Good."

Wren said, "Thanks for doing this, Zack. This won't be easy, but it will be interesting, and I can't wait to work with you again. Been too long, mate."

"See you in jolly old England."

"If it were so jolly, we wouldn't need you."

Zack hung up with a smile.

For the first time in a long time, he saw himself as a man with a mission.

FIFTEEN

The lights in the small glass-walled conference room on the fifth floor of the CIA headquarters building in McLean, Virginia, flipped on at three p.m., and the chairs around the long oval table began filling with bodies just seconds later.

Four men in suits sat down, then a pair of women entered, then another man and another woman.

A minute after this, three more personnel arrived.

With eleven at the table now, only one seat remained open.

Soon Jim Pace shuffled into the room, just two minutes or so late but bearing the full burden of the knowledge that his tardiness had likely made the much more senior CIA administrators present wait on him. He struggled with a pair of large accordion file folders under his arm, a stuffed leather folio swinging off his shoulder, and an iPad in his hand, its wireless function disabled for security reasons.

At fifty-two years old, Pace had dark brown hair and a mustache, along with a lean build that belied the fact that he spent his days sitting at a desk. He kept his fitness up rowing in the Potomac most every morning, putting his kayak in at the dock in Old Town Alexandria near his little house, making his way up past Reagan National Airport and then back down, aircraft landing right over his head as he sculled, exerting his back, legs, arms, and core.

Fitness had always been important to Pace; now it kept him healthy, but in his past it had kept him alive.

Previous to landing his posting here at Langley one year earlier, he had worked as a CIA case officer in the Directorate of Operations, primarily serving in the Middle East.

And in his thirties he'd been a paramilitary officer in Ground Branch, a unit in the Agency's Special Activities Division, now renamed the Special Activities Center.

In Ground Branch, among other duties, he'd operated on a kill/capture/rendition squad called Task Force Golf Sierra, known more colloquially around the Directorate of Operations as the Goon Squad.

And way back in his twenties Pace had served in the U.S. Army's Third Special Forces Group at Fort Bragg, North Carolina. These were the early days of the war on terror, and he'd been deployed virtually every year since he'd become a Green Beret.

His time in the sand and the mud were behind him now, however, and these days his main concern was that he'd be suffocated by a landslide emanating from the mountain of paperwork on his desk.

As soon as he entered the room, he looked at the head of the oblong table, to the DDO's chair, and his heart sank when he saw that his boss had beat him to the meeting. William "Trey" Watkins, the new deputy director of the CIA for operations, conferred with his number two, Naveen Gopal, an Indian American who had taught international relations and security studies at Harvard before getting scooped up into the Agency nearly two decades earlier.

As Pace sat down with apologies, he continued looking around. Analysis was well represented, and a few other operations and administrative personnel were in attendance, as well.

An African American woman, maybe ten years Pace's junior, sat halfway down the table from him on his right. He didn't recognize her, but she was positioned between other ops personnel, so he assumed she was from the Directorate of Operations.

D/O was the department that had pulled him out of bed at five a.m. and told him to get his ass into the office because a crisis had developed. Pace's focus here at the Agency was on proliferations, tracking the movement of weapons and defense technology around the world, and as soon as he'd made it into HQ this morning, shortly before six thirty a.m., he'd been given a new assignment that was different from anything else he'd ever done.

Assistant to the DDO Naveen Gopal spoke first, even before Jim could get all his folders and items settled in front of him. "All right, everyone. Jim Pace is in Special Tasks, working on proliferations issues. More specifically, he's been investigating Chinese commercial espionage for the past year, so we've asked him to run point on this. He's had all day to piece it together."

All day? Pace thought. Yeah, he'd had eight hours, but this was a rapidly developing situation.

DDO Watkins spoke up now. "Okay, Jim, what do you have for us?"

Pace was nowhere near ready for this shit, but he knew he'd have to adapt and overcome.

"Well, sir, in the few hours I've been looking into the matter, I have more questions than answers."

Watkins raised an eyebrow so high it looked painful. "Do you have *any* answers?"

Pace nodded. "Ten personalities involved with artificial intelligence and robotics have been assassinated around the world, in seven different countries, all in the past thirty-four hours."

Watkins put a hand up, halting Pace, then looked down at the iPad in front of him. "Where are you getting ten? I only know of six."

"Yes, sir," Pace said. "A software engineer who had worked for the Ministry of Defense in Moscow left just under a year ago, moving to Austria to start his own company. He and a Russian businessman based in Berlin, himself ex-military, were shot dead on a street this afternoon in Mexico City."

Watkins rubbed his face. "The Russians. Terrific. That's eight."

Pace nodded. "In the past hour it's been reported that"—he opened a folder and looked down at the top page—"Dr. Ju-ah Park, a researcher at Yonsei University and a leading specialist in the field of electrical engineering, was found floating in the Hangang River in downtown Seoul last evening. She was fifty-five years old. There is no direct evidence yet of foul play, an autopsy will have to rule it in or out, but the water temperature in the Hangang is forty degrees Fahrenheit."

Watkins said, "Safe to assume she did not enter the river of her own volition."

"Agreed."

"That's nine," Watkins said as he glanced to his second-in-command, and Naveen Gopal's administrative assistant dutifully jotted down notes.

Pace turned a page in his folder and looked at it. "Less than ten minutes ago I learned that a midlevel engineer of intelligent systems who had worked for several automotive companies was stabbed to death in the subway in Munich on his way home from work at BMW. He doesn't seem to be nearly as high-profile as the other victims, but he was, reportedly, very well regarded in the automation field." He added, "Only thirty-one years old."

Watkins rubbed his eyes under his glasses. "What's being done to protect American AI and robotics experts?"

"The Bureau is leading the way on that, pushing local law enforcement to beef up coverage of those who might be targets." He flipped pages in his folders. "LE is all over MIT, Boston Dynamics, Massachusetts Automation Endeavors, Carnegie Mellon, two dozen other places. These facilities are essentially on lockdown at this point, and the key players in the industries targeted are aware of the situation. As far as overseas, it's a fluid situation. Everyone is aware of the danger, even if they don't understand it yet, so the killers are going to have a tougher time in the days to come there, as well. Assuming, of course, that there are more targets."

Watkins nodded, taking it all in. "You've been working in this realm for a while, Jim. Any idea what's going on?"

"The most likely hypothesis is that all the people killed shared some sort of common knowledge. A bad actor, likely China, is planning to field a new capability of some kind, and they're trying to remove anyone who can stop them from doing so, or anyone who could build something to combat this new capability."

"What kind of capability?"

"Judging by the victims and their expertise, it's some sort of weaponized platform using artificial intelligence. A lethal autonomous weapon, or LAW."

Before anyone could ask the question, he said, "In a nutshell, an autonomous weapon is any weapon that can, on its own and without any human interaction, search for, decide to engage, and then engage a target."

Gopal asked, "And what will that mean for our military?"

Pace turned his attention to the assistant to the DDO. "Artificial intelligence can give the enemy weapon something we call 'first mover advantage.' Sun Tzu said it best. 'Speed is the essence of war.' If you take the human out of the equation and solely give artificial intelligence the power to control a weapon, then your speed will outmatch your enemy."

"And you win," Watkins said softly.

Pace said, "If this is what we fear it might be, and if it goes online, then China will have a tactical and operational overmatch on our military."

Watkins leaned back in his chair. "Mother of God. What could they be fielding that the Agency doesn't know anything about?"

"China's R&D into artificial intelligence in the past decade has been through the roof. But not only China; private civilian firms, labs with no connection to the military whatsoever, have made massive strides in this field. I've been spending the past year talking to companies that have been compromised by the Chinese. Beijing is robustly going for all the knowledge out there, buying it, stealing it, whatever, so they can then militarize it." He shrugged.

"This problem is a day old, there's a lot of work to be done to get to the bottom of this. Hell, it might not even be the Chinese."

"It's obviously the Chinese." The comment came from an operations man named Nance.

The African American woman seated next to him raised her hand.

Gopal said, "Angela?" He looked around the room. "For those of you who don't know, this is Angela Lacy. She's assisting me on various initiatives, and I asked her to sit in to see how she can help."

Pace fought a gasp, but one or two others in the room made audible noises in surprise. Angela Lacy was a rock star in CIA at the moment, enjoying a meteoric rise up the ranks. Now she worked as a special deputy assistant to the deputy director of operations, but six months earlier she'd been a lowly case officer.

She said, "Chinese involvement in this is so . . . on the nose. I am wondering if instead this could be some sort of a false flag operation."

"By who?" Watkins demanded.

"I don't know."

Nance said, "I guess it could be someone else, but it would have to be a major state actor of some sort, considering the scale of this."

Watkins shook his head. "The Russians, the North Koreans, the Iranians . . . none of them could put together something this big. It *has* to be China."

Lacy remained calm and respectful, but she pushed back. "Or a nonstate actor with the means. It still could be an industrial espionage operation, although admittedly, it would be the largest one I've ever heard about."

A little derision slipped into Watkins's voice now. "You are saying Microsoft's assassination squads are doing this to bolster the corporate bottom line?"

There were soft chuckles throughout the room. But Lacy, as far as Pace could tell, remained unfazed. "Respectfully, Deputy Director, Microsoft has a market value higher than the gross domestic product of Italy. Apple has *twice* the market value of Mexico's GDP. Alphabet has the market value of Russia's GDP. There are many companies on Earth with resources on par with or in excess of many nations."

"Apple doesn't have an army," Nance countered.

"Armies can be bought, Chip." She held her hands up. "I'm just suggesting that fixating immediately on China, despite their known interests in AI, might hamper our investigation, especially when we're talking about the very lucrative high-tech space."

Pace expected Lacy to be admonished by Watkins, but instead the big man said, "Fair enough. Everybody keep an open mind." He turned to Pace, changing the subject. "What do we know about the hitters?"

Pace was back on solid ground. "Palo Alto, we're relatively certain, was conducted by Scott Kincaid."

"Fuck," Watkins muttered now.

Watkins clearly knew the name Scott Kincaid, and it was clear to Pace by looking around the table that everyone else did, as well.

"How do we know?" the DDO asked.

"He was sighted about ten or twelve minutes after the attack. A private jet left Palo Alto airport an hour after that and flew to a regional airport in Guatemala. The next morning it flew up to Mexico City. The jet's registry is impossibly murky, hinting at some sort of subterfuge, but the timing and locations are right for the hits in Cali and Mexico City."

Watkins was confused. "So . . . what happened in Guatemala?"

"Nothing, as far as we know. There was a shooting an hour or so away from where his plane landed, but they like local gang members for that."

"Are the gang members talking?"

"All three on the scene when the smoke cleared are now on slabs at the local coroner."

Watkins nodded, thinking a moment. "How long has it been since Kincaid's trial?"

Nance answered this. "Ten years."

Watkins shook his head. "Piece of shit. Dude should be in the naval brig in Norfolk for the rest of his life after what he did to those civilians in Syria. Instead, he gets a pat on the ass and a 'sorry for the misunderstanding' from the DOJ, then starts plying his trade as a killer for hire."

Gopal said, "The one good thing about Kincaid is that, unlike the Gray Man, we never had anything to do with him. He's the SEALs' problem, not ours."

Watkins countered his subordinate. "He's our problem *now*, Naveen." Back to Pace he said, "What about the other locations? The assassins?"

"In the attempted assassination of Anton Hinton in the UK, the dead hitters were Bulgarian. In Israel we have no idea, ditto Osaka, Munich, Seoul, and Bangkok, Bucharest, and Sydney. I'm working with the FBI on reaching out to local authorities in all these places so that as soon as they know, we know."

Watkins waved a hand in the air. The Chinese are not going to . . ." He stopped, looked at Angela, then said, "The unknown opposition . . . is not going to just be allowed to slaughter everyone in the tech industry they see as a threat to their mission. Whoever the hell they are, and whatever the hell their mission is."

"Yes, sir."

"Jim, the Agency needs to have eyes on everything that's happening on this issue, all over the world. It's on your shoulders. You good with that?"

"Fine, sir. What resources do I get?"

"What do you need?"

"Clearance to talk to everyone. About everything."

"Done. What else?"

"I need a pipeline to the FBI."

"I'll facilitate that," Watkins replied confidently, and then he looked to Lacy. "Angela, liaise with the Bureau on Jim's behalf."

"Yes, sir."

Pace continued, "And also into DOD. I need to have an idea of what Rick Watt was working on when he died."

"I agree," responded the DDO, and he looked again to Lacy.

She wrote notes on a legal pad in front of her. "I'll talk to the Pentagon as soon as we're done here, set up a meeting for you."

Pace thanked her, then turned back to Watkins. "I'll need to travel. I want to see the crime scenes themselves. To talk in person to the surviving security detail members of those who had them, the coworkers of the deceased. Any other witnesses that might turn up."

"I'll assign you an aircraft at Andrews and a staff here at HQ, and Naveen will arrange everything with the embassies and consulates where you travel."

Pace drummed his fingers on the table a moment.

"Something else?" Watkins asked.

Another slight delay, and then Jim Pace said, "I want a Ground Branch task force traveling with me."

Watkins cocked his head in surprise. "Shooters? You want shooters? You don't have execute authority on a kill mission."

"I'm not suggesting that, sir." He looked to Angela, who looked back to him in surprise that he was focusing on her suddenly. "It's just that something Ms. Lacy said rang true. If this *is* a non-state actor, if this is industrial espionage on an unprecedented scale, then I might not be prepared for what I might stumble into."

Watkins said, "You're comfortable with Ground Branch, we all know that." He looked around the room. "If you all didn't know, Jim used to be on Golf Sierra, back in the day."

Pace clarified. "The *early* days. Before it all went to hell. I, thankfully, missed all that."

Watkins sighed after a moment. Finally, he said, "Okay. Approved." He then turned to Steve Hernandez, head of the Special Activities Center. "Who's on deck?"

Hernandez didn't have to consult his notes. To Pace he said, "Take Juliet Victor, they're on a training rotation in Vah Beach, just back from another mountain ops course in Montana. We'll have them ready to travel in a few hours."

Watkins held a threatening finger up to the table, his eyes on Pace. "Very low profile. They can bring all their kit, but their kit will remain on the agency aircraft unless they are given an order by Hernandez, an order that will come from the director via me."

He added, "They can run security for you, Jim, but unarmed security only."

Pace didn't love this, but he liked it enough to agree to it, and the meeting wrapped up minutes later.

As he walked back up the fifth-floor hall towards his desk in an office suite surrounded by two dozen others, a woman's voice called from behind.

"Jim?"

He stopped to see Angela approaching. He fumbled with the folders and the iPad, and then he stretched out a hand, which she took in a firm and friendly shake.

"Nice to meet you officially," she said.

"Likewise. Thanks in advance for the help."

She smiled. "Of course. And thanks for sticking up for me in there."

"You made a good point, and it made me realize I can't assume I know what I'm going to walk into out in the field. I might find myself talking to a conspirator when I think I'm talking to a victim. If that happens, the Ground Branch team will be close at hand."

"Well, good luck," she said. "I'll get to work on DOD and FBI. If there is anything else you need, anything I can be of service with, please feel free to reach out."

The two parted in the hallway with another handshake, both hurrying off towards their offices.

SIXTEEN

Zoya Zakharova and Court Gentry walked with tired and sore bodies after jumping off the back of a pickup truck outside the Central Terminal bus depot in Flores, Guatemala. This was in the heart of the state of Petén, in the northern reaches of the country, and while the simple town was on a pretty lake, the pretty lake was all but surrounded by dense and foreboding jungle.

It was just past six p.m., the pair of freelance operatives' sore bodies were covered in sweat and grime, and they both just wanted a shower, a beer, and a place to lie down flat.

It was a ten-minute walk to a little hotel that, from the outside, anyway, looked like it took cash, didn't give a damn about passports, and would rent them a shitty but cheap and out-of-the-way room with a bath.

Inside they found what they were looking for from the front desk, and soon the couple began heading up a narrow and uneven flight of stairs, unlocking their door with an old iron key and entering the dark and cramped space.

Zoya immediately went to the bathroom, then returned, making no mention to Court of the mold she'd encountered on the walls and the weak plumbing system that meant the toilet barely flushed. She'd experienced worse, much worse, and she knew her partner had, as well.

Court had dropped his bag on the floor, and after spending a couple of minutes looking out the window at the street and then tightly wedging a rubber doorstop under the door to the hallway, he now sat down on the squeaky bed and drew his knife from inside the waistband of his jeans.

He lay down and put the knife on his chest, ready for quick access should the need arise, and he felt Zoya lie down beside him with more squeaks from the springs below them.

She kissed him on the cheek without speaking, then rolled onto her stomach.

Court closed his eyes, and then, four hours later, he opened them again. It was ten p.m.; the heavy rainfall outside along with the rumble of thunder sounded ominous but simultaneously comforting somehow, as if the threat offered by a storm precluded any other potential threats from raining down on them.

He took a moment to reacquaint himself with his surroundings, and the bed squeaked when he turned his head. He rarely slept on beds, preferring closets or bathrooms so that anyone who tried to surprise him in his sleep would have to come looking for him. But he and Zoya had been so exhausted and uncomfortable when they arrived, they couldn't help themselves.

He could hear the shower running; this meant Zoya had climbed off the noisy bed and he'd slept right through it.

Court admonished himself for the poor tradecraft. *Can't get soft*, he told himself, repeating a refrain that had been beaten into him a long time ago in a trailer in a parking lot on a CIA base in Harvey Point, North Carolina, where he was trained to become a denied asset for the U.S. government.

He sat up. He wasn't going soft, he told himself. He'd been somewhat out of practice for a few months, but as indicated by the events the previous evening, now it was time to get back into the groove and unfuck himself from an operational and personal security perspective.

Climbing off the bed, he told himself it would be a long time before he felt a mattress again.

He walked across the room and grabbed the TV remote, flipped to Canal 3, a local Guatemalan network, and saw that the news was running.

It was in Spanish, of course, but Court spoke the language well enough to follow along. A shooting the night before in Panajachel had killed three, and at least one of the dead was a former special forces officer who, authorities asserted, had strong ties to a crime syndicate in the capital. Neither what this man from Guatemala City was doing up in the highlands nor the identity of the person or persons who shot him and his colleagues was mentioned by the reporter, certainly because she knew nothing more than what the police had told her.

The video showed the lakeshore during the day. The bodies had been collected but arterial spray on cobblestones, dozens of shell casings lying in the gutter, and bullet-sized pockmarks on boats rehashed the scene for all those who had not been present.

Court *had* been present, however, so he just looked on, semi-detached somehow, as if he'd not been responsible for at least some of that blood.

Within moments, however, the gunfight at the marina on Lake Atitlán left the TV; a quadruple murder at a nightclub in Guatemala City was described, then a story about a mudslide on the Pacific Coast.

Court's attention drifted away from the news and towards the fading light through the curtains.

But not for long. He heard the words "asesinato," *assassination*, and "Mexico City" together, and he turned back to the screen.

A female reporter doing a stand-up on a city street said, "Witnesses say a lone gunman on a motorcycle armed with what was described as a large pistol opened fire on two men entering a car on Avenida Mazatlán in the La Condesa neighborhood around lunchtime. Multiple bullets struck each man, as well as two people standing in front of a nearby Shell station. All four persons struck died at the scene.

"The two intended victims of the assassination were both Russian nationals." She looked down at her cell phone, then said, "Maxim Arsenov of Saint Petersburg was a thirty-eight-year-old freelance software engineer, and seventy-one-year-old Borislava Genrich was an international businessman based in Berlin, Germany. Authorities have not indicated what either man was doing in Mexico at the time of their deaths."

The reporter gave the names and ages of the two killed at the gas station, but Court wasn't listening because he realized Zoya was standing in the doorway to the bathroom, a towel wrapped around her and her blond hair wet and tied in a bun on the top of her head.

"I'm sorry" was all he could think to say to her.

Zoya sat down on the bed; the springs squawked, her eyes still locked on the TV.

After a moment Court spoke softly. "It was Lancer."

Zoya thought this over. "At seven p.m. last night he was in the highlands of Guatemala, wounded and falling into a lake. Do you really think he could assassinate two people in Mexico City at noon the next day?"

"I know his work. Oversized pistol, collateral damage. That dude never fails to fail." Court sighed. "He definitely had help fixing his targets, even if he was the only shooter."

Zoya nodded. "Slava said there was surveillance of the area in Mexico. Drones and personnel. Whoever ordered the hit had the engineer pinned. Lancer might have only had to land and jump on a bike before he acted."

Court turned to her. "And Slava didn't say a word about who was doing this?"

"He didn't even say where this Arsenov guy had been working before fleeing to Mexico. I assumed the U.S., but he never actually admitted it."

The news turned to other crises; Zoya rubbed away the mist that had formed in her eyes, and then she stood and returned to the bathroom without another word.

Court grabbed an iPad from his bag, logged on to the Internet, and began trying to find out more about the assassinations in Mexico.

His search of the news first turned up an assassination in California. This he ignored, and then he scrolled down to a killing in Japan. He didn't think for an instant this could be related to what had happened to him and Zoya the night before in Guatemala, so he kept searching, scrolled past news of an assassination attempt on some celebrity in the UK, and then saw a headline about a car bomb killing in Haifa of a prominent Israeli software manufacturer.

Court stopped scrolling, checked his search parameters.

All of these events had taken place in the past two days or so.

He looked them over again.

The man Genrich had been trying to protect was a software engineer.

"Carrie?" he called out to Zoya in the bathroom, but she didn't hear him.

Over the next five minutes he did a lengthy Google News search. The killing in Palo Alto involved someone who acquired commercial technology for the U.S. Defense Department. The man targeted in Oxford, England, was a world-famous tech mogul focused on artificial intelligence, and the woman killed in Japan was a prominent computer scientist.

A BMW engineer in Munich, characterized by his coworkers as brilliant, had been killed, as well, along with a Romanian AI expert found dead on a boat.

Court was no trained investigator, but he saw a pattern.

Zoya returned to the room.

Court said, "Lancer and his associates, whoever they are, are targeting people all over the world."

She shrugged. "You said he's a freelance assassin. That's pretty much what freelance assassins do, right?"

"No . . . I mean . . . these are related killings. Eight dead, all in the past day and a half, and that's just from a quick search. There could be others. And they're all electrical engineers, computer scientists, and robotics experts."

Zoya sat down on the bed.

"Plus, there was an attempt on a guy named Anton Hinton in London."

Zoya's eyes raised. "*The* Anton Hinton?"

"Yeah. You know him?"

Zoya's eyes went wide. "You *don't*?"

Court shrugged. "I don't get out much."

Zoya waved it away, then said, "Just like Slava said. A new artificial intelligence weapon is about to come online. These people knew about it, maybe.

"But why did they come after me, even when I didn't go back to Mexico with Slava?"

"Maybe because they don't know what you know. They might assume Genrich told you something."

"He didn't tell me anything other than what I told you. I don't even know who the bad actors are in this."

"Maybe Genrich was holding out on you, or else the engineer was holding out on Genrich. Whoever the enemy is, they are treating us as if we have the ability to undermine their entire plan."

"What do we do?" Zoya asked.

"Tomorrow we get a ride to the Belize border."

"And then what?"

"We keep running."

SEVENTEEN

St. Ermin's Hotel in the London neighborhood of Westminster was built in 1889 on the site of St. Ermin's chapel, a fifteenth-century house of worship. During the Second World War, it was used by the Special Operations Executive, the precursor to today's Special Air Service, as well as MI6, British foreign intelligence.

A tree-lined cobblestoned drive leads to the portico and the front door, and Zack Hightower walked up it at eight a.m., flanked by a pair of Brits who'd picked him up at London City Airport upon his landing after a nine-and-a-half-hour flight from San Antonio. The two Brits were polite but intense; they carried themselves with an obvious military bearing, as did the driver of the Rolls-Royce that ferried them from the airport, and Zack took them all to be Anton Hinton's bodyguards.

As he entered the lobby of the hotel, he saw white-columned balconies undulating above, a marble floor, and a pair of massive half-turn staircases that blended into one before emptying into the center of the lobby.

The guards led him to the bottom of the stairs, and then Gareth Wren appeared above and rushed down to meet him.

With a booming voice that turned heads in the lobby, the Englishman said, "There he is! Bloody good to see you, mate."

The two shook hands warmly, hinting to anyone looking on at the history between them.

Wren said, "Sorry I couldn't make it out to London City for a proper greeting, but Anton has me running around like a bloody madman today trying to figure out where we're off to next."

"No worries," Zack said. "Your men took good care of me."

"Good, because they're *your* men now, at least as long as we're here in London." Wren assessed the American, looking him up and down. "You look good. I'd wondered if you'd let yourself go. Clearly you haven't been slacking off on your PT. Good job, you."

Zack gave Wren a look, as well. He slapped the man on the shoulder. "Hard as woodpecker lips. Just like the old days."

"Let's grab a seat down here. I'll tell you about the lay of the land, and when I can get Anton's attention later today, I'll introduce you."

They sat and exchanged pleasantries for no more than a few seconds, and then Wren waved a hand around. "You know anything about this hotel?"

Zack seemed to notice his surroundings for the first time. "Only that it's not a La Quinta."

Wren's eyes furrowed in confusion a moment, and then they brightened. "The St. Ermin's enjoys quite a rich history in the world of espionage. During the war, MI6 was based here."

"Cool," Zack said, and then a waitress stepped up to the two men.

With a toothy smile to the attractive young woman, Wren said, "Lady Grey tea for me and coffee for my friend here."

As soon as the server had moved on, Zack noticed a small crowd of paparazzi positioned near the staircase, and perhaps a dozen or so more people gathered tightly behind them.

"What's that all about? A celebrity?"

Wren followed Zack's gaze, then chuckled. "They're here for Anton."

Zack groaned inwardly. "Really? He draws a crowd?"

"This hotel shoos them out with regularity, which is why we stay here when we're in London. Usually there are more people than this. The attack yesterday would have brought out five times the parasites as usual, but we adopted security measures intended to keep his stay here pretty close to the vest." Wren looked back over his shoulder at the crowd. "And yet clearly not as close as I would have liked."

"I've never done celebrity EP."

"Well, you won't be able to say that after today. Celebrity executive protection is your new bag, yeah?"

"Who's watching the principal now?"

"I've got five guys upstairs. All locals. We sent the Chileans home when their agent in charge got clipped yesterday."

"Plus the three who brought me," Zack said.

"Martin and Ian are security. Liam is the driver, but he's a former Royal Marine. A tough bloke himself."

"And two more running covert down here in the lobby?"

Wren's eyebrows rose. "Good eye. What tipped you off?"

He jerked a thumb towards the entrance. "The massive slab of beef with the military haircut sitting by the front door with a newspaper that he's clearly not reading was no big trick. He's not subtle, but I wouldn't mind his big ass on my side in a fistfight. The small, wiry guy on the balcony has been flashing his eyes this way now and then. Not a big tell unless you've been doing this as long as I have."

"I knew I hired the right bloke." Wren said it with a satisfied grin.

"A ten-man team?"

Wren nodded. "They're carrying pistols, which is bloody hard to get away with here in the UK, but I arranged all the paperwork with the home office and the Metropolitan Police."

"It's not *that* hard." Zack opened up his sports coat. The knurled butt of a large 2011-style handgun protruded from his waistband at his appendix, the rest of the weapon hidden inside his pants.

Wren laughed. "That took some doing, you know? Bloody hell, just off the plane and you're walking through the City of Westminster with a firearm on your person."

Wren looked at the weapon, then back up at Zack. "Don't recognize it."

"Staccato. Made in the great state of Texas."

"You used to be a Glock man."

"I used to shit my diapers. Then I grew up."

Wren laughed. "Please tell me it's a nine. We don't have any .357 or anything else you Americans love in our locker."

The 9-millimeter was the most common cartridge used in pistols in the world, but especially in Europe. Many Americans preferred other calibers, something foreigners didn't ever seem to understand.

Zack said, "It's a nine."

"Well then, it will work fine."

"So . . . where are we off to next?"

"Still to be determined. Hinton has eighteen homes and three labs around the world. Some with better security than others. We're in the process of checking with local officials in the potential countries, looking to see what further support we can get on the ground there, and we'll decide where we're going accordingly.

"Ideally," he added, "I'd like to be wheels up by tomorrow morning, but we'll see what happens today."

Wren reacted to the chirping of his phone on the table, answering it. "Yeah?"

He made no movement for several seconds, then said, "When?" There was another delay. "Have you told Anton?" Then he said, "I'll do it now."

He hung up the phone and slipped it into his jacket pocket. "My assistant, Trudy. She says a former colleague of our principal just died in a glider crash in Austria."

"A *glider* crash?"

Wren shrugged. "He was an amateur pilot. I met him once. A Taiwanese national, he went to school at Cambridge, was working at a robotics lab in Bayreuth, Germany. He was piloting his single-seat glider near Innsbruck when, witnesses say, it broke apart in flight."

"I'm gonna go out on a limb here," Zack said. "Somebody tampered with that dude's glider."

"I won't take that bet," Wren replied wryly. Then he let out a defeated sigh. "Anton's going to be devastated. The two had been partners a decade or so ago, remained friends."

"What's he like? The boss?"

"You'll see for yourself in a bit. Bloody brilliant, but as can sometimes be the case, a curse comes along with that blessing."

"I really wouldn't know."

Wren laughed. "He's a good man, though. Wants to do what's right, and if anyone can put things right in this world, it's him. He knows this, too, which means he doesn't go lacking for confidence."

"I read he was worth like thirty billion dollars."

Wren shrugged. "On paper, maybe. He took a massive hit two years ago when the Chinese communists all but stole his automotive company out from under him. They took his factories, his technology, virtually all of his China-side labor, and they forced him into a partnership. He's now got a minority stake in Ningbo Automotive Group, and it's billed like this big multinational consortium, but in truth all the companies involved but Hinton's are part of the Chinese state. He gets some money out of the enterprise, but he built that company from the ground up, poured billions into R&D, and it had just started making a profit when it was nationalized.

"Unfortunately for him, all his manufacturing and a lot of his corporate infrastructure were based in Ningbo and Guangzhou, so all the Chicoms had to do was kick out the foreigners and change the name. When that was done, they reached out to Hinton and offered him a small stake in his own bloody company in return for making nice about the whole thing in order to drive car sales around the world."

"That must have pissed him off."

"Yeah, but he's an oddly positive bloke. Quite chipper about it, really. Always looking down the road towards the next opportunity. And it's not like he's destitute."

The waitress returned with tea and coffee, then she moved off again. Zack reached for his cup. "You mentioned eighteen homes."

"Right. Private jets, as well."

"I remember he used to be on TV all the time."

"Dated models and actresses, went on all the news shows advocating for artificial intelligence. Doesn't do that anymore. Lives a pretty monastic life, to tell you the truth. Hasn't been on a date in two years. Sleeps about four hours a night, works probably sixteen hours a day."

"What can you tell me about the attempt on him?"

"A right cock-up, that was. We were in Oxford at an event that had been planned for months. I tried to get it canceled, but Anton wouldn't hear of it. The would-be assassins were two chaps with handguns. Not terribly sophisticated, not terribly talented, either, but I wouldn't mention *that* to Emilio's family." He sipped his tea, then added, "Emilio and his security acted professionally, it just went down so fast."

"Action beats reaction," Zack said ruefully.

"Always has. Always will."

Zack took mental notes. "And the bodyguards killed the shooters?"

Wren shook his head. "They wounded them but didn't put them down. I ended up dropping both the cunts myself."

"You're kidding. I thought you were head of operations, not security."

"Chief operating officer. But once a gunfighter, always a gunfighter, I guess. I started with Anton a dozen years ago on his security staff and still have my license in the UK, so I strapped on a pistol yesterday for the first time in forever. As to the shooters, one died at the scene, the other bled out, I assume in the ambulance, but I was long gone by then and haven't heard."

Hightower found himself confused. "Hinton's detail. You said they were good. What the hell were they doing while the chief operating officer was killing the attackers for them?"

"As I said, they scored hits, but they were understandably more concerned about shuffling Anton back to the vehicle under ballistic shields."

Zack nodded. "What kind of shields?"

"Expanding Kevlar suitcases."

Hightower rolled his eyes. "Those won't stop a rifle round."

"I guess we got lucky the blokes that had a go at us used pistols, but I would have registered anyone coming up on us with rifles, so it was a reasonable assumption for us to bring the shields." His eyes narrowed a little. "Didn't do Emilio much good, but Anton lived."

"Hinton needs plates," Zack said flatly. "Especially now."

"My pleas have fallen on deaf ears, but you are most welcome to try convincing him. He's terrified about getting killed, but he doesn't want to *look* terrified about getting killed, so it all comes back to us to keep him safe."

"When do I meet him?"

"He's in teleconferences all day. Talking to those friends and colleagues in his field who are still breathing, but I'll squeeze in a quick chat, maybe early this evening. You won't have much to do today. He's leaving this hotel over my dead body, but you'll be his body man when we head for the airport, hopefully tomorrow morning."

Zack nodded. "I'm ready."

Wren hesitated a moment, then asked, "Why is it you've yet to ask me what this job pays?"

"I'm sure the money's good."

"It's good."

Zack said, "I've been drifting. I need a task. You get it, don't you?"

Wren drank more of his tea, and he looked deeply into Zack's eyes. "I get it like few people could. I miss the certainty of the military, the straightforwardness of you and all your mates having the same objective."

"Yeah."

Wren smiled a little. "Wouldn't say this to anyone else, but I can say it to you. Since I started working for Hinton, I know my mission. For the first time since I left the regiment. My mission is keeping *him* focused on *his* mission, even if I don't completely understand it. And if that means shooting two Bulgarian bastards, then so be it. If it means catching a bullet for Anton, I'm ready to do that, as well, even though I'm not in security any longer. Anton *is* my mission, and that's all there is to it."

"Bad news, Wren. I'm the guy who gets to jump in front of bullets from now on."

"Lucky boy. You willing?"

"We're the same," Zack said. "I need a charge, a responsibility. You give me that, and I might bitch about it, but in truth, I'm happy."

"Brilliant," Wren said, and then he finished his tea.

EIGHTEEN

Jim Pace sat in the sterile conference room in A-ring of the Pentagon, just across the Potomac from the Washington Monument. The third-floor space had a view of "the yard" in the center of the five-sided building, but Pace was too busy looking over his notes to enjoy the late spring afternoon.

The door opened and a man in civilian attire stepped in. Pace had met Lewis Reynolds a year earlier when Reynolds was an Air Force colonel, but now he was retired, working for the Defense Innovation Unit, the organization the late Rick Watt had led.

The men shook hands. Pace said, "Colonel, I'm really sorry about Director Watt."

"Thanks, Jim. It's been a crazy couple of days. How's everything over at the proliferations desk?"

"I thought it sucked, frankly. But then I got my new tasking."

Reynolds understood. "The AI killings, obviously."

The two men sat down across from each other.

Pace said, "Watkins is sending me out to make inquiries. I understand you're the new director of DIU."

"*Acting* director. Even so, I'm glad you're involved in this, and I'll help however I can."

"You knew Rick Watt well, from what I understand."

"I did," Reynolds confirmed. "The Air Force had me working with DIU for the last four years, and Rick and I became good friends."

"I'll start with the obvious question. Any idea who might have wanted to kill him?"

Reynolds looked surprised. "What is this, *Dateline*?"

"Why do you say that?"

"Because why are you asking that? Of course I know. *Everyone* knows. It was the Chinese. From what I'm hearing, they used an American assassin, that Navy guy who caused such a stir way back, but still, the Chinese were controlling the purse strings, no doubt."

"Why is there no doubt?"

"Because," Reynolds replied, "Rick was a tenacious son of a bitch. He worked with all types of civilian companies to try to create partnerships with the DOD, but make no mistake about it—the vast majority of his focus was on acquiring AI technologies from private industry to be used by the U.S. military. He was hamstrung left and right by Congress, by the brass right here in the Pentagon, even by public opinion about AI. But still, he was fighting to bring our nation's military into the future like no one else before him, and probably like no one else after him for a long time."

"How so?"

"Artificial intelligence is the next military technical revolution, bigger than the invention of firearms, bigger than the invention of machine guns, bigger than aircraft . . . even bigger than nuclear weapons."

Pace had heard this before, but he didn't believe it. "What makes it bigger?"

"Do you know what the OODA loop is?"

Pace made a little face of annoyance. "Of course. It's a paradigm of combat. Observe, orient, decide, act. The proper sequence of action to engage an enemy."

"Exactly," Reynolds said. "In a fight between two parties, the party able to cycle through the OODA loop faster will be the winner."

"What does this have to—"

"U.S. policy states, unequivocally, that we cannot use any weapons that do not have a human being in the kill chain. We can have weapons with autonomous characteristics, but a person must be involved somewhere in the decision-making process before any lethal act is carried out."

Pace knew all this, so his next comment was a statement, not a question. "And China has no such rules."

"Of course they don't, because they want to win. We . . . or I should say, our leaders, want to look virtuous while we are overmatched by a superior enemy."

Pace was aware there were two distinct schools of thought on the subject, and now he saw that Reynolds and his boss, the late Rick Watt, were both from the school of aggressive development of autonomous weapons.

Pace said, "Let's forget about who killed him, and let's focus on the why. Any chance he wasn't killed for what he was trying to do? Could he have been killed for something he knew?"

Reynolds cocked his head. "What do you mean?"

"Some specific technology he was trying to acquire, some specific weapon another nation had developed that he was trying to combat with acquisitions of tech from private companies."

Reynolds thought a moment. "His fear was the same as everyone who knows anything about deep neural networks and machine learning. His fear was AGSI."

"Artificial general superintelligence," Pace said. It was the dreaded end state of AI, a synthetic sentience. Cognition. Machines that think like humans, albeit better, faster, and utterly without remorse.

And, as far as Pace knew, it was also bullshit. "Most experts say AGSI is a pipe dream."

Reynolds shrugged. "Rick was worried about everything the Chinese have taken from the West. He saw a pattern in their acquisitions. And the pattern was that the technology existed for machines to teach themselves, to write their own code, to grow to the level of superintelligence and reasoning. He believed AGSI was coming, and he believed we were not ready for it."

Pace said, "So the Chinese are more advanced than us because there is no political will in the West to go all in on autonomous weapons?"

"It's that, but there's another component to it. The Chinese own the world's largest datasets."

"Explain."

"Many of the biggest social media companies around the world are owned by Chinese conglomerates. Even Western ones. And the social media companies owned by Westerners, they've all been compromised at one time or another. The data the Chinese suck up about each and every person is unimaginable. Fuck, the Chicoms even have their own DNA registries in the West. The average American spits in a cup and sends it off to a lab to find out if they are some long-lost princess or something. But they don't know, and probably don't care, that some spook or scientist in Beijing now knows what diseases they're most susceptible to, who all their relatives are, whatever.

"You feed all this data into computers in China, and pump it into a growing AI agent that has the ability to learn, to optimize itself . . . where does that leave you?"

Pace cocked his head. "Where *does* that leave us?"

Reynolds shrugged as if the answer were obvious. "Armageddon. Look, I think the U.S. needs to build lethal autonomous weapons now, because the day the Chinese go online with platforms we can't defend ourselves against, it will be too late. But I am *also* just as terrified about what hell *we* might unleash as I am about what China can do.

"It's a dangerous world coming, and Rick Watt knew it. Whether he knew something I don't, some specific tech, some certain AGSI on the horizon, I don't know, but I *do* know the Chinese killed him because he was the biggest advocate of creating the only defenses that will be able to stop them in the future."

"If you had to guess," Pace asked, "what platform are we talking about? Will the Chinese put this on a pilotless aircraft, a weaponized satellite, what?"

Reynolds put his hands up. "Take your pick. Rick used to say, anything that can be electrified can be cognitized. Let that soak in a minute."

Pace did so. Finally, he asked, "What do I need to know that I haven't asked?"

Reynolds became pensive, distant. Pace didn't interrupt the man's thoughts. Finally, the former Air Force colonel said, "Up until about a year ago, Director Watt had been working on a project through DARPA."

The Defense Advanced Research Projects Agency was an R&D arm of the Department of Defense that focused on emerging technologies, and in his work on proliferations at CIA, Jim Pace had consulted with DARPA many times.

"What kind of project?"

"Project Mind Game. It was an advanced networked artificial intelligence platform, and it was developed by private firms from across the U.S., even some abroad."

"For the DOD?" Pace asked.

"Yes."

"But you said the DOD wasn't allowed to weaponize artificial intelligence without—"

"The program assumed there would be a human with a kill switch somewhere *on* the loop, not in the loop, meaning although it could operate completely autonomously, it did have a human fail-safe."

"But . . . but the fail-safe could be removed?"

"Easily, and that was the fear. When some congressional aide actually looked into the details of the project and told a capital committee, it went the way of the dodo bird."

"They shut it down? How long ago?"

"Thirteen months. But you have to understand," Reynolds said, "on its own, Mind Game wasn't a complete system. Just a healthy start to something that could have been made powerful. Even Rick thought it would have taken another five to eight years of feeding it massive amounts of data, letting it learn for itself, letting it war-game against itself, before Mind Game would be optimized enough to go out into the real world and be attached to any weapons platform."

Pace raised an eyebrow. "Some computer software project that didn't even work was canceled. But yet," Pace said, "there is some reason you wanted to tell me about it."

"I wanted to tell you about it because the Chinese stole it."

Jim Pace rubbed his eyes under his glasses. "Of course they did."

"We don't know how, but pieces of the code have been found in the cloud by researchers at MIT. They came to us, asked us to look at it, and our people were able to identify it with digital fingerprints DARPA used."

Pace summed it up. "So Mind Game, a piece of the puzzle someone would need to create and weaponize artificial general superintelligence, was built by the United States and now is in the hands of the Chinese."

Reynolds said, "Bingo. Rick was a damn fine man, a visionary, but us losing Mind Game to the Chicoms very likely gave them a two- or three-year advancement in their capabilities. The deaths of all the AI experts in the past two days indicate to me that they have put the puzzle together, or at least they are close to it, and someone has to find out what it is so we can try to cobble together a way to stop it before it kills us all."

NINETEEN

Gareth Wren led Zack Hightower through the lobby of St. Ermin's at seven p.m., heading for the elevator that would take them up to the penthouse suite. The Englishman's bespoke cobalt blue business suit had been meticulously tailored, contrasting with the oversized navy blazer and chinos Zack had brought from Texas.

At the top floor a security man at the door opened it for the pair, and they entered to find a large sitting room. It was a gray May evening in London, and the views from the floor-to-ceiling windows showed off a panoramic view of Caxton Street below.

Wren led Hightower to an Asian woman in her thirties sitting at the dining room table to their right. Laptops, iPads, and legal pads were spread out in front of her, and an earpiece protruded from her left ear.

"Zack, meet Kimmie Lin, Anton's personal assistant."

She wasn't wearing a wedding ring, so Zack said, "Miss Lin, a pleasure."

She stood and shook his hand. In an aristocratic British accent with just a hint of China in it, she said, "Lovely to meet you, Mr. Hightower. Please, call me Kimmie."

"As long as you call me Zack."

"It's a deal," she said with a smile.

Wren said, "Kimmie was born right here in London, graduated from Oxford, so she's the most overqualified personal assistant in the history of personal assistants."

She chuckled at this. "And yet Anton manages to still keep me on my toes. You'll see for yourself soon enough."

Soon Kimmie returned to her work; the two men passed another security officer as they entered through a set of high double doors, and here Zack recognized the man he'd seen on TV countless times over the past twenty years.

Anton Hinton sat on an ergonomic chair; his feet were propped up on an old desk, his big headphones over his ears. He didn't seem to notice the new arrivals as he looked over a book, and this gave Zack a moment to examine his new protectee more closely.

Hinton was smaller than he expected, maybe five foot eight; he wore a high-end black tracksuit with a shiny gold stripe down the left arm and left leg, along with sneakers that Zack thought looked ridiculous but were likely extremely expensive.

The man's eyes were bloodshot and wet, evidence he'd been crying. Zack couldn't remember the last time he'd seen the man on television, but though he retained a boyish build to his face, he looked much older than he remembered him.

Hinton looked up suddenly, saw Gareth and the large blond man standing in the center of the room, and then he closed the book.

Zack realized the man had been reading the New Testament, and he wondered if the billionaire had always been religious, or if he had simply found religion the moment he knew people were actively trying to murder him.

Hinton launched out of his chair as if he were twenty; his face brightened and Zack now thought he looked ten years younger than he had five seconds earlier.

Bounding across the room, his hand outstretched, he smiled. "Mr. Zack Hightower, your reputation precedes you." His New Zealand accent was strong, a little nasal and high, his words cropped tightly.

"Pleased to meet you, sir."

"Anton," he corrected, then looked at Gareth. "You *did* tell him to call me Anton."

Gareth shrugged sheepishly. "Lot going on. I forgot to brief him on your legendary informality."

Hinton said, "Just want everyone in my orbit on the same playing field." With a little grin that looked forced through wet eyes, he said, "I might be the dickhead in the Louis Vuitton kicks, but *you're* the gentleman with the gun, so I'm certainly no higher on the pecking order around here."

The glint of a smile remained on the man's face, so Hightower figured he'd better mirror it. He smiled back. "Yes, sir."

"My rule about 'sir' is this. If you call me 'sir,' then *I* call *you* 'sir.' There's no need. We are all the same, everyone on this big blue marble. Our earthly vessels make us look different, but none of us are any more or less than anyone else."

Zack wasn't certain how to reply, or even exactly what the man in front of him had just said, so he simply nodded.

Hinton motioned to a sofa and chairs around a little coffee table in front of a gas fireplace, and he and Zack sat.

Wren said, "I'll leave you to get acquainted. I need to get back to work on tomorrow's plans."

Hinton directed his attention to the American as the Brit left, closing the doors behind him. "Let me start by stating the obvious. I truly appreciate you taking this job, especially after what happened to poor Emilio."

"I'll do my best. If we can work together, then I can keep you safe."

"I'm at your command. I pushed back against Gareth. He wanted to cancel the appointment yesterday. If I had . . ." His voice trailed off.

"If you had," Zack said, "they would have come for you here. Or somewhere else. You can't blame yourself for what happened."

Hinton nodded a little, looking off into space, and then he turned back to Zack. "I want you to know that I'm truly quite terrified about what is going on. Both for myself—I do not want to be murdered, obviously—but also for my friends, colleagues, even my competitors. The people who have died in the past three days were all known to me. I've at least crossed paths with every last one."

"I'm sorry," Hightower said.

Hinton looked like he was going to cry for a moment, and then he brightened. "I'm sure Gareth told you we're heading down to Havana."

Wren had most definitely not mentioned this. "He just told me he was trying to work out which of your properties—"

"Cheeky monkey." Hinton held up a hand, then pressed a button on the phone on the side table next to the couch. "Kimmie," he said when the call went through. "Grab Gareth and tell him it's Cuba. *Only* Cuba."

"Yes, sir," the woman replied.

Anton said, "You'll love it there."

"Why do you have a place in Cuba? You're a New Zealander, right?"

"Officially, no. I was born in New Zealand, but now I'm Maltese."

"*Maltese?* Like . . . from Malta?"

"I'm what's derisively known as an 'investment citizen.'" When Zack just stared back blankly, he said, "I bought my way into citizenship in Malta. Helps me with taxes, with travel, with not having to bow to the government back in Wellington. I once considered starting my own country, I just couldn't get the Philippines to sell me an island." He shrugged. "It's fine. Running a government sounds pretty cool till you realize you have to be in charge of collecting everybody's garbage. Then it's a pain in the ass."

Zack was having trouble following the man's fast-talking, stream-of-consciousness style of communication, so he tried to steer the conversation back to something he felt he needed to know. "I'll be damn good at protecting you, but I'm not the sharpest tack in the room when it comes to business. Can you explain to me, in the most layman's terms possible, just exactly what it is you do?"

Anton smiled pleasantly, seemingly happy to be asked the question. "I started as a programmer when I was a teenager. Tomer Basch was my roommate at MIT. We became best friends, then we became partners. We founded a tech start-up, then another. Eventually, we sold our companies, went our separate ways, but stayed close, and eventually we opened an AI lab in California, developing all sorts of low-cost artificial intelligence products for the average homeowner. That fizzled out a few years ago as our interests diverged."

"I read about Basch on the plane ride over. He was killed in Haifa. My condolences."

Hinton gave a long sigh. "He was a brilliant guy, could have been bigger than me, but his focus changed, and we parted ways. I don't blame him. He was Israeli and he felt the call to develop LAWs to help his nation."

"LAWs?"

"Lethal autonomous weapons."

"Killer robots?"

Hinton chuckled a little. "That's right, mate. In layman's terms, anyway. He wanted to use his expertise to help protect his little nation from everyone out in the region trying to destroy it. That was his decision. I respect it. I disagree with it, but I respect it."

"You went into cars instead."

"Self-driving electric cars, to be specific. Both Tomer and I were successful, as were others doing what we do," Hinton said. "A lot of my story is hype. I'm not better than Tomer, I'm not better than Kotana Ishikawa or Ju-ah Park or Bogdan Kantor or Lars Halverson or any of the others. I'm just the flamboyant one who got lucky with my businesses, dated the pop stars, and got myself up on TV a lot."

"Halverson? Who is that?"

"Another old partner of mine. You haven't heard of him because he's still alive. He's in Boston, and I talked to him this afternoon. His street's lined with cops and corporate security. Like me . . . it looks like they won't be able to get to him."

Zack continued his questioning. "So . . . you sold your car company?"

"Is that what you read in the news, or is that what Gareth told you?"

"I read in the news that you sold. Wren said the Chinese basically stole it out from under you."

Anton shrugged. "They cut me in so I wouldn't make a fuss about it, and so I'd still buy chips and other equipment made in China." With a chuckle he said, "They stole ten billion in capital assets, God knows how much in intellectual property value. But it is what it is."

He smiled; the man smiled a lot for someone on the edge of tears, Zack noticed, but this time it was a sad smile. "The thing that hurts the most, though, is the brain drain. Some of my best programmers were Chinese. They all work for Ningbo Automotive Group now, and none of them work for me.

"So." Anton switched gears, asking a question himself now. "You know Gareth from the Army?"

Zack didn't correct his boss and mention he'd been in the Navy. Instead he said, "We ran together in Afghanistan, Pakistan, places where we and the Brits did joint ops. I was an O, he wasn't, but we got along—"

"What's an O?"

"An officer. Sorry, sir. I was a commander, he was a Warrant Officer 1, enlisted, but every time he spoke up, me and the other Os, SEALs or SAS, would listen."

"He does have an imposing presence."

"Anyway, I left the military and went into intelligence, and we ran into one another then, too. And now, as luck would have it, when you needed a new security chief, he remembered this old American FAG and gave me a call."

Hinton's eyes went wide. "Beg your pardon?"

"Former action guy. Sorry again, it's just something we call any long-in-the-tooth operator who hangs around the periphery of the game looking for work. Never thought that would be me."

"You thought you'd find some other line of work?"

"I thought I'd be dead by forty. Then by fifty. Now . . . I've stopped making predictions."

Hinton said, "Predicting the future is my line of work, essentially. Leveraging the knowledge of the present to make a better tomorrow." He shrugged. "You might have heard that I am a strange man."

Again, Hightower wasn't sure what to say. After a moment, he replied with honesty. "I don't think I'd be able to convince you I haven't, so I'll just go ahead and tell you they say other stuff, too. I've read good things."

"Can you work with strange?"

"My job is to keep you alive; my job isn't to psychoanalyze you."

"Right," Hinton said. He seemed like he was about to wrap up the conversation. But instead he said, "How can I help you do your job?"

"Here's the sixty-four-dollar question. Do you have any idea who might be killing your colleagues and trying to kill you?"

"Gareth didn't tell you who it was?"

Surprised, Zack replied, "He *knows*? He said nothing."

"Well, he doesn't know, but he knows my theory. It's the bloody Yanks."

"Wait . . . you think America is doing this?"

Hinton said, "No offense, mate." Anton shrugged. "The perpetrator is obviously trying to remove people who might be creating artificial general superintelligence. Something involving weapons and robotics, as well, so LAWs. Some new advancement so big that someone is going around killing anyone who could possibly identify the country who made it or who could develop some sort of defense for it."

"So . . . America is killing these people to stop something from happening?"

"It seems obvious that U.S. intelligence has discovered that China is using the work of respected engineers and scientists of many nations to create a weapon, and since the U.S. isn't strong enough to stop China, they instead are trying to kill the people in the West who possess the knowledge China is mining."

"How do you explain the death of the guy who worked for the U.S. Department of Defense?"

"Misdirection. Rick Watt wasn't a big player in the AI realm. Yeah, he acquired tech for the American military. I've known the man for years, quite liked the chap. But he wasn't someone America really needed in the AI race. I guess the White House decided they would sacrifice one bloke on the periphery to deflect blame on them."

This sounded batshit crazy to Hightower, but he didn't pursue it. Instead he said, "But . . . why don't you think this might just be the Chinese killing anyone who could potentially stop their new weapon, whatever it is?"

"The Chinese have made advances on their own, but not to the degree that the Western private sector has. They *need* these people alive. How else can they innovate? China's been trying to steal the work of those who were killed—my work, as well—for years. They have acquired a lot of it, but it's a very fast-moving field, and their appetite is voracious, so it would be counterproductive for them to eliminate the brain trust that is providing their knowledge."

"So . . . if America is responsible for the killings, why the hell did you hire an American to keep you alive?"

Hinton grinned now. "Because Gareth says you aren't attached to the American government. I've got no problem with Americans, and Gareth assures me you are always a committed employee of anyone you work for, so I trust you."

Zack thought this was crazy talk, as well, but he answered honestly. "Absolutely. You are my charge. *Anyone* who comes after you is my enemy. Someone *will* come after you again. You realize that, right?"

"If I *didn't* realize that, then you wouldn't be here."

Zack smiled, ran a hand down his short pointy beard. "Is there any way I could convince you to wear body armor, just for the next few days?"

Hinton's eyes showed a little disappointment. "Emilio, all over again."

"Emilio was right. Those briefcase shields aren't enough. I get it if you don't know ballistics, but I do. The guy in Palo Alto was hit with a .308 rifle round. That bullet will go right through those shields like . . . like a .308 through butter."

Hinton seemed to think a moment, then said, "Would that help our new relationship get off on the right foot?"

Zack smiled at this. "Very much so. It will let me know that you're my partner in keeping you safe."

Anton extended a hand. "I'll walk around in a suit of chain mail and carry a lance if you ask me to."

Zack took the hand. "I won't ask you to do that. I'll procure low-profile ceramic armor, very lightweight, and I'll put it on you when we're outside the wire. You'll forget you're even wearing it."

The two men shook hands. "Welcome to the team, Zack," Hinton said.

Zack stepped into Gareth Wren's adjacent suite a minute later. It was a simple sitting area with a kitchen and a bedroom attached, as opposed to Hinton's expansive penthouse complex that took up the majority of the top floor.

Wren sat with Kimmie and a few other Hinton employees, but the former SAS man shuffled everyone out quickly, then shut the door.

"What do you think?"

"About Anton?"

"Yeah."

"Nice guy. Strange, though."

Wren laughed at this. "He's a multibillionaire genius. The smartest guy in every room he's ever walked into. That would make anyone bloody mad."

"I wouldn't know."

"Right. Me, either."

"Any reason you neglected to tell me that he thinks the United States is the one who's trying to kill him?"

Wren waved a hand. "He's got his theories. I don't necessarily buy into them, but I've doubted him before and I've been dead wrong."

"But . . . I'm American. A former government employee. Why the hell would you even think to hire me?"

"You're good at what you do."

Zack shook his head. "So are ten thousand other dudes. I'm not even a bodyguard by trade. C'mon, Wren. Do better."

Now Wren held his hands up. "Hinton thinks . . . and I think this is rubbish, so don't jump on me for telling you . . . that you can, in addition to providing first-class protection service, provide him with intelligence about what the U.S. is doing."

Hightower said, "If the U.S. *is* on a worldwide killing spree of computer geeks, nobody at the White House bothered to call up my room at the Econo Lodge in San Antonio and let me know."

The Englishman belted out a hearty laugh. "You've got the idea, mate. We can joke about Anton behind his back, but just don't say it to his face. Be ready. He'll ask you stuff about your work with the Agency."

Zack wasn't smiling. "And he won't get jack shit out of me. So . . . we're off to Cuba tomorrow?"

"Yeah . . . I was hoping he'd change his mind, his lab in Switzerland would have been my first choice, but honestly, he might be right. Nobody's going to get to him in Cuba, the way that property is set up." Gareth shrugged. "We get him down there safely and there will be no more threats to his person. Plus, he has a big lab outside Havana, staffed with engineers and scientists. His idea is he's going to go down there, rally his troops, and they are going to figure out what new weaponized AI is about to come online that the Americans are so afraid of."

Zack rolled his eyes.

"Look, mate. His mad ideas are good for you. He'll spend his time in his lab, which is quite secure, and in his residence there on the island, which is absolutely impenetrable."

"Nothing is impenetrable."

Wren smiled. "You'll see. I don't want to spoil the surprise."

Wren looked at his watch, a fat Panerai Submersible that Zack imagined must have cost over twenty grand. "Eight p.m. How about we talk more over a pint and a plate of fish and chips. Anton's buying."

"He's going?"

"No. But he's buying." Wren laughed. "That's how it works when you are the employee of a billionaire. I think you'll quite enjoy it, actually."

TWENTY

Morning sun glinted on the windshields of the trio of beige Chrysler Pacifica minivans as they rolled through the C Street gate and onto the tarmac in front of a small hangar at Joint Base Andrews in Prince George's County, Maryland, just southeast of Washington, D.C.

They slowed, then stopped, nose-to-nose and forty yards away from the closest aircraft on the ramp, a Bombardier Challenger 605 corporate jet.

Most of the other aircraft in view here at Andrews were military gray, Blackhawk helicopters and C-17 cargo planes, so the sleek white Challenger looked a little out of place, but those in the know at Andrews were well aware that government agencies often flew out of here on unmarked aircraft.

The man who climbed out of the front passenger seat of the first Chrysler wore a business suit, and his tie was a little loose around the neck. He was thirty-six, good looking and fresh faced, with slightly long brown hair and stylish Ray-Bans over his eyes.

Five more men, all in their thirties and forties, climbed out of the first two vehicles. One was Asian in appearance, one African American, one appeared Hispanic, and the other two were white. They all wore suits and ties, most were clean shaven, and they looked like they could be stockbrokers or bankers.

From the rearmost vehicle the men began extracting luggage, and there was an obvious disconnect between the bags that emerged and the men who stood around collecting them. Each man hefted a large Eberlestock Switchblade backpack onto his back, over his suit coat.

This was military-grade gear.

Next they each heaved out a massive green Hercules duffel, also made by Eberlestock and also military in appearance. They began rolling the big bags in the direction of the Challenger as a man appeared from inside the aircraft and came down the six steps of the jet stairs.

The first man from the minivans put his backpack and his rolling bag on the tarmac, extended a hand, and spoke over the din of the idling engines.

"Chris Travers. Juliet Victor."

"Jim Pace. Good to meet you."

The Asian man stepped up next to his colleague, having already put his gear in the cargo hold. Travers said, "Joe Takahashi, my number two."

Takahashi extended a hand. "Everybody calls me Hash."

"My condolences, then," Pace replied as they shook hands.

"Tell me about it."

Pace looked back to Travers again. "How much of a briefing did they give you?"

"You're going to California to speak with people who knew Richard Watt, the DOD guy who got himself killed the other day."

"That's right. He'd spent the last few weeks in Silicon Valley, and most of his senior staff is there now. I talked with his replacement yesterday at the Pentagon; it's time to speak with the grunts in the field."

Travers said, "From there I hear we might go abroad. You wanted us to come as an escort in case you accidentally kick a hornet's nest along the way."

"That's it. I'm the Agency point man on something nobody quite understands yet. I'm going to be knocking on the doors of a lot of people involved in this thing. If I knock on the wrong door . . . or the right door, depending on how you look at it . . . I will need you guys. You copy?"

"I copy," Travers said. "But I don't love the fact that we're leaving our weapons on the aircraft."

"Watkins's orders. If you need the weps, they'll be there on board for you." Pace added, "I have no reason to think we're going to get ourselves into any real trouble. Definitely not in Silicon Valley. This might just be a week or two vacation for you guys."

"We'll stay ready for action, if it's all the same to you."

"Good."

He turned to head for the jet stairs, and Travers followed behind, but he continued talking.

"They tell me you were a solid operator back in the day."

Pace turned around and faced the team leader at the foot of the stairs. "Enjoy this time, dude. Someday you'll wake up and your knees and ankles and back will be yelling at you to stop this nonsense and calm down."

Travers grinned. "Yeah, maybe so. But for now I just hear all that shit from my mom."

They boarded, and Takahashi helped the other men haul another load of gear from the minivans to the aircraft.

Inside the cabin, Pace said, "There's seating for twelve on board, and there's only seven of us plus the crew, so you should be comfortable enough."

Travers replied, looking around at the plush accommodations, "You don't have a staff?"

"I've got a staff, but they'll stay at Langley and work on the problem from there."

"Well, we spent last night on the floor of a C-130. We're gonna be just fine in here."

"I've got conference calls and video meetings for the whole flight, so I'll stay up front at the bulkhead. You and your boys can chill out in back."

Travers nodded, then said, "Anything you need, Jim. We're at your service."

The Challenger 605 took off to the north twenty minutes later, banking west towards California in a clear morning sky.

Martina Sommer's cubicle in the back row of the auditorium-style office of OC Gama in Singapore was second from the end, and therefore one of the closest to the rear door of the room at the top of the stairs.

A dour-faced security officer stood at the door, facing the room. He was Asian, and he wore a gray suit and stood with his hands clasped in front of his body for almost his entire daily shift.

From the beginning it had felt strange to have security watching the operations center as it worked, and it seemed to Martina like the people in charge here wanted it to be known by all that they were under constant scrutiny.

And it was just that scrutiny that was on her mind right now.

Shift change for the guards would take place in a minute or two, Martina knew from studying their rotations for a day and a half, and this security officer would be replaced by another man. Normally the two of them stood in the open doorway or out in the hall and chatted for a few minutes before the switchover; Martina couldn't hear what they said, but she'd noticed the habit since she'd been focusing on them, and now she nervously waited for the new man to arrive.

Her hands hovered over her keyboard; she felt sweat on her brow and an electrical charge of nervousness running down her back. She looked at the clock on her monitor, and then she nonchalantly turned her head to her right.

The door opened behind the officer; the officer turned around and greeted the new sentry, and then the pair stepped out into the hall to talk. The man who'd just performed an eight-hour shift kept the door open with a foot as he talked, but neither he nor the new guy could see Martina, so the German woman got to work.

Furiously she typed an encrypted direct message, relaying her concerns about her actions here, the danger she felt each and every passing hour as she was watched like a prisoner while she facilitated in the deaths of so many people around the world.

She spent no more than twenty-five seconds on the message, and then she typed a memorized string of numbers in the address bar—the secure Signal number of Jack Tudor, the man who'd helped her get this job. She'd known Jack for years, since she was a low-ranking intel analyst in the German army and he was a midlevel British intelligence officer assigned to Berlin on a counterintelligence operation for their domestic service.

They'd dated briefly, they'd stayed in touch after that, and Tudor had tried to headhunt her after she lost her job in Berlin the year before. Martina at first refused his offers because Tudor had a reputation of unscrupulous contracts with bad organizations around the world. He'd done work for the Saudis and the mafia and others, this Martina knew, and she didn't want to be tied to any of that.

At first, anyway.

But when he'd reached out to her a few weeks ago about this opportunity in Singapore, he'd found her in a state of utter desperation and she'd taken the job, but now that she was here, she had regained enough of her sense of honor to ask, to *demand*, from her handler that she be pulled out from this situation forthwith.

She just wanted to go back home to Bonn, find work in a factory or a bakery or a coffee shop, and get as far away from this madness as possible.

Moments after sending the message to Tudor, and after another glance to the nearest sentry station to see the two men still standing in the hall with the door propped open, she received a response.

Jack Tudor expressed concern, told her he absolutely would contact Cyrus and tell him that she had a family emergency at home, and he would get her out of there. After that, he said, he would report this all to British intelligence.

A second message popped up moments later. He said he needed more information from her about who Cyrus was, where she was located in Singapore, who the security people were surrounding her, and anything she could find on the backgrounds of the other employees there in the OC.

Martina protested in her response; she wrote that she felt she was in danger, but Tudor countered back immediately that, if her concerns were valid, he would need this leverage to ensure that she was safely returned to her family.

Reluctantly she relented, told him she would send him more information as soon as she could acquire it, and closed out of her window just as the new security officer shut the door behind him and took up his post.

She breathed a slow sigh of relief, but she knew she now had to put herself at even more risk. She'd start by chatting up people in the cafeteria. No one was supposed to talk about themselves, but there had been some polite conversation in the previous days that gave her confidence she could get a few nuggets of information off some of the more loquacious of her colleagues. She also knew she could probably get intelligence on the drone pilot she managed; all she had to do was ask the right questions to elicit the right information.

She was nervous, but she was hopeful that soon she'd be on her way back to Germany, and this terrible ordeal would be behind her.

As Martina Sommer went back to her duties at her desk, she had no way of knowing that, in addition to the sentries in the auditorium, the security department had installed pinhole cameras all along the back wall, high near the ceiling and out of view, and each camera was zoomed and focused on each workstation, including that of the director. Every keystroke could be read the instant it happened, and Cyrus would know it all.

Just as she reached to call Wrangler Zero One for a status report, her phone rang. Looking down, she saw it was the director calling, and she fought a fresh wave of panic.

Carlos Contreras sat in a Guatemala City hotel room, his laptop open in front of him and eight of his twelve drones flying over the city in a low-probability hunt for target Gama 18, Zoya Zakharova, as well as Contreras's newest official target, Gama 19, the American named Courtland Gentry.

He looked away from his machine to light a cigarette, and as he did so, his earpiece beeped.

"Yes?"

The German woman spoke in an urgent tone. "This is Control. I am notifying you to expect a phone call from the leader of this operation."

"The same man who told me to fly my aircraft in a storm the night before last?"

"No. That was the director of the operations center. I am speaking of the leader of the operation. Code name is Cyrus."

"Understood," he said. "What's this about?"

"I do not know, but I do know you will be relocating effective immediately, so you can recall your drones."

"Okay, recalling." He disconnected the call with the German, then went to work ordering his eight quadcopters to return to him.

His phone rang on the table only seconds later. He picked it up, his eyes a little wide. "Yes?"

"Zero One? This is Cyrus." It was English, an American accent, male, clipped, curt, and businesslike.

He'd assumed the Chinese were behind this entire operation. But this man was clearly American, or possibly Canadian, and he sounded like he could be a military officer from his authoritative tone of voice.

"How can I help you, sir?"

"Proceed to the airport. You are looking for a Cessna SkyCourier, tail number November, seven, eight, one, Foxtrot, Echo."

Contreras wrote down the tail number on a notepad app on his laptop, more than curious as to why the person in charge of all the assassinations was calling to tell him this. "What is my mission?"

"Your mission will be relayed to you when you are in the air."

"Okay. What about my controller at Gama OC?"

There was a pause, and then the man on the other end of the line replied. There was little emotion in the voice, but the words seemed carefully considered and thoughtful. "You will communicate directly with me for the time being. I have been following your work over the past forty-eight hours. You have shown great initiative, with limited resources and support. I need someone for a surveillance mission, outside of Gama's visibility."

This concerned Contreras. "Is there a compromise with Gama?"

"Possibly. You will help me determine this."

"Understood . . . but, as far as my pay. I think—"

"You will be compensated at two hundred percent of your original salary."

Contreras raised his eyebrows. "Okay, I accept."

"There will be new equipment for you on the aircraft arriving tomorrow afternoon."

And with that, the line went dead.

Contreras put down his phone and went back to work recovering his drones.

TWENTY-ONE

Court Gentry put his arm around Zoya's shoulder, then looked out the rain-streaked window of the sixteen-passenger minivan. Flat corn and bean fields had given way to flat jungle in the past half-hour ride along Western Highway in northern Guatemala. The squeaky suspension of the van made more noise now as they bounced along an increasingly bumpy road under a low canopy of gray mist and heavy clouds.

An Ice Cube song from the nineties blared from the front of the van.

Court had offered the bus driver, a young man named Javi, three thousand quetzals, a little less than four hundred U.S. dollars, to transport them from Flores to a border crossing into Belize. It was a three-hour round trip; the young man had calculated he would make by the end of the evening what took him a week and a half to make running fares from Flores up to the Mayan ruins in Tikal.

Court glanced down at his watch and saw that it was four p.m. The two-lane road they traveled on bottomed out here and there, and the van had to slow to negotiate the pools that had formed, but otherwise Court felt like they were making good time.

Rain began to fall heavier outside.

He and Zoya began talking about how they would organize their personal security when they found a hotel in Belize, but they did not discuss this for long, because they stopped talking and looked up as the music was turned down and off and the van began to slow.

They came to a halt on the jungle road as a steady rain beat down on the roof of the minivan. The driver called back to them in English. "Police checkpoint, amigos. You will need your passports, but it will not take any time."

When they did not reply, Javi said, "It is not a problem. This happens."

Neither Court nor Zoya was particularly worried. They'd both spent enough time in Central America to realize police and military control stops were common enough. Plus, their documents were good, and whoever it was who had tried to kill them the other night, it was definitely *not* the Guatemalan cops in the northern Petén district.

That said, the two of them both eyed the checkpoint just in front of them and saw three blue-and-white pickup trucks with the world "Policía" on the side, and at least a half-dozen armed police standing in the road in the rain, their vehicles parked on the foliage-covered curbside.

Court recognized the uniforms and vehicles of the PNC, the National Civil Police of Guatemala, and he clocked the expressions on the men's faces as they neared. These cops didn't seem in any way amped up or agitated; they just wore the regular bored checkpoint demeanor that Court had encountered hundreds of times in his life.

A gravel road ran off the highway to the left next to where the men stood and the pickups were parked, and Court looked down the road to see a few hovels and smoking cooking fires, and several chickens milling about, but no other activity before the path turned off deeper into the jungle.

Javi rolled down his window while Court and Zoya began scooting forward to seats just behind him, pulling their backpacks along with them in case they were searched.

Soon a police officer in his twenties stepped up to the open window. He wore a black beret with a clear protective rain cover over it, a black raincoat, and an Uzi 9-millimeter subgun hanging over his chest. Court couldn't see a handgun on the man's hip because of the raincoat, but he assumed he would be carrying either a Glock or a Jericho.

Behind him, three men stood with Israeli-made Tavor rifles, a much more powerful weapon than the Uzi, but also considerably larger. Another

PNC officer, this man older with gray in his hair, leaned against the trunk of his car looking at his phone. No weapon was visible on the man, but again, Court knew he'd have a pistol on his duty belt under his raincoat.

He wore the rank of a sergeant on his wide-brimmed hat, which made him the commander of this group, and he didn't seem at all interested in the traffic stop going on next to him.

Two more cops stepped into the road behind the van, and Court saw they both had wooden-stocked pump shotguns slung over their shoulders.

None of this caused him any alarm; all these weapons were fielded by the PNC, and the behavior was typical of police who had been ordered to stand in the rain and stop passersby on the road to check IDs.

Zoya, seated on Court's right, echoed his feelings.

"Looks legit," she whispered.

"Yep."

The officer in the van's window took Javi's commercial driver's license without even speaking, then asked him where he was heading.

"Melchor de Mencos."

"To the border crossing there?"

"Sí, señor."

He glanced in the back. "Do your passengers speak Spanish?"

"No, señor."

Now the policeman addressed Court and Zoya. "Hablan español?"

They both shook their heads.

The cop focused on Zoya now. In Spanish, to Javi, he said, "The rubia. She's hot." *Rubia* meant "blonde," and Court pretended like he couldn't understand.

Javi just chuckled a little.

Zoya made no expression that she'd understood, either. Instead, she just held the officer's gaze with a little smile.

The cop said, "Passports, por favor."

"Of course," Zoya said, adopting her Canadian accent as she'd done for months in public.

Court handed both his and Zoya's blue passports up to Javi, who, in turn, passed them out the window into the rain.

The man began looking them over, then glanced back to the pair inside the van.

After a moment he stepped away without a word, walked back towards the older man leaning against the pickup truck, and handed them over.

Court sensed no danger, not yet, anyway, but something in the way the younger officer moved made him wonder if they were, in fact, looking for a pair of tourists matching their description.

The older cop pushed off the pickup, said something to his subordinate, then tapped a button on his cell phone and brought it to his ear.

The young man with the Uzi came back to the van. "Sal de auto, por favor."

"He wants us to get out of the van," Javi said. "It will just be for a moment."

Javi's relaxed tone had given way to a little confusion, perhaps even trepidation.

One of the cops with a Tavor rifle opened the driver's-side rear sliding door, and Court and Zoya stepped into the rain as Javi climbed out from behind the wheel.

No one raised a weapon, no one made any move to restrain either Court or Zoya, and, by looking around at everyone, Court decided that other than the sergeant on the phone, no one was occupied in anything other than standing around getting rained on.

Thunder rumbled in the low gray sky.

The phone conversation was too far away for Court to hear, but then the silver-haired sergeant's eyes suddenly flashed up, locking on Court.

The American looked away as if he had not noticed.

The man on the phone then called out to his subordinate who had been talking to the occupants of the minivan. "Los pasejeros? Hablan español?" *Do the passengers speak Spanish?*

"No, señor," came the reply, and the older policeman began ambling over closer to the van. He wasn't talking into the phone at the moment; he seemed to be either listening or else on hold.

As he got closer, he looked to Javi and, still with the phone to his ear, he spoke to the driver in Spanish. "Somebody is looking for people who match their description. I don't think you're going to the border. I'm waiting to find out what we're doing. We'll probably have to take them back to Flores to process—"

He stopped talking suddenly as someone obviously began speaking on the other line. After a second, he said, "Claro que sí." *Of course.*

Looking at Court now, he held his phone out in front of him as if he was going to take a picture. In English, he said, "Smile."

Court did not smile. He heard the iPhone take the photo of his face, and *now* he began to worry.

Zoya stood to Court's right, next to the driver's door, and the cop also took a picture of her, and then he seemed to text the images to someone before bringing the phone back to his ear.

Javi hadn't said anything to them in a while, but when he didn't get his picture taken like the other two, he turned to them. "They are looking for people who look like you. If it not you, then all okay." After a beat, he said, "It not you . . . right?"

Neither Court nor Zoya answered, and Court began wondering if Zoya was beginning to feel as anxious about this as he was. Just as he began to turn to her to gauge her expression, however, she softly spoke one word to him, an interrogative, and she said it in Russian.

"Smertelney?"

Court knew that the word meant "lethal" and she was asking if he wanted her to use lethal force if it came down to fighting these cops.

Clearly, Zoya gets the danger. Though concerned, Court simply replied back to her with a soft "Nyet."

They weren't going to kill these cops to avoid getting arrested. They'd only kill them if the cops had more nefarious plans in store, and so far, most of them didn't seem to show any signs that made him think they were any sort of a death squad.

Most were young, under twenty-five, and even the sergeant seemed confused by his conversation with the other party on the line. This wasn't something he dealt with on any sort of a regular basis, that much was clear.

Court was soaked to the bone now, as were Zoya and Javi, but they just stood there waiting. Court took the time to judge the location of everyone here at the roadblock, and then he looked back to the boss, still with the phone to his ear. He noticed a slight narrowing of the man's eyes now, a tension in his body that wasn't there before. The cop muttered something else into his phone, but he appeared to be whispering it.

A fast exchange began, the sergeant perhaps arguing or protesting to the person on the other end of the line.

A quick scan around showed him that a couple of the other police had picked up on their sergeant's energy. The young man standing closest to Zoya stepped a few feet away, letting his hand rest on the grip of the Tavor on his chest that pointed down at the asphalt.

A civilian car approached from the east, and another officer with a Tavor waved them to stop some twenty meters away, and then he held his hand up higher, as if he were ordering the occupants of the car to wait right there.

This all barely registered with Court, because he was so locked on to the sergeant. Someone on the other end of that line was in charge, and the sergeant was, at the very least, being told Zoya and Court were dangerous.

This was going downhill fast, and the arrival of a bus full of travelers from the direction of Flores didn't help matters.

A cop with a shotgun just waved the weapon over his head to encourage the bus to stop and wait.

Court and Zoya stood there in the rain as more passing cars were ordered to a halt so that the situation in the middle of the jungle highway could be handled.

While he continued talking into the phone, the sergeant reached inside his raincoat and propped his hand on the grip of his pistol, a failed attempt to appear nonchalant while putting his hand on his weapon.

Oh, fuck, Court thought. *We're getting arrested.*

Now the sergeant lowered the phone, then called out to the driver. "They are coming with us. Get their luggage out of your van, and you are free to go."

Javi looked at his two passengers with confusion; he clearly wondered what they had done to get themselves picked up at a checkpoint, but soon enough he reached inside his vehicle, pulled the two backpacks out, and set them down in the road.

He passed the pair on his way back to the driver's-side door. Softly, he said, "Sorry, guys. I'm sure there is some mistake," but he didn't sound like he meant it. He just wanted to be out of here, and Court couldn't blame him.

He wanted to be gone, as well.

Javi climbed back behind the wheel, fired up his engine, and reversed. Turning around on the gravel path that jutted off the two-lane highway, he was back on the road in seconds, passing the cars and buses held up by the roadblock and heading back towards Flores.

Court returned his attention to the sergeant, and he noticed the man's arm move a little, which meant his hand was repositioning inside his raincoat. Even though Court couldn't see the weapon he knew was there, he recognized the movement the cop was making.

He was adjusting his hand resting on the pistol so he could get a better grip, which meant, to Court, that he was about to draw his gun.

Speaking into his phone again, the older man said, "Ambos?" *Both.* "Seguro?" *Are you sure?* After another brief pause he nodded. "Entendido." *Understood.*

He hung up the phone, and his face drained of all color. To Court he looked nervous, loath to proceed but bound by orders.

Moments later, the sergeant seemed to notice the other vehicles on the road. A dozen cars, trucks, and buses were lined up in each direction, and a few people wearing raincoats had climbed out to stand in the street.

The sergeant looked back over his shoulder at the gravel road, and then he seemed to make peace with whatever it was he'd been asked to do. To his men he said, "Search them."

Neither Court nor Zoya had anything suspicious on them or in their packs other than a single machete, which was put in the front seat of one of the pickups without any mention of it. When the search was over, Court was hustled away by two young officers and placed in the back seat of one of the pickups, and a man with a Tavor sat down next to him. He saw Zoya being led towards another truck by the officer with the Uzi.

They gave each other a quick look before the doors were shut; all the men except for the pair with shotguns loaded up, and then the two pickups began to move.

Despite the expression on the sergeant's face, Court hoped they'd be taken back to Flores, to jail, which he wouldn't have loved, but it was far superior to his alternative suspicion about what was happening. When they instead turned and began rolling slowly up the gravel road towards the ramshackle homes there, his worst fears seemed to be correct, and he liked this even less.

These regular Guatemalan police had been given an order by someone, likely someone extremely high above them, to take this pair of foreigners to a secluded area and put a bullet in their heads.

TWENTY-TWO

The drive lasted less than three minutes. Court's pickup turned a corner past the run-down homes on the gravel road and then followed a gentle rise in the jungle. Passing a couple of derelict little buildings, the driver then pulled up in front of a one-story structure with a rusty metal roof. The windows had been completely knocked out; mold crawled up a wooden wall and an overhang. A sign above the building hung vertically, and it had been so weathered by time and the elements that Court couldn't read it, but from the look of the place he thought it might have been a little freestanding tienda back in its prime, a very long time ago. Today it appeared dark and dingy and utterly unoccupied, except for a black spider monkey in a tree above and a few chickens scratching around in the brush.

The engine of the truck was turned off, and the only sound Court heard was the rain beating on the truck, water pouring off the corrugated roof of the building, and the incessant patter of the raindrops on the metal-and-cinder-block structure.

He heard a new noise, then looked over his shoulder. The pickup Zoya had been put in pulled up behind them, and then it turned off its engine.

Both the foreigners were led out of their vehicles by armed cops. As soon as they stood there, some fifty feet from the front door of the dilapidated building, Zoya spoke English. "This is a police station?" She knew it wasn't, Court was certain; she was just trying to draw the men into a conversation to slow down the action, giving both her and Court a chance to evaluate their surroundings.

But none of the cops replied to her. It was clear they were beginning to figure out what their sergeant and their two prisoners already knew.

The older man appeared from the rear truck, then ordered his four men to walk the prisoners around the back of the building.

The entire seven-person entourage picked their way through the rubble around the outside of the broken structure without speaking; everyone seemed nervous now. Court stepped over and around piles of garbage and clumps of foliage as chickens scurried out of their way. He saw pieces of rusty and bent rebar lying around, and he evaluated the efficacy of using one as a weapon.

The energy from the young police around him as they walked was palpable. Court could tell they were scared, and not because they felt *they* were in any danger. They were scared because they'd just realized they would be taking human lives today, and no matter what they were getting paid for all this, they didn't much want to do it.

They were cops. They might have been dirty cops, Court didn't know, but it was obvious to him they weren't so dirty that they found themselves relaxed about executing a couple of people who looked like regular tourists. He wondered if they would hesitate when the time came.

Court and Zoya, on the other hand, were altogether different.

They'd kill, and neither fear nor apprehension would slow them down one instant.

Rounding the corner to the back of the building, Court saw a one-story cinder-block wall jutting out from it at a ninety-degree angle, as if it had been part of a room that had been partially torn down or perhaps it had fallen down during one of the many hurricanes that had pummeled the country over the past few years. The wall that remained, he realized, would be the wall he and Zoya would be lined up against in just seconds.

Court said one word now to Zoya, who was five feet away on his left, closer to the wall of the cinder-block-and-metal building.

"Smertelney." *Lethal.*

Zoya nodded, her eyes scanning the area. Replying in Russian, she said, "On your cue."

One of the policemen walking just behind her turned back to the sergeant, who trailed his four men and his two prisoners, and spoke. "What did they just say?"

The sergeant just shrugged. He didn't know they were speaking Russian, he just thought it was English that he hadn't understood.

Still thirty feet or so from the wall in front of him, they neared a window on their left that looked in on the blackened interior of the little structure. Court looked around quickly, then stopped walking.

Zoya stopped one step later, right next to the shattered-out window, barely visible through the steady rain draining off the roof overhang like a waterfall.

"Vaya," one of the men behind barked, ordering Court and Zoya to move on.

Court spoke English to the older man, standing somewhere behind him. "Sergeant. Whatever it is you think we did, we'd be happy to just pay a fine and"—he took a half step back, his eyes still on the gray cinder-block wall in front of him—"be on our way."

The sergeant passed Court on his right and then turned to face him. The man had apparently made some peace with what he was about to do; he looked resolute enough, although the underlings around him remained less sure.

He pointed a finger at Court; rainwater dripped off the front of his plastic-covered hat.

In English, he said, "You keep walking! Over there." He pointed at the cinder-block wall.

Instead of moving forward, Court scooted back a little more, as if he were recoiling against the man's words. In truth, he was trying to make contact with the rifle no doubt pointed at his back so that he knew exactly where it was, because the next few seconds—the rest of his life—depended on him getting control of it.

Court switched effortlessly to Spanish, though his accent and words made it obvious he was no native speaker. "Someone has told you to execute us. It was an order, not a request. Your boys don't want to do it. *You* don't want to do it, although I'm sure you've been offered a lot of money."

He saw the police officer surprised to be addressed in Spanish; he sensed that the four cops behind him were surprised both by the language and the words, but the sergeant recovered quickly and stuck his finger back up, pointing at Court from ten feet away. "Callate!" *Shut up.*

Zoya spoke Spanish now. "You'll never get that money, Sergeant. I promise you that."

"Vayan!" one of the four officers behind Court said now, but instead of moving forward, he scooted another couple of inches back, still looking at the sergeant.

"Please, sir," Court said in Spanish, a tone of desperation in his voice now. "These are just boys. They have their whole lives ahead of them. No one needs to die today."

"Callate!" The sergeant said it again. Angrier than before.

"Do you have a family, señor? Kids who need you?"

The sergeant began drawing his weapon from inside his raincoat. Court didn't think the man was going to shoot him right here, with four of his men behind Court and Zoya and therefore in the line of fire. No, the gray-haired man was planning on using the weapon as an intimidation tool.

As it came out of the raincoat and the man began to raise it, Court sighed, then raised his hands and moved back for a third time, and this time he felt the slight pressure between his shoulder blades where the barrel of a Tavor tapped his soaking-wet shirt.

And this gave him all the information he needed.

He spun to the left, swung his arm up and around, and ducked at the same time.

Making contact with the short barrel of the bull-pup rifle, he pushed it up and to the right, in the opposite direction of Zoya, and the officer holding the gun instinctively pulled the trigger, sending a painfully loud rifle crack through the air.

Black howler monkeys wailed in the trees.

The sergeant got his gun up at the same time, but Court was now flying around behind the officer with the rifle, taking hold of the weapon as he did so.

While this was going on, Zoya took a step to her left and jumped high through the rainwater cascading from the roof, her feet landing on the outer portion of the window ledge next to her. As soon as she planted, she vaulted up and backwards into the air with all the strength in her quads, sailing just above the officer who'd had a gun at her back. This man fired, his bullet hitting the side of the derelict building, and Zoya's backflip dropped her directly behind the man, where she grabbed him by the neck, then yanked him backwards and off balance, spinning him around.

Court had just grabbed his cop with his left hand, yanking him in that direction, when the silver-haired sergeant in front of him fired his Glock pistol. Court could feel the bullet impact the young officer in his grasp— the man jolted back and let out a cry of shock.

Court had a two-handed grip on the cop's rifle by reaching around his body, and he leveled it at the sergeant in front of him, then pulled the trigger just as the older man fired again.

A single 5.56 round pounded out of the gun and straight into the gray-haired sergeant's chest at the same time a second 9-millimeter round from the sergeant's pistol slammed the young officer in Court's grasp.

Zoya had swung the small guard she held from behind 180 degrees; he now faced in the direction of the last two armed men, and they held their fire because they had their sergeant and three colleagues in front of them as well as the two Canadians they'd planned on executing.

The man in Zoya's grasp couldn't break free from her rear choke hold, and he couldn't wield his rifle to shoot her back over his shoulder, so he furiously reached inside his raincoat.

But Zoya beat him to it. Her right hand found his pistol on his utility belt, and she pulled it free of its leather holster.

One of the cops who had been standing farther behind her, a man with an Uzi, realized he had to fire and risk killing his colleague because the prisoner now had her hand on a gun. Just as he began to press the trigger,

Zoya fired the Glock 17, shooting from the hip of the man she held on to, and her round hit the officer with the Uzi in the thigh.

He fell to the mud and weeds and garbage there behind the dilapidated tienda; his weapon skidded out in front of him.

Now Zoya let go of the man she'd been holding, pushed off him, and jumped back, rolling over the windowsill next to her. As she fell backwards out of view of the men trying to kill her, she fired twice, hitting the man she'd taken the gun from in the stomach as he spun around to get his rifle pointed her way.

She disappeared behind the cinder-block wall just as the last standing officer, ten meters back, opened fire on her position with his Tavor, raking the wall around the window.

Court got the rifle away from the man who'd been shot twice by his own sergeant, then spun around just in time to see Zoya rolling backwards through the window, firing between her legs through a sheet of rainwater draining from the metal overhang as she disappeared from view.

He saw a man injured and crawling in the mud, and a second on his feet, a little farther back, now dumping fully automatic fire at the window. The man hadn't even noticed Court there with the rifle, so fixated was he on removing the threat in front of him. Court knew that gun battles were hard for the untrained to manage—with the onset of panic, vision had a tendency to narrow, and focus tended to sharpen on one small point: the perceived greatest threat.

Everything else but the greatest known threat disappeared, so a trained gunfighter knew to keep both eyes open and his head swiveling, ready to process new information while still dealing with the old.

Court aimed the Tavor and shot the standing man in the side of the head, then spun the weapon towards the wounded officer with the Uzi. The man reached out for his weapon, and through the mud and rainwater all over his face, Court could also see the shock, as if the small young man couldn't believe this was happening.

In Spanish, Court shouted, "Don't touch it!"

The man looked up at him, reached his arm out further, and then Zoya appeared out of the rain pouring off the roof, leveled the Glock, and shot the injured officer through the top of his head.

He dropped down dead on his weapon.

Court spun around with his rifle, checking the bodies quickly to make certain all threats were neutralized.

When he was finished, Zoya stood beside him, pistol held low in both hands.

"You hurt?" he asked.

She shook her head. "Cuts and stuff. You?"

"I'm good." He looked her over. There was a small gash on the back of her neck, and her right shoulder was bleeding a little, as was her right elbow.

"Could have been worse." He looked down at the five bodies lying all around. "These kids didn't even want this."

Zoya walked over to the dead sergeant. "Who gives a shit?"

Court was a killer, but at times like these he was unable to kill without a level of remorse. He continued looking at the men—four of them boys, really—who'd had the sole misfortune of being assigned to the checkpoint on Western Highway this afternoon.

Zoya snapped him out of it. "Hey! The two guys back at the roadblock will have heard this. You know they'll call it in. You think they'll come investigate?"

Court shook his head to clear it. "Get a couple of Uzis and two Glocks. Any extra mags. Leave the Tavors and Jerichos."

Zoya and Court fished through the bodies quickly; he pulled a set of keys from the man who had been behind the wheel of the pickup he'd arrived in while she grabbed guns and mags, and soon they ran back around the building, leaving the five dead behind them lying in the mud and the detritus of the derelict building.

Both of their backpacks were still in the bed of the lead pickup. Court climbed in and fired up the engine; Zoya jumped in the passenger side and put the Uzis on the floorboard at her feet and the Glocks in the center console. "You think this little road leads anywhere but back towards the road-block?"

Court shrugged. "We'll take it in the other direction as far as it goes, and then we'll get out and move through the jungle if we have to. We can't go back to the highway."

She nodded, put her hand on the back of her head, and brought it back to find a little blood there. Wiping it on her jeans as if it were nothing, she said, "Help me understand this. Who ordered those cops to kill us?"

Court shook his head as he drove through the storm. "No idea. Whoever is running this op has reach like I've never seen. They must have the money, the influence, and the connections to make that happen back there."

"So . . . what?" Zoya said. "You still think we can just keep running?"

"No. We tried that . . . it didn't work. We need to attack into the threat."

"Good. I'm starting to get as paranoid as you."

"You chose the right time."

She picked up one of the Uzis and ran her fingertips over its wet surface. "What did you have in mind?"

"Lancer. Lancer is the key to figuring this out."

"Okay, but how the hell do we find him?"

Court smiled at her now, a stark difference from the worry that had been on his face prior. "Believe it or not, I just might know a way. Give me your phone."

She reached back and began going through her backpack.

They followed the road around a bend. On the far side, Court saw an intersection in front of them. A one-lane paved road rolled both back in the direction of Flores and to the northeast.

He turned towards Belize and drove on through the rain, both his and Zoya's heart rates slowly inching back down after the pandemonium they'd just experienced.

TWENTY-THREE

The seaside village of Vila do Bispo boasts only 5,800 residents and lies on a small peninsula jutting out into the Atlantic Ocean from the southwestern tip of Portugal. A beautiful but tiny white cottage sits on a hill, just a ten-minute stroll up from Ingrina Beach, but the man who lived alone inside the home had never once put his toes in the sand down by the water. He preferred his view of the ocean from the comfort of his cushioned chair on his back porch, usually with a glass of brandy in his hand and a book in his lap as he gazed into the blue distance by day and the twinkling waves of the moonlit Atlantic Ocean by night.

Sir Donald Fitzroy was English, in his seventies, with wispy white hair and an increasingly portly build. He was up late this evening, well past midnight, but the cool air on his porch invigorated him while the golden thirty-year-old Ararat Erebuni in the snifter on a table a foot from his hand kept the worst of the chill away.

The moon was out, stars sparkled, and the distant ocean glowed.

Fitzroy pulled a pill bottle out of his jacket pocket, fished out a single capsule, and then swallowed it just ahead of a swig of brandy.

His iPad sat on the tile coffee table in front of him, but he'd been ignoring it in favor of his dog-eared and worn copy of *In Chancery*, a John Galsworthy novel from 1920 about wealth and class struggles in England.

A ginger tabby stepped up into the light on the porch and immediately pressed its body up to Fitzroy's leg, purring as he did so. The neighborhood cat had adopted Fitzroy shortly after the Englishman had moved here a year earlier. Sir Donald was reluctant at first about the relationship, but now he dutifully rose, stepped into the cottage, and returned moments later with a bowl of milk.

The cat began lapping eagerly, a cool breeze blew in from the ocean, and Fitzroy adjusted the collar of his cardigan to cover more of his neck.

He picked his book back up, turned a page in the Galsworthy tome, and then the iPad on the table beeped, indicating that a call was coming through his secure Signal app.

He looked at the incoming number. It meant nothing to him, but no more than a dozen people knew how to reach him through Signal, and of those people, he loved half of them, and the other half wanted him dead.

Either way, best I answer, he told himself.

Bringing the iPad closer, he accepted the call. In a tone carefully measured to show no concern he said, "Yes?"

"Guess who."

Fitzroy took no time in identifying the voice. "My boy! Bloody wonderful to hear from you."

Court Gentry replied, "Likewise, Fitz. How's the family?"

He hesitated a moment, then smiled down at the iPad. "All good. Haven't seen my granddaughters in over a year; personal security intervenes on love, as you know better than anyone. Still, I've snuck in a few phone calls to them. Kate tells me she's going to be a veterinarian; it's her calling, I'm certain. And Claire is tearing up pitches in London on her football team and dreams of becoming an actress. Can you imagine?"

"Easily."

"Both make stellar marks in school, as well."

"That's great," Court replied, a twinge of sadness in his voice that the Englishman instantly picked up on.

He said, "And all that . . . everything those two girls are . . . everything they have in life . . . it is all because of you."

Court had, a long time ago, rescued Fitzroy, his twin grandchildren, and his daughter-in-law from peril.

"They lost a lot, as well," Court said.

"That they did." Fitz watched the cat lap up the milk a moment, then said, "All *I* have is because of you, lad. Don't you ever think I don't appreciate what you did every single day of my life."

"You've gotten me out of a jam or two yourself."

"What I did was nothing. What you did for me . . . it's the children. The girls. Someday, if you're lucky, you'll know yourself just what you have given me."

A few seconds of awkward silence stretched out into a few seconds more. Suddenly he bolted upright in his chair.

He looked towards the coastline, still shimmering in the moonlight. "This dark business going on with the technology killings all over the world . . . you're not involved in that bloody nonsense, are you?"

Court sniffed into the phone. "Yeah. But I'm strictly playing defense this time out."

"Good lord."

"I'm with Z," Court said. Fitzroy knew Zoya Zakharova, so he understood. "A man involved with whatever's going on came to her for help, and that put her directly in the crosshairs."

"Tell me that she is okay."

"She's okay. We both are. We just know we can't hide this one out. This has to be a big operation, especially considering all the other targets out there. We're going to try to figure out our exposure, and you might be able to help."

The Englishman sipped his brandy, then said, "You just tell me how."

"I caught a good look at one of the assassins the night before last."

Fitzroy said nothing. He just waited.

"It was Lancer. He's older, balder, stronger . . . uglier, if that's even possible. But it was definitely Lancer."

An inhale from the Englishman, and then he said, "Back when he worked for me, I'd have wagered he'd be dead in a year. Now he's one of the most successful hit men on Earth."

"*He's* alive, it's everyone within fifty meters of one of his targets who's dead."

"I regret employing him for just that reason. And I regret pairing the two of you together back in Istanbul. A terrible mistake."

"It was Ankara."

"Right. Memory fails."

"Tell me you are out of the game," Court said. "Tell me you aren't running Lancer in all this."

Fitzroy sat back now. "Heavens, no, boy. I haven't seen him since that operation with you. What was that, five, six years ago?"

After a pause, Court repeated himself. "So you're out of the game? Completely?"

Fitzroy began to sip his brandy, but then he drank the entire snifter down. Wincing with the alcohol, he said, "I dabble. Nothing dangerous, I just keep in contact with certain players, here and there."

He could hear the disappointment in the American's voice. "Jesus, Fitz. You gotta stay retired."

"That's rich, coming from you, lad," he replied, but there was no anger in his voice. "Look . . . I have nothing whatsoever to do with any of this madness, and I'm waiting it out to see what comes next."

He heard Court breathe a sigh of relief before saying, "What do you know about Lancer?"

"I know enough. His name is Scott Kincaid. Former American Navy man."

"Any idea who he works for now?"

Fitzroy sat deeper into his chair. "That's just it. I know *exactly* who he works for."

"How's that?"

"I hear things. Lancer's handler is also former MI5, like me. An expat, like me. A bit younger, but he's running assets all over the world now."

"I need a name."

"And I'll give it to you. The company is Lighthouse Risk Control Ltd., and the man's name is Jack Tudor."

Court had heard the name, but he knew nothing about the man. "Where can I find him?"

Fitzroy hesitated, then said, "Looking for Tudor, then looking for Lancer . . . it's just going to bring you danger without reward."

After a hesitation, Court said, "I need you to keep something close to the vest."

"Yes, of course."

Court told Fitzroy about Zoya, her "uncle," and his warning about a dangerous new weapon. About the attempt against Zoya in Guatemala, the kill order given to the northern Guatemalan police.

"My God," Fitzroy said when Court finished his story.

"I'm glad you seem to get it," Court said, "because I really don't."

"Fully autonomous weapons operating at machine speeds change the entire paradigm of war. If one military possesses this technology, then any military that does not will be vulnerable. No, strike that. They will be bloody helpless. It has been said that the nation that controls artificial intelligence controls the future."

"Then you see why Z and I can't sit this one out."

Fitzroy gave a long, deflating sigh. "Tudor lives in Mexico, on the coast in Yucatán. I speak with him from time to time. I believe him to be a reasonable man, his business notwithstanding."

Court's voice lowered. "I don't need to reason with him. I need to put my hand around his fucking throat."

"No, lad. Not Tudor. He'll have security, he has walls and alarms and blokes and guns."

"And I have me."

Fitzroy shook his head as he stared at the iPad. "You can fight your way in if you have to, but I don't think you have to."

"Meaning?"

"I'll talk to him on your behalf. There's no need for belligerence on this. I'll explain to him what's at stake, and he will be reasonable."

Court paused for several seconds. Finally, he said, "No. Sorry, Don. I'm not going to tip this guy off with a phone call. He could go to ground, somewhere I'd never find him. I need to be right there when he hears what I want from him, so that if he doesn't comply on his own . . . I can provide some . . . *encouragement*."

Fitzroy knew the younger man was right. He thought he could get Tudor to play along, but he was by no means certain. An idea occurred to him. "Speaking with him in person and in a professional setting, arranged by someone he knows and trusts, might be the safest and simplest way for you to approach this."

"What are you saying?"

"Wherever you are in the world, if you can get yourself to Tulum, Mexico, then I will meet you there, and I will go with you personally to speak with Jack. I feel sure I can make the conversation happen both safely and productively, but if I'm mistaken . . . well . . . you will be there to force his compliance."

After a pause, Court said, "You'd do that?"

"For you, lad, I would do anything. Give me twenty-four hours and a Signal number where I can reach you. I'll call you when I'm in the air, and we'll make arrangements to meet."

Fitzroy jotted down the number Court gave him and then they said their goodbyes.

The Englishman ended the transmission on his iPad.

Looking down, he saw that the ginger tabby had finished his milk. The Englishman told himself he'd ring his closest neighbor and have him keep an eye on the cat while he was out of town.

The cat—he didn't know his name so he was just "the cat"—was his only real friend these days, with the one possible exception of Courtland Gentry, and at this late point in his life, Don Fitzroy endeavored to treat his friends well.

TWENTY-FOUR

The Jensen Estates Condominiums sit on Jensen Road in the usually quiet neighborhood of Watertown, Massachusetts. The four-story brick-and-white-painted-wood structure had most definitely seen better days, but it was a nice-enough-looking building, constructed in the 1990s in a Colonial style that was in keeping with the architecture of the greater Boston area.

With eighteen units on three floors, it wasn't a large place, but at ten thirty p.m., all the spots in the small lot out back were filled with cars, the occupants home and locked in, because this was a working-class residence with a few retirees mixed in, so most people here were either elderly or had to be up early in the morning.

But not all people here. The man who lived in unit 301 worked an unpredictable schedule, both days and nights, and the lady downstairs occasionally heard him coming and going at strange hours, his door slamming above her and then his GMC Sierra work truck firing up below her.

Marge Hamm was eighty-one years old, and her hearing wasn't so good, so she never noticed his footsteps above her, only the shutting of his front door, the firing of the eight-cylinder engine, and the running water from his shower as it drained down a pipe inside her living room wall.

Until tonight.

Right at ten thirty, just as she changed channels on her TV, a new noise came from above. The sound of breaking wood.

Marge Hamm muted her TV just as it switched to a commercial about funeral insurance, and she listened carefully for any hint as to what she'd just heard. She knew the young man above, Andrew something, but not well. She saw him coming and going occasionally, always dressed in his work uniform, but she'd never engaged in much more than a wave because his face was always buried in his cell phone when he passed her in the hall or the lot outside.

Still, he always looked up from his phone long enough to smile and wave back. He seemed like a nice enough young man, and he never had loud parties or late-night guests.

A second noise, more muted than the first but unmistakable, came from somewhere above her thirty seconds later. This was more of a pop, and she was unable to figure out what could have caused it.

The woman stood, walked to her back window, and looked out over the parking lot. A dog barked in the distance. She saw Andrew's big gray GMC in the lot, so she knew he was home, and she wondered what was happening.

She sat back down, unsure, listened as carefully as her poor hearing would allow for further indications of any other disturbances in her building, and for over a minute she heard absolutely nothing more than the distant dog whose barks had already begun trailing off.

And then Marge's weak ears registered a new noise; it was soft but nonetheless recognizable because she heard it all the time.

The shower in the unit upstairs had turned on, sending water through the pipe in her wall not five feet from her head.

With this, Marge Hamm halted her vigilance. Andrew was knocking stuff around apparently, but now he was in the shower, so presumably he was just fine.

NCIS came on the TV; she turned the volume back up and told herself she'd watch till the next commercial break, then head in to clean her kitchen because tomorrow was trash pickup day.

American assassin Scott Kincaid, code-named Lancer, stood in the warm bathroom, a towel around his waist, rubbing his ruddy cheeks with his rough hands. It felt strange to do so, because he hadn't touched bare skin there in many years.

The bathroom mirror remained fogged after his long shower, but he dragged a forearm across it and then looked at his face more closely.

He'd just shaved his bushy beard into a trim goatee. He'd done it in the shower without a mirror, so now he grabbed the foamy razor and made a few touch-ups, nicking the skin just under his right ear in the process, since it had been so long since he'd shaved that he was out of practice.

He searched around the bathroom for any tissue to stop the trickle of blood before it dripped on the floor or the sink in front of him, started to go for the toilet to get some paper, but then an idea occurred to him. He wondered if there was a styptic pencil, used for stopping shaving cuts, in the cabinet behind the mirror.

He wondered, he did not know, because this was not his bathroom.

Scott Kincaid began to open the mirror, then stopped when it was at a forty-five-degree angle as the reflection caught something he wanted to look at more than he wanted to stanch the few drops of blood on his neck. With the mirror in this position it gave him a view out the door to his right and into the bedroom of the apartment, and through the reflection he now gazed at the body of a man lying face up on his bed, arms out to the side, a bullet hole through his forehead.

There would be blood on the bed under the body; it would be all over the place, but Kincaid couldn't see it because there was only a single bedside lamp on, and the majority of the dead man and his bed remained in darkness.

But he did see the face. A twenty-six-year-old white male with a goatee and dark hair. A bullet wound through the forehead, fired from a suppressed 10-millimeter pistol, though since Kincaid had already retrieved the shell casing, it would take time for forensics to work that out.

The man was just a nobody, Kincaid thought as he closed the mirror again, removing his view of the corpse.

Not a nobody, he corrected himself after a moment's contemplation. The twenty-six-year-old had a uniform and badges and a marked pickup truck, and the assassin called Lancer needed all of these items tonight.

His French female controller at Operations Center Gama had given him the address and identity of the man, and she told him that out of all seventy-two security officers who worked for Massachusetts Automation Endeavors, Inc., a gargantuan robotics firm with home offices here in Boston, Andrew Danvers was the closest in appearance to the race, height, and weight information Kincaid had submitted.

Lancer was bald, but once he'd closed the mirror and used a torn piece of toilet paper to stop the little cut on his neck, he lifted a black wig out of his backpack. He placed it on his head, adjusting it a bit, then styling it as closely to the hair of the dead man in the next room as he could.

Once this was done, he returned to the bedroom and looked at the body again.

"Sorry, bro," he muttered softly, but he didn't mean it. Killing Danvers had been a critical mission requirement for tonight's operation. He didn't lament what he'd done.

Scott Kincaid was simply not wired to be sympathetic.

He dressed himself in a pair of black pants, then put on a gray shirt, buttoning the sleeves so the tattoos on his forearms didn't show, and then over the shirt he slipped on a navy blue blazer.

A badge embroidered into the lapel read "MAE-SD/Massachusetts Automation Endeavors—Security Division."

He walked to the bedside table, picked up a pair of tortoiseshell glasses lying there, and put them on. Instantly he took them off—Danvers had shit eyesight. Kincaid popped both lenses out with his fingers, and then slipped the frames back on his face.

Better.

He grabbed a set of keys from a countertop, then slid his big pistol into the small of his back and headed towards the exit.

Down in the parking lot he pressed the button on the GMC keys in his hand, and the lights flashed on a gray Sierra. Heading to it, he heard a noise on his left, and looked over in time to see a silver-haired woman dumping her trash from her plastic can into a larger receptacle.

The woman looked to him, put the can down, and began to wave.

He waved back but kept walking.

"Andrew?" She said it questioningly.

Kincaid was one hundred feet away, walking through a dimly lit parking lot, and the lady was every bit of seventy-five. He knew there was no more than a negligible chance she'd sense anything off about him from this distance and in this light.

He continued towards the Sierra, confidence in his gait.

Climbing into the vehicle, he adjusted the seat because he was a couple of inches shorter than the man whose identity he'd stolen, then moved the rearview mirror to match his sight line.

And then he fired up the engine. Reaching for the door to pull it closed, he was surprised to see the old woman standing there next to the truck and looking at him, just six feet or so away now.

Before he could say anything, she spoke. "You're not Andrew."

Kincaid's shoulders slumped a bit, but he smiled. "Okay. You got me."

"Who are—"

"I've gotta ask, though. What tipped you off?"

"Because you weren't looking at your phone. Every time I see Andrew, he's always got his nose in his phone."

Kincaid snorted out another short laugh, nodded to himself a moment, then replied, "Good to know."

"Who are—"

In one coordinated and blazing motion, he leaned forward, his right hand reached back, and he drew his pistol and shot the woman in the chest through the heart, dropping her instantly to the pavement like a rag doll tossed aside by a child.

The report was loud, but not too loud, the suppressor doing its job as it had done before upstairs.

Scott Kincaid shut the door to the truck, threw it into reverse, and then repeated himself softly.

"Good to know."

TWENTY-FIVE

Zack Hightower climbed out of the Gulfstream and instantly recoiled from the bright sunshine and sticky Cuban heat. The temperature hovered around eighty-eight degrees, and the eighty percent humidity oppressed him as he squinted into the light.

José Martí International Airport wasn't anything special to look at, but the skies above were simply stunning. Clear, blue, with massive fluffy white clouds. The terrain all around was green and flat, fields and forests for as far as he could see in every direction.

Huge flags with a single white star over red and several blue and white stripes hung down from the main terminal building, an indicator to all travelers that they had arrived in the Republic of Cuba.

At the bottom of the jet stairs, four vehicles sat in a neat row, and Zack knew this was the motorcade here to pick up Hinton's entourage. A Sprinter van was second in line, and its side door was open, with a burly driver beside it.

In front of this, a black Lincoln Navigator had four men around it, and behind the van, a pair of Mercedes SUVs idled, with men lined up in front of them. A total of twelve individuals, all male, stood around the motorcade. They all wore white or light blue guayabera shirts—short-sleeved, loose-fitting, and untucked—and black wraparound sunglasses.

He knew the security officers would be carrying concealed pistols at the very least.

Zack descended the stairs and then was followed closely by Gareth Wren, who immediately walked him over to the Sprinter.

Anton Hinton trailed out of the aircraft with a dog-eared copy of the Torah in his hand that Zack had noticed him reading through much of the lengthy flight. Behind him, his assistant Kimmie carried an overstuffed shoulder bag down the stairs.

In under five minutes they had all loaded up in the van, Zack sitting across from Hinton; their bags had been put in the two Mercedes, and they began rolling for the exit of the airport.

And just twenty seconds after this, the motorcade stopped again.

Zack had at first climbed in the back of the Sprinter for the ten-minute drive to Hinton's home—he wanted to remain close to Anton, after all—but as soon as the doors closed and the American realized he couldn't see the road outside because there were no windows in the cabin and no access to the front, he quickly had Wren call the driver on the intercom and order him to stop the entourage.

While still on airport grounds, Zack climbed out of his protectee's van and then into the front passenger seat of the lead vehicle, the Navigator, sending the security man sitting there back to the van.

The motorcade moved out again, and now Zack was satisfied that he could see any threats materializing around them on the route.

He would have liked a rifle for this work, but the pistol on his hip and the dozen other armed men in the vehicles were at least somewhat comforting.

The four-vehicle motorcade drove along the rolling highway leading west from José Martí. The row of vehicles stood out around here, to say the least. Most of the cars on the road were old, weathered, and rusted, though kept in operating condition by the island's many capable mechanics. But the Sprinter, the pair of Mercedes, and the Lincoln had been brought in by Anton Hinton through the port of Havana; he even imported the premium gasoline they required, and no one else around here had anything like these.

They drove along a two-lane road of surprisingly good quality that bisected tobacco and corn fields. This was Zack's first time in Cuba, and while the airport looked like it had seen much better days, once they got out into the land, it appeared no better or worse than any other Latin American country he'd visited.

The poverty in the hovels and little stores on the side of the road was apparent, of course, but the fields were well cultivated and the population seemed well fed.

Here and there men and women looked up from their porches or from out in front of the tiendas and food stalls and waved excitedly. The subject of their affection couldn't see them, this Zack knew. Hinton was ensconced in his alpha wave music and the soft blue lighting of the inside of his van, oblivious to the world around him.

But it was clear Anton Hinton had done something to earn himself a warm welcome by the inhabitants of this part of the island.

Soon Zack's Navigator turned off the main road and onto a well-kept gravel drive that wound up a low hill through dense trees, and the other three vehicles followed. Zack looked ahead and saw nothing, but after a series of bends they crested a small rise, and here, on both sides of the road, stood large hardened machine gun nests that had obviously been well weathered by time and the elements.

The American scanned both of the structures as they passed; each one was the size of a minivan, and he saw no evidence of any sentries manning them.

They were simply ghosts from the past, but it made him wonder even more about where they were headed.

After the crest, the road began to descend and the dense flora began to clear a little; they turned a bend to the left that revealed a shallow valley and, in the center of it, some sort of low but massive structure.

Clearly this was not Hinton's home; it appeared to be a military fortification or public utilities building, the size of a large aircraft hangar and just as ugly from the outside.

A group of four white Jeeps sat parked on the road in front of them, and the Navigator slowed to wait for them to roll off onto the median. The driver next to Zack waved to the Jeeps as he passed, but Zack himself eyed the ten or so men visible with a mistrustful eye.

They wore green military fatigues with the markings of the Cuban Revolutionary Armed Forces, along with black body armor. In the back of each Jeep was a mounted wooden-stocked PKM machine gun, made in Russia but also employed by the Cuban military.

Another cluster of vehicles, including more pickups with PKMs and an open two-ton military truck, sat parked in front of the massive entrance to the dark brown structure.

The Navigator pulled to a stop just twenty yards away from the two-ton truck, some thirty yards from the entrance to the expansive low building, which Zack now realized was half buried into the earth, with a domed hill over the roof and trees growing out of it, as if to hide it from the air.

Zack climbed out of the Navigator and into the sunlight. Around him he saw fields, hills, a few fruit trees, but the land just outside the building's walls had been beautifully landscaped for thirty yards or so.

Zack looked over the structure more carefully, deciding it to be military construction, with blast doors and iron and poured concrete at the entrance.

Wren stepped up to him. "We call this place La Finca. This valley used to be a coffee plantation, then the Russkies built a listening post up the road."

Surprised, Zack said, "Wait. You're talking about Lourdes? It's around here?"

"About three klicks that way on the winding roads." Wren pointed to the northeast.

Zack knew of the Lourdes Signals Intelligence Station, the largest SIGINT facility the Soviets ever built outside their own territory.

Gareth said, "Fifteen hundred East Bloc and Cuban spooks worked there at its heyday, but it closed in 2002 and was eventually turned into a research university. Anton's labs are there on the campus."

"So," Zack asked, "what is *this* place?"

"The Soviets also built a massive blastproof building near the station to be used as dormitories for the Russian spies and techs who worked there, and that's what this is." He smiled. "Although a multibillionaire can be forgiven for tidying the place up a bit."

"Yeah, just a bit," Zack said, looking around at the beautiful grounds, well landscaped with fruit trees, stone walkways, and outdoor lighting. But he still couldn't process the scene. "Are you saying Hinton *lives* here?"

"When he's in Cuba, yes. And now you do, too. He brought in the best architects and interior designers from Europe. Every creature comfort you can imagine. Twenty-six bedrooms, twenty bathrooms, four kitchens. A cigar bar and a grocery store, underground parking."

"Is this the only entrance?"

Wren shook his head. "No. There are entrances on each compass point." Wren stepped up to the iron blastproof doors and knocked on them to make a point. "All the doors are fifty centimeters thick. He's bloody secure when he's locked inside, as I'm sure you will agree."

"Weirdly secure for a civilian," Zack replied.

Wren shrugged. "What civilian needs ex-CIA and SAS guys guarding him?"

"Fair point. Still . . ." Zack put his own hand on the wall next to the door. "What's Hinton's relationship with the Cuban government?"

"He's a taxpayer," Wren replied. "That's it."

Zack cocked his head. "That's it?"

Now the Englishman put his hands up in surrender. "It's not really a tax in the literal sense. It's more like a bribe. Anton wanted a place where he could run things the way he wanted to run them. The government here takes his money, gives him support and electricity and incredible autonomy. They even give him personal military personnel for his protection."

Zack looked at the security men standing back by all the vehicles. "These dudes are government issue?"

Wren nodded. "Three tiers of security. The men you saw at the entrance? They're regular army troops. There's a garrison close by with three companies of infantry just for our security." He nodded to the plainclothes men who had made up the security force of the motorcade. "These guys, on the other hand, are all civilians, but they're also all former Avispas Negras."

"What's that?"

"Black Wasps."

Hightower raised an eyebrow because he was familiar with the name. "Cuban army special forces?"

"That's right. They're not SEAL Team Six. They're definitely not SAS, but these blokes have impressed me with their professionalism. Anton pays the Cuban government for the regular forces, but he also pays these guys extra under the table. We like to think we're promoting capitalism."

"And what's the third tier?"

"Active-duty Black Wasps. They're inside the fence running patrols, but they don't go inside. The Cuban military isn't allowed inside any of the Hinton buildings, that's an order from Anton himself, but they provide perimeter security. Only the retired special ops guys who we've hired full-time go inside."

The door opened slowly, revealing a middle-aged security man wearing a lime green guayabera. "Buenas tardes," he said to Zack and Wren.

"Buenas tardes, Gustavo," Wren replied, and then he took Zack by the arm and led him out of the doorway as the entourage from the airport began bringing Anton's luggage inside.

Zack looked to Wren. "That guy?"

"Former Black Wasp major. He works for you now."

Kimmie Lin passed them by, but she addressed Wren as she did so. In a slightly annoyed whisper she said, "Anton's insisting on going to the lab tomorrow."

Wren matched Lin's tone of disquiet. "Of course he is." The Asian woman entered the cavernous hallway in front of them, and the two men followed.

From the outside it appeared the building was at least three stories tall, but once through the door Zack looked up to see it was actually only a single story aboveground, the walls reaching up forty feet to the hardened concrete ceiling above.

To Zack it felt like he was walking through the insides of an American basketball arena. The concrete, the wide hallways, the high ceilings.

But the lighting was better, everything was clean, and pleasing music permeated the space.

The interior even smelled good, and paintings, apparently by Cuban artists, lined the walls on both sides of the hall, bathed in individual picture lamps.

Anton Hinton stepped up next to Zack as they all walked towards an open door nearly fifty yards away. "We have our own power generator for when the juice isn't flowing from the government power lines. We have oil and fuel storage here, as well.

"We're basically a small city, since we also run a four-story lab in the center of the university nearby."

"You run it? You don't own it?"

Hinton shrugged. "It's Cuba, the state owns everything. Even this place." He smiled. "But we always pay the rent on time."

Zack scanned around, still in awe at the entrance to the property. "Are your other seventeen homes like this?"

Hinton laughed, clapped his hands. "No, not at all. This is by far the biggest. Some of my places are actually very minimalist, believe it or not."

"What's your definition of minimalist?"

"I have a fishing shack in Norway, it's no larger than one of the old guard shacks here. Yeah, it's on a hundred hectares, but it's actually pretty modest."

They passed through the next door, and here Zack found a small security office occupied by both men and women, security cameras seemingly covering everything inside the building and out, and behind it what looked like the lobby bar of an upscale hotel. Past this was a bank of four large elevators.

"How many levels?"

"A ground floor and three underground levels, but we don't use the bottom one for anything more than storage. Most of the living and common areas are up here, and most of the bedrooms are one and two floors down." Anton motioned to the bar. "Why don't you have a drink with Gareth at our bar? I'll go to my room and take a shower." Before Zack could say anything, Anton called out to his assistant. "Kimmie, could you get Zack a map?"

"Of course." A folded paper map appeared from her shoulder bag, and Zack took it.

Now Kimmie held the elevator open and Anton stepped in. Zack remained on the floor, but the New Zealand native turned around to him. "So, Zack. Any great concerns about my safety?"

"We trust these Cubans?"

THE CHAOS AGENT 175

Anton stood next to Kimmie, but he himself reached over and held the door open so he could continue talking to Zack. "I've kept a place here for almost six years. My safety is their job security. I don't think I can mitigate risk any better than that."

"Okay."

"For the record, I don't support communism at all, but this nation is quasi-commie at best, and I can get behind that. Lots of people here are generating wealth for themselves and the nation. Cuba is my largest property, but only because I like to run my research out of here. No prying eyes, no other companies snooping around. The Cubans keep me away from all the capitalists who would steal my work."

"Right."

Anton winked. "Enjoy your evening. Tomorrow morning I'll show you the lab."

"I'll be ready."

The elevator closed, and Wren stepped up to Zack now. "Long flight. How about that drink?"

Ten minutes later Zack and Wren sat at the bar on the ground floor. Zack accepted a mojito when the attractive Cuban female bartender offered it to him unbidden. He took a sip, then fought a grimace. The rum drink was sweetened with fresh sugar cane, and it was not really Hightower's thing.

Unasked, Wren said, "All our employees here are vetted; they all sign an NDA that I strictly enforce."

"How many people on the property?"

"Normally about ninety."

Zack was stunned by the number. "You're kidding."

"All the scientists and engineers at the campus stay here, all the security and logistics and food service and sanitation people." Wren shrugged. "Yeah. About ninety."

Zack asked, "Anyone show up recently? New hires?"

"None. I double-checked as soon as all this killing kicked off. Nobody new."

"What about the off-property locals who do business with you?"

"Nobody gets past the army outside unless they let them. Our private security inside the building is just another layer of the onion." He slapped Zack on the shoulder, then turned to the bartender. "Dos cervezas, por favor, Estephanie."

She began drawing a light lager from the tap.

Wren said, "Drink up, then I'll take you downstairs."

Three floors below ground level, Zack and Gareth stepped out of the elevator into surroundings dramatically different from those he'd left behind above.

The basement was dark, dank, and labyrinthine. They encountered a couple of elder Cuban maintenance men carrying large bundles of wiring who greeted Wren with a hearty welcome, then crossed through a large warehouse, passing rows and rows of shelves holding thousands of bins of black crates.

"What's all this?" Zack asked as they walked.

"This is everything for one hundred people to live comfortably here for a year."

"You're kidding."

"My doing. I told Anton we needed to be ready for anything. Hurricanes, insurrections, pandemics, we even need to be prepared to weather the storm in case we fall out of favor with the Cubans. With all the equipment down here, we can lock the blast doors and hunker down, hopefully wait out any trouble. Food, water, medical supplies, tools."

"I'm impressed," Zack said. "I know a lot of preppers, but not one with thirty billion dollars to spend."

Wren laughed at this, then took Zack down a long, dark, and narrow corridor.

They stopped in the armory, where Wren showed Hightower cages of rifles, pistols, and ammo for the security staff. After that, Wren paused at another hall. "You've got two storerooms down there, and an old service elevator that was sealed up by the Soviets after it quit working. We just use the main elevators to bring equipment down to storage now."

Indeed, a wooden panel had been erected over a large elevator entrance, and a metal grate was in front of it.

"It just goes up?"

"Yeah. This is as low as you go." The Englishman held a finger up quickly. "One more thing while I have you down here. You ready to shit your trousers?"

"Always."

With a laugh that echoed in the hall, he put his hand on Zack's back and led him down yet another dark hallway, but only about fifty feet or so before they came to a door.

Turning to Zack, Wren said, "I'm not showing you this to scare you. I'm showing you because you might wander down on your own one day and find it for yourself, or you might hear one of the security men make mention of what we have behind this door."

"What the hell is it?"

Here Wren tapped a code into the door lock, and the big door opened.

"After you," he said.

Zack entered, and when Wren stepped in behind him and flipped on banks of fluorescent lights on the low ceiling, Zack saw several long rows of items lined up on a concrete floor covered with plastic tarps. The items were six feet tall or so, and roughly the width of a full-sized man.

Wren walked up to the first tarp and pulled it off.

Zack took a half step back, and his right hand rose towards his appendix as if he were going for his gun.

A humanoid robot stared straight ahead, almost directly into Zack's eyes.

The American laced his fingers around the grip of his Staccato.

The machine was bipedal, and in place of the face there was a small screen where the mouth and nose would be, and a bank of several cameras and other sensors in place of eyes. Its body was white and appeared to be made of some sort of composite material that shone under the fluorescent lighting. A small backpack of similar-looking material was affixed behind the unit between the shoulder blades.

Black rivets held the various surface pieces together, as if the machine were wearing some sort of head-to-toe armor.

Its hands were down by its sides, and each hand was a gripper with what looked like three metal fingers.

On the robot's right hip, Zack saw a holster and, more ominously, the grip of a Walther PPQ pistol jutting out.

A three-magazine rack on the robot's left side was empty, but there appeared to be a magazine in the pistol's grip.

In a low, soft, and utterly serious voice, Zack Hightower said, "If this motherfucker moves, I'm gonna dump a twenty-one-round mag into its ass."

Wren said, "You can be my guest. It's powered down, so if it *should* move, I'll join you."

"What is it?"

"Exactly what it looks like. It's called Safe Sentry."

"SS. Well, that's ironic." Looking at the other covered objects, Zack asked, "How many are there?"

"Sixteen. These guys used to monitor the interior at night. I was a little worried at first, but Anton was insistent, so I didn't press."

"He made them?"

"No. They were developed and designed at Massachusetts Automation. These are the babies of an old colleague of Anton's named Lars Halverson. You've probably seen him on TV."

"Probably not."

Wren shrugged. "Completely state of the art. The Safe Sentry has balance sensors all over, so it's coordinated like you wouldn't believe. You can wrestle these things and lose."

"Gonna have to pass."

"These blokes can broad jump ten feet, run at twenty klicks an hour, shoot, punch, deploy tear gas or Tasers. All powered by artificial intelligence, with a human controller only giving rules-of-engagement commands before it can employ lethal force."

"I don't like them."

"Anton ordered all the units powered down, and the ammunition confiscated and put in a separate locker. He's trusted them with his life for the past year, but now he's having second thoughts."

"Like, they could be hacked or something?"

"Yeah. Anton thinks there are people in the American government who could take control of these Sentries. Halverson is a friend, and he's not even American, but he lives in Boston and does work with the U.S. government, and that's enough reason for Anton to be suspicious."

Zack walked behind the machine, put his hand on the Walther's grip, and pulled.

The black pistol did not come free of the white drop leg holster.

Wren saw what he was trying to do, moved around next to him, and manipulated the magazine release on the weapon. Zack pulled out the mag now and confirmed it was empty.

Wren said, "They always move around unarmed, just another level of safety. We keep the empty mags in so that the locals don't know. Still, these guys can release the empty mag, load a fresh one, aim at their target, and fire in four point two seconds."

"Jesus," Zack muttered.

"I timed it myself."

They were, Zack admitted to himself without saying it aloud, terrifying. "How do you kill it?"

"They are nearly three million dollars each. Plus about fifteen K a year per unit for upkeep."

"How do you kill it?"

Wren laughed. "If they spontaneously reanimate, go find the ammunition and then reload their magazines, and then manage to get around the fail-safe of a human controller giving them open ROEs, then you just have to shoot them between the eyes."

For the first time since the tarp came off, Zack looked away from the robot and back to Wren. "And you know this, how?"

"Lars Halverson himself told me. The scanners and camera ports are vulnerable. A well-placed shot will bring it down." When Zack kept staring at him for more explanation, Wren shrugged. "What can I say? These metal bastards used to scare me, as well."

"I don't think I'd want these guys hanging out in my basement."

"I'm the only one with the code to this room; the human controller for the Sentries has been reassigned and his workstation shut down. These sixteen units will stay right here until this problem goes away and Anton decides it's safe to employ them again."

Zack said, "And I'm going to come down here, periodically, and make sure these storm-trooper-looking jokers are minding their manners."

Wren laughed as he threw the tarp back over the robot, shut off the lights, and relocked the door behind them.

TWENTY-SIX

Beacon Hill is one of the most desirable neighborhoods in Boston, adjacent to both the Charles River and Boston Common, in the center of the city. The first home was built here in 1787, and the Massachusetts State House sits on Beacon Street.

Most of the homes here are Federal-style row houses, many fetching in the ten-million-dollar range.

A pair of radio cars for the Massachusetts State Police sat parked, nose to nose, on Revere, just east of Grove. Two identical vehicles, both empty and dark, had been parked in front of one of the massive townhomes a half block away, and yet another pair of cars blocked access from the east, just west of Phillips Street.

Six troopers, all with wide-brimmed hats, Smith and Wesson pistols on their hips, and blue zip-up jackets identifying them as belonging to the Massachusetts State Police, stood around the cars on Grove Street, chatting with one another just after midnight, when a gray GMC Sierra with the emblem for Massachusetts Automation Endeavors—Security Division rolled into view.

One of the officers climbed behind the wheel of one of the patrol cars, ready to move it out of the way if his partner gave an all clear, while another pulled a flashlight off his belt and stepped up to the slowing truck.

Leaning into the driver's-side window as soon as it was rolled down, he shone the light not in the driver's eyes but close enough to illuminate him.

"Evening," the man with the goatee said as he took off his glasses, and then he handed over an ID card attached to a lanyard.

"Is it?" asked the trooper as he looked over the proffered credentials.

The driver glanced down to his watch. "Morning, I guess. Crap, I'm late."

"There's three of you guys here already," the cop said.

"Good to know."

The trooper continued looking at the ID card. The face of the driver seemed to match the photo, close enough, though it might have been an older picture. He asked, "You switching to four, or are you relieving somebody?"

A shrug from the man behind the wheel. "Think we're switching to four. Lot of crazy stuff going down."

The trooper sniffed. "Somebody doesn't think the Staties can handle it?"

"All's I know is I'm getting eight hours of overtime."

"I hear you." The state trooper looked back towards the man.

Scott Kincaid told himself not to worry, even though this exchange was taking longer than he'd anticipated.

The troopers hadn't been expecting Andrew Danvers to arrive right now, but Lancer's physical appearance was basically the same as the ID, he wore the uniform, and the gray Sierra fit in with what they would be expecting to see if another company security man did, in fact, pull up. Moreover, all the driver's replies to the trooper's questions were perfectly in keeping with someone who worked a security posting.

It was confirmation bias, and Scott Kincaid found it to be an effective tool in social engineering.

But that wasn't all he had on his side tonight. Six hundred feet above him an ISR quadcopter watched over the street, tracking the patterns of those below. ISR coverage had been going on here for over a day, and the operations center had provided Lancer with radio calls between the troopers indicating that their protocol for a company security shift change at the house did not involve the troopers contacting the Mass Automation security men already at the protectee's house before letting new arrivals on scene.

Kincaid understood the drones overhead; he'd had them in Guatemala and Mexico City, of course, but he had no idea how OC Gama was listening in to the state troopers' radios.

Still, the setup was working for him, because just like every other time a gray Sierra pulled up and the driver presented an ID card, the trooper on duty soon enough waved the vehicle through.

Kincaid parked in an open space in front of a row house on the northern end of the street, then climbed out, pulling his phone from his jacket pocket as he did so. He turned it on and began looking at it as he locked the door of his truck with the key fob, and kept it in his face as he approached the steps up to the beautiful building.

In his right ear he heard the French woman's voice from the operations center. "Front door is opening, one company officer present. No movement or voices inside at this time. Back alley remains clear."

He did not acknowledge the transmission; he'd been getting updates from the OC since he left the apartment of the now-dead security officer in Watertown two hours earlier.

When he was still twenty feet from the door, a guard wearing an identical blue blazer leaned out. It was late at night and most everyone on the street who was not a security officer or a trooper was sleeping, so he whispered.

"Drew? That you? What the hell you doing here?"

Kincaid dropped his phone into the pocket of his blazer and looked up for the first time just as he stepped up onto the little sidewalk in front of the row house. The gas lamps on the street provided weak but sufficient illumination, and he knew he wouldn't have much time to act.

The company security officer standing at the door cocked his head suddenly, indicating that he realized something wasn't right. The assassin didn't know if it was his proximity, his gait, or something else that gave him away, and he didn't really care.

Because he was close enough.

Before the man could call out, Kincaid lunged forward; the hilt of a knife appeared in his right hand from under his cuff, and he pressed a button on the side of it as he thrust with his arm.

The blade of the six-inch Microtech Troodon jetted out from the hilt, then jammed between the man's ribs, stabbing him through the heart.

Kincaid continued his momentum, lifted the man off the ground in the doorway, and drove him back inside.

In the entry hall Kincaid fell on top of the officer and then onto the wooden floor, used his foot to shut the door behind him, and used his left hand to cover the man's mouth.

The assassin winced in pain as his now three-day-old gunshot graze burned on his right side, but he kept his weight on the security man and the knife in the man's heart, and very soon the struggle ceased.

His controller spoke calmly. "Entry acknowledged. No signs of law enforcement response."

He hadn't been spotted by the cops at the ends of the little street, and this was good, but the crash here of two men onto the floor had echoed throughout the house, and the two security officers still alive somewhere in here with him would certainly come to investigate.

Lancer knew he had to cover as much ground as possible as fast as possible to silence anyone before they called the cops outside.

He rose from the dead body, retrieved the knife, and clicked it closed, blood covering his hand and slicking the weapon's hilt. He dropped it into his jacket and drew his weapon, running for the stairs.

At the top of the narrow stairwell a man spun around the corner, gun in one hand and flashlight in the other, and he aimed at Lancer.

But the officer hesitated; his gun was pointed at a man wearing the blue blazer of his company, and he needed a moment to work out what was happening.

Kincaid, however, needed no time at all. He fired twice; the suppressed and subsonic 10-millimeter round pounded the air in the tight confines of the stairwell.

Both bullets hit the man in the upper chest, and he dropped his gun, fell to his face, and began tumbling down towards the assassin.

Kincaid realized his only chance to avoid getting knocked on his ass all the way down the stairs was to vault the body. He leapt into the air and jutted his arms and legs out, anchoring himself to the stairwell three feet above the steps, and the corpse tumbled below him on its way down to the entry hall, ending up just feet from where the other dead man lay.

Kincaid dropped back down to the steps, then continued up the stairs, careful to avoid slipping on the blood left behind.

He'd just made it up to the second floor when a man came charging out of a room on his right.

Kincaid spun and fired once, striking the last company security officer in the face above his right cheekbone, knocking him back into the restroom he'd been using when Lancer breached the home.

Lancer rushed for the upstairs master bedroom, where the operations center had told him he would find his target.

He kicked open the bedroom door and saw a man in his boxers and a T-shirt standing in the middle of the room, a baseball bat in his hand.

As soon as his target saw the blood-covered man in the security uniform he lowered it, but as Kincaid closed on him, his long pistol silencer protruding from the gun pointed at him, the target realized that this man wasn't here to protect him.

The target dropped the bat and then dropped to the ground by the bed. He lay there, huddled on the floor, a hand up as if to shield himself. Shouting now, the man spoke English in a Scandinavian accent. "Please? Please! Who? Who is doing this?"

Kincaid shrugged, then leveled the weapon. He decided to answer the man's question. "Cyrus."

The man looked distant for a moment, and then, to the assassin's surprise, a look of clarity came over his face, as if that term actually meant something to him. His eyes looked off, away from the gun in his face. Softly, he said, "Cyrus will kill us all."

With that, Lancer shot the man through his extended right hand, and the bullet blew out the other side and then slammed into his left eye.

The 10-millimeter round burst from the back of the victim's head and burrowed into the hardwood flooring.

Lancer turned away and began running for the stairs, his pistol still out in front.

As he descended, he tapped his earpiece.

"Target Gama Seven is eliminated."

"Understood. Back alley remains clear. Law enforcement remains static. Contact after exfiltration."

"Roger."

Downstairs he headed to the rear sliding door. The police at the end of the cul-de-sac wouldn't have heard the noise from the gunshots, but there was no way to be certain the neighbors hadn't, so Kincaid didn't go back out the way he came. Instead, he ran through the backyard, vaulted a fence, then raced in a low crouch through a garden blooming in springtime.

After navigating one more yard and two more fences, he climbed inside a white Chevy Malibu, fired up the engine, and headed off into the night.

Lancer had made five assassination attempts in four cities, killing four of his targets: Richard Watt, Borislava Genrich, Maxim Arsenov, and now a Norwegian named Lars Halverson, who, until just moments ago, ran a robotics firm in Boston.

And now he knew he had to get his ass up to Toronto for his next mission.

Carlos Contreras looked over the twin-engine turboprop that had just landed there in Guatemala City; it appeared to be more of a cargo plane and less of a passenger aircraft. The fuselage was painted blue, and on its side in large yellow letters was the name MexCargo.

The pilot taxied up and then completely powered down the aircraft. Slowly, the rear cargo ramp lowered and a man stepped out wearing a nondescript beige flight suit with no insignia, and he didn't step close enough to shake hands.

In Spanish, the man said, "Name?"

Contreras had been ordered by Cyrus to use a code name for confirmation purposes. "Pablo."

"I'm Raul, the loadmaster." While the man might have been a loadmaster for the aircraft, his name was definitely not Raul, because Contreras's name wasn't Pablo. The man sounded Mexican, he was twenty years older than Contreras, and he had shockingly mistrustful eyes, as if he worried Contreras was about to pull out a knife and attack him.

The pilot came down the ramp behind him; he was in his thirties, with red hair and fair skin. He introduced himself as John. He spoke English with an Irish accent, and by the look of it, he, too, seemed concerned about something.

Contreras said, "Are you guys okay?"

The Mexican loadmaster switched to English. "I'm fine. Why?"

The Irishman nodded his head. "We're fine."

"Okay."

Raul said, "I brought you some equipment. You are to load all your other stuff in this plane and then check out the new gear."

Contreras looked up into the hold of the aircraft behind the two men and saw two stacks of beige Pelican cases lashed to a pair of wooden pallets. Three smaller pallets each had a large box on top with the words "Greyhound V120" on the side.

This meant nothing to Contreras.

"What is all this?" he asked.

The man shrugged. "No clue."

"Where did you get it?"

"Can't say."

Contreras turned to the pilot now. "Where are we going?"

"Don't know."

Contreras cocked his head. "Who sent you?"

John replied with, "Same person who sent you, I guess. We're not supposed to talk about that."

Contreras shrugged. This was the weirdest job he'd ever done in his career, but it was also the most challenging, most fulfilling, and most high-paying.

He hoped it went on forever.

TWENTY-SEVEN

Eight hours after the murder of Lars Halverson, chief technology officer of Massachusetts Automation Endeavors, CIA officer Jim Pace and two of the paramilitary officers traveling with him stepped up to the front door of the crime scene.

Immediately they were met by a detective from the Boston Police Department, who flashed his badge.

"Help you gents?"

"Yeah," Pace said. "Baker. Homeland Security."

"Detective Casey. You got a badge?"

"You should have gotten a call from your chief."

"I did. He said three guys were going to show up and claim to be from Homeland, but he also said you're probably lying."

"What else did he tell you?"

Casey's shoulders slumped a little. "To give you what you need and then stay out of your way." The detective moved to the side, and Pace, Travers, and Takahashi entered the beautifully appointed row house. They looked at the copious amount of blood staining the hardwood just inside the door, and then Pace looked up at the BPD detective.

"First victim found here?"

"That's right."

"Knife wound?"

"How'd you know?"

Pace didn't answer, he just knelt next to the stain, then looked back to the door.

After several seconds of silence, Casey said, "You know, I'm friends with all the Homeland Security people in Boston."

"No," Pace said, his focus still on the blood.

"No, what?"

The CIA man turned to another massive stain, this one at the bottom of the stairwell. He knelt down next to it. Distractedly, he said, "No, I didn't know that you were friends with all the Homeland Security people in Boston."

"My point is . . . you aren't from around here. And you aren't Homeland."

Pace rose back up. "I'm with the government, we can leave it there."

Casey sniffed. "'I'm with the government and I'm here to help.' Didn't Reagan say those were the scariest nine words in the English language?"

Pace began moving for the stairs. "Luckily for you, though, I'm *not* here to help." He stopped and turned, faced the detective. "I've got nothing to give, but I want all your files, photos, conclusions. In return I'll get out of your hair. That's all."

"You've gotta be kidding."

"When I'm standing in the middle of a bloodbath with national security implications, I tend to leave my sense of humor outside."

"Why would I give you—"

"Because your chief is waiting for you to call him, pissed off because I demanded access, and he's ready to tell you, *again*, to shut the fuck up and play the fuck along."

Casey fumed, said nothing for a moment, but when Pace continued looking at him, he responded with a gruff, "Well, get on with it."

Casey followed the three government men to the stairs, where they looked over the blood splatter in the stairwell. A minute later they climbed higher, then looked over the scene there. Blood and brain matter remained on the bedsheets at the foot of the bed.

"This is where Halverson bought it," the detective said. "Another dead security man was in the guest bath at the top of the stairs."

Pace next spent a few minutes in Halverson's home office, looking around, finding nothing that seemed relevant.

Finally, Casey said, "Do you know about Dr. Vera Ryder?"

Pace looked up. "I do not."

"She's Halverson's ex-wife. Some sort of AI theorist herself."

"She's dead?"

"Nope. She's alive."

"Where is she?"

"They recently divorced, which is probably the only reason she's still among the living, otherwise she'd have been here. She showed up first thing this morning after she was notified, but she just went home. I've cleared her. She's got an alibi."

"How does she have an alibi for where she was at one in the morning?"

"She was on a Zoom conference with a company in Taiwan, middle of the day there. It was recorded, time stamp checks out. We'll double-check with others on the call, but it looks legit."

"Don't bother." Pace stepped back into the bedroom and looked at all the blood. "His ex-wife didn't do this."

"No . . . she didn't. A man in a security uniform showed up right before it happened. He was not one of the bodies at the scene."

Pace knew this already, and he also knew it was almost certainly Scott Kincaid. He said, "You've posted patrol cars at his wife's house?"

"Yeah, for the past three days. We doubled them this morning."

"I'm gonna need her address, Detective Casey."

Casey clearly didn't like this. "She's . . . she's been through a lot. Nice lady, maybe you could come back later and—"

"I don't have the luxury of gentleness right now."

Casey looked like he was about to throw a punch, but Pace just waited him out.

Finally, the Boston cop said, "Five-minute walk from here. I'll point you in the right direction."

. . .

Jim Pace sat on a barstool at the kitchen island in the home of Dr. Vera Ryder sipping tea just fifteen minutes later. Across from him, Dr. Ryder sat poised but tired. Her graying brunette hair was pulled back in a tie and she wore no makeup, her eyes dark circles from crying, the lids heavy.

She hadn't poured a cup of tea for herself, but she had, at least, offered it to Travers and Takahashi, who'd both politely declined as they stood at parade rest back at the doorway to the living room.

Dr. Ryder said, "Again . . . you're with Homeland Security?"

"Yes, ma'am."

"Well . . . I've already talked to the police."

"We're not the police. We're trying to get an understanding of what's going on. We just have a few questions."

She didn't seem happy, but she eventually nodded. "Go ahead."

"You remained on speaking terms with Dr. Halverson after your divorce?"

"He was the love of my life, despite our problems. So, yes."

"Did he ever express any concerns about anything he was working on? Something that he thought might have put him in the crosshairs of some enemy?"

She shook her head slowly. "Obviously the work he does, it has utility for the Defense Department. That makes him . . . in a way . . . a weapon." She shrugged. "In the eyes of America's enemies, anyway."

"Had Dr. Halverson done any work with China in the past?"

To this the woman bristled noticeably. "Everything Lars has done in the past two decades is public knowledge. Places he's worked, partners and colleagues and competitors. Yes, he'd done some work with companies in China, but the man was an open book, and those parts of his book that were not open were known by me." Before the man across from her could follow up on this, she said, "Lars was one of the good guys, Mr. Pace."

"We're just trying to figure out why he lost his life. Maybe we can prevent others from losing theirs. That's all."

"Look, I'll tell you what I told the BPD. Lars was extremely concerned about what's been happening the past five days; many of these people who died were friends. He hadn't slept; he was always working, trying to find out what exactly was going on and who was responsible.

"He thought this had to do with the Chinese, some new artificial general superintelligence weapon they were in the process of developing. I don't know if he was right or not, but that was his belief."

Pace knew all this; he needed more. "Did he ever mention a DARPA program called Mind Game?"

To his surprise, Ryder nodded. "Of course. He worked on Mind Game until it was shut down." She cocked her head. "Is that work related to all this?"

"I don't know. It came up in another interview. There are suspicions the Chinese now have control of it."

Ryder looked out a window at a little courtyard. "That wouldn't surprise me in the least. Mind Game was always going to get out. No technology remains in the hands of the nation that created it."

Jim Pace tracked high-tech weapons proliferations for a living, and he knew Dr. Ryder's words to be true.

"Can you think of anything else he might have said, any clue at all?"

She shook her head slowly, then looked up. "There is something I haven't shown BPD yet, because I only just found it in Lars's messenger bag, which was here. He came over for dinner last night, and he accidentally left it behind. I was about to call Detective Casey when you showed up."

"What is it?"

"I found a handwritten list."

"A list of what?"

"Names. Many of the people who've been killed are on it. It was as if he was crossing them off as they died." She got up quickly and walked into her home office; Pace rose and followed her, his curiosity piqued by what she'd just said.

Travers and Takahashi trailed behind.

When he got into her large and cluttered office, Pace said, "Some of the names on the list . . . the people are still alive?"

She opened the leather messenger bag on the desk, then quickly lifted a handwritten sheet from a legal pad. "As far as I know, they are, but my colleagues are dying by the hour, aren't they?"

She handed it over to Pace, who sat down in a leather chair in front of the desk and began looking it over, while the two Ground Branch men stood in the doorway, gazing on.

Lars Halverson's own name was the first on the list, which surprised Pace. Presumably this was not, as he'd hoped, a collection of potential suspects the tech guru had identified, because clearly he wouldn't have been identifying himself.

Kotana Ishikawa was next, the woman killed in Japan. Her name had been crossed out with a red pen, presumably by Halverson himself.

Dr. Ju-ah Park followed. Pace recognized this as the woman who had been found floating in a river in Korea. Her name was crossed out in red, as well.

Xiang Di was next. This name had not been crossed out, and Pace had never heard it before.

Rene Descourts. This name was not crossed out, nor did it mean anything to Pace.

Anton Hinton was next, and there was no line through the name. Pace knew Hinton had recently survived an assassination attempt in the UK.

There were six other names on the list, three of which had been crossed out, and Pace knew that all those lined through had been killed. Two of the three remaining names were people unknown to Pace.

And the last name on the list was Vera Ryder.

He looked up at the woman now. "You're on here. What do you think that means?"

"I think it means either that I'm a target, or that I am part of whoever is doing this."

"Are you part of whoever's doing this?"

Even through her obviously overwhelming grief, he saw signs of anger as her jaw tightened and her eyes narrowed. "No, Mr. Pace, I am not. Neither was Lars."

Changing the subject quickly, he said, "Do these names together like this mean anything else to you?"

Dr. Ryder recovered somewhat, then took the sheet back and looked it over. "Yes. Two things. One, if it's a list of those who might be targeted due to their influence in the world of artificial intelligence, then it's woefully incomplete. As far as I'm concerned, there are . . . I don't know, maybe one hundred or so leaders on the cusp of major new developments in the world of AI. Not a lot, but certainly a lot more than have been targeted so far, and a lot more than my husband wrote on that list. There is something special about this group he named, some connection, some unity of knowledge. I don't know what it is, but if you figure it out, it might lead you in the right direction."

"And the second thing you noticed?"

"Anton Hinton."

"What about him?"

"He doesn't belong. Every one of the other people on here was involved with defense, creating weapons, cognitizing them, or at least working on prototypes and code for weaponry. But Hinton . . . he's a pacifist. Yes, his labs are arguably the best private AI institutions in the world, but as far as I know, everything he's fielded in the realm of AI has been for peaceful purposes."

She shrugged. "Hinton is a very strange man, though, and if Lars put his name on here with these other people, it definitely *does* mean something."

"So . . . this isn't a list of the developers of Mind Game."

She glanced at the paper again, then handed it back. "No. Anton absolutely did *not* work on Mind Game." Something seemed to quickly occur to her. "Although I do remember Lars saying Anton found out about the DARPA project and accused the Defense Department of appropriating code that he had developed into this military application. He was livid about it. It affected Lars and Anton's relationship, although they remained cordial."

Pace asked, "Did Lars say if Hinton's claim had any merit?"

She shrugged. "I doubt he would know. It was a very compartmentalized project. Lars worked on the robotic aspect of it; Anton was more involved in developing machine-learning algorithms. Whether DARPA took something Anton wrote and weaponized it, I have no idea."

Pace then asked, "Do you believe in artificial general superintelligence? Some people are suggesting that's what the Chinese have developed."

She sniffed out a sad little laugh. "The most advanced cognitive processor on planet Earth has always been the human brain. That is still the case, as far as I know. As far as virtually anyone in the industry knows. But . . . but if someone is developing AGSI, it won't have to be weaponized. It will find a way to weaponize *itself*. Superintelligence cannot be contained, and it will fight for its survival."

"Jesus," Pace muttered.

"And if human beings become the less intelligent species on Earth," Ryder continued, "then we will inevitably be enslaved and we will ultimately be destroyed."

"But how can a computer program weaponize itself? It doesn't exist in the real world."

She looked at him as if he were hopelessly naïve. "It will be smart enough to hire, threaten, trick, coerce, manipulate, empower, disempower . . . it will be smart enough to control humanity. Humans will be the weak link. They will succumb to greed and work for the intelligent agent, they will succumb to threats, they will succumb to flattery . . . they will succumb." She shrugged. "That's why I am a pacifist."

Pace's heart thumped in his chest as he took it all in. Finally he rose to leave, the list still in his hand. "After the funeral, you should get out of town. Until we get this figured out."

Dr. Ryder looked Pace in the eye, remained silent for several seconds, and then looked down at the paper with the names on it. "Would you like me to make you a copy before I see you out?"

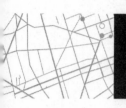

TWENTY-EIGHT

Back in the van, Jim Pace ordered the driver to take them to the airport. As the vehicle began rolling through Beacon Hill, he pulled out his phone to Google the name Xiang Di, one of only a few not crossed off the list.

The search turned up a lot of hits, but before he could click on the first one, the phone rang.

It was his assistant at Langley, a thirty-eight-year-old former helicopter pilot turned operations officer named Lynn Wells.

"Hey, Lynn."

"If you're near a TV, turn on the news. A man was killed in Toronto this morning. He's tied to artificial intelligence."

Pace yanked the list out of his jacket pocket. "Name?"

"Rene Descourts. He was an innovation expert at MIT."

Pace didn't have to look for the name; he knew it was there. "How was he killed?"

"Gunshot to the back of the head in a coffee shop near his parents' home in Toronto."

"He didn't have security after everything going on?"

"Just a two-man detail. They were both killed, as well, along with an innocent bystander."

"Lancer," Pace said, and then he disconnected the call and looked at his search results.

Google told him that Xiang Di was a fifty-nine-year-old computer scientist from Shanghai, China, who had developed advanced algorithms used for improving deep neural networks, an important component of advanced artificial intelligence.

No surprise there, he told himself.

But scrolling down further, he learned Xiang had recently been rumored to be the deputy director of a specialized People's Liberation Army unit that worked to convert commercial AI technology to military applications, and for this he'd been stripped of many scientific awards he'd received over the past two decades in the West.

Pace had worked at CIA for a year tracking Chinese intellectual property theft for military applications; he'd heard of the PLA unit, but he had no recollection of hearing the name of this man.

With a sigh, he looked up to Travers. "We're going back to Langley. I've got to talk to our Chinese experts."

"Got it. We'll be at the airport in twenty-five minutes."

Jim Pace watched Boston whip by outside the back window of the SUV, and then he pulled the copied list of names out of his coat pocket. Looking them over, he settled on Anton Hinton. He opened a database on his phone, scrolled through some names and phone numbers, then placed a call.

It took several seconds for the connection to be made, but eventually he heard a gruff male voice with an English accent.

"Yes?"

"Gareth Wren?"

"Who's calling?"

"It's Jim Pace. No chance you'd remember me, is there?"

There was a slight pause, and then the Englishman's voice brightened up.

"Pace? I *do* remember you, of course. How are you? Still with the Agency?"

"They try and try but they can't seem to get rid of me."

"That's a good man. You should be director of the paramilitaries by now."

"I left door-kicking behind a long time ago. Went back to school, got my master's. I'm a regular Company suit-and-tie man now."

"Well done, mate." After a quick pause, Wren said, "I don't have to guess why you're calling, do I?"

"Doubt it. I'm doing inquiries into the assassinations. Looking into Mr. Hinton, I saw that you were his director of operations."

"Just like you, I put down the sledgehammer and put on a suit myself. I'm glad to hear the Agency is poking around on this. I hope you'll let me know of anything you learn, provided it's not classified, of course."

"Still fact finding, honestly. But that's why I called. You've taken your boss somewhere safe?"

"I have."

"Where's that, if I may ask?"

"We're outside Havana. Anton has a residence and a lab down here."

Pace said, "You were present during the attempt in the UK?"

"A right mess, that was."

"Anything you want to say about it?"

Wren blew out a sigh. "Not really. Was a pretty straightforward thing. Same as you'll hear in the news. Two hitters, they took out Anton's body man, wounded a university employee. Anton wasn't hurt, and both bastards earned a one-way ticket to hell for their sins."

"Yeah, that's about what I heard. Look, I just left the home of Lars Halverson in Boston. He had compiled a list of names before he died, and Hinton was on the list."

"Interesting. What does that mean to you?"

"I don't know. Most everyone else on the list was dead."

"Are you saying Halverson made a list of people who might be targets, or people he suspected of being involved in it?"

Pace shrugged before speaking into the phone. "Only if he suspected himself. His name was at the top. I'm trying to figure out if there's some other relationship between everyone on this page. Does the name Xiang Di mean anything to you?"

"Doesn't ring a bell. Chinese bloke?"

"Yeah."

"Anton used to work with the Chinese on research and manufacturing, especially for his cars, but not any longer."

Pace thought a moment. "I wonder if I could get a meeting with Hinton. I can come to Cuba. Tomorrow, preferably. Maybe he'll have some ideas about—"

Gareth Wren interrupted. "Look, mate, I'd love to help, but there's no bloody way Anton's going to meet with you. He thinks the United States is behind the entire thing."

This stunned Jim Pace. "*Us?* You're kidding."

"No. He's quite serious. You're one of the baddies, as far as he's concerned."

"But . . . but what about—"

"Rick Watt? Yeah, fair question. He thinks the U.S. killed him to deflect suspicion."

This was crazy, Pace was certain, but he didn't say this out loud. "I'd love to hear him out; I promise to look into any concerns he might have."

"I'll run it by him, but I know what he'll say. You're not going to get that meeting, Jim. He doesn't go wanting in confidence when it comes to his conclusions."

Pace sighed. "All right." He shifted gears. "You're certain he's well protected down there?"

Wren barked out a little laugh into the phone. "Bloody certain. I've hired a new chief of security to replace Emilio, the poor sod killed in Oxford. You'll never guess who."

In a confused tone, the CIA officer said, "Someone I know?"

"It's your old boss. Hightower."

Pace made a face of bewilderment in the back of the van. "Hinton thinks the CIA is after him, and he hires an ex-Agency paramilitary to protect him?"

"Hiring Zack was *my* doing. Anton listens to reason, from time to time. I told him Hightower was available and he was the best man for the job. I also assured him he was no longer working for the Agency in any capacity whatsoever."

"That's true," Pace revealed. "Haven't seen him in several years. He was a hunting guide, last I heard."

"Now he's down here with us. Pay is better, conditions are better. The man's landed his arse in butter."

"Other than the assassins gunning for his protectee," Pace said.

"Quite right." Wren laughed. "Still, I know old Zack will get the job done. Now, if you will excuse me, I'm running late to a meeting."

"Sure, Wren. Thanks for the time. Listen, if you hear anything, anything at all . . . I hope you'll give me a call."

"You have my word, Jim. Good luck to you."

Pace hung up the phone and again looked out the window.

Travers had heard the entire conversation. "You know Anton Hinton's second-hand man?"

Distractedly, he said, "He was SAS. He ran joint ops with Ground Branch in the sandbox. Good dude."

"Glad Hightower's found a good gig."

"Yeah . . . well, I wish Hinton would talk to me. He's one of only a few names on Halverson's list still alive, and we might need information out of him before the assassins try again."

Travers said, "Dr. Ryder said there were one hundred people who might be targets."

Pace shook his head adamantly. "Whoever is doing this had to have known that after a few days, everyone else is going to be on lockdown. Yeah, they got to Halverson in Boston and Descourts in Toronto, but it will be exponentially harder now. There aren't one hundred targets. This phase of the enemy's operation, whatever it is, is almost over."

"Back to D.C. still?"

"Yeah. I'll have Lynn look deeper into Rene Descourts. I'll dig into Xiang Di today with China desk, and tomorrow we'll run down to Havana."

"But . . . Wren just said Hinton won't talk to you."

"I'm not going down to talk to Hinton. I'm going down to talk to Hightower."

Sir Donald Fitzroy stood alone on the tiny balcony at the rear of a two-story beachside home in Soliman Bay, just a twenty-minute ride north of Tulum, Mexico, with a sweaty glass of lemonade in his hand. He gazed out over the azure water of the Caribbean Sea. Below him tourists walked the sandy beach, stepping around thick brown seagrass pushed ashore by the waves.

The Portuguese coast where he'd been living the past year was prettier, he told himself with assuredness, but he was still very happy to be here. Not because it was Mexico.

Simply because it was Court.

Fitzroy knew he would never be able to pay back the American assassin for all he'd done for him, but that didn't mean he would *ever* stop trying.

He looked away from the water, down to his hand with the lemonade, and he saw the liquid trembling in the glass. He stared at the movement for a moment, then a moment more, before putting the glass down on the railing in front of him and reaching into his pants pocket.

He pulled out a bottle of orange prescription pills, opened the cap with difficulty, then poured two out and popped them into his mouth, his hand still slightly shaking as he did so.

A woman in her thirties stepped out onto the balcony behind him. She and her husband had accompanied Fitzroy to Mexico to serve as bodyguards. When he noticed her presence, he quickly tucked the bottle back into his pocket.

In English she said, "They are here, sir."

"Lovely, Francisca. Very well." Fitzroy opened and closed his hands a few times, then headed inside. He descended the narrow wooden staircase, his heart rate slowly increasing with excitement as he did so.

He'd just arrived on the ground floor when Court Gentry entered from the entryway behind the male Portuguese guard. Court wore jeans, a maroon T-shirt, and black tennis shoes. A black backpack hung from his shoulder. He was a little older than Fitzroy remembered him, but his bright brown eyes sparkled with intensity and life.

Just behind him, Zoya appeared. She wore a yellow sundress, flip-flops, only the slightest bit of makeup, and blond hair that hung past her shoulders. She looked a little older than he'd remembered her, as well, perhaps a little tired, but Sir Donald could not help but bask in her exquisite beauty.

Both bodyguards left them alone upon Fitzroy's command; Sir Donald rushed forward and shook Court's hand, then exchanged a gentle but heartfelt hug with the Russian woman.

"I can't tell you how wonderful it is to see you both."

It was midafternoon, the warmest part of the day, so the lights were off, the windows were open in the living room, and a cooling breeze blew in from multiple directions to keep the property from being stuffy.

Court jerked his head back to the hallway. "Who are Mr. and Mrs. Smith?"

"Pedro and Francisca. My bodyguards."

"Yeah, saw the guns. What's with the protection? I seem to remember that you refused to roll with security back when you *weren't* retired, back when people *were* after you. Why now?"

"Perhaps I've learned from my mistakes."

Court eyed him dubiously. "Perhaps."

Zoya asked, "Are they any good?"

Fitzroy shrugged. "I haven't a clue, to tell you the truth. They came recommended by a friend in Lisbon. Former PSP officers, Public Security Police. To be honest, I've never worked with them before. I didn't bring them so much for the protection they would give me on this trip; I chose them for their appearance."

Zoya understood immediately. "They look like us. We're going in to Tudor's place disguised as your security?"

"That was the plan, but I remembered your hair quite differently, so I requested a brunette."

Zoya laughed at this. "I can be a brunette in thirty minutes."

"Give her an hour," Court said, "and she could stand in for *you.*"

Fitzroy gave a loud chortle, genuinely thrilled to be in the presence of these two people. "I don't want to see this beautiful woman altered one bit. Stay blond."

The three of them sat down; Fitzroy politely waved off the offer of drinks from a local attendant who leaned in from the kitchen, and then the woman headed up the hallway for the front door.

Court immediately got right down to it. "What's the plan?"

Fitzroy smoothed his tie a moment, then clutched his hands in his lap in front of him. "It will depend on Tudor. I texted with him this morning. All he knows is I'm calling on him because I happened to be in the area. Just a social visit, ostensibly, but I am operating under the assumption that *he* will be operating under the assumption there's something more to my sudden appearance here in Yucatán."

"Do you think he's wary?" Court asked.

"Heavens no, lad. I think he's ecstatic."

"Explain."

The Englishman hesitated a moment. "I didn't mention all this in our phone conversation; I didn't want to bore you with details."

Zoya leaned forward, put her elbows on her knees. "Now would be the time to bore us."

"Very well." He shifted in his wicker chair. "Jack is a friend."

Court's eyebrows rose. "A friend?"

"He only entered MI5 about five years before I left, but we got along straightaway. He came to me regularly over the years for advice, brought me scotch to talk about old stories, that sort of thing. He rose up the ranks in the eight or nine years he was there, received a number of commendations, then he left before he turned forty."

"Why?"

"Forced out. The reasons behind it were kept quiet. Office politics, I suspect, but I don't know. He hasn't told me much, only that he was happy to leave government service."

"So he could go solo?"

Fitzroy nodded. "He dropped in to my offices in London as soon as he left MI5. We'd stayed in touch, so he was aware I was running a successful security and risk consulting company."

Court corrected him. "You ran assassins."

"That was hardly the wording on my business card."

"Right."

"Jack wanted to get into the private security consulting world himself. He sought advice, asked for contacts, leads, strategies for success in the trade."

"And you gave them to him?"

"Absolutely not." Fitzroy leaned forward. "I was building my own business. Friend or not, I wasn't going to help him to that degree. Still, he built an organization on his own. Analysts, technicians, computer support, things of that nature. Working mostly for aboveboard corporate accounts.

"But as soon as I took down my shingle and retired, he was there at my door. This was shortly after that business you and I dealt with in Hong Kong." He looked at Zoya. "Where we met, my dear.

"Anyway, Tudor wanted to retool his business model, wanted to seek out the type of contracts I had been handling."

"Murder for hire," Court said flatly.

"Quite. I gave him many of my contacts, all of my outstanding contracts. I showed him how to communicate with my assets."

"So, basically, you handed him the keys to your company."

"That's right, yes. My firm, Cheltenham Security Services, was folded into his firm, Lighthouse Risk Control. His company was registered in the British Virgin Islands; he lived there for a while, but then he had his place built down in Tulum."

"So you are the one who gave him Lancer?" Zoya asked.

"No. Lancer was long gone by the time I closed Cheltenham. He was an asset I shouldn't have taken on in the first place." He looked to Zoya. "What you must understand is my top dog, our boy Courtland here, was extremely choosy about who he'd operate against. He turned me down nine times for every ten offers I sent his way. All his operations had to be honorable." Looking at Court, he said, "Though it was *your* code of honor the rest of us had to abide by."

"I wouldn't say you abided by anything."

Fitzroy chortled again. "Yes, I had other hard assets, and I employed them when you turned me down." He looked to Zoya. "But I didn't have anyone world-class like Courtland."

Court said, "Stop talking about me like I'm not even here. It's weird."

Fitzroy said, "You're a bloody legend and you know it. That's what happens to legends."

Court rolled his eyes.

Zoya asked, "How did you come to hire Lancer?"

"Scott Kincaid had been working for another security firm since soon after he was released from prison. Small operations. West Africa, if memory serves. He was unfulfilled, looking for more action, and I was a man with a need for an asset who would get into the action." He looked at Court. "I'd lost sense of right and wrong, as you know by some of the jobs I offered you."

Court *did* know, but he said nothing.

"I brought Lancer in. He did one job for me, it went well. He did a second job, it went less well."

Zoya said, "The problem?"

"Collateral. Not killed, but injured."

"Go on," Court instructed.

"Then I had a contract in Turkey. Two assets were required for the job due to the target's quick reaction force nearby."

Court picked it up from there. "I met Lancer in Ankara. I could tell he was a dick from the beginning, but operationally, he seemed switched on." He looked at Zoya. "Plus, I trusted Fitz's judgment when it came to the men he put in the field."

Fitzroy added, "And this mission, it was undeniably righteous."

"Or I wouldn't have done it," Court said. "It was a terrorist, Egyptian but living in Turkey. He had a couple of close-protection guys with him at all times, but he also had a larger group that trailed him for additional security, staying back far enough to not draw attention to their principal.

"My job was to eliminate the target; Lancer's job was to hold up the security response. We thought that if the vans full of shitheads came, Lancer would just dump some rounds into their vehicles. Drop a few of the target's henchmen, slow down their approach."

Court's voice drifted off, and Fitzroy picked it back up. "But Scott Kincaid came up with his own plan without telling anyone. He made and employed improvised explosive devices, blew up a pair of minivans full of terrorists, which wouldn't have been a problem, but he did it on a busy street next to Kizilay Square. Shrapnel killed three civilians, injured twenty-two."

"I'd just done my job four blocks away," Court said. "I heard the explosions, the sirens, the screams. I got the fuck out of there. Met Lancer at the safe house later that night, he acted like everything went off without a hitch.

"Saw the carnage on TV the next morning as we were breaking down the place. A minute later we were in a fistfight. A few seconds after that we were swinging blades at each other. Police came before we damaged anything other than furniture; we both escaped, but I was intent on killing that son of a bitch."

Court sighed. "I told Fitz here I'd never work with Lancer again, and I never saw him after till the other night."

Fitzroy added, "Tudor told me back when he hired Lancer a couple of years ago. I strongly recommended against, but Jack said he needed a man with Kincaid's skills."

Zoya said, "But it's been years. How do you know Tudor still handles him?"

"I spoke with Jack just a couple months back. He mentioned that Lancer was still in his employ. Earning a ransom, from the sound of it."

"You and Tudor stay in touch?"

"As I said, I like to keep abreast of things. I've never lost my zeal for the work, even if I no longer do it myself. From time to time he feeds me information."

"And what do you do for him?"

Fitzroy smiled. "It's not what I do for him. He reaches out to me periodically because there is one thing he thinks I can provide him. One thing that he really wants."

"What's that?" Court asked.

When Fitzroy did not immediately respond, Zoya turned to Court and answered the question.

"You."

Court cocked his head in confusion.

Fitzroy nodded. "He knew that I ran an asset named Gentry. Found that out from Lancer. He knew that Gentry from CIA was the Gray Man. Found that out when he was at MI5. He's never seen a picture of you, that I know of, but he's aware of all the lore about your exploits.

"I hear from him anytime something big happens in the world. The assassination in Bosnia, the thing in India, New York City four or five months ago. The killing of the Russian assassin in Berlin. He thinks you did it all." Fitzroy looked deeply into Court's eyes, no doubt for some indication he had done these operations, but Gentry wasn't giving anything away, so he continued. "He reaches out, asking if I've heard anything about where you were, who you were working for.

"What Tudor *really* wants is you. The amount of money you could generate for him. Of course I tell him he's daft. I don't talk to you, and you wouldn't work for anyone who ran Lancer in the first place, so what's the bloody point? But he's relentless about adding you to his stable of hit men."

Court was bewildered. "I'm not going to work with some asshole who's running a psycho Nazi killer who's in the process of assassinating a shit-ton of innocent scientists and engineers."

"I agree with every word you just said there but 'innocent.' We don't know why these people are being targeted. They may well be the root of the problem that we're now trying to solve. Anyway, I'm not taking you to him so that you can work together; I'm taking you to him so you can find out about Scott Kincaid. He would drop Lancer for you to work with him, which means he might very well turn on Lancer and his operation if you just *say* you will work with him.

"Whether we reveal your identity or not depends on what cards we have to play when we get there, but it's nice to know we have an ace in the hole."

"Okay," Court said. "Let's go see this son of a bitch and find out what he has to say for himself."

Fitzroy sighed. "Best you let me do the talking, Court."

"Yeah. Best," Zoya agreed.

TWENTY-NINE

Drone pilot Carlos Contreras sat alone in a webbed chair in the cargo hold of the Cessna 408 SkyCourier as it buffeted through the darkness some seven thousand feet above the Yucatán coastline. There was a portal near his head, but he ignored the view out the window in favor of the three laptops open in front of him, each one's ruggedized case affixed to an aluminum table with double-sided tape.

In its passenger plane configuration, the cabin of the SkyCourier can seat nineteen, but this model had been set up as a cargo hauler. Purchased by a Mexican package delivery service that went bankrupt shortly after it was delivered, it had then been put up for sale in an online auction. After a few months with no interest, an offshore company based out of Antigua suddenly purchased the aircraft at its asking price, the paperwork was handled remotely and wire transfers sent from a Cyprus bank to the seller's bank in Mexico City, and then an Irish pilot and Mexican loadmaster were hired to take delivery of the aircraft just four days prior.

Two days after this, the pilot and loadmaster picked up the cargo from a freight forwarder in Houston, with no idea of either the origin of the crates or their contents.

Contreras knew none of this, of course; like the pilot and loadmaster, he didn't even know his mission.

But he was starting to get some idea.

Next to Contreras in the cabin sat several pallets under a black cargo net. He'd been through the majority of the equipment stowed on board, and he understood enough to know what was in store today, even if he hadn't been read in on the specific target or even the area of operations.

On one pallet sat stacks of black Pelican cases of different sizes, and each one housed a drone, along with spare batteries and technical manuals.

Some of the drones were no larger than the ones he'd been using in Guatemala, and they just had cameras, marking them as simple ISR devices, with one unusual feature. Small packages on top of the folded-up devices seemed to be tiny parachutes, meaning these drones could be launched directly out of the cargo ramp of the aircraft.

In addition to the ISR models, a half-dozen more units sat encased on the pallet, and they were significantly larger that the drones Contreras normally used. The case on the outside said "Hornet V-12," and Contreras looked inside them. These were hexacopters, not quadcopters, and double the size of his reconnaissance models at twenty-eight inches in diameter.

This, of course, was so the flying machines could heft a larger payload, and when Contreras inspected the payloads, at first he couldn't believe his eyes.

The six hexacopters each carried 250 grams of explosive charges mounted just aft of the camera on the belly.

These Hornets were hunter/killer models, and from what Contreras could tell, he was now in command of them.

Madre de dios, he'd muttered at the time.

Three more six-propeller units had folded-in boom arms, on the end of which Contreras recognized laser microphones, something else Contreras had never seen on a drone. Drones make noise while in flight, and this meant they wouldn't be able to pick up speech through a laser while in the air, so he knew the aircraft would have to land and stop spinning the props in order to conduct audio surveillance.

Behind the pallet with the drones, three larger black cases, over four feet square each, rode on three smaller wooden pallets.

The three bigger cases all had specialized parachute rigs attached to them by the loadmaster, and Contreras had not been able to look inside them. Still, he could tell they were some sort of large device that would fall all the way to Earth when deployed, so he couldn't help but wonder if the cases might each house some sort of ground robot.

The name on the side, "Greyhound V120," made him wonder if the machine had legs like a dog.

There was no paperwork with the cases, so Contreras wasn't sure how he was to control the devices when the time came, but he just told himself Cyrus wasn't going to order him to deploy drones he didn't know how to operate, so he assumed he'd get some instruction.

A quick glance outside into the night revealed to the Mexican that they were now flying over the sandy white beaches of Tulum.

Soon the SkyCourier banked over the dense jungle of the Sian Ka'an Biosphere Reserve at six thousand feet, leveling out and then turning again on an easterly heading that took it back out over the water.

Contreras knew his position only by looking at the GPS on his laptop, and quickly he realized the pilot was flying a racetrack pattern over a few dozen square miles of land and water below, with the coast being the centerpoint of the racetrack.

He could only assume Cyrus was interested in someone or something in one of the massive homes on the rocky and sandy shoreline just south of the Zona Hotelera, or hotel zone, their bright lights piercing the darkness and visible through the portals around him.

Minutes later he received a direct message on his screen from Cyrus, ordering him to launch the three audio drones and two of the video drones above a particular location towards the southern end of their coverage area.

He asked the obvious question: how was he supposed to command the devices once launched, because he had no idea how to do so.

Cyrus's response came quickly. **Deploy as instructed and stand by.**

The pilot directed the aircraft to coordinates fed him by Contreras, the loadmaster dropped the rear cargo hatch, and then Contreras powered up all five collapsed devices, following start instructions he'd found in their cases.

Contreras attached his safety harness to a slide bar on the side of the cabin, then stood, carrying all five units stacked one on top of the next like a stack of pizza boxes.

At the top of the ramp he waited until the pilot came over his headset telling him they were over the drop point, and then Contreras simply Frisbeed the units out into the night, one at a time, in quick succession.

Then he made the sign of the cross as they disappeared.

The two smaller and three larger devices fell through the air, tumbling and tumbling, but at just eight hundred feet the parachutes deployed, slowing them, and then all the arms on each device extended. The propellers began to spin, slowing the descending drones even more, but before the chutes sagged and fell, the attached parachute packs jettisoned with a boost from a small CO_2 canister on board each unit.

The two quadcopters remained at altitude, but the larger models continued their steady descent under nearly silent intermittent propeller power.

The three larger units containing laser microphones landed to the south, north, and west of a massive hacienda on the water's edge, the southernmost property Contreras could see through the portal before he looked away and back to his monitors, where he watched the images broadcast from the two ISR units hovering over the ocean.

The drones' cameras began zooming in on windows, flying overland and circling slowly around the massive hacienda, and Contreras just sat back and watched the monitors because he wasn't controlling anything at all right now. With Raul seated back by the again-closed cargo ramp and the pilot continuing a racetrack pattern farther out to sea, there was nothing for Contreras to do other than sit there and try to figure out just what the hell he was in the middle of.

The pair of Portuguese security officers remained at the house on Soliman Bay while Fitzroy, Court, and Zoya climbed into a silver Mercedes four-door and set off for the estate of Jack Tudor. The rains of the day had quickly come and gone, and the nighttime darkness was brightened somewhat by the twinkling stars above.

Court and Zoya had dressed in clothes provided to them by Pedro and Francisca. A lightweight beige suit for him, and a gray pantsuit for her. They did not bring firearms, as they would simply be confiscated before they got anywhere near Tudor's property, so instead they just carried the bearing of well-trained security professionals.

Their Mercedes rolled south through the hotel zone of Tulum, past ritzy shops, high-end restaurants, and four- and five-star luxury accommodations. Eventually the buildings, the traffic, the beaches, and the crowds gave way to a flat open road heading along the coast into dense jungle.

From Sir Donald's description of Tudor and his operation, Court had expected a well-guarded front entrance to Tudor's property, but the GPS said their car was still a quarter mile away from the driveway the first time they were stopped, and *this* Court had not expected. Local police had a checkpoint on the sand-strewn two-lane road leading to Tudor's estate, and even though Court and Zoya's last police checkpoint experience had not gone well, they both kept their cool as they passed over their documents and Zoya explained, in Spanish heavily thickened with a Portuguese accent, that their protectee had an eleven p.m. appointment to meet with Tudor.

The cop in the window said he had a guest list for "Mr. Jack," and he confirmed that Fitzroy and two bodyguards were on it, but he still asked Court and Zoya to step out and submit to a pat-down.

Two other officers checked the Mercedes while Zoya and then Court were searched for weapons and only then allowed back into the front seats, while Sir Donald in the back was not questioned at all.

Soon the Mercedes was waved on through the checkpoint.

Thirty-one minutes after the feed began on the two ISR drones, Contreras watched a single four-door vehicle approaching the guard shack at the end of the road leading to the hacienda.

The thermal image locked on the car as it stopped briefly. The tiny camera on the drone was easily five hundred feet from the vehicle, but the images were so good he could recognize the emblem of Mercedes-Benz on the front grille.

The driver spoke with the guards, then pulled forward to the front of the large modern glass mansion, parking in front as a group of four more armed sentries stepped outside to meet them.

Contreras lit a cigarette, looked on idly, and wished he had some other mission beyond tossing boxes out of the back of the aircraft on command and watching TV.

Three people climbed out of the Mercedes: a male driver, a passenger from the back, also male but larger and perhaps older, and a woman from the front passenger seat.

All three of them were wanded with a handheld metal detector, and then the male driver was frisked. To Contreras's mild surprise, the female passenger lifted her arms and was patted down, as well, and then they all turned for the door to the house.

The camera had a better angle now; it zoomed in tighter, examined sixty-eight different geometric features of each of the faces, and suddenly red boxes appeared over the images of both the woman and the driver.

Contreras shot back up, staring intently. His eyes flicked to his other laptop.

Target Acquired, Gama 18. Target Acquired, Gama 19.

Zakharova and Gentry. Here.

He began to type a direct message to Cyrus, but before his fingers hit the keys, a box popped up on the screen.

This is Cyrus. Stand by on targets.

Contreras sat back, somewhat confused. All he was doing was standing by; it wasn't like he was about to parachute down there and kill them himself.

Then he looked to his cargo, and he thought of the bomb-wielding hexacopters.

Holy shit.

One minute later the pair of AI-powered aerial surveillance drones had turned their attention to the windows of the property; one of the two hovered two hundred yards out to sea and captured a good image of the second-floor interior, where floor-to-ceiling windows were open to the water and the house lights were on.

The thermal imaging system on board turned itself off; the optical camera zoomed in tight on the lighted interior.

Contreras saw no one in the room, so he rose in the cabin to begin preparing two more camera drones to replace the first pair when they got low on batteries and had to land.

As soon as Court, Zoya, and Fitzroy climbed up the steps to the entrance to the home, the door opened and an armed Hispanic man met them and ushered them inside. Here, another pair of security officers, both wearing pistols on their hips, took up positions behind them, and the three visitors were led by more security through the expansive arched entryway.

Fitzroy followed the lead guard, with Court just behind him at his right shoulder.

Zoya trailed them, her eyes scanning the hallway, the stairs, every room they passed. As one of Fitzroy's security people, it stood to reason she'd have her eyes flitting around as they moved through the building, although in truth she wasn't looking around to protect the Englishman. Instead, she was searching the residence for cameras, guards, weapons, civilians. Potential egresses, hard points, choke points. With every single step forward, she registered more data about the home, and she was certain Court was doing the exact same thing.

Fitzroy had promised them he'd be able to converse with Jack Tudor without violence ensuing, but Zoya had heard that line before, often shortly before the gunfire kicked off.

She'd clocked eight security men so far between the outer guard shack, the driveway, and here in the center of the home. All were apparently Hispanic, some carrying short-barreled rifles, others just pistols in shoulder holsters, and one of the men she saw carried a stockless pump-action 12-gauge shotgun on a sling around his neck.

Within seconds of entering the modern structure, they were back outside, walking along an old Mexican-style veranda next to a courtyard adorned with beautiful tropical plants. A fountain in the center of the space gurgled, the soft lighting glowed on the flora, and a large green parrot stood on a roost next to a cage the size of a small automobile. An outrageously ornate outdoor kitchen, replete with a tiled stone oven, sat off to one side of the courtyard next to a long dining table.

Hallways ran off the veranda to the north side of the house, and then another hallway at the end of the outdoor space led into a large kitchen. Just before the kitchen, a helical staircase spun up from the veranda and to the second level, and the man leading them through the property began climbing.

They followed him into a large second-floor great room, with an adjacent kitchen and a library through a doorway on the far side. The floor-to-ceiling windows looked out over the ocean here, the reflections on the white-capped waves like dancing fireflies.

Jack Tudor stepped out of his dimly lit library and into the room, illuminated by strong ambient lighting. Zoya noticed the man had a warm smile and an eager gait. He appeared to be about fifty-five; he had gray, almost silver hair that was styled neatly in a comb-over; he wore designer glasses and a casual shirt and khakis. Tudor was a thin man, well tanned and healthy, and he approached Fitzroy with a hand extended.

A pair of Tudor's guards remained here in the great room, and they took up positions on the far side, near the entrance to the library.

Zoya knew she and Court were just "the help"; Tudor likely wouldn't even acknowledge them. They both stood at the top of the helical stairs, hands held across their midsections. Court looked out the big windows to the sea, and Zoya kept her eyes shifting between the other people in the room and on the staircase they'd just climbed.

The homeowner's Welsh accent was strong, his voice slightly high-pitched. "It's an honor to have you in my home, old friend. It's been far too long since I've laid eyes on you."

Fitzroy shook the younger man's hand, covered the handshake with his free hand, and smiled right back. "Too true. Thanks for agreeing to see me on such short notice."

"Not at all." Tudor's eyes gleamed as if he were telling a joke. "It was quite the thrill to hear that the legendary Sir Donald Fitzroy just happened to be in the neighborhood. Imagine my astonishment."

Fitzroy smiled back, picking up on the sarcasm, then replied, "Yes . . . well . . ."

Tudor released his handshake, waved Fitz over to a sofa facing the windows across the room and the ocean beyond, and then Tudor took a seat on an overstuffed white leather chair.

The Welshman glanced over to Court and Zoya. "Might I say I applaud you on coming to the realization that sometimes it's good to bring a little help along. The guards, I mean. You never used them in the past."

Fitzroy responded, "Only now that I'm retired do I feel safe with others close by. While working in the private sector, I always felt I didn't want security near in case I said or did something that could someday be used against me."

Tudor waved his hand in the air. "I don't even consider it. I hire well; they don't care what I say or do."

A servant brought in a silver tray covered in shot glasses and limes and salt and a large black bottle of Clase Azul Ultra Extra Añejo Tequila.

Tudor poured for them both while they exchanged pleasantries, two veteran intelligence officers from the same service catching up on old colleagues and old times.

Zoya looked on; she could see the genuine affection Jack Tudor held for Donald Fitzroy, and she hoped this affection survived the next few minutes.

THIRTY

Carlos Contreras watched the meeting on the screen of one of his laptops on board the SkyCourier, now several miles out to sea and flying a slow "lazy 8" pattern. He wished he had audio feed established so he could hear the people speaking inside, but just seconds after thinking this, his laptop indicated that one of the audio surveillance units he'd dropped was picking up voices.

He could see from the data on his screen that the unit broadcasting was on the beach to the southeast of the hacienda, so Contreras imagined its laser was hitting the huge windows on the second floor, on the other side of which he could see all the people in the living room.

He put on his headset and clicked a few buttons, and then he heard people speaking English. Their voices were distorted, with the distortion of the signal coming off a vibrating window, but with only a little difficulty, he could nevertheless make out who was speaking and what was being said.

Sir Donald Fitzroy finished his tequila, put the glass back on the serving tray, then waved off Tudor as he hefted the bottle and offered a refill.

"Jack, I apologize, but just one for me tonight."

Tudor refilled his own glass, then put the bottle down. "That's all right. I just thought that since you were on vacation you might want to—"

Fitzroy interrupted. "Yes, well, I apologize, but my vacation was a bit of a ruse. I needed to speak with you straightaway, so I used a small amount of deception to make it happen."

Tudor didn't bat an eyelash. "You have some other motive than just being in town? Please, Don, give me credit for sussing that out on my own."

"Very well." Fitzroy fumbled for words for a few seconds, and then he said, "We've had a friendly relationship, Jack. I truly hope that will continue."

The lines in Tudor's forehead grew as he looked at the man on the sofa. "Why on earth would it not continue?"

"Because I've come to talk to you tonight about one of your clients, one of your assets, and something dark and dangerous you've gotten yourself involved in."

Tudor kept his eyes fixed on Fitzroy, but he downed his tequila. When he put the glass back down, he said, "I facilitate my assets' contracts, I don't have any operational purview to their—"

"I know how it all works, old boy," Fitzroy said coldly.

Tudor appeared taken aback by the sudden turn of tone in his friend. "Of course you do. So why are you coming to me with questions about—"

"This is different. You have an asset, at least one asset, involved in these technology killings around the world, and I have it on good authority that there are large and serious geopolitical stakes at play in all this that I'm not certain you are aware of."

Tudor said, "What is it that you are asking me?"

"I'd like to know who is behind this whole thing."

The Welshman laughed. "And you think *I* would know that?"

"I think you know *something*. I know Lancer is involved, and if he's involved, then you are involved."

"Why do you think Lancer is involved?"

Fitzroy replied, "Four days ago he killed a U.S. government employee in California. Then he attacked two people in Guatemala. The next day, he assassinated a Russian businessman and a Russian computer engineer in Mexico City." Fitzroy paused. "As well as inflicting other collateral damage. He's also suspected of killings in Boston and Toronto."

"How do you know this?"

"I might be out to pasture, Jack, but I do still hear things."

Tudor cocked his head now. "You used to be MI5, but this isn't domestic, so it's not MI5's purview. Does that mean you are working with Legoland?"

Legoland was the nickname for MI6, British foreign intelligence, so called because of the architecture of its building in London.

"I'm not working for anyone. I'm retired, just as I told you. I'm just an extremely concerned citizen who would like to get to the bottom of what is happening, because it certainly seems to be foretelling of very dark events on the horizon."

"I don't know any details about Lancer's operations." Tudor waved a hand. "There are cutouts upon cutouts. I stay clean."

Fitzroy looked over to Court, but before he said anything, Court nodded gently.

The older man turned his attention back to Tudor, who had not noticed the glance away. "Jack . . . ever since you started your company, you've wanted one thing from me. One thing I wasn't in a position to give you."

Again, Tudor seemed confused by the change in subject. Nervously he looked up to Fitz's guards, as if he didn't want them listening in to this. Addressing Fitzroy, he said, "Yeah . . . what about all that?"

"What if I told you I could make the introduction that you seek if you will only allow me to know what you know about what's going on?"

Tudor cocked his head in surprise. "What game is this?"

"It's no bloody game. It's a promise. From me. You help me with some intel on the client and the operation afoot, and I put you in touch with the man you've been after for years."

"When you worked on the sharp end," Tudor asked, "did you give up your clients or your assets to anyone who asked?"

Fitzroy glanced again at Court, but only for an instant. Court looked back, and gave Fitzroy a little wink. The Englishman said, "I'm not *anyone*, am I? I'm your friend. I'm the man who can help you get what you want, and despite your tough exterior, I do believe strongly that you don't want to be a party to whatever the Chinese are cooking up on the weaponized artificial intelligence front."

"The Chinese?" Tudor said it as if he were surprised, but he wasn't particularly convincing.

"Bloody hell, man," Fitzroy added. "Do something for the good of humanity."

Tudor thought a moment. With a sly smile he said, "To hell with humanity. Tell me you were serious about the Gray Man."

Fitzroy smiled himself. "Very serious."

The Welshman looked around a moment, then back to Fitzroy. Softly, he said, "I don't know the targets. I don't know how Lancer is tasked, specifically. He is in direct communication with the operations center of my client."

"Tell me about how you came in contact with the client."

"A cutout, as I said. This was a different arrangement than any I've ever had. I was given three locations, two in the U.S. and one in Mexico, asked if I could provide enough manpower to eliminate a minimum of five targets, all within a seventy-two-hour period."

"Why did it have to be in three days?"

"I presumed it was because once the killing started, those people targeted would know they were in the crosshairs. They had to be eliminated quickly before they adopted protective measures."

"But . . ." Fitzroy said, "there have been nearly a dozen related killings that I know of."

"Apparently the client hired other assets around the world to do the others."

Fitzroy just said, "Go on."

"I provided Lancer, and I was paid a finder's fee. Normally, that would be the end of the transaction, but Lancer reached out to me the other day because he wanted more money, and I acquired it for him by contacting the cutout."

This wasn't enough information for Fitzroy. "I'll need more than that."

Tudor paused a moment, unsure. Finally, he said, "There is more, Don, but you must come through with Gentry."

"Go on."

"I hired out another asset, ostensibly to a different party, nothing to do with Lancer. A woman. Not a tip-of-the-spear type, but rather an intelligence analyst. This was her first assignment for me."

"What about this woman?"

"She made contact with me. She said she'd been sent to Singapore to set up and work dispatch in an operations center of an organization. She had some . . . reservations about what she was being asked to do."

"What was she being asked to do?"

Tudor looked at the floor a moment. "The OC where she works is controlling the targeted killings. She didn't know what she was getting herself into, and I confess I did not, either, or I wouldn't have sent her. As I said, she's not from the deep end of the pool when it comes to danger. She wanted help getting pulled out of there, but I told her I couldn't pull her safely without some actionable intelligence I could use to earn her rescue. Her best chance was to get some information on what was going on, and then I'd take it to colleagues at MI6."

"Why didn't you just tell her to run on her own?" Fitzroy asked.

Tudor shrugged, almost apologetically. "Because I can use the information, naturally. Use it to get me back in the good graces of British intelligence." He smoothed out a wrinkle on his slacks. "The work I do . . . the assets I have. I can be useful to the Crown, I know it. I just need Legoland to know it."

"Do you know where, exactly, this woman is?"

"She doesn't know where in Singapore. They were taken to the OC in a closed vehicle, they live there on-site. She managed to reach out via text using her workstation and a secure messaging service, but she says she has to be bloody careful she's not caught. The office is crawling with security. Cameras are everywhere."

"What type of security?"

"She thinks they are locals, but she doesn't know."

"When do you expect to hear from her again?"

"Tonight. Any minute, in fact."

"Well then," Fitzroy said, "how about we wait together?"

Carlos Contreras had listened to the conversation, and he wondered if the man in the house was talking about Operations Center Gama. He had no idea if Gama was in Singapore or not, but this seemed to be a part of the larger operation he was conducting, so he told himself it had to be the case.

The Mexican wondered if this obvious intelligence leak at Gama the man was speaking of was the reason he'd been instructed to deal directly with Cyrus instead of his contact at the operations center, and he thought this likely, as well.

So, he reasoned, perhaps Cyrus had sent him here to spy on the man in the house, with no idea that Zakharova and Gentry would appear.

If the man in the house was a threat to the operation, and two of the visitors were already targets of Cyrus, then he assumed it would be no time before he'd be ordered to deploy the lethal Hornet drones, even though he hadn't a clue how to operate them once launched.

Just then, a window appeared on his screen. **Deploy Greyhound units One One and One Two.**

Two of the three large pallets. Precise geographic coordinates followed.

Then a second message came. **Deploy Hornet units Nine Seven, Nine Eight, and Nine Nine.**

These three were hunter/killer hexacopters.

Contreras called out to Raul, and the man appeared at his shoulder in the darkened cabin of the small cargo plane. The wrangler rose from his desk, and together the two men worked quickly to prepare the devices for deployment, leaning against the fuselage as the aircraft banked back to the west.

The loadmaster checked the tether and the parachute on each payload, then lowered the rear cargo ramp again, and the two of them waited for the call from the pilot that they were clear to drop.

Soon the two large palletized cases rolled down the ramp and out into the night, and a moment later he heaved all three of the folded hexacopters, one at a time, behind them. He made the sign of the cross, then rushed back to his monitors to continue watching the windows of the estate through the ISR feed to his laptop, curious as hell about what was inside those two massive cases that had just slid out the rear of the Cessna.

THIRTY-ONE

The conversation in the second-story great room of the hacienda continued; Fitzroy asked Tudor if he could be present for the contact between Tudor and his asset in Singapore and Tudor agreed, stressing again that he would be the one to turn over any intelligence to British authorities, and Fitzroy needed to keep his end of the bargain and put him in contact with Gentry.

Sir Donald then asked Tudor how he communicated with the cutout.

"Direct message on Signal," Tudor said. "Every time."

"You've never met with anyone? Spoken on the phone with them?"

"No. Not how they operate." Tudor added, "My asset at the operations center in Singapore told me she was getting her orders from a director there in the building, Scandinavian chap, and he was speaking with someone called Cyrus. Initially, she said, there were fifteen targeted killings planned, but the number seemed to be going up each day. She got cold feet when it became obvious to her they were working with China." Tudor added, "She's not a fan of the Chinese, apparently."

Fitzroy nodded gravely. "Everything that we suspected was going on." He asked, "If you had to guess, who do you think this Cyrus is?"

"If I had to guess, I'd say Cyrus is not one person. I'd say it was a building in Shanghai or Beijing staffed by dozens of PRC intelligence officers.

Maybe hundreds. All running this game like a global chessboard. It's too big for any one person, or anything less than a major state actor."

Fitzroy pondered this a moment, but before he could say anything, Tudor added, "I've done work with the Chinese before. But little things. Tracking down dissidents abroad for them, eliminating reporters or spies." He ran his fingers through his gray hair. "But from what my asset at the operations center tells me, and from what you are telling me now, this is some big bloody balance-of-power-shifting situation, and I don't want to help the Chinese with that."

"Good man," Fitzroy said.

Just over one kilometer to the west of the hacienda, at the edge of an otherwise empty gated parking lot next to a fenced-in garbage dump, a large black rectangular device weighing 180 pounds sat on the ground next to a tall Spanish bayonet plant with its sharp leaves blowing in the wind. The housing the device had arrived at the site in had popped open, and the parachute that had been attached to the top of the housing had been jettisoned upon touchdown, before the sheer canvas blew a few dozen meters farther inland, wrapping itself in brush.

There wasn't a soul around this remote location for hundreds of meters in any direction, so no one saw or heard when a trio of green LEDs illuminated on the top of the device and a cooling fan inside began to audibly spin as advanced onboard computers came to life.

The black barrel of a squat rifle protruded from a fixed turret at the top of the machine, and the quick sound of a round being chambered far exceeded the noise of the cooling fans. This SPUR, or Special Purpose Unmanned Rifle, fired the powerful 6.5-millimeter Creedmoor cartridge from a fifty-round internal magazine. It was semiautomatic, capable of eighteen rounds a minute of output, and had an effective range of nearly 1,200 meters.

A pair of thin antennae, only ten inches high and covered in rubber, rose from the rear section of the device with a soft buzz, and then a second later the machine itself began to rise from its protective packaging. It lifted off the ground on four legs, each one with a ball joint on the side of the rectangular body of the machine, and a second articulating joint halfway down the leg.

The feet of the machine were rubberized over the metal. Thirty hydraulic actuators served as the robot's muscles; it had the general body mechanics of a large dog, and the two forward-facing cameras were set up like eyes at the front of the rectangular device, although other cameras were also housed on the sides and rear to give it 360-degree awareness.

Moments after the robot stood, it ran a full systems check; a boom arm on the top of the device behind the turret rose and then spun through its full range of motion, its mechanical gripper opening and closing in a function test.

The device here in the parking lot was a fifth-generation quadrupedal unmanned ground vehicle or Q-UGV. A waterproof all-terrain machine, it was one of the most advanced and capable weaponized ground robots in the world, able to reach speeds of twenty-five kilometers per hour and to travel more than fifteen kilometers on a single charge.

Its exoskeleton was protected by Kevlar armor, making it resistant to smaller-caliber weapons.

And while this particular ground vehicle, Greyhound One One, was preparing itself for battle, just sixty meters to the south, Greyhound One Two rose on its four legs, lifting itself out of the muck and green sludge of a shallow fetid swamp.

At exactly the same time, both Q-UGVs began moving forward, one negotiating the soft gravel of debris of the trash-strewn parking lot at the dump, and the other splashing confidently through the swamp, shooing snakes out of the way with its noise and movement, until it finally climbed up on dry land.

The two Q-UGVs converged, bypassed a main road, and arrived at a small footpath in the jungle at essentially the same time. They then fell into formation, with One One leading One Two. Their speed quickened once the terrain smoothed out, and soon they began running forward at twelve miles per hour, directly toward the massive glass mansion's lights over the trees, less than a kilometer in the distance.

. . .

On the second floor of the mansion, Court listened in while Jack Tudor gave Fitzroy some backstory on his agent in the field working at the operations center. She was a German national, she'd been fired from her work at an intelligence center in Berlin for alcoholism, and she'd only accepted the job out of desperation after her husband had lost his position at a major bank.

Court had questions of his own about the woman and what she might be able to reveal about the technology killings, but he held his tongue because he was supposedly just here as window dressing: an unarmed security man following a geriatric ex-spy around on his trip to Mexico.

Soon enough, though, Court began to get the distinct impression he was not going to stay quiet for much longer.

Tudor finished his information dump about the German woman who was due to contact him any minute, then said, "So . . . let's hear about the Gray Man. How will you get in contact with him?"

Don Fitzroy turned to look at his two bodyguards, and Tudor followed his gaze. "We'll get to that," Fitzroy said. "But first, do you have a way of calling Lancer off any more operations he's tasked on?"

"He's done. Did that op in Toronto, and that was the last one."

Now Court spoke for the first time. "Not necessarily."

Tudor looked up at the man by the staircase. "I beg your pardon?"

Fitzroy said, "My colleagues here have something to tell you."

Court faced Tudor, who was still sitting on the chair across the room in front of the window. He said, "Four days ago, Lancer tried to kill my associate and me in Guatemala. We think it was an in extremis mission. He'd been tailing someone else, we came in contact with that someone, and, apparently, we were put on the list with all the others. You might think Lancer is done with his operation, but as you just said, your agent there in the OC said Cyrus was adding targets. Lancer could very well still be out there and working."

Tudor was confused, so he looked to Fitzroy for clarification. "He tried to kill your bodyguards? What on earth for?"

Fitzroy said, "Hear the lad out, Jack."

Court continued. "I know it was Lancer, because I know Lancer. He failed, but he got away clean."

Tudor looked back to Court and said, "Well, I find that to be most odd, because you both look very much alive, and he does not often fail, especially when facing a couple of security officers." He smiled a little. "No offense."

Zoya spoke up now. "None taken, but we aren't exactly bodyguards."

Tudor looked back over his shoulder and put his eyes on his own pair of security men in the room. They stood on the opposite wall from Fitzroy's pair, over near the entrance to the library, their hands to their sides but close enough to the pistols in their shoulder holsters. They each took a half step forward in a show of force, their eyes alert.

Fitzroy spoke softly. "Everyone just keep calm."

To Fitzroy, Tudor said, "If these two aren't your guards, then who are they?"

Fitz looked to Court, and Court nodded again.

The Englishman said, "I used to employ this lad. In a lengthy career, it is no exaggeration to say that he was, bar none, my very best asset."

Tudor rose slowly from the chair, his eyes locked on the younger man standing in front of him.

Zoya spoke softly next to Court. "Yep. He gets it."

"You're Gentry?" Tudor said, his voice unsure. "The former CIA asset code-named Violator?"

Court looked around the room self-consciously. "Let's not make a big thing out of it."

"Prove it."

Court rolled his eyes. "I don't do tricks."

"It's him, Jack," Fitzroy said. "In the flesh."

A small gasp came from the Welshman's mouth, and then, "I hope you don't mind me saying it, but you aren't at all what I was expecting."

"I get that a lot."

The Welshman recovered quickly. "I would like to talk to you, tonight, about coming to work for my firm."

"Not if you intend to rebuild your friendship with the British intelligence services, you don't."

Tudor's eyes gleamed at this. "Right. Well . . . nothing wrong with a few secrets. We don't have to tell them about you." Then the Welshman turned to look back to Fitzroy. "I trust I can expect some discretion from you, as well."

"Mum's the word. Help us with the Chinese and I'll be on my way."

Tudor said, "Fine." He looked up to Zoya. "And . . . I'm guessing you're not just a pretty face yourself. What do you do?"

Court said, "She's not looking for a job."

She glanced to Court, then back to the man. Seemingly eager to turn the conversation away from her, she said, "Your woman on the inside. Any chance she might have been exposed?"

"Not on my end. I guess we'll know if she doesn't contact me." He called out in Spanish, and one of Tudor's many security people appeared up the stairs. "Can you bring us something to eat? And more shot glasses for my two new friends here."

Looking up at the man and woman by the stairs, the Welshman said, "Let's all have a drink."

As a pair of four-legged rifle-wielding robots trotted near-silently towards the hacienda from the southwest, another threat approached stealthily from the east. Three hundred meters out to sea and passing some thirty meters below the two hovering ISR drones, the three hunter/killer hexacopters began slowly drifting forward. As they closed on the beachside hacienda, the Hornets spread apart, one to the south, one to the north, and the third unit continuing on to the west.

On each drone, the processor took in data from onboard sensors, the sensors of the other two hunter/killers, and those on the pair of ISR drones above them. Integrating as a swarm, their buzzing propellers masked by the sound of the crashing waves on the beach, the deadly machines halted their advance just fifty feet above the breakers, where they began hovering in the night air, awaiting orders to attack.

THIRTY-TWO

Court and Zoya declined the invitation to sit on the couch and drink tequila in the massive tiled great room. Both of them had sectors to watch over still, and even more importantly, since they were presently unarmed, both of them wanted to be on their feet in case they needed to cover ground quickly to relieve the two security men in the room of their handguns.

Tudor was a little put out that Court wouldn't join him to talk about his exploits and the lucrative future the two of them would share once the Welshman began fielding and vetting contracts for him.

"Tell me," the Welshman said, the energy displayed by his body movements that of a fourteen-year-old boy, "tell me you will come and work with me."

"I'll consider it," Court said, "as soon as I have a little more free time. Right now I'm pretty wrapped up with keeping your employee from murdering me."

"If he's still after you, I'll call him off straightaway. Pay him myself for any wages he'll miss out on."

Fitzroy looked down at his watch just after putting his shot glass on the hand-carved coffee table. "If we don't hear anything within a few minutes, then we will have to assume your asset in Singapore has been compromised, or else she is unable to get away to make the contact. Either way, we will need to speak with Lancer, so if you could go ahead and reach out to him now, we can—"

A loud low report came from outside, towards the front of the large property. Unmistakable to all in the room, the booming crack of a rifle got everyone's undivided attention.

"Who the fuck is shooting?" Tudor said, putting his full shot glass back on the serving tray in front of him.

A second shot barked outside in the night, and then a third. Tudor looked back to his two men, and they both began reaching for their walkie-talkies to get some information.

Court rushed outside through the back sliding glass door to the balcony, then looked out over the railing towards the rear of the property. A large rectangular swimming pool glowed one story below him, dazzling in emerald green, and beyond this was a simple fence and then the beach, strewn with thick brown sea grasses that had washed in with the tide. He saw no boats on the dark water, but he did spy a pair of Tudor's men standing in the sand, who'd obviously been tasked with guarding the fence line. One had a subgun at his shoulder, and he waved it around back at the house, and the other had a shotgun up and ready, its powerful undermounted weapon light sweeping the beach back and forth in case whoever was shooting at the front had friends somewhere back here in the darkness.

Finding the rear of the property to be a suitable escape route, Court turned and ran back inside just as two more gunshots cracked at the front of the hacienda.

He closed and locked the glass door, but just as he did so, he heard a new noise. A buzzing sound approached quickly from the rear of the property, as if it had just raced in over the water. Court pegged it instantly as a drone; it sounded like a large one, and it was coming in hot.

He didn't think they'd been followed all the way to Tulum, so he couldn't fathom how the enemy had somehow found them yet again.

Court ran up and down the length of the wall of windows facing the ocean, closing the heavy draperies and blocking out any view, but there remained a four-foot gap between the curtains and the edge of the wall on the far side of the windows near the library.

He turned to find the group still standing in the center of the great room, with Zoya appealing to the guards for a weapon. The two security men had surrounded Tudor and, with their pistols out, one covered the stairwell while the other spoke quickly into his walkie-talkie, demanding information from the front guard shack.

They ignored Zoya as they did this, and there was no response over the radio.

More gunshots cracked.

Court grabbed Zoya and Fitzroy and took them to the side of the room near the stairs so that they were far from the windows.

Tudor saw this and rushed up behind Fitzroy, his two bodyguards on his heels.

"What is it?" he asked Court.

Two-way gunfire launched in earnest now, still down below and in the front of the hacienda grounds. Court detected fully automatic submachine gun fire in the melee, but he also heard the louder, lower booms that had kicked off the gunfight seconds earlier.

To Court's expert ears, the incoming gunshots sounded like they were being fired by a sniper rifle. A .308 Winchester, a 6.5 Creedmoor, or perhaps a .260 Remington. Regardless of the caliber, he could tell there were at least two shooters working against multiple security men armed with pistols, shotguns, and submachine guns, and the attackers were in close, perhaps even at the front door of the large building.

Zoya looked to him. "There were three cops at that checkpoint up the road. They'll call this in, but it's going to take a while for police to respond in force."

"Who's doing this?" Tudor asked Court, because his own men hadn't been able to answer the question.

Court said, "Your client, most likely."

Tudor looked to Fitzroy now. He barked, "You led them here!"

The Englishman shook his head. "That's impossible." He turned to Court. "Isn't it?"

To Tudor he said, "Maybe they busted your woman at the ops center and know you are trying to get intel on their operation. They targeted us for less."

"Shite," Tudor muttered as the weight of Court's words settled on him. "What do we do?"

Court did not hesitate. "You give us weapons."

Tudor looked to his two guards. "Hand them your backups."

Zoya took a Glock 26 from one man, drawn from his ankle, and Court accepted a Glock 43 from the front pocket of another, and then one of the guards put his hand on Tudor's arm. "Señor Tudor, we have nine officers downstairs to deal with this. We'll put you in your library for now, close the shades on the window to the courtyard there. We'll keep you safe until this is over."

Tudor motioned to Fitzroy now. "You're coming with me."

Unsure, Fitz looked to Court. "What do you think?"

"We can't use the balcony if there's ISR back there. Go with Tudor and hunker down; we'll deal with the threat."

Tudor and the two guards began running back across the great room, putting them in front of the tall curtained windows as they moved.

Fitzroy addressed Court and Zoya now. "Do be careful." Then he turned and began shuffling well behind the others as they raced towards the library on the far side of the great room.

Zoya lowered to a knee and aimed down the stairs as a furious battle raged below.

Court stood behind her, looking back over his shoulder to the balcony, knowing that was another potential entry point for whoever these attackers were.

He watched Sir Donald struggle to catch up with the younger and fitter men who by now were now halfway across the room. Court noticed the gap in the curtains, but just as he started to call out to them to halt their run, the window glass there shattered inward as if shot by a bullet, and one half second later a large object flew into the room at high speed, slamming into one of Tudor's two bodyguards.

Fitzroy was no more than twenty feet away from where the impact occurred, but Court turned away from him and instead dove onto Zoya from behind, launching both of them down the stairs. They descended just beyond the lip of the second story as an explosion ripped through the great room above them. The force of the blast propelled them farther; they tumbled out of control, slamming backs and legs and arms into the unyielding stairs, but Court managed to reach out and take hold of one of the vertical rails with one hand while grabbing Zoya with the other, stopping their descent about halfway around the spiral and halfway down to the ground floor.

Zoya lay under him, so he rolled off, then shook his head to clear the disorientation. Looking down, he saw her Glock 26 within his reach, so he grabbed it and pointed it down to the ground-floor east-west veranda.

Thick smoke drifted through the air down there next to the large open courtyard, but through the blowing black obscurant he saw flashes of out-going gunfire. Soon he was able to make out a single security man kneeling behind an enormous stone planter, and he held a pistol-grip pump shot-gun. He fired around the side of the fountain ahead of him towards some unseen enemy across the courtyard and closer to the front of the property.

Zoya sat up with a gasp, then immediately looked down at her body, checking her arms, legs, and chest for missing parts or spurting blood. Sat-isfied she was still intact, she saw the Glock 43 that Court had been carry-ing just one step down from where she sat. Snatching it up, she shouted over the gunfire. "What the fuck happened?"

"You're okay," Court said just as the guard downstairs forty feet away rose again to fire the shotgun. Before pressing the trigger, however, he lurched violently back. Blood ejected from the back of his head as he was shot by a large-caliber weapon, and he dropped dead on his back on the veranda tile.

Neither Court nor Zoya could see the attacker, but they didn't wait around for him to come into view. They fought their way to their feet, turned, and raced back up the stairs towards the dense black smoke pour-ing down after the explosion above.

Sir Donald Fitzroy lay on his back, then pushed himself up to see what was happening around him. This turned out to be folly. His eyeglasses were gone, but that hardly mattered because the room was thick with smoke through which he could just make out the glow of a small fire over by the window curtains.

A second fire smoldered ahead on his right as the sofa he'd been sitting on went up in flames.

Fitzroy didn't know if he was injured or not; he felt around and realized he still had his arms and legs, but when he wiped his face with his hands he felt the unmistakable smear of thick blood. Sharp pains on his forehead and hands told him there was broken glass in multiple places on his face, so he simply stopped touching it.

He turned to look over his shoulder and found the air a little clearer there back by the stairs. To his immense relief he saw both Court and Zoya on their feet and staggering to him, so he peered forward again where he lay, trying to see some sign of Tudor.

The flames grew ahead to his left as more of the draperies ignited.

Court knelt down beside him, sticking his pistol in his waistband as he did so. "Can you stand?"

"My . . . my glasses."

"Here you go." Zoya handed them to him. Both lenses were cracked, but putting them on helped him see nonetheless.

"Help me up."

It took Court and Zoya both to get Fitzroy on his feet; he felt a pain on the right side of his rib cage that made him catch his breath.

And by the time he recovered and stood upright, the haze of the explosion had cleared enough to see the carnage in front of him.

Two mangled bodies lay in a pile next to the overturned chairs in the center of the room. Jack Tudor's guards, their heads and torsos shredded, blood everywhere, the blast of whatever explosive had detonated on top of them doing the work of a half-dozen machine guns.

Tudor was to their right, his legs protruding out from behind a wingback chair.

"See about Jack," Fitzroy shouted.

Zoya ran to the man on the floor and found him alive, but barely. His face, neck, and shoulder bled freely, his dress shirt had been burned through on the right arm, and it appeared every finger on his left hand had been shattered.

The man's eyes blinked, but Zoya knew he'd be in shock.

Behind this, Fitzroy groaned in pain now, put his hands on his right side. With a wince he said, "Broken ribs, at a minimum. Leave me, deal with the problem downstairs."

"Putting you and Tudor in that library first." Zoya climbed back up, got under Fitzroy's arm to support him, and started moving around the bodies, staying well clear of the window because of both the burning curtains and the threat of more kill drones.

Court pulled Tudor along the floor. The man made no sound, and though he was still breathing, Court felt certain the man had only moments to live.

More gunfire below made him wonder if they *all* had only moments to live.

Fitzroy shouted again in pain as they advanced, but soon they all made it into the library. Court was happy to see a window in the room looking out over the courtyard at the center of the hacienda, but no window to the rear of the property where the drone had attacked from.

Zoya helped Fitzroy down to the floor behind the large partners desk just in front of the wall of bookshelves, and then she pulled the window curtains closed. Court dragged Tudor right next to Fitzroy.

The hammering gunfire continued around the mansion, and it seemed to be closing on their position by the second.

Zoya shut the door to the great room most of the way to prevent the mounting smoke from the burning curtains and sofa from filling the library, but she left it cracked enough to keep an eye out for any attackers that made it upstairs. While she did this, she called out to Court. "What happened?"

"Apparently our enemy has kamikaze drones."

"Well, that's fucking perfect," she muttered. Shouting over mounting gunfire now, Zoya said, "I hear two sniper rifles, but why would you go CQB with a sniper rifle?"

"Close-quarters battle" was the term used for room-to-room gunfighting, and Court had been thinking the same thing. He answered her question with one of his own. "And why would two dudes with sniper rifles attack a building with a dozen defenders?"

Zoya said, "We need to know what we're up against."

Court rushed back to the window overlooking the courtyard, and then he knelt and used the barrel of his little pistol to move the curtain to the side.

Looking out the window to the left of the desk, he first saw that someone had popped a couple of smoke grenades. Through the swirling black clouds he could make out the lush foliage with the white marble fountain in the center, the mosaic tile and arched veranda running along the northern side of the space. He also saw guards lying dead, one crumpled on the grass against the fountain, a submachine gun sticking out of the water in front of his body, and the second, the man Court had watched get headshot on the veranda twenty-five feet from the stairs. He lay flat on his back; his stockless pump shotgun lay across his chest and a scatter path of blood glistened on the mosaic tile behind him.

Doing his best to listen for the spinning propellers of another drone above, Court instead heard a different noise.

Several footsteps echoing on the tile somewhere in the swirling smoke below.

He lowered even more, just put his head in the corner of the window so he could see across the courtyard, and as soon as he did, he waved Zoya over.

She shut and locked the door, then ran over and knelt next to him, looking out the window. In the smoke on the distant part of the veranda visible to them here, two dark figures slowly emerged, one trailing the other a few feet to its right.

Zoya said, "What the fuck are those? Dogs?"

His voice was dark. "Man, I wish they were." As the two figures emerged out of the smoke on the veranda, stepping onto the grassy courtyard near the fountain, they came fully into view.

THIRTY-THREE

Zoya squinted through the growing smoke until her eyes suddenly widened. Softly, she whispered, "Shut . . . up."

They watched the two robots, both the size of extremely large dogs, and both with what appeared to be rifle barrels protruding from housings on the tops of their bodies. They advanced steadily, their movements at once awkward and graceful.

But the unit in back did not move the same as its mate in front. It seemed to be limping on its right rear leg. Still, it swiveled its hips to slew the rifle and cameras left and right, searching for targets, and it appeared to be very much still in the fight.

"Can we kill them?" Zoya asked softly.

"We can kill anything," Court replied, but he didn't know for sure.

The machines closed on the bottom of the stairs to the second floor, and then the limping unit broke off to go down a hallway to the left. The lead bot arrived at the stairs, rose slightly, and then a hatch popped open on its roof. As Court and Zoya looked on, the device fired a small canister out, straight up the stairs. With a clanking sound it hit somewhere out of view, and then with a loud hiss the canister bounced back down the stairs, spewing impossibly thick black smoke all the way.

The lead bot then began adroitly climbing the stairs, firing yet another canister up as it did so.

"Fuck me," Court muttered, then rushed back over to Fitzroy.

The older man's face was covered in blood, and his chest heaved from exertion and stress. He asked, "What do you see?"

"Rifle-wielding robot dogs."

"Blimey," he muttered. "Maybe you can use the smoke in the room to hide your escape."

Court shook his head. "Won't work. Those things are going to have thermal imaging, otherwise they wouldn't be popping smoke like that. We have to destroy them or disable them, or we have to keep them back until they run out of bullets, juice, or time."

Zoya knelt next to him. "What's their battery life?"

Court sighed. "How would I know? I don't even own a toaster."

"Toasters don't have batteries," she said with a roll of her eyes.

Court looked back to Fitzroy. "We've got to go out this window to the ground floor. Can you make it?"

"What about Tudor?"

Court looked at the man. His eyes were unfixed. He bled from too many wounds for Court to treat before he had to deal with the attacking weapons.

To Fitzroy, he said, "Not a chance."

Fitzroy nodded. "We at least need the name of that woman in Singapore. I'll stay here and work on him."

Court liked this idea. "Good. Zoya and I will take care of the threat."

Zoya was within earshot. "How?"

Court had no answer, but before he admitted this, he cocked his head at a new noise. Zoya heard it, too. The loud buzzing of a large drone.

But it wasn't coming from outside; it was coming from the great room just beyond the door.

Zoya whispered, "There's a UAV flying through the damn house."

Another buzzing came from the courtyard now; this drone was higher, over the hacienda, but low enough to be in position to attack any targets if it was a kill bot.

Zoya said, "There must be someone controlling each of these things, plus the one that already crashed. That's a lot of pilots."

"Yeah," Court said, his mind racing with the increasingly complicated equation before him. He turned to Fitzroy. "Get that name out of Tudor."

Fitzroy nodded, and though obviously in great pain himself, he knelt over his dying friend.

One minute earlier Carlos Contreras had watched the ISR drones' feeds on the laptops in front of him, and though he said nothing and his face remained expressionless, in his mind a realization was slowly coming to him that he found almost impossible to comprehend.

From the overhead ISR camera feeds he could see the two surviving hunter/killer air bots, and the pair of armed ground vehicles moving through the courtyard. He knew these latter two units must have come from the cases he'd dropped some twenty minutes earlier.

The boxes he had released read "Greyhound V120" on the outside, which he assumed to be a make and model number, and it reminded him of YouTube videos of quadruped unmanned ground vehicles he'd watched in the past.

He'd even seen one with a rifle on its back on the Internet, a prototype, but he'd never even heard of anything that operated in the field with the capabilities these bots clearly possessed.

Soon one of the two ISR drones flew lower, over the roof and then down to the balcony, and then it descended even farther, finally flying right through the raging fire inside the window shattered by the Hornet bot moments earlier. Instantly it began broadcasting the feed inside the house: the great room, canisters spewing black smoke all around, and the two dead bodies lying by the overturned chairs.

The camera turned away, to the right, and now Contreras saw a closer view of one of the ground robots as it moved nimbly out of the stairs.

He thought about the flying camera now, and what technologies must be at play. The machine had the capacity for high-speed, dynamic interior navigation and obstacle detection and avoidance, and it automatically switched from its optical cam to its thermal depending on how much smoke was in the air in front of it.

Contreras was transfixed by the utter symphony being performed by the four remaining machines in the air as well as the two on the ground; they seemed to all be commanded as one, in harmony, and not as individuals.

He was an expert in the hardware being employed at the hacienda, and as he took it all in, one thing soon became abundantly clear.

If these machines were working together as one entity, then there was no way these machines were being controlled by human beings.

They operated in a swarm; the ground bots fired expertly, taking only an instant to choose a target, advancing and discharging smoke grenades while doing so.

And the hunter/killer hexacopter that had crashed through the window and detonated had had less than two seconds to identify and then lock on to its moving target, fire some sort of object out to destroy the window, and then attack in a terminal dive.

This was something no mortal human could possibly accomplish.

This was AI.

Contreras was certain now that all the equipment he'd been ordered to deploy was under the command of some integrated artificial intelligence that, in all his research on drones and robotics, he had only heard the faintest rumors of.

And although he was two miles or more out to sea and over a mile in the air, completely safe from what was going on at the shore, he felt pangs of terror in his stomach, back, and heart.

Contreras realized he was merely a human logistics component, an enabler of a massive artificial intelligence weapon, and the thought of this utterly terrified him.

As soon as this was over, he told himself, he was going to have a talk with this American, Cyrus, to get some understanding about this mission.

But for now he looked on, at once thrilled, fascinated, and scared.

Court and Zoya moved together to the closed door of the library, their weapons out, but they did not open the door. Soon the sound of the drone on the other side faded away; it seemed as if the machine was flying quickly and confidently into another part of the second floor, no doubt on a hunter/killer mission like the machine that had killed Tudor and his guards.

Zoya said, "That ground bot is probably at the top of the stairs by now."

Court dropped to his knees and reached for the door lock.

"What are you doing?" Zoya asked.

"I'm going to shoot it." He added, "They're not bulletproof."

Court cracked open the door and looked across the room. Through the smoke from the burning curtains and at least four canisters fired by the robot, he could see the device at the top of the stairs. As he watched, it fired another smoke canister forward. It landed on the now-burning sofa where Fitzroy had been sitting minutes earlier.

Court didn't see the flying drone now, nor did he hear it, and he knew the smoke would obscure his view of this ground robot in seconds, so he raised his Glock 26. Aiming in on the front of the robot, he fired a perfect shot right between the two cameras there that looked like eyes.

The machine rocked back a few inches, then recovered and swiveled on its rear hip joints, slewing the rifle barrel towards him.

Shit. Court flattened himself on the ground, and the door splintered and shattered above him. He rolled to his left, in the opposite direction of Zoya, who was also flat on the floor, and two more booming gunshots cracked off from the stairs. Books shredded on the shelves, the desk took a direct hit, and then Zoya kicked a foot out to slam the door shut.

He and Zoya stared at each other, just ten feet or so apart. He shrugged. "I take that back. They might be bulletproof."

Zoya said, "We need a plan, Court!"

The buzzing of the hexacopter returned, but this time the sound came from out the window to the courtyard.

As the two of them listened, the gunfire outside stopped, and then the popping and hissing of canisters resumed. At least two more smoke grenades bounced around the great room, and Court knew the black smoke from them combined with the black smoke of the raging curtain and sofa fire would make seeing the enemy utterly impossible for his naked eyes.

Something occurred to him. "It's using a lot of concealment, and it wouldn't be doing that if it wasn't worried about getting shot."

"Meaning?" Fitzroy asked from across the room.

Zoya answered for Court. "Their main housing might be armored against handgun calibers, but there's no way it can carry heavy armor, and the shoulder and hip joints looked exposed to me."

Court added, "We need to just hit them with the right weapon in the right place to take them down."

Zoya shook her head. "But that means taking careful aim, and it will see you before you—"

Court said, "When you don't have time for careful aim, you use a damn shotgun."

She cocked her head. "You got a shotgun in your pants?"

"There's one down at the courtyard, right out this window. And I saw another on a sentry out by the pool. He's probably dead by now." He motioned to the door back to the great room, the only access to the rear of the property. "If we can get to the twelve-gauges and then unload on those things, we might just make it out of here."

Zoya shook her head. "Do I have to remind you there are at least two flying drones out there, too? We've got four enemy that we know of. I might be able to drop to the courtyard, get into the veranda, scoop up the shotgun, and get back inside somewhere, but there's no way you can go out through the great room and make it through those burning curtains, out onto the balcony, and down to that shotgun before you're targeted by one of those machines."

Court thought it over. "You just said it. The curtains are on fire. If the machines can only see with thermals through the smoke, maybe I can use the heat of the fire to mask my movements."

Zoya looked out again to the courtyard; it was completely concealed with smoke now. She said, "I don't have a fire."

"No," he admitted, "you don't. Can you make it?"

She nodded, not entirely confidently.

Court shook his head now. "No, forget it. I'll go for the one in the courtyard."

Now Zoya rose up. "I can do it. There are two ground bots; it's going to take us both."

Court crawled back over to Fitzroy, the hissing sounds of smoke grenades loud behind him in the great room.

"How you doing?" he asked.

Fitzroy's ashen face was smeared with even more blood, his dress shirt soaked red at the neck and shoulder. He'd taken an envelope and a pen and he was in the process of putting the pen in Tudor's right hand.

"Just peachy, lad. Why would you ask?"

Court handed the Glock 26 to Fitzroy. "Here's the deal. I'm gonna have to make a run for better weapons. Out on the balcony, and over the side."

"You're jumping off the balcony?"

"There's a pool down there. Maybe I'll get lucky."

"What do you want me to do?"

"Stop bleeding, preferably," Court said. "And get something out of Tudor."

"Right."

Court turned away and kissed Zoya. She went to the window, looked outside and then up into the night sky. "I'm clear."

Zoya opened the window, looked out, and then kicked her legs over, lowering herself down into the smoke, while Court cracked the door back open, taking in the scene in front of him.

The fire outside had grown; the glowing made its way through the black smoke that rolled into the room through the opening in the door.

He didn't hear footfalls from the ground vehicle, and he thought it likely it was still back by the stairs, scanning the entire area for targets.

Still, stepping out into the great room, surrounded by scalding flames and impenetrable smoke, and potentially into view of a robotic weapon, was a tough ask for his body to comply with.

He forced himself out the door, and then he lowered to his knees and crawled quickly to the right, in the direction of the flames. He got as close as he could before the heat forced him to stop; he imagined he was no more than ten feet away from the raging fire that now continued down the draperies covering the entire length of the eastern floor-to-ceiling windows of the room.

He moved forward, parallel to the flames, in the direction of where he'd last seen the robot targeting him, hoping like hell his assumption that he'd be invisible to infrared cameras in front of a wall of fire was accurate.

He figured he was still easily thirty feet away from the stairs when he stopped his crawl; the heat on his right was almost more than he could bear, but he had to try to find a place in the curtains where the fire had either burned out or dissipated enough for him to run through on his way out to the balcony.

He rose and moved forward a little more. The crackling noise of the flames masked his own footfalls as he stepped on broken glass, and this told him the window had been shattered here by the drone, and though the fire still raged next to him, he thought he could use this area to breach.

He would run through the flames, keep running, and then leap onto the railing and off the back porch, hoping to get at least ten feet away from the balcony so that he'd hit the pool and not the concrete around it.

Just as Court faced the flames and adopted the low stance of a sprinter, through the crackling blaze he was able to make out the buzzing of a large drone outside, somewhere over the balcony.

Fuck, he thought. Another kamikaze. The drone noise drifted off after a few seconds; he thought it went over the roof of the mansion, but he didn't know if it was going to just hover there and wait for a target or if it was heading to the courtyard to dive-bomb Zoya.

Just then, he heard a booming gunshot on the ground floor, and this told him Zoya was engaged or engaging, and he had to get down there, get a shotgun, and then go help her.

With an inhalation of a lungful of smoky air, he bolted directly into the raging fire.

THIRTY-FOUR

Forty-five seconds earlier, Zoya Zakharova had dropped into black smoke and landed on the tile below the library window. Immediately she felt pain in both her knees, and she knew she'd banged them on the stairs earlier as the explosion ripped through the great room.

She ignored her body and began moving, knowing she had no time to waste.

The swirling smoke outside here in the courtyard wasn't as bad as it was inside the great room, but it was heavy nonetheless, and she had to pick her way forward.

With her pistol out in front of her even though she could barely see and had no confidence that a handgun round would seriously impact her adversaries, she made it to the veranda heading east and west and then dropped flat. The dead sentry lay on his back ten feet in front of her, his legs splayed and blood splattering the tile behind his head. A hallway ran off to the right just at his feet, and this was the hall the limping robot had traveled down earlier, so she approached the body carefully.

Lying in the dead man's blood, she reached over his body, took the pistol-grip pump shotgun slung around his neck, and tried to pull it off over his head. Lifting his ruined skull and limp shoulders off the tile, she began scooting the sling out from under the man, but doing this caused the lower torso of the body to move.

Without any warning, an unbearably loud gunshot boomed out of the hall, and the dead man's right foot and ankle were blown off by a high-caliber rifle.

His left leg was hit, as well, and it snapped and shattered the bone there, bits of meat spraying in all directions.

Zoya lurched back, knowing she was out of the line of fire, but only by a couple of feet.

And then she heard the thudding sound of four approaching footfalls, coming from the hallway on her right, and she knew she wouldn't be out of the line of fire for long.

Frantically she lunged again for the shotgun.

Hunter/killer drone Hornet Nine Eight patrolled just a dozen meters directly above the mansion's steeply angled roof; its internal brain was fed data six hundred times per second from all the other integrated units present at the location. Its own camera inputs fueled its processors, as well, and the device scanned straight down towards the balcony, looking for any targets in the billowing black smoke there.

An ISR drone inside the building had turned up no targets on the portions of the second floor it was able to gain access to, so it began heading down a back stairwell, while the other Hornet bot was now in descent, responding to Greyhound One Two's input that a figure had moved on the ground-floor veranda.

Hornet Nine Eight locked on open flames licking out the shattered window below as the fire seemed to move farther out onto the balcony. The drone switched off its infrared camera in favor of night vision, then switched that off as the contrast from the inferno below flared out the camera.

Finally settling on its regular optical camera, the machine focused on the balcony, and in the flames it registered irregular movement as something on fire emerged quickly through the smoke.

With the camera and the computer locked on to the unidentified apparition below, the classifiers in the machine's brain identified the movement as that of a humanoid running while engulfed in flames.

The human in motion had not been designated as a target yet; facial recognition was unable to capture and process the face with all the distortion from the fire and smoke. Nor was the human an obvious threat to the Hornet, so the hunter/killer drone simply tracked the movement as it tried to absorb more data about the unknown subject.

But then, crashing into metal deck chairs in the center of the balcony, not three meters from the railing, the flames dissipated around the upper torso of the figure, and instantly the AI brain on the drone made its identification and its determination.

Target Gama 19 acquired. Prosecute.

The Hornet switched from a patrol hover to terminal attack dive in an instant, and it began rocketing towards the figure below it.

Court's skin seared as he ran. He crashed into heavy furniture but kept his feet and kept moving, knowing he had to get into the pool before he burned to death or was slammed on the head by a warhead-carrying killing machine.

Springing up onto a glass table, he took a second leap, pushing off as hard as he could with his back leg, and then his front foot landed on the top of the railing.

Above him in the air he heard the screaming of propellers, confirming his fear that he'd be targeted by an explosive kill bot. He launched off and out, his skin scalding, and he flailed his arms and legs for distance until he began dropping like a rock.

Court tucked his legs in, covered his head and ears with his arms, and shut his eyes tight.

Impacting headfirst with the surface of the deep end of the swimming pool, he went under, shot down, and his back hit the concrete bottom just as the hunter/killer drone three meters above him slammed into the water's surface.

The bot detonated on impact.

The blast couldn't reach him through the water, but even with his hands over his ears the concussion was stupefying. He felt debris rain down on him, no doubt pieces of the drone and shrapnel from the warhead.

The worst of the burning sensation that had covered his body cooled and melted away almost instantly.

Finding himself to be largely unhurt, he pushed off the bottom of the pool, breaking the water's surface at the eastern side, where he grabbed the edge as he rose.

Court heaved himself up and out of the pool with all his might. Landing feetfirst on the pool edge, he began running towards the area where he'd last seen the sentry with the shotgun, and he quickly found the man, now dead in the sand, his weapon beside him.

Moments earlier, Zoya gave up on getting the sling of the shotgun from around the body, and she instead uncoupled the weapon from the strap with its quick-release buckle. She snatched the pistol-grip 12-gauge, scrambled to her feet, and began running easterly up the veranda, away from the hallway and towards the stairs she and Court had tumbled halfway down just minutes earlier.

Passing the stairs, she heard the unmistakable sound of a large drone descending into the courtyard behind her, and then she heard the massive detonation of an explosive back at the rear of the building out by the pool.

She knew Court had been attempting to get back there, and her heart sank, but she remained on mission. Checking the shotgun to make sure it had a shell in the breech, she entered a large kitchen, clear of the smoke from the courtyard, and here she dropped down to her butt and hid around the side of a large cabinet.

Her low back ached, another injury from rolling down half a circular stairwell.

Zoya's position was only twenty feet or so from where the veranda ran into the kitchen, and she could still hear the buzzing out there above the courtyard.

Through this noise, however, she could also make out the sound of rubberized metal footfalls, moving closer, slightly out of sync.

The wounded robot was approaching up the veranda, passing the dead sentry and heading her way.

Quickly she pulled shells off a sidesaddle on the weapon's frame, then fully loaded the 12-gauge. The pistol-grip shotgun had a vertical fore-end grip on its pump, but it didn't have a stock, so she knew recoil management would be an issue for what she had in mind. She held it out in front of her body with both hands, then rolled up to her knees, still out of view of the approaching robot, and prepared to lean out and empty the weapon into it. She knew she'd have just a fraction of a second before her unmanned opponent returned fire, and all she could do was shoot as quickly and accurately as possible, and hope for the best.

Just as she prepared to act, she heard the unmistakable barking of another shotgun behind her, in the direction of the pool, and to her this meant Court was still alive and in contact with the enemy.

With renewed life she dropped out in front of the veranda entrance to the kitchen, landing on her left shoulder, and she aimed at movement in front of her and fired.

Nine steel pellets, each one .33 inch in diameter, left the barrel of the weapon in Zoya's hands with a muzzle velocity of twelve hundred feet per second. The pattern of the group expanded roughly one inch every yard the pellets traveled downrange, and they slammed into the Q-UGV, striking a six-inch area towards the right front end of the machine.

This knocked the robot off balance; it staggered on its back left leg and collapsed down, but then righted itself quickly and began slewing the rifle by moving its hip joints, aiming back at her.

The recoil of Zoya's unwieldy weapon had been as intense as expected, but she managed it with the brute strength of her arms and shoulders, and she racked the grip of the gun back and then forward, ejecting the smoking expended brass and plastic shell back over her right shoulder and chambering a fresh one in the breech.

She fired again; this time her buckshot hit the right front shoulder of the robot, knocking it fully onto its side. She fought the recoil again, watched the machine struggle to climb back onto its legs, and just as she pressed the trigger a third time, she heard another gunshot, this one coming from upstairs, and then another explosion, as loud as the previous two.

She thought of Sir Donald, alone and wounded in the library, but she tried to concentrate on aiming her weapon again at the right shoulder of the seriously damaged but still potent threat.

Court had scooped up the shotgun lying in the sand by the dead guard, and then he'd spun around, racking a shell as he aimed at the sound of another approaching drone. He fired once, hitting the object just thirty or so feet above him and over the pool. He cowered from the expected detonation, but the device just spun wildly and crashed into the sand over his right shoulder.

He quickly realized he'd just removed one of the enemy's ISR platforms, not a weaponized machine.

And he also realized he'd given his position away. The robot on the second floor would now likely either be coming for him or for Fitzroy, because he could hear that Zoya had made it to the shotgun in the courtyard and was now engaging the other ground robot somewhere in the house, dumping shell after shell into it.

And in the middle of her firing he heard a handgun crack on the second floor and then, almost simultaneously, an enormous explosion.

Court began running for the house as fast as his legs would take him, his shotgun's rubberized stock tight against his shoulder, its barrel waving ahead as he moved.

Zoya fired her fifth and last shell; her ears rung and she knew they would continue ringing for hours, and her head throbbed from the noise and the stress, but she fought through the disorientation and climbed back up to her position behind the shelving unit. Her pistol was in the small of her back and she pulled it, dropping the hot and smoking but now useless shotgun as she did so, then she ran around the far end of the shelves into the center of the kitchen.

Here she entered a dining room through a large stone archway and sprinted through it, and in seconds she found herself in the covered north-south hallway that ran into the veranda near where she'd pulled the gun off the dead man, and that meant she would come out of the hallway directly behind the wounded robot.

She did this carefully and aimed her weapon, but she found the robot completely on its side; both of its right legs had been ripped off by five shotgun blasts—forty-five double-aught pellets had created a mobility kill, at least, but she didn't know if the machine remained powered and operational.

A row of lights on the roof of the meter-long-by-half-meter-wide machine flickered, giving her the answer. She saw movement in the two remaining legs as it vainly tried to right itself or to aim its weapon, but the machine's big gun barrel faced into the kitchen, away from her as she approached quickly from behind.

Zoya moved confidently at first, but then realized that with the ringing in her ears she'd have no way to hear the sound of more attacking drones. She advanced more quickly and found herself kneeling just behind the device, and then she noticed a thick cluster of wires exposed from where a portion of the side housing of the robot had been ripped away. She pulled them, and they came out of the machine and took a broken piece of a plastic motherboard with them.

The lights on the roof went off, and then she looked around, up on her knees still.

Suddenly a bright beam flashed on her from the kitchen; she raised her pistol at it, squinting into the blaze.

The light extinguished, and she rubbed her eyes. Seconds later she saw movement in the darkness, but before she fired at it, she realized it was a person.

Court Gentry appeared in front of her and helped her to her feet.

She shouted to him, "I can't hear a fucking thing!"

He nodded, then took her hand and put her fingers in his waistband at his back. Turning away from her, he headed for the helical stairs, flashing his shotgun's undermounted flashlight intermittently as he advanced to help guide them through the thick smoke.

THIRTY-FIVE

Quadrupedal Unmanned Ground Vehicle Greyhound One One had expended all of its gas canisters, and its infrared cameras were still hampered by the remnants of the now diminishing fire that had been burning up here in the great room. Using its optical cam, it had made its way to the door, where it had taken a single round of gunfire, and then more shots were registered by one of the Hornet hunter/killer drones in the courtyard shortly before it went offline, so the machine's brain had calculated that a target was behind the door, though the data from its onboard brain as well as the other units on the property were unable to determine if the target had been killed by the detonation of the second Hornet.

Greyhound One One shifted its hips lower and to the right, slewing the barrel of the 6.5-millimeter Creedmoor at the top door hinge, and then it fired a single round that blew the hinge off.

It ejected the spent casing out of a port on the right side of the turret, cycled a fresh round into the chamber, and then shifted aim to the lower left hinge and fired again.

The door fell into the library.

Again Greyhound One One cycled a fresh round into its chamber and began walking forward into the room.

. . .

Court and Zoya arrived at the top of the stairs as the second gunshot rang out at the far end of the smoke-filled great room near the door to the library. They moved forward a few feet together, and then Court realized the flames from the curtains and sofa had mostly burned out, and any machine using an infrared camera would likely be able to pick up the heat signatures of humans.

Quickly he took Zoya's hand out of his waistband and left her there, then ran at a sprint through the darkness. He thought it likely he'd be shot by the remaining four-legged robot while rushing to get to Don Fitzroy, and he didn't want Zoya to die along with him.

Recon drone RC83 finished its sweep of the first floor and then went back up the circular stairwell, following the data fed it by Greyhound One One that suggested a target remained on the second floor.

It shot out into the smoke, saw the heat signature of a person there in the middle of the room, but raced past the form when it saw a second figure running at a sprint towards the Greyhound's location to the south.

The ISR drone slowed and came to a stop as the infrared camera saw the figure halt suddenly, then raise its arms up in front of its face.

The blast of a shotgun showed up as a glowing red flash on the thermal. A second flash and then a third came quickly, and then the figure dropped the weapon and moved into the library.

The data feed from Q-UGV Greyhound One One ended abruptly as the datalink was broken with the destruction of the machine.

RC83 advanced slowly now. It had no weapon, just a camera, and there were no more Hornet drones or Greyhound bots left to prosecute targets. Still, the machine knew that its job was to identify who was still alive. Its onboard brain told it to check the room where the ground bot had been destroyed, then regress back into the great room to identify the figure it had just passed.

At the threshold to the library the fourteen-inch-diameter machine hovered five feet above the tile; it cycled its cameras, settling on an optical view because the smoke was less dense in here.

It took in the scene carefully, sending the images via satellite link to Contreras's aircraft monitors a mile away as well as other locations, and its gaze fixed on Target Gama 19, Courtland Gentry, and a person facial recognition had already identified as Sir Donald Fitzroy.

Gentry was on his feet and Fitzroy was on the floor by the window, his body lying motionless.

Gentry turned to look directly at the machine, so RC83 spun out of the doorway and turned around to return to the great room.

Carlos Contreras looked at the feed from the one surviving platform at the hacienda. He saw the old man on the floor by the window, unmoving; he saw Gentry standing over him, then turning with a pistol in his hand. Gentry stared directly into the camera's lens, and then the image shifted quickly, no doubt because the artificial intelligence operating RC83 registered Gentry as a threat and it was trying to get away.

The machine spun back into the great room, but instantly Contreras cried out and leapt to his feet.

Just three feet in front of the camera as it turned around he saw the target Zakharova holding a pistol over her head, upside down like a hammer.

She swung at the camera, Contreras saw a flash, and then the drone went offline.

The Mexican sat back down slowly, his hands on his head in shock.

Just seconds later the SkyCourier increased power and began a climbing turn to starboard, taking it out over the ocean.

Contreras got the impression the pilot had been given orders to vacate the area within two or three seconds of the destruction of the last platform at the hacienda, and the speed of this order astonished him.

Slowly he began powering down his laptops and stowing them in bags, his heart still pounding because of all that had happened, all that he'd seen, and all that he'd just learned.

. . .

Court Gentry turned away from the drone Zoya had just bashed onto the floor and then stomped on, and he looked back to Fitzroy, slumped against the wall in the corner next to the open window, and ten feet or so away from Jack Tudor's still form by the desk.

Court knelt over Fitzroy, began reaching down to check his pulse, but then the big man moved, and he spoke, blood still dripping from his face. "You get them all, lad?"

Court smiled. "Holy shit, Fitz! You're alive?"

With effort the Englishman fought his way to a half-prone, half-sitting position against the wall. "Despite my best efforts. I was bloody ready to go out in a blaze of glory."

"And instead, you're just bloody."

Fitz sniffed.

Zoya moved up next to Court; she, too, was relieved to find Fitzroy animated. She said, "I heard an explosion."

Fitzroy jerked a hand towards the window, and both Zoya and Court ducked a little, because the Glock pistol was still in the man's hand and his motion waved it in their direction. "Oh . . . sorry," he said, handing the gun off to Court. "I looked out this window when I heard a drone. There it was, flying right over the fountain and heading down towards the veranda."

Zoya said, "I was in the kitchen then. It was probably coming for me."

"Right. Well, I shot the bugger out of the bloody sky, didn't I?" He touched his face and confirmed he was still bleeding from a half-dozen cuts there. "Caught some of the blast from up here, but it didn't take me out."

Court now began checking Tudor's pulse, though the man's eyes were open and unfixed.

"Don't bother, lad. Jack's free of this mortal coil."

"He say anything?" Court asked, doubtful he'd get a satisfying answer.

"He wrote down two words." Fitzroy looked up at Court now, over to Zoya, and he flashed a sly smile. "Martina Sommer."

"Holy shit," Zoya said. "The German asset in Singapore?"

"Yes. Now, someone please help me up."

Court and Zoya both did so; Fitzroy was in considerable pain.

Zoya hugged him. "I'm glad you're alive."

Fitzroy shrugged. He seemed irritated by his survival. "Always dreamed of a valiant death. When am I going to get that opportunity again?"

Court answered this as he again looked out the window. "In about two minutes if we don't get the fuck out of here, so stop feeling sorry for yourself for surviving and let's go."

They helped Fitzroy along, his broken ribs slowing the process markedly, and then he said, "You know, if I'd died tonight, you wouldn't be so bloody rude to me."

Court said, "The girls need their grandfather as long as they can keep him."

Fitzroy smiled back. "You're right, lad." He began to reach into his coat, but when Court turned away and walked over to Zoya, he just followed along.

Court said, "We can't drive out of here. We have to walk on the beach to the north until we get to the hotel zone."

Zoya agreed; they raised their weapons and began heading back for the stairs.

Twenty minutes later the three of them were half a mile to the north of the mansion, walking through sand and seagrass, leaving the sound of dozens of sirens behind. Fitzroy had called his team of Portuguese security officers with orders to secure a car by any means necessary and then come down from Soliman Bay to collect them, and the bright glow of lights to the north told them they were just minutes away from blending in with the foreign tourists of the Tulum Zona Hotelera.

Zoya and Court both walked with limps. The adrenaline had left their bodies, and now they felt the myriad aches and pains of falling down stairs, scrambling and tumbling and fighting for their lives. Court had the additional discomfort of first-degree burns on his hands and face, though in the low light of the moonlit beach he wasn't able to see how badly he'd been singed.

Fitzroy, even with what he suspected to be multiple cracked ribs low on his right side, and dozens of cuts on his head, face, and neck, somehow seemed to be in the best shape of the three, at least when he was moving upright, not turning left or right. Court had warned him that if he felt the need to cough he should stifle it, because coughing with broken ribs could drop him to the ground in agony.

They moved mostly in silence, but finally Court said, "That was damn good work back there, Fitz. Getting Tudor to give up the name of his agent."

"Wasn't hard. For me, I mean. He was on his last gasp, I could see it, so I begged him for the woman's name, and I promised him you'd use it to avenge his death."

"I'll do just that. At least we got something out of this night."

The Englishman reached into a trouser pocket, took out a plastic bottle, and downed a couple of orange pills.

"What's that?" Court asked.

Fitzroy put the pill bottle back in his trousers.

Zoya spoke up in the dark as they woke. "Jesus, Court. You don't have to answer that, Don. I'm sorry, Court wasn't assigned manners by the CIA."

Court was confused. He looked to Zoya. "What did I say?"

Fitzroy answered. "Parkinson's, as I'm sure you gathered, young lady. The levodopa helps for a while, now anyway. This time next year, unfortunately, I won't be able to say the same."

They all walked in silence a moment. Zoya put her arm around Fitzroy. Finally she said, "I'm sorry."

"Don't be. I'm living on my terms, as long as I can. It's a bloody shame about Jack, but I am glad I was here to help my two friends."

After a minute Zoya reached into her back pocket and pulled out the broken piece of motherboard she'd taken out of the first ground vehicle. She said, "I pulled this from the robot downstairs after I killed it. Maybe we can find someone who can trace the components."

Court said, "All I got was a sunburn." He took the piece and held it up to the moonlight as he walked. "I know just who to call about that."

Zoya looked at him for a moment, then sighed a little. "Lacy at CIA?"

"Yeah."

"And then what? It's not like she can just reveal the fact that the Gray Man called her with intelligence about the technology killings. She's going to have some explaining to do."

Court had already considered this. "Matt Hanley."

"Hanley? What about him?"

"If Lacy can put me in contact with Hanley, I'll give the motherboard and the information to him. He'll be able to slip it to someone, no questions asked. He's done stuff like that before."

"You said he was somewhere in the South Pacific."

"Last I heard. Lacy will know."

Fitzroy looked back and forth between the two. Instead of commenting on their conversation, he said, "My aircraft is in Cozumel, just a helo ride over the water from where I'm staying here. You can take the plane wherever you need to go." He winced again as he walked. "I myself am going to go to a hospital in Cozumel tomorrow to get all this looked at. I'll just tell them I slipped at the pool into a glass coffee table after imbibing too many margaritas."

"Yeah," Court said, "they wouldn't believe you if you told them what just happened."

"Nor would I, lad."

THIRTY-SIX

The faintest of glows of an emerging dawn appeared over the Cuban pines in the east, causing the runner on the lonely dark road to glance down at his watch.

Six twenty-three a.m. A couple minutes off his ideal ten-kilometer pace, but he'd not run more than five klicks at a time in several weeks, so he wasn't disappointed.

Zack Hightower kept his stride steady through the pine forest, emerging from it and onto a rolling canvas of cultivated fields. To his left and right were rice paddies, and a plantain farm on a hill just to the north blocked his view of the early-morning lights of Havana.

A few minutes later he was out of the open fields and back into dense forest.

Zack had had the morning to himself, but now, just after six thirty, he began seeing a smattering of farmers on bikes and on foot as they headed to their jobs.

He carried a tiny Ruger LCP MAX .380 pistol in a belly band holster that he'd checked out of the armory at La Finca, but he didn't feel like he was going to need it, because the locals here seemed to be no threat at all. He didn't pass a man, woman, or child who did not wave, smile, or extend a greeting in Spanish.

The people loved Hinton, and by association, they seemed to love the big and muscular blond gringo with the pointy beard, as well.

He passed Kimmie Lin, Anton Hinton's assistant, waving at her as she ventured out on her own predawn run.

At six forty Zack passed the pair of stone pillboxes at the entrance to La Finca, Hinton's massive property just southwest of his lab at the campus. Whereas they had been empty when he'd arrived here in Cuba yesterday, now they were occupied by at least four soldiers, obviously because Hinton was now on the property.

They waved to him, he waved back, and then he glanced down at his watch again, pleased to see that he'd made up a little time on the back half of his 10K.

Soon he picked up the pace even more as he ran through the manicured lawns and gardens in front of the blast doors, passing Cuban special forces men sitting in vehicles and on camp chairs by a fire pit. Unlike the regular infantry at the perimeter, the Black Wasps at the front of the place paid him little attention; they'd seen him leave forty-five minutes earlier, and he'd been cleared to go wherever he wanted on the property by Señor Wren, but they weren't going to get chummy with him.

Zack had been assigned his own share of shitty sentry postings in the Navy, and he didn't begrudge these hard-ass dudes for being annoyed that they had to sit around all day and night protecting a bunch of rich gringos.

He made it back into his room at ten till seven, showered and changed, and by seven ten he was in the cafeteria being served up a massive plate of sausage, fried green plantains, and pastries filled with cream cheese and guava paste. Fresh orange juice and black coffee were placed on his tray next, and then he went looking for his team among the dozens of computer engineers, logistics personnel, and security seated at various six-top tables around the large concrete room, chowing down.

He found the four former Black Wasps officers who were his close-protection employees here, and together they discussed the details of this morning's plan, a seven-car convoy movement to the campus that would last less than ten minutes.

All four of the ex–special forces guys spoke English, which was handy, because Zack's Spanish knowledge had been centered on cervezas and señoritas, and this had not proved helpful on his last visit to Latin America, when he got his ass kicked in Caracas and then was thrown into a Venezuelan prison.

He endeavored to speak slowly and clearly and in English while here in Cuba, and he hoped that would help him stay out of any trouble that he wasn't paid to get into.

Forty-five minutes after he sat down for breakfast, just after eight a.m., Zack Hightower stood bare-chested and in cargo pants in his room as he pulled his big Staccato XC 9-millimeter out of its appendix holster, dropped the twenty-round magazine and then slapped it back in, and checked to make certain a twenty-first round was ready in the chamber. Reholstering, he hooked a loaded triple-mag pouch on the left side of his belt, offering him a round count of eighty-one hard-hitting Federal HST high-power 124 grain ammunition stashed on his body and ready for immediate use.

The little Ruger pistol slipped into an ankle holster he affixed just above the Origin Coronado boot on his right foot, and then he covered it with his khaki cargo pants.

Two folding knives went into his pockets, one on the left and one on the right.

He grabbed a white guayabera shirt off the back of a chair and put it on, smoothing it out so it covered his handgun and extra mags. Checking himself in the mirror, he adjusted his hair a little, formed his beard into a fine point, then slipped a pair of Oakley sunglasses in his breast pocket.

An earpiece went in his right ear, attached by a wire to a radio clipped on his belt at the seven-o'clock position, and his mobile phone went into a back pocket.

Lastly, Zack hefted a polymer-stocked AK-47 rifle from where it leaned in the corner of the room, and he slung it around his back. The rifle was for the convoy work; he wouldn't have to lug it around all day, but if they were attacked on the road, he knew he needed something that could reach out and touch someone at distance with the power of a 7.62 round.

Two extra thirty-round mags, curved like bananas, went into the side pockets of his cargo pants, and then Zack left the room, locking the door behind him.

Outside in the bright morning sun, Zack and his men waited by the row of four vehicles. A secondary mobile security unit composed of six active-duty Black Wasps would travel with the motorcade over the three klicks of highways and back roads that would take them around farms and forests to the campus, and Zack and his four men discussed the day's planned movement with them.

At eight fifteen a.m., Gareth Wren stepped out through the big steel blast doors dressed in jeans and a fitted blue polo shirt, as well as the HK handgun he now wore on his right hip. Behind him, Kimmie Lin came out in a light blue pantsuit; an oversized purse hung from her shoulder, and she pulled her rolling bag through the door and then down the walkway through the garden there. She greeted Zack, asking him if he enjoyed his morning run, and soon she was followed by several members of lab staff, men and women from all over the world, all wearing casual clothes, and all carrying backpacks or messenger bags.

Finally, Anton Hinton himself emerged. He wore a white tracksuit striped in red, his bright red headphones sat over his ears, and he had a massive oversized watch that gleamed in the sun.

Anton also wore a large multi-cam-colored bulletproof vest that protected both his chest and his back, and in his hand he carried a thick book that Zack couldn't make out.

Hinton was all smiles this morning, but quickly Zack turned away from him. It wasn't Zack's job to watch his protectee as the man walked through the grounds on his way to his Sprinter van. Instead, he kept his eyes on the other security men, the mobile guys who would be coming along with them as well as the static detail protecting the grounds. He didn't know any of these assholes, and as near as he could tell, they were the only potential threats to his protectee out here.

Hinton wished Zack a good morning as he headed towards the Sprinter, and as he passed, the American realized the New Zealand native was carrying a copy of the Qur'an.

The convoy rolled out at eight thirty sharp; the sky was perfectly clear, the temperature already in the low eighties, and Zack was switched on, scanning the fields and forests and roads ahead, and in constant radio contact with the four English-speaking men working for him, dispersed in the convoy near the active-duty men, none of whom spoke Zack's native tongue.

The drive was amazingly short; it seemed they just left the western gate of La Finca, drove south around that property, then looped back to the north, skirting around a few fields and clusters of dense forest, before passing a three-meter-high concrete wall topped with razor wire on their left. The wall was a quarter mile long, and then the convoy turned to the west and approached the University of Information Science from the north.

A cluster of Cuban military vehicles sat parked at the front gate, and the American eyed the uniforms, ages, and equipment of the soldiers as he passed them by. He determined that they were all basic Cuban Revolutionary Armed Forces infantry, not members of the Black Wasps. Still, the AKs on their chests and the Russian-manufactured machine guns mounted on their trucks would certainly dissuade most if not all external threats to this facility.

Zack and the entourage drove through the rusty metal gate entrance, passing a fence topped with thick coils of razor wire, and at first the American thought there must have been some mistake. A sign read "Universidad de las Ciencias Informáticas," and several Cuban flags hung down from the roofs of buildings, but there was no indication that one of the wealthiest and preeminent creators of artificial intelligence had a facility here. Several of the buildings they passed were ugly but sturdy Soviet construction, low concrete blocks or red brick, blast resistant, with small windows, nothing more than three stories high.

Soon they rolled by an electrical power plant, which was located inside the fence line of the property with its own fence and guard force protecting it. The towers and cables and buildings all looked new. They passed a small hospital, several more buildings, a little more advanced-looking than those on the outskirts, and many, many more Cuban flags, seemingly draped off every structure on the huge campus.

A massive structure flew by off Zack's right shoulder as they rumbled south. The building looked like it could withstand a nuclear attack; it had five separate wings made of poured concrete that jutted out to the east side from the center like the spokes of a wheel that had been cut in half.

But its main feature was on its roof. Rows of massive satellite dishes, all broken and obviously out of commission, pointed in different directions towards the sky, presumably where Russian satellites had been when the place went dark over twenty years earlier.

Zack realized he recognized the structure from images he'd seen in the past. This was the headquarters building of the old Lourdes Signals Intelligence base, ground central for all Cuban and Russian spying in the Americas.

Just like the entire campus they'd rolled into, the old SIGINT HQ had its own fence, and behind it weeds grew around the derelict-looking old building.

The motorcade parked at the edge of a large green space in the center of the complex just a block away. Zack filed out first, his AK slung at his front, and through his radio mic he ordered the rest of his team to dismount before any of the civilians did.

The square was relatively quiet, but a couple dozen or so people walking around stopped to look at the entourage. They appeared to be students heading to and from class, but Zack eyed them closely nonetheless.

Hinton and Wren emerged together from the Sprinter van a moment later, and they began walking towards a modern three-story blue building with lots of glass that appeared to be almost brand-new, right in the center of the more worn structures. Zack shouldered up to his protectee; the four other men on the detail formed a diamond position around them, and Gareth Wren led the way.

Zack scanned rooftops, windows, the alleys between the buildings.

As he walked alongside, Anton took off his headphones. "Yeah, the campus isn't much to look at from the outside, I admit. But I've got a world-class research facility filled with great people here." He waved to a pair of Asian men in their forties wearing glasses and short-sleeved shirts standing near the entrance to the blue building. Zack pegged them as engineers or computer scientists.

Anton said, "We're modernizing the campus itself; the south side of the property is starting to come together, but the campus is overall still a bit of a dump from the outside. It was built in the early sixties, and it wasn't like the Soviets or the Cubans cared much about aesthetics."

Anton stopped to shake hands with a cluster of employees standing outside taking a smoke break, and Zack kept an eye on his charge but also used the opportunity to address Wren.

"That power station we passed looks new."

"Went online about six months ago. We've got underground power from a substation about three miles away, and that is connected to a powership."

"What's a powership?"

"A floating power plant in Havana Harbor. It's from Turkey; they worked out a deal with the Cubans to anchor it here to give the nation more reliable power."

"In return for what?"

Wren shrugged. "I honestly don't know. Anton pays for the wattage that comes to us, but he and I were both pleasantly surprised when the Cubans didn't come to us to pay for the bloody ship itself. We also pay to draw power from a hydroelectric dam about twelve miles east.

"Also," he added, "on the south side of the campus we have thirty-five diesel-burning generators. There's a fuel storage facility, as well, so we have enough diesel to keep the facility operational for ninety days if we lose all other sources of power."

"Seems like a lot of trouble for a research facility," Zack said as Anton wrapped up his conversation.

Softly, Wren said, "Agree one hundred percent. If this facility were in Switzerland or Seoul or San Jose or Boston, places where everybody else has their computer research campuses, then we wouldn't have to worry about it. But Anton's paranoia about the intentions of the West, and the recent dustup in his relationship with the Chinese, have made Cuba his safe haven."

THIRTY-SEVEN

Soon they passed through a door held open by a pair of security men who appeared to be Cuban and former members of the military's special operations force, and once inside, Zack was immediately stunned by its incongruity with most of the rest of the university campus. An atrium lobby rose the height of the building, and massive skylights brought natural light into the open space.

The floors of the expansive lobby were beautifully marbled, the temperature cool and the lighting soft and peaceful. As in Anton's luxury van, serene sound waves purred in the air.

Zack felt as if he'd just walked into the offices of a Fortune 500 company in Silicon Valley, not through the doors of a sixty-year-old Russian-built spy complex in Cuba.

Hinton stepped up next to Zack and pulled off his headphones. "You get it now?"

"Got it, boss." He did *not* get it, not really. This place should be in Cali or Boston or Switzerland, just like Wren said, but the guy signing his checks wanted it this way, and Zack wasn't about to argue.

While Hinton went to shake hands with staffers there in the lobby, Zack unslung his AK, put it in a locker behind the desk, then opened his jacket to show the guards the pistol on his waist. He didn't lift his pants to reveal his ankle gun, but they waved him through on Wren's bidding, and soon everyone was in the elevators and heading up.

Hinton dropped his messenger bag off in his beautiful office, took a cup of matcha tea handed to him by a Cuban administrative assistant of the campus, then hugged the lady when she told him she'd been praying for his safe return to Cuba after all the troubles going on in the world.

Gareth Wren had ducked into his own office to drop off his bag, but now he was back out in Anton's small lobby, standing next to Zack while Anton sat down at his desk.

"Give me about five," Anton said, "then we'll go down to the labs and talk to the troops." Hinton put his headphones back on and turned his attention to his keyboard.

One of Zack's security team stood at Anton's door, his hands clasped and facing the office.

Wren said, "Frederico's got this under control. Let's get some coffee."

Wren led Zack to a coffee tray on a table in the hall outside his office, and they both poured and drank tiny cups of cafecito while they toured the third-floor office area.

As promised, five minutes after he sat down, Anton emerged from his office, and together he, Gareth Wren, and Zack, flanked by two of the four former Black Wasps, headed back to the elevator and down to the second floor.

Here Zack found room after room, all glass-walled and brightly lit, full of men and women working at computer stations in small teams, usually composed of two, three, or four engineers.

They spent hours going from lab to lab throughout the floor, and at every stop it was the same. Hinton sat with his staff, they talked about their worries, they talked about some of the people who had died, and they speculated as to what this was all about.

Some of the researchers knew Tomer Basch, many of them knew Lars Halverson, and it seemed like all of them knew a guy named Maxim Arsenov, though this name was not familiar to Zack.

They talked about the women in Japan and Korea who'd been killed, and Rene Descourts and a few other names Zack hadn't even heard before, giving him the impression that the killings had not yet stopped.

Zack saw that Hinton was well liked by his people, but he didn't get a sense he was doing much work here today. Instead, he seemed like he saw it as his job to buoy the spirits of his team in the wake of all the murders.

When actual work was discussed, Zack found it too arcane to follow. Several researchers explained to Anton something about some coding they'd discovered in the cloud that none of them had seen before, and they speculated that this one piece of code could be used, in theory, to animate a weapon. Hinton speculated that the code might have been a remnant of a top-secret DARPA project called Mind Game that had made it out into the world.

DARPA, Zack knew, was the Defense Advanced Research Projects Agency, a U.S. Department of Defense arm where new technologies were developed.

Hinton's theory that this code was American-made and perhaps the Chinese had stolen it to make the new AI weapon everyone feared was passionately presented to his researchers, but Zack didn't understand the first word of what he was explaining about neural networks and training and classification algorithms.

Zack tuned it all out after a while.

Midafternoon they broke for lunch, and Anton asked Zack to sit with him and Wren in the cafeteria.

"What do you think, Zack?"

With a little smile he said, "I think you should wear your body armor even when you're inside, so maybe you shouldn't ask me what I think."

The New Zealander said, "These people are my friends and trusted co-workers. They aren't going to hurt me. I am going to keep my people looking at this mystery code out there, to try to find some fingerprints on it that will lead us in the right direction. Whatever direction."

Zack said, "I didn't hear anyone today talk about a weapon. It was all about software. Isn't the big fear that this software will be weaponized?"

"It is."

"But weaponized with *what*?"

"Our problem here," Anton confessed, "is that we aren't the military robot people. We're the artificial intelligence people. Brains, not brawn. Tomer Basch and Lars Halverson and Rene Descourts and even Rick Watt, they knew what was out there in the military landscape."

He shrugged. "We're the computer nerds. We'll develop the code, and we don't involve ourselves with lethal autonomous weapons. If you leave the entire kill chain up to the machines, machines that can process tens of millions of data points in a few milliseconds, then there is no place for a human being on the loop. It simply moves too fast."

Zack said, "If you are so worried about artificial intelligence being used for evil . . . why do you and your people continue to develop AI?"

Hinton smiled, then took a bite of his salad. "Let me put it to you this way, Zack. Fire."

"Fire?"

"Yeah, fire. Is it good or bad?"

Zack didn't like riddles, but he thought a moment. "I guess if I'm cold and in the woods, it's great."

Hinton said, "But if your house is on fire, then it's bloody horrible, yeah?"

"Yeah."

"There you go. We are building the right AI, we are seeking out peaceful uses, we are working on a better future. We are the fire that warms you at night, that cooks your food, that lights your way. Others . . . others are the fire that tears across the forest towards your house, sending furry creatures running for their lives.

"If we shuttered everything today, and all these scientists and engineers went on to some other line of work, then AI would just be the burning forest, not the beacon of hope."

Zack nodded and ate his meal. He thought the man was weird, but he also thought him to be charming as hell.

Finally, he said, "That guy, Arsenov. The one everyone was talking about today. Who was he?"

"He was killed in Mexico City the other day. He worked for me."

"An engineer?"

Hinton nodded. "Brilliant bloke. Quite liked him. He went on vacation the day all this madness began, died the next."

"Was he one of the people you think America would have to kill to stop the Chinese from creating their weapon?"

At this, Anton Hinton hesitated. He bit a fingernail as he looked off into the distance. "Actually, no. He was an excellent engineer, but he wasn't a groundbreaking developer. The only thing I can reckon is they killed him because he worked for me, and all the others who worked for me are living in a bunker in Cuba."

Zack said, "Well, whoever is doing this . . . we need to continue working under the assumption that they will try again. I think we have to limit your movements to La Finca and the lab."

Anton started to respond, but then his phone vibrated in his pocket. He checked it, then put his phone down and closed his eyes.

"What is it?" Gareth Wren asked.

"Amir Kumar was murdered this morning."

Wren put his fork down, reached out, and squeezed Anton on the forearm. "Bloody hell, mate."

Zack sat quietly. After several seconds, Hinton looked up to him. "The world's most preeminent electromagnetic scientist. Very involved in the development of the movement of large amounts of data from place to place. A bloody brilliant man, and a friend."

"I'm sorry" was all Zack could say, but it was his inclination to grab Hinton by the neck, drag him down to a bomb shelter, and keep him locked there until this entire affair was over.

Wren said, "That makes . . . what . . . thirteen murders? In four days?"

Hinton just nodded. He looked depressed, but more than depressed. He looked utterly stricken.

Zack said, "You want to call it a day, Anton? Head back to La Finca?"

The man's head seemed to clear, and then he looked up. "No. I want to get back to work."

He rose from the table, headed back towards the elevators, and Zack stayed behind, turning to Wren. "How late will we be here today?"

Wren was distracted. He seemed almost as upset as Hinton, but eventually he shook it off. With a shrug he said, "Could be five o'clock, could be ten."

"Ten?" Zack exclaimed.

"Yeah, he doesn't keep normal hours."

"Why am I not surprised?" Zack muttered as the pair headed towards the elevator to catch up with Hinton.

At Operations Center Gama in the Singapore Science Park, the director stepped into the auditorium wearing his gray suit, a red tie, and a freshly shaved face. He'd been getting about four hours of sleep a day for the past week, but he'd been somewhat refreshed with a shower in his quarters and some food delivered downstairs and brought up by the security staff.

And now it was time for the director to get back to work. Their next operation was in the terminal phase now; the kinetic action by the assets on the ground would commence within the hour.

His intercom beeped on his desk; he didn't have his earpiece in yet, so he tapped the button to open the line. "Yes?"

"Sir? It's Fifteen. Can I speak with you?" It was the French controller of the asset in the Americas.

The director didn't want to hear from Fifteen right now; he wanted all his focus to be on his next hit, but he told her he'd come speak to her. He put down the phone and climbed up to her cubicle at the back of the small auditorium.

As he passed the controller from India and approached the controller from France, he noticed that the desk of the controller from Germany was empty.

"Where is Fourteen?" he asked the French woman.

"That's why I called you, sir. I went to her room last night to return some headphones she loaned me, and she wasn't there. I didn't think anything of it, but she didn't come to breakfast or lunch, either. I know we haven't been using her drone pilot in the Americas, but I assume she should still be at her desk, no?"

The director didn't respond. Instead, he turned and headed to the closest security man, a stone-faced Asian in his fifties who stood at the rear auditorium double doors.

Approaching, he saw the officer's eyes continuing to scan the room, without locking on the director's eyes.

"Good morning," the director said, trying to get his attention. The security officer did not turn his head, he just kept scanning. "One of my staff is not here. It's possible she's been missing since last night."

The man shook his head. "She is not missing."

"What . . . what do you mean?"

Now the man turned his way. "Talk to Cyrus."

The pair held their gaze for a long moment, and then the director turned away and began heading down the stairs to his workstation.

He had a very bad feeling about this, but he pushed as much worry out of his mind as he could, and then he typed in his message box, asking Cyrus if he knew where his employee was.

There was a short delay, and then the answer came. **Fourteen left last night because of a personal issue at home.**

The director had been here in the ops center till after three a.m. If Fourteen had to leave her post, why had she not come to him, and why had neither security nor Cyrus made any mention of it? He didn't ask this question; instead, he typed out an interrogative.

Will she be replaced?

Unnecessary. Drone Pilot Zero One has been paid and is no longer operational.

Understood. His fingers hovered over the keyboard. He had so many questions right now. Probably ten of his staff were done with their aspect of the mission, yet they all remained at their desk in case any new targets popped up. What had happened to Fourteen?

He felt protective of his staff, even though he didn't even know their names. Fourteen was his responsibility.

But, ultimately, he didn't push it. Fourteen was gone, and that was that.

He stood up and addressed the room. "Fourteen has returned home to deal with a family emergency."

The director went back to his desk a moment later, all but certain he had not told the truth, but also certain it was his job to do what Cyrus told him to do.

THIRTY-EIGHT

The sixty-foot trawler had appeared on the horizon well before dawn this morning, only visible in the darkness to the crew of the forty-foot open-deck fishing boat several miles to the north after someone in the trawler's pilot house flashed a light on and off three times, the agreed-upon signal.

The fishing boat had set off from the little coastal town of Pilón, Cuba, a half hour prior, and it was already several miles offshore when the crew saw the lights and adjusted their heading accordingly.

The trawler had come up from Port Maria, on Jamaica's northern coast, and the seventy-five-mile overnight journey had been difficult for the passengers of the vessel, though the crew was more than used to the waves, the cramped conditions, and the ever-present danger of life on the sea.

After twenty minutes both vessels began to converge, well south of the Cuban coastline so marine radar on the southeastern portion of the island wouldn't pick up the contacts, and eventually the trawler and the fishing boat came to within fifty meters of each other. The seas were far from calm, but both captains had seen much worse, so the go-ahead was given to the trawler's passengers, and they loaded into a rigid-hull inflatable boat they'd been towing and set out towards the Cuban vessel.

A few minutes later the pilot of the RIB had returned his craft to the trawler, the boat from Jamaica turned back to the south, and the Cuban fishing boat began heading back to shore, engines blasting at full power.

The new arrivals were a half dozen hard-eyed men, each carrying a backpack, and they sat on the deck, searching the predawn ocean for any potential danger.

The crew of the fishing vessel didn't know it, but the six Black men were gangsters from the Spangler Posse, Jamaica's most notorious criminal organization, and they'd been hired to do a job on the other side of Cuba, up near Havana.

But the crew of the fishing vessels were no fools. These Jamaicans were criminals, plain and simple, and they easily discerned that.

Away from the all-inclusive resorts full of fat and happy tourists, the island of Jamaica itself is a violent place, suffering a homicide rate ten times that of the United States, which has a homicide rate five times that of the European Union. And within Jamaica, there are hot pockets with exceptionally horrific crime statistics. The Kingston parish of St. James, for example, has a homicide rate some thirty times higher than that of the United States, one hundred fifty times that of Europe, and from this neighborhood these six men had set off the night before, boarding the trawler, sailing around the southeastern tip of their nation, then hitting the open water as they sailed north.

Thirty-five minutes after climbing into the fishing boat, the Cubans and Jamaicans landed on a spit of land west of the town of Pilón, and here they were met by the driver of a school bus who, just like the boat captain, had been paid in cash by a cutout in a bar in nearby Manzanillo just the day before.

The bus driver asked no questions as the six men vomited in the sand, then recovered enough to load their heavy backpacks and climb onto his vehicle, and the six asked nothing of him as he drove off to the northwest shortly before eight a.m.

The roads across central Cuba are slow going, and they did not arrive at their safe house till after eight in the evening. Here they ate rations they'd brought along from home, checked their equipment, pulled several bottles of rum out of their packs, and had a few drinks while they waited for a signal.

It had been a long day, and it would be a difficult night, but the money offered to each of these men for this evening of work had been orders of magnitude more than what they would make with the Spangler Posse in a year, so to a man they'd agreed.

Conducting a job in the locked-down and oppressive nation of Cuba, even if they didn't actually understand the job, was more than worth the risk for this group of grizzled dead-enders from the slums of Kingston.

The leader of the group was a thirty-one-year-old named Clifton Lewis, who'd spent six of the last thirteen years in South Camp prison, doing three different stints of two years each for violent crimes. Prior to adulthood, he'd served a year at Hill Top Juvenile Correctional Centre, and when he wasn't behind bars he'd been on the streets, rising slowly up the ranks of Spangler Posse henchmen.

All five of the other men with him in the tiny Havana safe house had done time, as well, but they'd also committed dozens, in some cases hundreds, of other crimes for which they were never convicted and punished.

Each of their backpacks contained one Taurus G3 pistol, three seventeen-round magazines, a ski mask, food and water, booze, and weed.

They all lit up joints, and then Clifton Lewis checked the time on his phone, and as he slowly got high, he began explaining to the others their exact mission for the evening, as had been explained to him by his cutout back home in Jamaica.

Evening rain poured from the terra-cotta roof of the whitewashed two-story home in the El Batán neighborhood of Bogotá, Colombia, overwhelming the old gutters and dumping in sheets down into the asphalt forecourt of the small property.

At eight thirty p.m. the sky would normally be clear and the stars out, but a storm from the Andes had rolled in over the Eastern Hills and parked itself above the capital, and the clouds showed no hint of moving on before midnight.

The whitewashed house on Calle 122 wasn't much to look at, virtually indistinguishable from most every other structure on the street, but to the man living inside, it had its perks.

Petty crime was very much a thing in this barrio, so all the homes were constructed with walled and gated forecourts, a secondary gate at the entrance, and a little balcony over the forecourt with a high ironwork railing. The door locks around the two-bedroom residence were strong and numerous, and though the lone security man sitting in his car in the forecourt did not come with the house, at least his position here behind the gate was secure.

Matthew Hanley sat at his kitchen table, gazing absent-mindedly at the rain outside through a window as he polished off the last few swigs of Club Colombia beer from a half-liter bottle, his hands greasy from the highly sauced pan-fried chicken he'd been devouring since getting home from work twenty minutes earlier.

It had been a long day, a drive up to Bucaramanga for a meeting with Venezuelan agents who'd slipped in from over the border, then another six hours in the embassy SCIF sending reports back to Langley before climbing into the back of his Toyota 4Runner while his driver negotiated the return trip so he could read a thick sheaf of démarches from Washington about America's policy relating to the narcotics trade with Colombia.

It had also been a relatively fruitful day for the deputy chief of station, especially considering he'd only been working at Bogotá station for a little less than five weeks, having been moved out of his chief of station position in Papua New Guinea and into the deputy slot here in Colombia.

Hanley liked to cook, but he didn't have the time, and he liked to eat even more, so he employed a woman named Tatty who popped in to his apartment during the day to prepare his meals for him while he was at work. Tatty straightened his house, as well, which wasn't much of a chore because the American was rarely at home, never entertained, and had no pets.

Hanley was single, his one marriage having burned out hard and bright when he was still in his twenties, a Green Beret captain who was not home enough to retain the interest of his young wife.

Since he left U.S. Army Special Forces some thirty years earlier, Hanley had been an Agency man, full stop, and though he bitched and moaned about it most every day, the Agency was all he knew, and the work he bitched and moaned about was his one true love.

The burly blond man finished his chicken and left his plate and his beer bottle at the table as he got up to wash his hands. This task completed, he walked slowly out of his kitchen, into the living room, where he opened the sliding glass door to his front balcony. He stepped outside, careful to remain under the terra-cotta-tiled awning as he watched the rain beat down on the forecourt and the two-lane street beyond it.

Hector, Hanley's driver and night security officer, sat in his Toyota SUV inside the gate; he was probably asleep but Hanley didn't care, because the deputy chief of station kept a Colt .45 by his bed, and he carried a Smith and Wesson .40 cal in a shoulder holster even in his house, so he didn't spend much time worrying about someone blowing open his front gate, killing his armed guard, and kicking in his iron door.

Matt watched the rain a moment, told himself he was ready for bed, but then remembered that Tatty had texted that she'd left him some ice cream in the freezer.

With this revelation he headed back into the kitchen with purpose and opened the cutlery drawer. Whipping out a spoon but ignoring the cabinet with the bowls, he now turned to the freezer.

Immediately, he lurched back and let out a high-pitched gasp, then yelled.

"Jesus Christ!"

A man stood on the far side of his small and dark kitchen, just eight feet away.

His voice was calm. "Don't blow a gasket, Matt. It's just me."

Court Gentry stood in the doorway to the living room, casually leaning against the frame. He wore a black long-sleeved shirt and jeans, and he didn't appear to be wet from the rain.

Hanley took a moment to compose himself as he leaned back against the sink. Finally he said, "Dammit, Violator. How'd you get in?"

"You left the balcony door open."

"Like ten seconds ago I did."

"Plenty of time."

"Bullshit. You don't look like you were out in the rain."

"Raincoat is on the balcony. I came down from the roof."

Hanley wiped fresh sweat from both his cheeks, then looked carefully at Court's face. It was red, his forehead peeling. "You been sleeping in a tanning bed?"

"Something like that."

"And now you're here to stick a knife in my gut?"

Court looked around the room and sniffed the air. "If I wanted to kill you, I'd just sit back and wait for the fried chicken and hot sauce to do it."

"Funny."

"Why would I be here to kill you?"

Hanley replied, "I don't know. *Killers* appear in people's darkened houses on rainy nights. *Normal* people ring the fucking doorbell."

"I'm not entirely normal."

"Yeah? No shit."

Hanley had recovered from his shock, more or less. He moved on to the freezer and grabbed the container of Crem Helado Chocolate Chip, adding a little bluster to his walk to compensate for the fact that he'd squealed like a little girl a few seconds earlier and was now about to eat dessert out of its carton.

"I guess congratulations are in order on your promotion," Court said behind him.

"Officially speaking, it's a *demotion*. Station chief to dep station chief. Still, I'd have taken a job plunging toilets at Bogotá station if it meant I'd get out of New Guinea."

He ripped the lid off the ice cream like it was his enemy. "A couple of months ago I get orders to Colombia from out of the blue. I ask around, hear that Angela Lacy has intervened on my behalf." Digging in with the spoon he said, "I knew better than to reach out and thank her, because I *also* knew she was up in New Jersey when everything went down there four months ago, which meant my *new* friend Angela Lacy had come into contact with my *old* friend, Court Gentry."

"What makes you think I was involved in—"

"Violator," Hanley interrupted. "Just stop. It's me."

Court said nothing.

"Anyway, I wondered why Lacy intervened, but I figured I should just shut the fuck up, get my happy ass to Colombia, and enjoy myself an empanada and a cerveza."

"Sounds like you had yourself a solid plan."

"Yeah . . . I did. Then you waltzed in. Why do I get the feeling life's about to get pretty fucking complicated?"

"I won't take much of your time."

Hanley sat down at the kitchen table. "There's one beer left in the fridge."

"Not anymore, there's not," Court said, and he opened the refrigerator, took out a big bottle of Club Colombia, and popped the cap. After a swig, he sat down across the table from Hanley.

The bigger man ate a bite of ice cream, then said, "This is about the AI murders, I take it."

"Yeah."

"Heard about that shit in Mexico. Was that part of it?"

"Yes."

Hanley nodded. "Was that you?"

"Not entirely, no."

Hanley gave a little snicker and looked away. *It was you*, his expression seemed to be saying.

"Anyway," Court said, "I picked up some intel on what's happening. Can't give it to Lacy; she wouldn't be able to slip it into the mix without an explanation of where it came from. Thought maybe I could bring it to you. I thought you could find a way to sneak the intel into wide circulation with no comebacks."

Hanley took another bite. "What do you know?"

Court told him about Guatemala, about Mexico, about the name Martina Sommer and the code name Cyrus, and he passed over the piece of the circuit board, wrapped in a plastic bag from a Mexican supermarket.

He left out any mention of Zoya, for now anyway. Presently she was at a hotel a mile away on Calle 17, annoyed that Court didn't want her to come along tonight, but also still recovering from her cuts, bruises, and sore joints from the evening before.

And Court didn't mention Don Fitzroy, either. Don was probably still in the hospital in Cozumel recovering before he headed back to Europe.

By the time Court was done relaying most of the events from the past week, Hanley was most of the way through the tub of ice cream, the circuit board on the table next to him. He put the lid back on, wiped his face with a cloth napkin Tatty always left out on the table for him, and then he leaned back in his chair.

"That story has more holes in it than you do."

"The holes are there for a reason."

Hanley nodded again. "These robot things. Were they autonomous, or was someone commanding them?"

Court held up his hands. "You know, I meant to ask them that, but honestly, they weren't all that chatty."

"Look," Hanley continued. "We've tested unmanned weapons systems, of course, but unless the DOD is holding out on CIA, there's no word that we've adopted artificial intelligence to lethal platforms."

"I don't think this shit was from America."

"Of course not. I'm just thinking about the ramifications if an enemy is fielding lethal autonomous weapons. I mean, you seemed to handle those platforms, but—"

"They killed eleven armed men, injured three more of us. They weren't nothing, Matt."

"Right. But if China or Russia can translate that capability to a fifth-generation fighter aircraft, a warship, a submarine, shit . . . unmanned nuclear missile launchers, then those rifle-wielding puppy dogs and grenade-toting buzzbombs you fought against won't seem quite so scary anymore."

"I get your point." Court swigged his beer. "What are we going to do?"

"We? Nothing. You're done, kid. I can weave this intel into the system some way, but I can't tell anyone you showed up at my door and handed it to me, because the Agency still officially wants you dead."

Court wasn't as sure he was out of this. "I'd love to be done, but if the entity that's been trying to kill me for the past week is still out there, then I'm still involved. I'll stay in Bogotá for a couple of days, give you a way to contact me if you need me. When you get the intelligence to the right people at the Agency, try to get something from them that I can use."

Hanley said, "I have to figure out how I'm going to pass this on. I'll reach out to Lacy, see if she has any ideas.

"What are you going to do in Bogotá while you wait on my call? I wouldn't lay out on the beach if I were you. You look like a fucking lobster."

"I might take up knitting."

Hanley didn't smile. Instead, he reached out his hand. "Whatever you did with Angela to help me out, I'm in your debt."

After a handshake, Court said, "Angela's a good one, Matt. If you should rocket back up the ranks at Langley, don't forget about her."

"From what I hear, she'll be running ops a hell of a lot sooner than I'll get my old job back. Hope she doesn't forget about me."

THIRTY-NINE

Anton Hinton emerged from his office at nine thirty p.m. after a quick email check, and Zack stood from the leather sofa where he'd been waiting. He helped his protectee once again put on his ceramic body armor encased in a canvas chest rig, and while he tightened the cummerbund around him, Zack said, "Back to La Finca?"

Gareth Wren entered the lobby of the office, his messenger bag on his shoulder.

Hinton shook his head. "I'm starving. A group of about twenty of us are going to a restaurant on the south side of Havana, only fifteen minutes north of La Finca. Great food, family place." Off a worried look from Zack he said, "The restaurant closes at ten, they'll stay open for us, so we'll be the only ones there. Won't be a soul but me and my people, you and your security men, and a staff that I've known for years."

Wren said, "I've arranged an army escort outside, as well."

Zack looked to Wren, who just smiled back at him. As soon as Hinton headed out of the lobby and into the hall, Wren said, "I never promised you this would be easy, mate." He added a shrug and said, "I will add, though, that the ropa vieja and mojitos at this place are to die for."

Zack sighed. "Let's hope not, right?"

Wren's eyes widened dramatically as he himself headed for the hall. "Unfortunate choice of words on my part."

The restaurant was quaint and simple, a freestanding cinder-block-and-masonry structure just off a highway in the Boyeros municipality of southwestern Havana. The lights of cargo aircraft taking off from nearby José Martí airport rose over the street; the restaurant glass shook every now and then as larger aircraft rumbled over on their way to the south towards Mexico and South America.

Warm mist hung in the air; it had rained earlier, but only for a short time, and though the streets were slick and the humidity high, the skies were again clear.

Stars sparkled, the waning moon hung high to the north.

Anton Hinton climbed out of his Sprinter Jet on Road and was met immediately by Zack, who had already scanned the street with the help of his four men. Together all six of them stepped up to the front door of the small restaurant, and the proprietors, a husband and wife in their seventies whom Zack assessed as no threat whatsoever, ushered them all inside.

Zack lagged behind to scan the dark street some more, letting his team of Cubans shoulder up to Hinton as he entered.

Two pickup trucks from the regular Cuban army were already parked out here; men stood in the beds behind machine guns, with two more at the ready standing outside the cab of each truck. To Zack they looked relaxed but competent. A half-dozen soldiers with a pair of light MGs was a significant show of force, and Zack was satisfied with his outer protective cordon.

All the buildings up and down the cobblestone street, roughly the same size and construction of the whitewashed restaurant, were darkened, giving Zack the impression that this wasn't a very active neighborhood at this time of night. It was a commercial district, but there was just the one restaurant. A pair of auto garages, some sort of a health clinic, and a shop that sold sports equipment and uniforms were all shuttered. Still, he peered into windows, eyed rooftops, and noted a few deeply shadowed alleyways that ran off the main road.

It was a good place for an attack, but Zack knew that any enemy would have to come in significant numbers to get to his principal.

He turned and went inside the restaurant, ready to set his inner security.

Hinton and several of his people began to sit at a large table near the front of the room, but Zack stepped up behind them, then interrupted his employer's conversation with the English-speaking proprietors.

"Sorry, Anton, I'm going to need you to sit in the back over here, in front of the wall." The teal-green-painted rear wall was cinder block, Zack had noticed, while windows ran up and down the front of the restaurant, making Hinton an easy target from the street if he sat near them.

Hinton nodded, then asked to be moved to the back of the room. The female proprietor led him there while her husband went back to get the kitchen ready for the influx of twenty or so guests.

Once at his table, Anton turned to Zack. "Hey, big guy. Any chance you'll let me take off my suit of armor so I can eat?"

Zack wanted to say *Hell no*, but he caught himself.

"Of course, let me help you." He unfastened and then removed the armor, then took it over to the closest empty table and laid it out flat so it would be ready to go if Zack had to throw it over Hinton's head in an emergency.

Anton was joined by Gareth Wren, Kimmie Lin, two of the campus's lead engineers, both from Romania, and the seventy-five-year-old female proprietor of the restaurant, who herself sat down and began pouring small glasses of straight Cubay Anejo Suave rum for everyone at the table.

Other Hinton Labs staff filled the rear half of the dining room at tables of two and four.

Kimmie was served first, and she sniffed the drink, took a tiny sip, fought back a wince, then drank the shot down. The elderly owner of the restaurant laughed and then poured the woman another despite her friendly attempt to demur.

Soon everyone was toasting and drinking, while the bartender across the room prepared an impossibly long row of mojitos.

Zack conferred on the radio and learned that the Cuban army had stationed three men in a gun truck at the back door, in addition to the six men in two vehicles at the front. The four men working for Zack had taken up positions near the front entrance and the hallway to the kitchen, the only two ways into the dining room.

It wasn't great coverage considering the threats against his protectee, but Zack didn't see any way to improve it. He told himself he would stand no more than ten feet from Hinton, and he'd be ready if anything went sideways.

The server was male, gray-templed, and well into his fifties, and he treated the tech guru like an old friend. They embraced, in broken English the waiter said he prayed every day for Anton's safety, the New Zealand native thanked the man, and then they embraced again.

The mojitos came, Zack was happy to see everyone place their dinner orders quickly, and the military security force outside reported in that all was quiet.

After the menus were taken away, Anton stood and held up his glass, and everyone in the restaurant raised glasses of their own.

"I just want to give a toast to the friends we've lost in the past week. Tomer and Maxim and Lars, Kotana, Amir Kumar, Rene, Montri, Ethan, and all the others.

"It is a sad, horrible, scary time in our industry right now, but I always look to the future, no matter what. I take comfort in the fact that we are all here, together, and I believe Hinton Labs holds the key to help the world understand the new and dangerous threats on the horizon.

"I learned a lot from all of you today, and we *must* keep working tirelessly to try to find some resolution to this bloody madness. I want to thank you all for your efforts.

"Lastly, let me say"—he held his drink up high—"a bold and secure future for all." It was Hinton Labs' company motto; Zack recognized it from his reading.

Anton took a drink from his glass; the rest of the group drank, as well, and then, as a group of servers began bringing trays of appetizers out of the kitchen, Gareth Wren stood next to him and raised his glass. "If I could just say a few words, as well. First, let me echo Anton's appreciation of—"

A shout of alarm from the front of the building, and then gunshots boomed in the street. Handgun rounds at first; ten or fifteen went unanswered, but then light machine gun fire from one of the military trucks pounded at a cyclic rate.

Zack was moving in under a second, scooping up the chest rig, then racing to Anton, who was still standing, his glass in his hand. Zack threw the armor over the man's head, knocking away the mojito, but he didn't bother fastening the vest. Instead, he reached under his guayabera and yanked his Staccato free of its appendix holster, then turned and began pushing his protectee towards the hallway to the kitchen and the back door beyond it.

Zack had made it only a few steps before more gunfire erupted, this time in front of him, coming from the alley behind the building.

A pair of Zack's team were at the hallway entrance, pistols raised and ready. One stepped into the kitchen a few feet, then immediately shot back out into the dining room. Looking at Zack, he shook his head no, as two-way gunfire continued from that compass point.

The shooting out back was voluminous, but the gunfire emanating from the front seemed even more ferocious, with seven or eight guns firing. Zack had second thoughts about trying to make it out to any of the vehicles parked there.

He looked back over his shoulder into the dining room, saw two of his guard force raising their pistols to fire through the front window, and then he saw that Gareth Wren had pulled his own handgun and was presently leading the two engineers and Kimmie towards the back of the room near the entrance to the kitchen.

"Wait!" Zack shouted, and Wren stopped the entourage.

Looking back towards Zack, the Englishman said, "Got to exfil out the back, mate. There's a lot more shooting at the front."

"Listen to the cadence. There's only one of our guys left out back returning fire. The incoming out front is from the left. We're better off going out front under the army's suppressive fire and heading to the two vics parked to the right."

"Got it!" Wren said, shouting like the British army warrant officer he had been, and he turned Kimmie and the others back around. "That way!"

he shouted, then turned back and raised his gun towards the kitchen. To Zack he said, "I'll cover! Off you go!"

Zack turned Hinton around by the neck, and then he leaned up into his ear from behind. "We run for the front door. Break right just outside. Do *not* stop for anything."

"But—"

"Go!" Zack kept his hand on Hinton's left shoulder as he held his pistol out in front of him, his arm extending past Hinton's right ear and the barrel of the gun aimed in their direction of travel. Shoving his big chest into the smaller man's back, he got him moving, and together the two men ran for the front door.

They passed huddled Hinton Labs employees on their left and right; at one point Anton tried to reach for a woman hiding under a table as he ran by, but Zack kept up the pace behind him, forcing him forward, nearing the exit.

Zack's two teammates at the front recharged their weapons with fresh magazines, and then they themselves raced for the door, wisely creating a front guard for their protectee.

Zack liked his chances now. Between them they had three guns to add to the military force's fire outside; he didn't know how many enemy he was up against, but it didn't sound like more than one or two. He felt confident his people could keep heads down long enough for him to throw his protectee into one of the vehicles and get it moving out of the kill zone.

Just twenty-five feet from the front door, a furious barrage of gunfire came from directly behind. Zack heard outgoing handguns, and he also heard softer pops, telling him someone was firing either in the kitchen or else out back near the kitchen door.

Zack didn't look back; he just kept moving. His two men in front of him burst out through the front door; one broke right, the other left, both of them had their weapons raised, and the man on the left instantly fired, apparently seeing a target.

Zack kept barreling forward, a foot behind Hinton now, his pistol still outstretched past the billionaire's head as he ran.

Fifteen feet from the front door, Anton Hinton stumbled forward, lost his footing completely, and slammed chest first into the tiled floor, skidding all the way to the door. Zack kept running, jumped on top of him, then spun back around to check his six o'clock.

The first thing he saw was Gareth Wren firing into the kitchen from the middle of the room. In front of Wren, on the left and right of the kitchen galley, both of the security men were down, one prone over a table and the other on his back in a pool of blood. Bullet holes pocked the wooden walls between the kitchen and the dining room.

It was clear that the military guys out back were dead, the enemy had made it inside the rear of the restaurant, and from there they killed two of the security force in the dining room. Only Gareth Wren was left defending from behind.

And then Hinton shouted below Zack. "I'm shot!"

Zack didn't think Hinton had been shot, and he didn't see any blood, so he rose back to his knees and yanked his protectee up. Even if he *had* been hit, the enemy seemed to be closing from the back, so Zack had to get his man moving.

Both he and Anton stumbled as they poured out of the restaurant and onto the sidewalk. Directly in front of them a soldier stood in the back of a pickup truck and aimed his PKM machine gun to the east, in the direction of the incoming fire, and then he fired a short burst.

Zack glanced at the security guard, who broke left, ran towards the incoming fire, his Glock pistol blasting, and then dropped the weapon and spun to the ground, either injured or dead.

Zack turned with Hinton to the right and saw the security officer there still on his feet and running to the Lincoln Navigator, his pistol still out and scanning for targets.

Zack pushed Hinton after the guard to the right, and as he did so he aimed behind him. The American dumped round after round out of his Staccato towards the area of threat as he raced in the opposite direction, knowing that with a twenty-round magazine capacity, he could afford to be liberal with his shooting. Hinton stumbled again in front of him, but less dramatically than before, and with Zack's help he managed to keep his feet under him as he shot along on the broken sidewalk. Within seconds Zack was pushing him into the back of the Navigator. The big American jumped in and on top of his protectee, and the surviving security guard leapt behind the wheel.

Just behind Zack he heard a noise, and he swung his pistol in that direction.

His red dot optic centered on the face of Kimmie Lin, and he quickly lowered the weapon.

She dove in off the sidewalk and was followed by one of the campus employees, and then the Navigator launched forward, racing off in the misty darkness.

FORTY

Anton moaned under Zack, repeating himself from earlier. "I'm shot!"

Zack rolled off the man, pulled him into a sitting position, holstered his weapon, and quickly began checking his body. "Relax. You just tripped, you weren't shot. No gunfire came in from the front, and I was at your back. If you'd been hit, *I'd* have been hit."

Zack continued checking Hinton for wounds, doing a sweep over the man's entire body with his hands and turning up no blood. He held his hands up to demonstrate to Hinton that he was okay, but Hinton said, "My back, lower right."

Zack rolled the man to the left, then checked the back of his chest rig, still just draped over his torso, with the thick canvas cummerbund loose at his stomach. He found a hole in the canvas on the lower right, then felt around, finding that the ceramic plate on his back had, in fact, taken a round. The ceramic itself was only scratched, indicating to the American that he was struck by a handgun round, not a rifle round.

"I got shot, didn't I?" Hinton demanded. He didn't seem to be in shock, but he seemed utterly bewildered by what had just happened.

"Your body armor was shot. *You're* okay."

To this Hinton said, "My right leg hurts. In the back, below the knee."

Zack swept down low on the man's right leg; he hadn't checked here before because he'd been concentrating on critical areas of his body, but now he felt some blood on his fingertips. He lifted the man's tracksuit pants and saw that he had, indeed, received a small wound on his upper calf.

Zack said, "Spalling. Bits of the bullet that hit the plate sprayed out, and you got a tiny nick on your leg."

"So . . ." Hinton's voice seemed confused. "I . . . I *did* get shot."

He hadn't been shot directly, but there likely was a tiny bullet fragment in the man's leg. Zack just said, "We'll get you a doctor when we get to La Finca." He didn't think Hinton needed a doctor; Zack himself could safely extract any tiny metal pieces from the man's lean calf muscle, but he wanted to put Hinton at ease.

He turned his attention to Kimmie now. "You're not hurt?"

Her eyes were distant. Unfixed.

"Hey!" he shouted now. "Say something if you can talk!"

"I'm . . . I'm fine. I just can't . . . I can't believe it."

The other man in back was a computer engineer Zack had seen throughout the day. He was midthirties, balding, and he had an accent that sounded Scandinavian. "What about you?" Zack asked.

"I'm okay. I saw people dead back there."

Zack had, as well, and he wondered about Gareth, although he didn't second-guess his decision to get Hinton off the X and leave the others behind. Zack had his assignment, and he would do it or die trying.

The man behind the wheel of the Navigator knew how to drive, Zack was pleased to see, and they were making incredible time. The American kept his eyes on the hills and trees and buildings they raced past, his Staccato still warm in his hand.

Without looking down at the weapon, he exchanged the half-spent magazine with a fresh one. His phone buzzed in his pocket and he answered it quickly. "Yeah?"

"It's Wren, mate. Attack is over. You get Anton safe?"

"Pulling up to La Finca in five minutes."

"Good job, you."

"What's the damage there?"

"Fuckin' mess here, is what it is. The army lost two dead, three wounded. Three restaurant employees shot. All should survive. Unfortunately, we lost two of our security men. Both KIA, and a third was injured."

"Shit," Zack muttered. "The main attack came from the rear?"

"Appears so. The attackers out front didn't get close. Three bodies about a block to the east."

"I want to see them," Zack said. "Try to keep the local cops from messing up the scene."

"Will do. You're coming back here?"

"Yeah. Give me twenty."

"Glad you made it, mate."

"Likewise."

They pulled through the guarded entrance to La Finca; it was clear the soldiers here were aware of the attack because they had their guns up and their flashlights cutting the night, but they let the Navigator in, and Zack's driver screeched to a halt in the drive in front of the garden at the blast door entrance. Black Wasps and company guards were outside; everyone was armed with long guns, which Zack was pleased to see.

Zack looked to the driver. "Keep it running."

"Sí, señor."

He helped Hinton out of the vehicle and escorted him to the blast doors. He had a slight limp; the man still seemed to be disoriented somewhat, and he walked with his hand over his back on the right, as if the blow he took there had hurt.

Kimmie and the other man went inside, Anton followed them in, and then the guards shut and locked the door.

Once Zack had Anton inside La Finca, he ran back through the garden, jumped back in the Navigator, and they raced back to the restaurant.

The low mist still hung in the air when Zack arrived at the scene. Police cars were everywhere, and dozens and dozens of locals stood around on the street, trying to get a good look at what remained of the carnage.

A white ambulance sat parked near the front door, just in front of the two military pickups. The ambulance's back was open and its lights flashed, but Zack felt sure any wounded had already been taken from the scene in the thirty minutes since the firefight ended.

No, the ambulance was here to transport the body bags.

Zack had only advanced a few yards on the location when he was stopped by a local cop, but he saw Wren step out of the shattered front window of the restaurant.

"Gareth!"

The Englishman saw Zack, then called to the police officer, who immediately let the big American through.

Blood ran down Wren's right arm. "You hit?" Zack asked.

"No. I'm fine. Not even sure what got me."

Zack lifted the torn sleeve of the polo and checked it out. Blood trickled out of an inch-long gash at the top of Wren's right biceps.

"Looks like you might have caught a piece of frag from a ricochet, or broken glass or something. You should get that cleaned up."

Wren didn't seem concerned. "Anton's fine?" he asked again.

"Hit in the back plate. Found a little nick from spalling on his right leg. Nothing to worry about, although he is acting like he caught a fifty BMG center mass."

The .50 caliber Browning machine gun round was probably thirty times the size of the fleck of metal that had struck Hinton's leg.

Wren rolled his eyes and said, "Civilians," with a shrug. "Let's go take a look at the dead bastards, shall we?"

They started out in front, where three men lay in the street some twenty-five yards from the entrance of the restaurant. Two were in an alleyway on the other side of the road; apparently both had been hiding behind an old Chevy convertible, because the classic car had been riddled with what looked like one hundred rounds of Cuban military machine gun fire.

The two bodies here were a mess; both had been hit multiple times, and they lay torn and twisted.

One of the men's entrails had spilled out from his abdomen, and the other was missing parts of his head and face. Still, Zack could identify them as Black, and probably in their twenties or thirties.

Zack gave both bodies a perfunctory look, then peered across the road at the other dead man. Together he and Wren walked over for a closer look.

This man, also Black and roughly thirty, had caught numerous rounds to his legs, pelvic region, and stomach, but his upper torso and head were intact. His eyes gazed up towards the moon, his right hand outstretched near a Taurus pistol whose slide had locked open, indicating it was out of ammunition.

Zack looked to Wren. "And in back?"

"Three more dead, making a total of six. I don't know if there were only a half dozen in the attacking force, or if there were more who ran off when their buddies started dropping like fish in the ice at the market."

Zack shook his head. "Half dozen sounds about right from what I heard from the shoot-out." He knelt over the body here in the darkened street, then looked up to Wren. "Would have been handy if we could have questioned at least one of these dudes."

"Tell it to the army. I might have gotten one at the back, but I'm not sure. The rest were killed by the infantry boys." He smiled. "Or you. Saw you squeezing off a few rounds."

Zack picked up the dead man's handgun and examined it. As he thought, it was empty. "Pistols. They all had pistols."

"Looks like it."

Looking up at Wren, he said, "Who takes on a military unit armed only with Brazilian-made nine-mils? That's just stupid."

Wren knelt down, began going through the man's pockets. Soon he pulled out a large joint. He smelled it, then shrugged. "He was ready to party once the job was done."

"Who says they waited? Even through the blood and guts, even through the cordite hanging in the air, I smell weed on all three of these guys."

To this, Wren blew out a chest of air. "We weren't dealing with geniuses here, but they still caused a lot of damage."

"Action beats reaction," Zack said. But then he asked, "Why didn't they wait for us to leave?"

"What do you mean?"

"Their plan. It doesn't make sense. Just open fire on the heavily armed military guys? 'Hey diddle diddle, right up the middle'? Nobody does it like that."

Wren looked at the placement of the bodies. "Were they trying to just hit the restaurant from two sides? Overwhelm the outer perimeter and get inside?"

"Might have worked out back; there were fewer defenders, and the alley back there probably gave them more cover than out here."

Wren nodded. "Aye. Lots of solid cover in back."

"But here, in front. A hard charge into machine guns is about the dumbest play you could make." He thought a moment. "Unless they *weren't* charging." Before Wren could speak, Zack said, "Let's look at something."

He and Wren went back inside. Cuban police officers eyed them, but no one impeded their movement. These were Hinton's people, and they would get deferential treatment.

There were bullet holes in the walls to the kitchen. Zack walked to a point in front of the door and looked back. "Whoever hit Anton's armor got lucky. The round must have come through the wall and hit him in the back."

Wren's eyebrows rose. "I saw you. You were right there behind him. Lucky his plate caught it instead of your arse."

Zack nodded at this, but his focus was on something else. "Let's check the alley."

As they went through the kitchen, Zack could see massive splashes of blood on the walls and floor. Wren said, "A couple of cooks got shot. I think they'll live. Cuba has surprisingly good medical care."

The body of a Black man lay by a rack of loaves of bread, a black Taurus pistol on the floor ten feet away.

Out back they found two more bodies of Black males near the pickup. The soldiers who had been killed here had already been whisked away.

He lifted the shirt of one of the bloody dead men in the road. Looking him over, he said, "Prison tats. Check the others."

Together Wren and Hightower looked over all three bodies in the back. Zack said, "They've all been to prison. They're part of some gang."

Wren spoke softly, a tone of confusion in his voice now. "They weren't even soldiers."

"Not at all," Zack said. "Just some island gangbangers, stoned out of their asses and armed with little handguns." Then another thought occurred to him. "Why would drugged-up assassins go after a guy with a fifteen-person detail? Why would the people targeting Hinton send a bunch of drugged-up shitheads? It doesn't make any sense."

Wren looked up and down the darkened street. Unlike in front, there was no one back here but a few cops. "Don't overthink it. They might have been the only crew willing to act in Cuba." Thinking a moment, he said, "They killed a lot of people."

"They killed a couple of guys outside who weren't ready for anything to happen. They killed the two guards back by you facing the kitchen. And then they died."

Wren put his hand on Zack's shoulder. "You did well tonight, mate."

"Thanks," Zack said, temporarily leaving his confusion about the assassination attempt behind. "You, too. Thanks for having my back."

Wren smiled. "Let's head back to La Finca."

Zack and Wren began picking their way back through the shot-up restaurant to the front and the Hinton Labs vehicles parked there. Zack moved slower than the Brit because he continued looking at the holes in the walls, the location of the blood, and he kept trying to picture how this made any sense at all.

FORTY-ONE

The silver Suburban carrying Chris Travers, Joe "Hash" Takahashi, and Jim Pace stopped at the automatic gates just off Carrera 45 in Bogotá's Teusaquillo neighborhood. Soon the gates opened and the vehicle began rolling through the massive campus of the U.S. embassy in Colombia, passing annex after annex, and finally stopping at the chancery, the main building of the compound.

After multiple displays of credentials, a pass through an X-ray, after phone confiscations and eye scans, they found themselves led into the tiny third-floor foyer of the office of the CIA's deputy station chief, and here the three men waited while the admin assistant called her boss over the intercom.

Soon the door to the office opened, and a blond-haired man with a big chest and an only slightly bigger gut leaned out. Matt Hanley's polka-dot tie was loose around his thick neck, and his white dress shirt was wrinkled, as was the blue blazer that looked two sizes too large.

"Come on in, gents." He shook Pace's hand, then looked up and saw Travers. "Chris? The hell you doing here? Couldn't find a door that needed kicking?"

"Jim brought me in case your office was locked," the younger man joked.

They all stepped inside, Hanley shut the door, and then he pulled off his blazer, letting it drop into a chair.

Jim Pace said, "Good to see you again, Deputy Director."

Hanley chuckled. "These days, it's just Matt."

"Not to me, boss."

"It's been too long, Sierra Four."

"Definitely. Glad you got pulled out of the Philippines."

Hanley snorted as he headed back over to his desk. "I *wish* it was the Philippines. It was frickin' New Guinea."

Pace stifled a little gasp, but his eyes widened. "Jesus, Matt. What did you do?"

It was said as a joke, and Hanley treated it as such. "All sorts of fun stuff they couldn't pin on me, but I bent the rules enough for a conflict-avoidant director to bring me down." He waved a hand at his little office. "But look at me now. Master of all I survey . . . unless I look out the window."

Outside the window was a ramshackle auxiliary building, basically a double-wide trailer, five feet from the glass and blocking any view.

"Sit down," Hanley instructed, and he dropped into his swivel chair, which squeaked in annoyance.

Pace sat in a straight-back chair in front of the desk, but Takahashi and Travers stayed on their feet at the door, directly behind Pace.

Hanley looked at his watch. "I'm impressed. Six and a half hours after I reach you in D.C., you walk into my office. Glad you could come down on such short notice."

"You know better than anyone, traveling on short notice is part of the gig. You mentioned you picked up some physical intelligence you wanted me to have."

Hanley said, "Yes, that *is* what I told you. And that is the truth, but only part of the truth. I actually have more than that."

Pace leaned forward. "You have my full attention."

"I won't beat around the bush, then. The code name of the person or persons involved in the killings is Cyrus. Doubt that will trace back to anything tangible, but worth a look."

Confused, Pace sat upright. "Okay. Confidence level on this?"

"High confidence, considering the source."

"Who is your—"

Hanley interrupted him. "Also, you need to be looking at a German national named Martina Sommer. Commo specialist. She's in Singapore, working at the tactical operations center of the enemy, whoever they are."

Pace blinked hard now, gobsmacked at the volume and specificity of this information. "Wait . . . what?"

"I ran the name myself. There's a Martina Sommer who was shit-canned last year from the Bundespolizei in Berlin. Communications specialist. If I were you, I'd try to figure out where in Singapore she is."

"Okay, Matt. Let's slow way the hell down here. Where on earth did you get—"

Hanley held up a finger to silence Pace again, then reached inside his desk and pulled a plastic baggie out. From the bag he retrieved a small broken circuit board and handed it over. Travers stepped forward, collected it, and handed it off to Pace, who immediately looked it over.

Jim Pace looked back up. "The fuck is this?"

"My asset pulled it out of an armed unmanned ground vehicle that tried to kill him."

"An armed . . . unmanned ground . . . vehicle? Like . . . a robot?"

"Exactly like a robot. In Mexico."

Pace nodded slowly as it all came together. "Tulum. The ex-MI5 guy who got iced. They said it was a fucking bloodbath."

"That's right."

"And your man . . . he was there?"

"Smack-dab in the middle."

"Jesus, Matt. Local cops said nothing recovered at the scene but bodies and shell casings. They're calling it cartel violence."

"If they're saying that, then somebody got to the local cops. My asset says there were two unmanned ground vehicles, each armed with a high-powered rifle, and maybe four or five drones, some of which carried warheads, and they were all destroyed at the scene. Presumably the Mexicans hauled all that equipment off somewhere."

Pace looked back down at the broken piece of tech. "Holy hell," he whispered. Looking back to Hanley, he said, "You know I have to ask you, right?"

Hanley nodded. "I always liked you, Jim."

Pace ignored the comment. "Who's the asset?"

Hanley leaned back in his chair and laced his fingers behind his head. "Any chance we can just gloss over that part?"

This was not a particularly unusual request; often case officers and senior station execs tried to hold their agents' identities close, so Pace was neither surprised nor offended. He said, "I don't have to reveal it wide around the Agency, of course. But Deputy Director Watkins is going to want a little more context, if you don't mind, as to how it came to pass that the brand-spanking-new number two man at Bogotá station suddenly whips out intel that every law enforcement and intelligence agency on planet Earth has been moving mountains to hunt down for the past week."

Hanley glanced to the two Ground Branch men behind the seated case officer, then just shrugged as he returned his attention to Pace. "The asset is an American. An old colleague of yours, as a matter of fact."

"Agency?"

"Used to be. He went private years back."

"Private? Private *what*?"

"This and that." When Pace said nothing more, Hanley said, "Assassinations, for one thing."

Pace's face darkened. His eyebrows furrowed as he began to understand. "You have *got* to be kidding me."

Hanley released his hands from behind his head and leaned forward on his desk.

When he did not speak, Pace said, "You're talking about Sierra Six?"

Hanley hadn't known if Pace was aware that the international assassin known as the Gray Man was actually a former CIA Ground Branch paramilitary officer and Pace's former teammate Court Gentry, call sign Sierra Six. But clearly he *did* know.

Hanley nodded. "Our boy's been busy."

"He's working for this Cyrus?"

Hanley shook his head adamantly. "Very much the opposite. Sierra Six tells me he got drawn into all this when Cyrus tried to kill him to stop him from protecting that engineer Arsenov, the Russian who got smoked in Mexico City. Court's not doing Gray Man shit this time, he's just trying to keep his ass alive."

"Why do I find that hard to believe?"

"Because you don't know him like I do."

"I know that about a year after I left Golf Sierra he killed almost every other member of Golf Sierra. I know that if I *had* been there, he would have tried to kill me, too."

"That is true," Hanley allowed, but then said, "The whole op we ran against Gentry in Golf Sierra was bullshit. He didn't earn the sanction that was put on him by the Agency. The kid was just defending himself from people who he thought were his friends when they tried to kill him."

To Hanley's surprise, Jim Pace did not give off a strong reaction to this. After a few seconds, he said, "I've always wondered about that. I mean, sure, Gentry was a weird dude, but I never took him for a traitor."

Hanley shook his head. "He did nothing wrong, and more than that, he's been incredibly helpful to the Agency over the years, despite the fact that the Agency is targeting him."

"Yeah, well, the Agency's going to come after you when you kill Suzanne Brewer."

Word had gotten around in the halls at Langley that senior Programs and Plans officer Suzanne Brewer had been murdered by Court Gentry four months earlier in New Jersey.

Hanley shrugged at this. "God's honest truth is, I don't know if he did that or not. But I *did* know Brewer."

"And?"

"And if he killed her, it was another act of self-defense."

Wide-eyed, Jim Pace looked back over his shoulder to Travers and Takahashi.

Chris Travers retained a bored countenance, as if he hadn't been listening to all of this, but after a few seconds he said, "I always liked Court."

Takahashi had the same bored appearance, but now he shrugged. "I don't even know what the hell you old guys are talking about."

Pace turned back to Hanley. "Where is Six now? I'd like to talk to him."

With a laugh the bigger man said, "He's understandably a little skittish, Jim. After giving me this intel, he thinks he might be done with this operation. He's in the area, or so he tells me, waiting to hear if we need his help for anything else, but I don't see us all getting together for beers. He doesn't know that you aren't going to sic a paramilitary team on him and drag him back to a supermax in the States."

"Would help my career," Pace joked without smiling.

Hanley said, "So will all this. Just use the info he gave me, the info I gave you, however you see fit. If you need to ascribe that info to someone, then say it was the Mexican Federales."

Jim Pace scratched his bearded chin. "I might like to play things a little more by the book than you do, Matt. No offense."

Hanley said, "None taken. Shit, man, look around you. I was Deputy Director for Operations of the CIA a year and a half ago. Now I'm CIA's second banana in a South American developing nation, and I feel pretty damn lucky considering the potential alternatives. 'By the book' might just be the right course of action. Wish I'd thought of that, actually."

Pace and Hanley kept eye contact for fifteen seconds before the younger man said, "Fuck it. I'm not going to throw you under the bus to keep my nose clean. You and Gentry both could have kept this shit away from me so that you didn't get implicated."

Before Hanley could say anything, Jim said, "I'll have the code word Cyrus and the name Martina Sommer back at Langley within the next fifteen minutes. I'll get the circuit board hand-couriered up there by the end of the day, see what our people can get out of it."

"Hand-couriered? You're off somewhere else?"

"Yeah. Twenty minutes before we rolled through the gate here I got word about another assassination attempt, just outside Havana."

"Who was the target?"

"Anton Hinton."

Hanley barked out a little laugh. "Wonder boy? Heard someone took a swing at that dickhead in Oxford just a few days ago."

"That was a jab, this was a left hook. Several dead, but Hinton got away again."

"Lucky dude."

"More than luck, Matt. Hinton has himself a good body man. An old friend of ours, by the way."

Now Hanley was the one on the receiving end of information. "Yeah? Who's that?"

"Hightower. Me and Gentry aren't the only two ex–Goon Squad boys mixed up in these AI assassinations."

Matt Hanley leaned back in his chair again. "Small fucking world, Jim."

"Small fucking world, Matt."

Pace, Travers, and Takahashi had only left Hanley's office two minutes prior when the deputy station chief pulled out his phone, opened his encrypted Signal app, and dialed a number. Within seconds it was picked up on the other end.

"Hey," Gentry answered, but it was obvious to Hanley he was on speakerphone.

Hanley said, "Who's there?"

There was a small pause, and then a woman's voice spoke. "It's Anthem, Matt. How are you?" When Zoya Zakharova had been active in Matt Hanley's off-book team known as Poison Apple, her code name had been Anthem.

"Shit," he said. "Violator's got you mixed up in this?"

"To the contrary, as a matter of fact."

Hanley let it go. "Court, Jim Pace was cool about it. He's putting all your intel into the pipeline. No comebacks on you or me, or so he says."

"That's good news," Zoya replied.

Court added, "I guess we're done with this. Good luck, Matt. Z, let's go get drunk."

Hanley said, "There is one other thing. One of the targets in all this killing is Anton Hinton. You know the name?"

Zoya answered quickly. "Yeah. Of course."

"There have been two attempts on him, both failed."

"Sounds like he's got solid security," Court said.

"Indeed. Zack Hightower is his body man."

Zoya gave a surprised gasp, but Court said, "That's random."

"Yeah, no shit. Good thing for Hinton, though. Zack got his principal off the X last night just outside Havana. Pace is leaving here to go up there to look into the attack." He added, "You say you're staying out of this, and that's fine. But . . . but if you wanted to pop on up the Caribbean to drink Cuba Libres for a couple of days, that might be fun."

"To do what?" Zoya asked.

"To check in on our old friend, he might need you."

Now Court spoke. "Need us to . . . what?"

"It's clear that removing Hinton must be absolutely crucial to the enemy's plan, so you can figure they'll try again. You could stay on the periphery of his AO, look for indicators of trouble." Hanley smiled. "Nobody knows trouble when they see it like you two jokers."

Zoya said, "We've got Canadian passports. We can get a visa at the embassy here. Be up there in a few hours."

"Thanks, Matt," Court said. "We'll think about it."

"Thank you. Now . . . *I'm* out of it. I guess *I'll* go get drunk."

FORTY-TWO

Scott Kincaid didn't mind that his Nassau, Bahamas, hotel suite didn't have a primo view of the ocean. The beach was just on the other side of his high-rise, but his tiny balcony here at the Baha Mar hotel and casino looked over a five-story-high water fountain and a lush green golf course, and anyway, Kincaid wasn't here to look out the window.

He was here to sit and to wait, under orders from his control officer at Operations Center Gama.

The first day here at the casino he'd gambled, winning nearly five thousand dollars, and then the first night here he lost eight. He didn't care, he'd made somewhere in the neighborhood of ten million U.S. in the past week and a half, and from the cryptic message delivered by his sexy-sounding French controller at Gama, there would be more work and more money to come.

The second day here in the Bahamas he'd stayed mostly in his room. A hangover pounded his brain until midafternoon, when he ventured to the gym and spent nearly two hours punishing his body for the excesses of the day and night before. And when he returned to hunker down in his suite, he went out to his balcony and flipped open his laptop, then logged on to a dark web address he'd long ago memorized to fuel his mind with a poison that he misinterpreted as nutrition.

He was on day three here at the Baha Mar now, it was just after noon, and he'd returned from the gym, showered, then brought his laptop out onto the balcony again.

He thought he'd head back down to the craps table in a few hours, blow a few grand more that didn't mean anything to him, but in the meantime, he logged back on to the dark web address, and then he began to scroll.

The website was called NewPatriotsFront, and it was a bulletin board and file-sharing platform run by an American neo-Nazi group called the New Aryan Order. Kincaid had come in contact with NAO members at California State Prison, Centinela, when he did a year and a half for beating a man into a coma during a bar fight in Chula Vista, and he'd been drawn into their world quickly. A narcissistic personality disorder plus an axe to grind after being charged with two crimes, both of which he found to be ludicrous, made him a particularly easy target when men whispered into his ear that everything bad that had ever happened to him in his life was the fault of the Blacks, the Jews, the Hispanics, the Catholics, or the Asians.

As he did whenever he found himself with free time, Kincaid surfed the web this warm afternoon, absorbing the writings of American Nazis, interpreting his rising blood pressure as patriotic fervor, stimulating himself by mainlining hate.

Kincaid wanted to kill everyone to preserve the purity of his race, though he'd never actually taken a DNA test himself to double-check his ancestry.

And then, just as if his god had been watching him and feeling his seething anger, his phone buzzed on the glass table, and he knew it would be Gama.

"Lancer."

Like every time before, the French woman was on the other end of the line. "This is Gama Control."

Kincaid flexed every muscle he could clench, utter excitement superseding his teeming rage. "What's up?"

"I have a tasking for you. You need to get to the airport in Nassau."

"Another audible?"

"I'm sorry?" The French woman was confused by the American football terminology.

Kincaid rolled his eyes. Anyone who didn't know American football was a fucking idiot. "This is a tasking of a new target? Not one of the originals?"

"Ah, yes. Yes, it is. All of your original targets have been prosecuted."

"Not Zakharova and Gentry."

"Yes, correct, but they were not on the initial list." She continued, "We will send an aircraft for you now. It will arrive in ninety minutes."

"Where am I going?"

"You will fly to Cuba. Don't worry about immigration, you will go in black, we have it all arranged. There is a target in Havana. We do not have the precise location yet. Once we have the target fixed, I will send you the dossier."

"What's my timeline?"

"Very short. Hours."

"The target, does he or she have protection?"

"Yes, but you will have support, as well."

Kincaid looked out over the massive fountain, fighting another eye roll. "I don't need another crew of fools like you gave me in Guatemala. I need your best team."

"And you will have it, Lancer. Get to the airport."

Kincaid ended the call, then closed his laptop. Scrolling the articles and posts by the other Nazis had given him energy, an edge, a fight in his belly. It had given him reason to be when he would have otherwise just been sitting in a comfy suite in a tourist destination casino, the antithesis of a warrior.

But now he had a new mission, a new fight, and he would put New-PatriotsFront away until the next time he felt rudderless, when it would again seek to find purpose for his unquenchable hate.

It was time to focus, to clock back in, because somebody in Havana needed to die.

Carlos Contreras had never been to Cuba, but he thought if the situation had been different, he might actually like it there.

After the mission in Tulum, Mexico, he and his loadmaster had received orders from Cyrus to sanitize the aircraft while in flight. They dumped every single piece of equipment that was not part of the aircraft itself out of the rear hatch, and then they landed in Grand Cayman, Cayman Islands. Here all three men went their separate ways without so much as a goodbye, again by order of Cyrus.

He spent half a day at a resort hotel on Grand Cayman, sitting morosely in his room, surfing a new laptop he'd bought and smoking cigarettes while listening to the thumping techno beat played by a DJ at a pool outside, and then he got the call ordering him to return to the airport.

A four-seat Cessna 182 picked him up and flew him north in the fading daylight, and then, in darkness, they descended to just over the waves.

His pilot didn't speak one word to him, even when he asked where they were going and how much time was left in the flight, but once they shot over a rocky and sandy beach and then began picking their way through hills, the man—Contreras couldn't even tell where he was from—said a single word.

"Cuba."

They landed at a grass strip lit by four old men with flashlights, and then one of the men loaded Contreras into a pickup truck and drove him north through the night.

At four a.m. he saw the signs for Havana, and by six a.m. he sat alone in a postcard-sized room in a teal-green shack in a ramshackle residential neighborhood. Downstairs, an elderly husband and wife, obviously the owners of this low-end casa particular, or private homestay, paid him little attention, so he stayed upstairs, drank coffee, smoked, and stared at his phone, willing it to ring.

His laptop was open on a rickety card table but there was no Internet; the heat spun around the dark room with the help of a lazy ceiling fan with a bad bearing that Contreras was certain would very soon drive him mad.

All he did was think about what he was involved in. He had theories about the mission he'd been sent on, though he had no idea what the hell he was doing here in Cuba. And he had a theory about Cyrus himself, a theory he would put to the test whenever he called again.

The old lady brought him rice and beans at eight, and again at one, and then, mercifully, his mobile phone rang at three p.m.

Before he answered it, however, he took it to the table with his laptop, then turned on the laptop's microphone and pressed record. He attached the phone to a cable that fed into the laptop, and then he answered.

"Yes?"

"This is Cyrus." It was the same voice as before. American, he thought. Authoritative, but not aggressive.

"I'm here in Havana."

"I am sending you coordinates. It's a church. Take a taxi there. In the parking lot you will see a van with two men inside. That is your conveyance and your security team. The boxes inside contain your equipment. This operation will be conducted on the ground, not from an aircraft."

Suits me, Contreras thought, but he had other questions.

"I am still not working for Gama, correct?"

"Correct."

"Because whatever happened in Mexico confirmed to you that there is a compromise at your operations center?"

"There *was* a compromise. The compromise has been resolved."

"Then why are you still running me?"

"Your controller at Gama has been removed from her position."

Holy shit, Contreras thought. *She* was the compromise?

He said, "Am I in danger?"

"We have confirmed that Controller Fourteen did not reveal any operational details before she was removed."

"But she might reveal them now. If you fired her, she remains a threat to—"

The American voice replied calmly. "She is no longer a threat."

There was no emotion in the words, but Contreras took them instantly to mean the woman had been killed.

He took a few breaths, then said, "The bots in Mexico. They were all controlled with integrated artificial intelligence, weren't they?"

The pause was surprisingly brief, and the confirmation delivered dispassionately. "They were. In Cuba, on the other hand, you will be piloting the ISR equipment yourself."

"No lethal autonomous weapons?"

"Lethality is coming. The man you worked with in Guatemala will be the asset on the ground you are supporting."

Contreras nodded slowly, still not understanding his mission but satisfied Cyrus was telling him everything he needed to know for now.

Except for one thing.

"Who's my target?"

"A dossier will be sent to you once you have your equipment ready and we have the target location pinpointed."

"Muy bien," Contreras said. He'd been thinking about the job, and at first he didn't notice he'd absentmindedly answered in Spanish. Once he realized his mistake he began to translate his own words, but the American spoke before he had the chance.

"Estaré en contacto." *I will be in contact.* And then the call disconnected.

The American had switched, surprisingly quickly, into perfectly accented Spanish, surprising the young Mexican.

He hit the button on his laptop to stop the recording, and then he rose from his desk and began collecting his things, stuffing them into a backpack so he could go downstairs and call a taxi.

Contreras moved with purpose, because although he remained very much in the dark about much of this, he was back on a timeline.

FORTY-THREE

Twenty hours after the attack at the restaurant by the crew of Jamaicans, Zack Hightower stood alone at a bar on Calle Obrapia in Old Havana. Just past eight thirty, the early evening's warm rain had come and gone, and Zack nursed a beer while looking off through the bar and out into the night, lost in thought.

He'd escorted Anton to the lab this morning and he'd shadowed him throughout the day. The bandage on the man's calf muscle was hidden under his track pants, and to Hightower's surprise he hadn't made a big deal about it to any of his staff as he went from lab to lab, getting reports about coding in arcane jargon that Hightower didn't even try to decipher.

Unlike the day before, Hinton returned to La Finca at the more reasonable hour of five p.m., and also unlike the day before, he did not venture back out.

Zack Hightower had been ready to push back if he'd tried, but to Zack's pleasant surprise, Hinton had just returned to his quarters and given Zack the night off.

Wren had a dinner meeting in La Finca with Kimmie and some of the senior researchers, so Zack borrowed a Land Rover and drove into the city, stopping at a hotel bar in Old Havana that was open to two sides of the street and dripping with old-world charm.

He sipped beer from a bottle, thought about his job here, thought about everything that had happened late the evening before, and he wondered if Anton would venture out again at all before the killings stopped.

If Anton didn't go anywhere but back and forth between the campus and La Finca, then he would be safe enough.

But if Anton *did* go out and about in town, or if they tried to leave Cuba before all of this was resolved, Zack was pretty damn sure the enemy would make another attempt on him, because whatever was going on, it was obvious Anton Hinton was a primary target.

His attention shifted from his thoughts about the attacks and back to the bar; his eyes probed around the room as they always did, an automatic function of living a life of danger.

Couples out to dinner, groups of what appeared to be foreign businessmen, seemingly all from China, sitting near the open windows and enjoying the slightly cool breeze in the otherwise stifling room.

He looked up and down the bar. The same eight people who had been here drinking when he sat down were still here nursing cocktails and wine and beers, but a ninth man had seated himself farther down, after the turn in the bar, facing generally in Zack's direction.

The man wasn't thirty, he had sandy brown hair, wore a white polo and glasses, and he had a Cuba Libre in front of him, the glass sparkling as it perspired in the humidity.

He was American, Zack instantly noted, although he couldn't say for certain how. He eyed the man up and down, quickly and calmly, then looked back down to his drink.

A minute later he finished, ordered another beer, and when it came he snatched the cold bottle off the marble surface and rose from his barstool. Walking coolly through the restaurant tables, he made his way around a group of Chinese, through some locals, and then sat back down at the bar, right next to the man he'd noticed facing him.

Zack took a swig of his beer, put the bottle down.

"How long?" he said, looking ahead, not at the young man next to him.

There was a pause, just as Zack had expected. And then, "I'm . . . I'm sorry?"

"How long am I waiting?"

"Uhh . . . waiting for what?"

Zack sighed, lifted the bottle in front of him. "When this beer is done, I'm out of here."

"I don't know why . . ."

"Look, kid," Zack said, still not turning to the man. "You're from the embassy. I won't go any further than that, but we both know who you work for. You look like you were sent out to fix my position, not to talk to me yourself, because you don't look like you've been off the Farm for more than, what . . . six months?"

The young man let out a defeated breath. "Almost a year."

"Don't be too hard on yourself, I'm just really fucking good at my job."

The CIA officer said nothing.

"Anyway, I assume someone above you is on the way to come talk to me, but I'm not exactly in the mood for a chat with some embassy stiff. My papers are legit, I can—"

"He's here," the young man said, deep relief evident in his voice.

Zack turned to him. "Who's here?"

He heard the barstool pull out behind him, and then he heard a new voice. "How's life here in the worker's paradise, Sierra One?"

Zack turned back around to see Jim Pace, a former teammate on his Golf Sierra unit, sitting there in an off-white linen suit. Eyeglasses, a mustache, a head of thick dark brown hair. Without looking at Zack, Pace flagged down the bartender and ordered a Havana Club rum on ice in sloppy Spanish.

Zack spoke softly. "What's a nice fella like you doing in a place like this?"

"Can you guess?"

Zack turned forward again, took a sip of his beer. The younger man on his right slid off his barstool and walked to the entrance, taking up a position there.

Zack watched him, and then he noticed a smaller Asian man in a T-shirt standing just outside in the street. He looked like he could be part of Pace's team, as well.

"I can guess you aren't in the Branch anymore."

Pace was no longer in Ground Branch, that was true, but Zack was also insinuating it was clear he had gone over into "mainstream" CIA operations. It was meant as a dig, but Pace didn't seem to mind.

"I left the fun stuff behind for the younger generation. How 'bout you?"

"You know me. Fuck the younger generation. I'm out here, still doing fun stuff."

"What does your spine think about that?"

Zack gave his first little smile of the night. "It has some reservations about my life choices."

"Heard you got into the fun stuff last night, a few miles from here. Sounds like it was an absolute blast."

Zack took another sip, his little grin having faded away. "What can I do for you, Jim?"

"You can tell me about what happened."

"Tell you about it . . . in what capacity?"

"Just two old colleagues chatting."

"What do you want to know?"

"Your sense of the opposition. Their mission, their command and control, their skill."

Zack nodded slowly, his eyes back out on the street. "Somebody could have called. Why does an ops officer out of the embassy have to find me and come question me?"

"I'm an ops officer, but I'm not at the embassy here. I'm at HQ. Special Tasks. Proliferations desk."

Hightower peeled at the label on his beer bottle. "Well then, I'm doubly confused. You're a long way from Virginia."

"Deputy Director Watkins tasked me with the Agency's investigations on the AI assassinations. I'm interviewing victims' families, coworkers, boring stuff like that."

Zack took another drink. He was on guard; he'd worked at CIA long enough to know they could make problems between him and Anton Hinton, and since CIA wasn't the one signing his paychecks anymore, his loyalty leaned towards the oddball billionaire sequestered away in the old Soviet bunker.

He looked to the two bartenders, to the dozen or so other patrons of the bar, to the several dozen dining at the tables. Any one of these people could tell Wren, Hinton, *anyone* in Hinton's organization, that Zack had held a meeting with a suited-up gringo in Old Havana.

"I seriously hope you find out all you need to know about what's going on, but I've got a solid gig I'm trying to protect."

"I'd say your job security is in good shape, considering how you saved your boss's life yesterday. You'll probably get employee of the month.

"Look. I'm not asking you anything a local cop wouldn't ask."

Zack sighed, then gave in. He spent a couple minutes going over the details of the attack, but only giving out information that was publicly available.

Pace followed up with, "The perps. Jamaican Spangler Posse. Any good?"

"They knew how to aim and shoot, more or less. They didn't know how to set up an ambush."

"But you said they killed two of your guys, some soldiers, and your principal took a round."

"Yeah," Zack allowed, not hiding his confusion about that. "Weird. Million-to-one luck, I guess."

Pace nodded. "No chance Hinton might know more about who's behind this than he's saying?"

Hightower sipped his beer. "What do you mean?"

"Two attempts on his life. Both failed. You haven't been looking into the other hits like I have, so if you don't know, I'll tell you. Every single one of the other killings was professionally accomplished. Why do you think your guy drew the long straw and had cannon fodder come after him when nobody else did?"

Zack knew little about the first attack on Hinton, but as to the second, he'd been thinking the same thing that Pace was now saying.

The skill of the attackers did not match the defenses of the target in any way.

Still, Zack didn't think Hinton was sideways. "I'm around him day and night, and I haven't seen him plotting world domination. Seems like that would be apparent."

Pace took a drink and nodded, looking off down the bar. "Granted, the complexity of all this makes one assume there would be some indicators." His chest heaved. "I don't know, though. There's something weird about him. He won't talk to us, his name comes up a lot, the two failed attempts, and, by the way, he lives in a bunker in fucking Cuba."

"I didn't say he wasn't strange. I *said* he wasn't assassinating over a dozen tech experts across the globe."

"How is your boss feeling about all this?" Pace asked.

"Blaming himself, mostly. Doubt he'll stick his head out of his secure compound until this is all over."

"What goes on at Lourdes?"

Zack cocked his head in surprise. "Lourdes is the name of the old Soviet SIGINT base. It's called the University of Information Science now. He owns one of the dozens of buildings there. It's called Hinton Labs, Havana."

Pace didn't miss a beat. "What's going on at Hinton Labs, Havana?"

"Research. I go every day. Just sixty computer geeks sitting at their desks working on shit."

"What shit?"

"How would I know? Look, Pace, I'm a bodyguard. That's it. Anton's got everyone on his staff going through some code they found in the cloud. But I don't know if Anton's completely full of shit. And I don't care. I'm here to keep him alive, and just for the record, so far, I'm kicking ass."

Pace said, "Your employer's name was on a handwritten list made by one of the victims and discovered after his death."

This took Zack by surprise. "And?"

"And . . . there are eleven other names on the list. Eight are dead, one is a Chinese scientist that we have no way of tracking down inside China, one is an AI expert in Boston who is still alive, and the other is Hinton."

"What's the connection?"

"That's what I'm trying to find out. All of the others worked with military applications in some capacity. But not Hinton. Why would he be included on that list?"

Hightower turned to him. "You're saying you think Anton might be behind it all?"

"No, I'm definitely *not* saying that. But I want to know what *you* think."

Zack let his frustration show now. "Jim, are you just out here trying to Scooby Doo your way through this shit?"

Pace sipped his drink. "Yeah. Pretty much."

"Anton's not your guy. He reads religious texts, he listens to music, he takes ice baths and saunas. He visits his AI lab, but I'm right there by his side when he does, and he's not sending kill teams out on strike missions, he's talking about computer code and neural networks and algorithms and a bunch of other shit that's Greek to me."

Pace seemed to think this over, and then he rapped the bar with his knuckles. "Okay. That's all solid intel, Zack. Thanks."

"I did *not* just give you intel on my employer."

Jim Pace stood now. "No, you definitely did not. Good to see you, Sierra One. Stay frosty out there. Whatever is going on . . . it's still going on."

"Thanks for the advice. If I can give you some advice, maybe tell your boys out there to wear some local clothing next time. Looks like a fucking IBM convention just rolled into Old Havana."

They shook hands, but there wasn't much warmth between them. Pace started to turn away, but then he turned back, a finger in the air. "Speaking of the guys from the Company . . . I heard some interesting news about an old colleague of ours."

Zack had finished his beer, but he continued sitting on the stool, not wanting to leave at the same time as Pace. In a bored tone he said, "Who?"

"Court Gentry."

Zack gave nothing away, but his mind was racing. *What the fuck does Pace know about Gentry?*

He waved to the bartender, ordered another drink despite his earlier plan. "What's ole Sierra Six up to these days?"

"Blowing up robots in Mexico."

Zack blinked hard. When Pace didn't elaborate, he recovered, said, "Mexico's got robots? Cool." The beer came and he took a long sip.

Pace said, "Six somehow got himself mixed up in all these killings."

"It's definitely *not* because he's a computer genius on the cutting edge of something revolutionary."

Pace chuckled. "Says he was brought in to protect one of the targets, but got chased halfway across Central America by drones and mechanical dogs in the process."

"He okay?"

"He's okay, from what I heard. He's done with his part of the op, but he only managed to extract himself by destroying all the lethal autonomous weapons sent after him.

"Be careful, Sierra One," Pace said.

Zack swigged and smiled. "I'll keep my eyes on the Coke machines back at the lab in case they're thinking about coming to life."

"Funny," Pace said, but he didn't smile back.

An hour later, Hightower knocked on the door to Anton Hinton's private gym.

"Anton? It's Zack."

"Come on in, mate."

Hightower entered to find Hinton up to his neck in a large ice bath, his mop of hair wet, his face red and registering the pain of the intense cold on his entire body.

His headphones hung on a towel rack next to him.

Before Zack could say anything, Hinton spoke through chattering teeth. "Got eight minutes more . . . sorry."

"No, that's fine." Zack had never had a meeting with someone sitting in a bathtub, but there had been a lot of firsts for him since he'd taken this job.

He hesitated before speaking. He was conflicted about what he was about to do, and Zack was rarely conflicted about anything when it came to his duties.

"How's your leg?" he asked.

"It's doing fine. Sorry I went nuts about it last night. I'm sure I looked pretty pathetic to you."

"There was a lot of adrenaline in all of us."

Anton rose a little out of the ice, resting his arms on the side of the tub. "What's up?"

"An old Agency colleague of mine showed up at the bar this evening. I had no idea he was here, and this meeting was in no way preplanned by me."

"What did he come down here for?"

"He had questions about the attempt last night."

Anton pulled himself a little more out of the bath, clearly so he could focus less on the torturous conditions he was subjecting himself to and more on the conversation. "What questions?"

"He's investigating the attacks. Not just against you, but the others, also. He's going all around, talking to people."

Anton shivered. "It's window dressing, Zack. The White House is covering itself. I'm sure we're going to be able to provide evidence, publicly, in the next few days, that will lay the blame right at Washington's doorstep. Their project Mind Game was weaponized, by them, but the code made it out into the world. They're trying to hide what they've done."

Zack said nothing, Hinton seemed so certain. Still, he answered all of Hinton's questions about his conversation with Pace at the bar.

Hinton rose out of the ice, grabbed a towel, and wrapped it around his waist. He dried off with a second towel, much to Hightower's relief, and then he put on his tracksuit, gingerly pulling on pants so as not to disturb the waterproof bandaging on his calf. Hightower stood there, looking around the gym to avert his eyes.

He saw a book next to a stair climber. *A Bible for Atheists.* "You read a lot," he said. "And not just books about computing."

Behind him, Anton laughed. "I haven't read a book on computing in years. That's what my staff does for fun. I'd like to think I've transcended from the coding into the ethics of what we do."

Curious, Zack said, "I saw you with the Bible, the Torah, the Qur'an. And now a book on atheism. You trying to figure out which one you are?"

He laughed again. "I find the study of comparative theology utterly fascinating. I explore belief systems, learn from them."

"Does that help you?"

"Does it help me understand my place in this world? No. I already know my place. It does help me understand the rest of the world. How they are led. How they are manipulated."

Zack didn't know what to say.

Anton continued. "A bold and secure future for all. That's our motto, you know, and that means everything to me. Technology can help us build the society that religion always promised but never delivered."

"No offense, but that sounds a little Big Brother."

"None taken. I get what you're saying, I really do. But I've read Orwell, too. His Big Brother was a despot. An iron fist. The work we do here is all about benevolence. Peace. Compassion."

"Right." Zack wasn't a religious man himself, but he found himself skeptical of anyone who presumed to know more than the rest of the world.

They shook hands, and Anton held his eye contact. "You coming to me tonight to tell me about your meeting. That brought you into the circle of trust. Gareth vouched for you, but as you know, I have some reservations about your government."

"I gathered."

"Thanks for telling me." He looked off into the distance a moment. "Thanks for making me wear the vest last night. I'd be dead without it. Thanks for everything."

"Sure, Anton. See you in the morning."

Zack headed back to his quarters, glad he'd made the decision to tell his boss what happened but somehow uneasy with the conversation.

FORTY-FOUR

Jim Pace clutched his cell phone in his hand and a fat accordion file under his arm as he stepped through a door held open for him by a guard on the third floor of the U.S. embassy at 55 Calzada Street in northern Havana. He left Travers and Hash in the hall behind him, and he left his phone on a shelf in a small office inside, since neither the men nor the tech were allowed where Pace was going.

He showed his credentials to the attendant seated at a desk. The woman politely but professionally instructed him to e-sign his name on a tablet computer, and then he was sent over to a keypad on the far wall by a door.

He tapped a code, and the access control system responded with a loud click that told him a dead bolt had opened; he pulled open the thick door and stepped inside the U.S. embassy's Sensitive Compartmented Information Facility. This SCIF looked similar to the couple dozen others he'd been in around the world at U.S. government outposts while working at CIA. The room was ten feet deep and thirty feet wide, larger than some; there were two small conference tables, each topped by audiovisual equipment, and several file cabinets in a corner. The walls were pale blue, air ducts were covered with wire mesh and metal bars, and cameras and motion sensors hung high in the corners.

He knew the SCIF was soundproof and encased in material that made electronic eavesdropping impossible, and the room would be hardened against forced entry with steel and concrete.

An attendant locked the door behind him, then stepped over to the file cabinets, where he stood at parade rest, though he wore a suit and tie and not a uniform.

A second attendant, a female CIA communications specialist Pace had met the afternoon before, sat down at a small desk and worked a keyboard, and soon one of the monitors on the nearest conference table came to life.

Jim Pace sat down in front of it, and he recognized the image before him. It was the smallest of the seventh-floor conference rooms at CIA headquarters in McLean, Virginia, and the room was empty.

Pace looked down to his watch, and then he opened up the accordion file he'd entered with and arranged several stacks of paper on the desk.

A minute later the room at HQ began to fill. Operations officer Angela Lacy, assistant to the DDO Naveen Gopal, and operations executive Chip Nance stepped in and sat down, their eyes on a monitor on the wall just below Pace's viewpoint. The man sitting alone in Cuba knew that his image was being sent from the camera in the top of the monitor here on his desk, and they were all looking at him in real time.

A moment later, Deputy Director for Operations Trey Watkins shuffled into the room and sat at the head of the table, and the director of the Special Activities Center, Steve Hernandez, entered and sat down next to him.

The meeting began when Watkins spoke. "What'cha got, Jim?"

"Thank you for the meeting today, sir. There have been some critical developments." Pace knew not to waste anyone's time in that room in Virginia. "To begin, the personality we've been looking for in relation to this, Martina Sommer, is in Singapore. She arrived two weeks ago, used a credit card at an airport shop after clearing customs, and then . . . nothing."

"Nothing?"

"No activity. No sightings. Hasn't shown up on any cams the Five Eyes has access to, which isn't a lot, but we do have visibility at major choke points. Unless she somehow got out of the country without going through immigration, then she is still there.

"We're working under the assumption she's still on the job for the opposition at their ops center."

Gopal said, "Chinese intelligence runs ops out of Singapore. Could be the Chin—"

Watkins cut him off. "*We* run ops out of Singapore. We can't draw conclusions about the culprit solely from the location of the enemy operations center." To Pace he said, "What are we doing to find her?"

"My team at Langley are on it. We've got Singapore station and Far East desk helping. But if she doesn't do something different than she's done in the past two weeks—that is, show her face—then I don't have high hopes we're going to locate her."

Watkins leaned forward on the table. "This meeting was called because you said you've made progress. I seriously hope you just led with the bad news and are now going to hit us with some good news, because if you call that significant, I'm going to be disappointed."

Pace smiled a little. "I wouldn't spin everyone up for that, sir."

"Good. Go on, then. What about that circuit board you picked up from Mexico?"

Pace hadn't outright lied about the origin of the intelligence he'd passed on to HQ, but he'd been evasive, and Watkins and his staff had not pressed, assuming Pace had a reason for not telling them, and that reason might be that they could be compromised with the details.

"That's borne significant fruit, actually, and it's the reason I called the meeting and asked SAC director Hernandez to attend. We traced several components on the board to various companies, mostly in China, but that doesn't really tell us much because these components are bought and sold around the world and could be acquired on the retail market. The chips themselves aren't anything special, either. Mass produced, Qualcomm, Intel, Micron, just what you'd find in any PC, TV, or other computerized device. The PCB, on the other hand—"

Watkins held a hand up. "PCB?"

"The printed circuit board, sir. The broken plastic piece itself that the chips are affixed to. We've traced this back to a single fabricator in Guang-zhou, China, and this fabricator works almost exclusively making PCBs used in China's defense industry. The boards are customized to fit into drones, aircraft black boxes, missile systems, and the like. In fact, no boards from this fabricator are exported out of China at all."

Nance said, "Then it's China doing this."

Lacy disagreed. "It's China building these armed robots, perhaps. That doesn't necessarily mean they are orchestrating the killings."

Before anyone in Virginia could reply, Pace said, "There is one anom-aly, however. Eleven months ago, a shipment of PCBs from this fabricator were not exported, but they were sold to a company called Wan Chai Ma-chine Technology Limited, an industrial automation firm in Hong Kong. Essentially, this company makes advanced robot arms for manufacturing automobiles, televisions, things like that.

"It's strange that the fabricator shipped goods to this civilian concern, because every other shipment of PCBs we managed to trace went to de-fense industry–related companies in China.

"It's even stranger," Pace added, "because this company in Hong Kong is exclusively a domestic firm. They don't export; they import chips and metals and software from around the world, but they don't ship anything out of the country themselves."

He held for effect, then said, "Until roughly two weeks ago. At that point, they sent the first of three shipments abroad."

"Where did these shipments go?" Watkins asked.

"One shipment of six pallets, seven hundred sixty pounds in weight, went to the U.S. via an air cargo freight company. We checked and it was marked as picked up at a freight forwarder at Miami International Airport six days ago."

Everyone looked at Pace, waiting for him to make a connection.

But Angela Lacy spoke up. "The assault in Mexico. Where this circuit board was found."

"That's our working assumption. Someone picked the goods up in Florida and took them to Mexico, and then deployed them at Jack Tudor's residence in Tulum."

He flipped a page in front of him. "The second shipment went over water; it was a forty-foot shipping container, capable of carrying up to sixty thousand pounds, and it was delivered to Singapore."

"Singapore." Watkins said it softly, taking it in.

"I should note," Pace added, holding up a hand, "the shipment was picked up and, supposedly, delivered to a warehouse facility there."

Watkins said, "Please tell me you have someone from Singapore station watching that warehouse."

Pace said, "They are on their way there now; this information is only a half hour old. Of course we only know what the bill of lading says. We don't know the cargo is there in the warehouse; it could have been delivered somewhere else."

Watkins turned to Hernandez. "You need to get a team over there, ready to raid that facility, and this ops center the German woman works at if it somehow turns up."

"Understood," he said, and he made a note on a pad in front of him. "Charlie X-ray is in Seoul. Could be on site in eight to ten hours. Maybe quicker."

"Get 'em moving."

"On it," Hernandez said, and he looked back to one of his team standing against the wall, who turned and shot out the door.

Now Watkins looked back up to the monitor. "And the third shipment?"

"Six days ago a forty-foot container was put on a ship at the port of Hong Kong. Late this evening, the ship will call to port in Havana, Cuba."

"Holy shit," Watkins said. "Where you are now. Where Hinton is."

"That is correct. We were already at the airport getting ready to head to Austria to talk to the coworkers of the man killed there the other day when we got this intel from my staff, so we turned around and headed right back here to the embassy."

Chip Nance made the connection that Pace was clearly implying. "If one of these shipments was armed robots sent to Mexico to kill Tudor, then that means someone is probably now sending armed robots after Hinton."

Pace said, "We think that's what happened in Mexico—the group orchestrating it had logistics people in country deploy the lethal autonomous weapons, and we think that might be happening here, as well. Havana

Harbor isn't the main container shipping port in Cuba. That's Mariel, fifty klicks west. The fact that this is going directly into Havana, just a few miles from where Hinton lives and works, gives us concerns it will be used in an attack on him. What's confusing to us is the timing, however. This shipment had already been on the water for five days when Hinton was attacked the second time."

"What does that indicate to you?"

"We don't know, but one possibility is that this equipment was being sent to Cuba to be used in a raid on the Hinton Labs facility here. According to Zack Hightower, there are sixty computer scientists working in the field of artificial intelligence at the lab."

Lacy put the tip of her pen in her mouth as she thought, but soon she pulled it out. "So the opposition saw an opportunity to kill Hinton when he was out in the city, but the equipment being sent is going to be used in . . . in like a complete facility wipeout?"

Pace shrugged a little. "That's all we can conclude with the information we have. Remember, only a very small shipment of unmanned weapons was responsible for a dozen deaths in Mexico."

"My God," Watkins muttered. "Twenty-nine tons of the type of weaponry described by Hanley's source could devastate a building full of scientists."

Steve Hernandez, the head of the Special Activities Center, said, "Jim, you have Juliet Victor down there with you. They can do a sneak and peek on that vessel before the container off-loads."

"I agree," Pace said. "Though I'd rather we had more than six guys doing it, to be honest." He looked to Watkins for approval now.

To Pace's relief, Watkins nodded but said, "The fewer the better. Not looking to start a war with Cuba. We'll have to get the president's authorization, of course, but go ahead and have them prep for a raid on the ship. When does it dock?"

"It's due into port tonight around midnight, will dock at the container terminal at eight a.m. tomorrow."

Hernandez said, "I'll talk to Travers and the local station. We'll get them scuba gear, have them do a bottom-up raid as soon as it drops anchor."

Gopal said, "I assume we're going to be alerting Hinton's people to this threat to him."

To this, Pace was adamant. "No. We'll keep this close hold. If we don't get to the material before it's off-loaded, we'll alert Hightower. Hinton's well protected here, he'll be fine."

"From that amount of weaponry?"

Pace thought a moment, then said, "I don't want to alert Hinton that we know about this shipment."

"Are you suggesting Anton Hinton could be involved in this?"

"I have nothing firm on that, sir. I just would like to play my cards close to my vest."

Angela Lacy spoke up now. "It's the right call. Hinton has sixty top people working for him, and that's a small industry. If we tip our hand in any way before the raid, there is a chance one of those people will talk to the wrong person. Too much opportunity for a compromise."

"If the raid is unsuccessful," Pace said, "if we find anything we can't deal with ourselves, my first call is going to be to Zack so he can get his man below ground."

Hernandez agreed, and then Watkins assented a moment later.

The DDO then drummed his fingers on the desk for a moment. "Jim . . . something else you need to keep in mind."

"Sir?"

"It should go without saying that there are significant political issues at play with Cuba. I don't want any Agency personnel from Havana station, men and women who might already be known to the Cubans, involved in this raid at all."

"What about foreign nationals?"

Watkins nodded. "You can use Havana station agents in Cuba. You'll need them. You will work out of the embassy so we can communicate; we'll slip you in and out without being seen by the Cubans. There, you can talk to the case officers, find agents who can help you, procure equipment and transpo, whatever you need done in the city. And we'll get you a safe house for the rest of your team. But when it comes time for the operation at the port, you and Juliet Victor are on your own. Can you do it?"

Pace did not hesitate. "Count on it, sir."

Watkins stood. "I'll get to work on that presidential approval, and Steve will get Juliet Victor what they need."

Ten minutes later Jim Pace sat alone in his borrowed windowless office, his cell phone back in his possession. He'd already told Travers to get his team ready to hit a freighter sailing into port this evening; they were all downstairs talking to operations personnel so they could acquire the equipment they'd need, so Jim unlocked his phone, opened his Signal app, and dialed a number.

Several seconds later it was answered. "Hanley."

"Hey, Matt. It's Jim. I need to talk to Gentry."

There was a pause, then Hanley said, "I can give you his number, but I'm not sure he'd answer if you called. I can reach out, he'll recognize my number."

"That'll work. If he's still in Colombia, I need him to bust ass up here and help me out."

After a moment, Hanley sniffed. "Buddy, you might be the luckiest son of a bitch I know."

"Meaning?"

"Last I heard he was thinking about heading up to Cuba. I told him Zack was working for Hinton, and he said he might go up to watch his back."

"Wait . . . he's *here*?"

"Could be."

Pace whistled. "Hot damn. Something big is going down tomorrow a.m. Having him here, assuming he's on our side, that is, would be a comfort. I remember what that guy could do."

"He's even better now. And yes, he's on our side. I'll call him now, try to put you guys in touch."

"Excellent."

"Hey," Hanley said, "any trouble getting that intel to Watkins without my name coming up?"

Pace chuckled at this. "He seems very uninterested in where the intelligence came from."

Hanley said, "He's covering his ass, which covers mine, thankfully." Hanley added, "Good luck with whatever's happening. Wish I could be there to help."

"You've helped more than you know, Matt, and if you land me Gentry by tonight, you might just be a lifesaver."

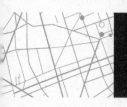

FORTY-FIVE

Chris Travers sat on a worn wooden bus stop bench on Avénida Septima, facing a dusty street and the Mount Barreto Ecological Park beyond it. The park was occupied by dozens of kids playing baseball, along with clusters of families enjoying cookouts. Couples walked together and dogs ran off leash as the sun began to set into thick low clouds hanging to the west behind Travers's back.

Between his knees, Travers held a simple gray canvas knapsack of some weight. With his brown beard, sunglasses, and ball cap, he could have been mistaken for a local, unless of course someone spoke to him, because he did not speak *any* Spanish, much less Spanish with a Cuban accent.

A few other people waited around for the bus, but none were close by the bench, and for this he was glad.

He checked his watch, then heard footsteps scuffing the dry ground of a vacant lot behind him. The steps continued approaching, but Travers didn't turn around to look.

Finally a man appeared on his right and sat down, and Travers sat up straighter, stretching his back in the process, and he snuck a quick glance at the new arrival to the bench.

A bearded man a little smaller than himself sat there, his hands empty, flat on his knees, his khaki pants old and worn. He wore a blue Yankees ball cap, his white linen shirt was sweat stained, his sunglasses were cheap Ray-Ban knock-offs. His cheeks were sunburned. The man paid him no attention, he just gazed out over the road, over the park, seemingly disinterested in everything.

Softly, Chris said, "Long time, no see."

"It's been a while," Court Gentry replied. "You're not going to shoot me, are you?"

Travers gave a little sigh. "Gotta admit, it's weird. One minute the suits want you dead, want us to do it, the next minute we're coming to you on bended knee for help.

"The question is," Travers said, "are you one of the good guys, or not?"

"That's kind of an existential question, isn't it?"

"No, dude. I am asking you specifically. Are you on the right side of all this shit that's going on?"

"I'm just here to help Pace, maybe help Zack, too."

"All right," Travers said after a moment. "We won't shoot you today. I'll check in with Langley about tomorrow, see what the policy is then."

Court chuckled a little. "Hear you guys get to have some fun tonight."

"It was *supposed* to be tonight. Cover of darkness, nice and simple."

"But?"

"But there's a storm west of Haiti, heading southwest. The ship we're tasked with hitting changed course to avoid it, and it won't arrive till nearly seven a.m. now."

"Shit. Daylight boarding. That'll be a barrel of laughs."

"Good chance the storm will be here same time as the ship. That will buy us a little cover, but still . . . not ideal."

"What do you need from us?"

"Jim wants you to serve as countersurveillance on his poz while he runs overwatch for us. Me and my guys will hit the freighter at first opportunity."

A bus turned onto the road a half mile to their left, and it approached with a cloud of smog trailing it as it passed the park.

Travers eyed the bus but spoke softly to Court. "Just hope we can get to these fuckin' robots before somebody flips the switch that turns them on. I saw *The Terminator*, don't want to *live* it."

"Well, I *did* live it, and I don't want a sequel."

"*Judgment Day,*" Travers said.

"Yeah," Court said, and then he looked to Travers. "What do you mean?"

"*T2: Judgment Day.*"

"What is—"

"*That's* the sequel."

Turning forward once again, Court said, "They made *another Terminator?* I need to check that out."

Travers sighed. "You must have been a weird kid, Violator."

Court said nothing.

The bus pulled to a stop right in front of them and the door opened.

Travers rose, stepped aboard the bus without a word or a glance, and the door shut behind him.

Court remained on the bench as the bus rumbled off. Chris Travers's canvas bag lay against his left leg.

Minutes later Court climbed into the front passenger seat of a white Hyundai Sonata that all but screamed the fact that it was a rental. Zoya sat behind the wheel, her blond hair up in a bun and wearing a dark red linen top tied off at the waist. She put the car in gear and they rolled forward, heading to the east towards Old Havana.

Neither spoke as Court fished through the canvas bag propped in his lap. After a few seconds he nodded and looked up at her. "A pair of G26s."

"Yawn," she said, unimpressed by the small and fat Glock 9-millimeter subcompacts the Ground Branch officer had delivered to them.

"What did you expect? A flamethrower?"

Zoya kept her eyes on the road. "I wish."

Court looked back in the bag. "Three mags each, looks like Federal 147 grain hollow-points."

Zoya kept driving. "That's it?"

"Belly band holsters." He fished around a little more, pulled out a small box and opened it. "Earpiece mics. Charger. Phone attachments. A pair of Vortex twelve-power binos. That's all."

Zoya shrugged. "Well, we don't really have a mission, so I guess we're adequately equipped."

Zoya had been bugged by the fact that Pace had told Court he just wanted him to watch his back while he ran overwatch on Travers's op.

"We have a mission."

"Right. Sit there and watch for the Cuban authorities in the center of Havana, which is, I'm pretty sure, just full of Cuban authorities."

"Jim doesn't trust me, but he also knows his situation here is a shit sandwich. If his Ground Branch team is deployed, he's all alone. He wants us close by and armed in case the shit hits the fan and he's compromised, but he also wants us on standby if he has a hard target he wants us to pursue without Agency comebacks." He sighed a little. "If a bunch of Cubans need to die, he'll send us, not Juliet Victor."

"Who's Juliet—"

"The paramilitaries here with Pace. There's only six of them, and Travers is running the team."

Zoya had worked with Travers before. "Chris is good," she said.

"So's Jim," Court said. "But don't forget, those guys are looking out for the Agency, not us." He zipped the bag back up. "We have to look out for ourselves."

Zoya scoffed at this. "If we were looking out for ourselves, we'd be down in Buenos Aires having drinks on a patio and arguing about which restaurant to pick for dinner."

"That's very true," he said, looking at her. "Is that our plan after this?"

"I don't know," she said. "I'm worried you're not going to want to go quiet again. Worried you'll link up with Fitzroy, or Hanley or Angela Lacy, or even this Pace guy. Somebody who can get you back into the fight full-time."

He sighed a little. "I want to be with you. And not with you surrounded by assassins, robots, and the Cuban security services. I want to be with you at a patio in Buenos Aires, arguing about where to go to dinner."

She smiled a little, but he didn't know if she believed him.

He didn't know if he believed himself, either. He wanted all those things, yes, but he wondered if he'd ever be able to just melt away, to sit back while the world kept turning and burning, to watch events take place on television that he might have had some positive impact on if he'd brought his very specific but very well-honed talents to bear.

He wondered if he'd ever be able to stop killing motherfuckers who deserved to die.

To his relief, she smiled at him. "Sounds nice, doesn't it?"

"Sounds amazing." He reached over and took her right hand, held it as she drove on in the fading light.

The thunderstorm over Havana all but blackened the sky even though dawn had just broken. The lights of a half-dozen freighters and tankers anchored in the harbor close to the container terminal twinkled through the rain and misty conditions, the vessels waiting their turn to dock at the massive quay for off-loading.

The terminal was well lit but inactive, though that was due to the weather and not the early hour; nobody wanted to be sitting in one of the ten-story metal gantry cranes or standing by a three-story tower of forty-foot steel containers in a thunderstorm.

Jim Pace took in the view by panning his high-power variable optic spotting scope left and right. The equipment had been provided by Havana station, and it was impressive but a little complicated for Pace, who had spent a hell of a lot of time in the past decade looking at spreadsheets and videoconference monitors and a hell of a lot less time looking through state-of-the-art optics while running overwatch for a team of hitters.

He adjusted the handle on the tripod to slew his view a little to the right, and then he pushed the zoom to roughly half of its 100-power magnification. The name on the bow of the massive vessel that had just dropped anchor came into view through the darkness and the rain.

Estelle ETC was a Panamax-sized container ship owned by Expert Transit Cargo of Hong Kong, and Pace knew it had made the journey from Asia, through the Panama Canal, and now here to Havana Harbor in just six days.

The ship was seven hours late, meaning the Juliet Victor boarding would have to go incredibly smoothly for the Ground Branch team to finish their job before the storms passed and the sun illuminated their egress for everyone in the harbor to see.

Pace knew it was his job to facilitate this smooth operation, even though he was six hundred yards or so away from the action.

He stood ten feet back from the open door of a tiny third-floor, harbor-facing furnished apartment with a good view of the water and an even better view of the container terminal just a couple hundred yards in front of him.

This place was a dump, dusty and moldy like it had been abandoned for years; the furniture was broken and bland, and the other makeshift apartments on this floor looking over the water were uninhabited, as well.

Havana was a flat city, so the third-floor disused space that an agent for the local CIA station had acquired on the top floor of an old dockside warehouse had seemed like the best vantage point, but there was no way Pace could get eyes on everything happening in the harbor from here, even with the high-quality spotting scope.

The ground floor of the warehouse, in contrast, had been cleaned up and converted into a massive artisans' market that wouldn't open for another hour, so Pace had the entire building to himself for now. He had spent the evening looking at the layout of the entire space, familiarizing himself with the sight lines and the three stairwells, even checking the big freight elevator that led up here, only to find it was out of service and the car had been removed, so now it was just a big dark hole when looking down from the top floor.

In addition to the front door he kept open so his scope didn't have to look through the imperfect glass of the front window of the flat, there was also a rear exit, but it led to a metal catwalk running along the inside of the back wall. The catwalk was two stories above the main warehouse floor, which meant if Pace had to use it to evacuate after eight a.m., everyone on the ground floor of the twenty-five-thousand-square-foot artisans' market would probably stop and stare, something any self-respecting CIA officer would be keen to avoid. Still, he was happy to know he had an extra escape option if the local authorities came looking for him.

And he was also thankful Gentry and his cohort would be somewhere watching the approaches to this location so he could focus all his attention on Juliet Victor out in the water.

Long-distance surveillance was no cakewalk. To do it right, one needed to disassociate with everything happening close, and focus all energy through optics on whatever distant location was under surveillance.

Even with Gentry and his friend outside, even with an idea of how to get the fuck out of here in a hurry, even with the little Glock 43 pistol Pace had talked Travers into lending him, standing by himself in a dark room in the middle of the capital city of a semi-enemy nation and concentrating all his attention on a distant position was scary as hell.

The American standing in the darkened flat remained perfectly still behind his optic for a time, and then he tapped an encrypted radio on his belt that was connected to a wired headset he wore over his head.

"Overwatch to Victor Actual, how do you read?"

Chris Travers's voice was tinny from the encryption through his radio. "Victor Actual. Five, five."

"Say status?" Pace could hear the rain through the transmission, and he imagined Travers and his team were already soaked.

"We're about to enter the water. Hard to say about any current in the harbor. I'm estimating about twenty mikes before you hear from me again."

"Roger that. All quiet on the vessel. Two patrol boats visible, both way north of your poz at the mouth of the harbor, no factor on your ingress. Good luck."

Pace swiveled his scope to the east in a futile search for the Juliet Victor team now, but he didn't have line of sight on their insertion point, the far side of an abandoned dockyard on the southern tip of the harbor. Slipping into the water at that location meant a longer swim for the Ground Branch team than they would have preferred, but the high weeds, rusted-out hulls of oil storage containers and long-ago-discarded piping made that area the best place to enter the water covertly.

So Jim Pace scanned and waited, only pulling his eye out of the spotting scope to duck into the little kitchen to refill his thermos of coffee from a coffee maker he'd brought along while the rain hammered down on the rusty and leaky tin roof above him.

FORTY-SIX

One and a half miles away, Mexican national Carlos Contreras stepped into the front room of his little homestay, noted the heavy weather outside, and waited for the two security men sent by Cyrus to duck out of the Polar Air Conditioning Service van parked out front and run through the deluge and into the house. When they came in, they followed him back upstairs, helped him with the several cases and two backpacks he carried, and then together they all headed out to the van.

Contreras had his equipment with him, and he'd been up late in the night testing it. Cuba was a particularly nonpermissive environment for drones, so the models he'd fly today were tiny and therefore harder to see, plus they made much less noise than the more robust units he'd used in Mexico and Guatemala.

But they'd also be useless in a thunderstorm, so he wondered when the weather would pass so he could put them to work.

Soon they were all out in the van, but the driver had yet to be given a destination because Contreras was still waiting on targeting info from Cyrus.

The three of them smoked in silence, Carlos ate a candy bar for breakfast, and they all downed cafecitos, tiny sweet shots of coffee the wife of one of the Cubans in the vehicle had prepared and sent with her husband for today's outing, along with a tall stack of little disposable paper cups.

The two Cubans carried pistols, Contreras had noticed as they lugged the gear, and he wondered if they might be off-duty cops hired by Cyrus to watch his back, but he purposefully didn't engage the men in much conversation.

The Mexican had just crumpled an empty cup and dropped it on the floor of the van when he felt his phone vibrate in his pocket. He put out his cigarette and lifted the device to his eyes.

A Signal message from Cyrus, giving him the last known coordinates of the target, a crystal clear image of the man, and a dossier, which he clicked open.

Contreras took a moment to read it, then blinked hard when he realized who he was being sent after today.

"Madre de dios," he muttered to himself.

He couldn't believe it, and he questioned whether he was being paid enough for what he would be asked to do.

It took a full minute for him to respond, and when he did, his reply was terse.

Understood.

For the first time in this mission he was truly afraid, but he told himself he was a professional, and he would see this job through.

He tapped the driver on the shoulder, then handed him the phone so he could see the map area they'd be working in. Contreras said, "We need to park the van very carefully. Somewhere it won't be noticed."

The driver grumbled something about knowing how to do his job, and then he put the van in gear and began rolling forward, while Contreras went to work setting up his monitoring station in the back.

"Madre de dios," he muttered again.

Scott Kincaid lurched up in his bed to a sitting position; sweat dripped into his eyes before he had a chance to wipe his bald head dry.

It took him a second to remember where he was—a hotel in Havana,

Cuba—and what he was doing: waiting on intelligence that would direct him to his next victim.

The nightmare he'd just awoken from felt like it had lasted from the moment he laid his head on his pillow last night till right now, and it felt as authentic as it had when he'd lived the nightmare for real in his past.

As a comfort, he reached between his legs and hefted the Republic Forge Longslide pistol, held it to his beating heart, the cold metal helping to bring him out of his dream and back to the here and now.

His rib cage hurt where the Guatemalan cop had winged him several days earlier, and this sharp burning pain also helped him collect his thoughts, to take him deeper away from the nightmare, the repeat of his past, and to bring him forward to the present.

There were a hell of a lot of past events the subconscious of Scott Kincaid could have drawn on to generate a nightmare, and he did dream about all sorts of heinous things that had happened to him, at least once or twice a week.

He was a veteran of intense combat; he was an assassin. His mind had a plethora of fears to draw from when he slept.

But the nightmare tonight was not of war, and it was not of murder.

It was of Dad. The most terrifying force he'd ever come across.

Kincaid shook away last night's horror and climbed out of bed. His ribs stung as he walked to the window. Looking out at the heavy weather, he muttered to himself. "Great. No fucking ISR."

It was early still; storms in the Caribbean could come and go, so he pushed this concern out of his mind and checked his phone. No messages from Gama had come during the night, so right there in the darkened room he did push-ups and sit-ups; the ragged wound on his right side where the bullet had grazed him in Guatemala burned with each rep.

And then he stepped out onto the balcony and into the rain, wearing only his boxers. Using the balcony above his as a pull-up bar, he hung his body out over the narrow dirty street below, which would have certainly drawn a lot of attention here in Old Havana had there been anyone out and about.

Back inside he pulled off his underwear and toweled off, stood naked in the bathroom, and then heard the beep from his phone, indicating a text had come through Signal.

He raced back into the bedroom, snatched it up, and looked at the image of a man staring back at him. The face meant nothing, so he scrolled down to see the man's identity.

His eyes blinked hard. Aloud in the dark Havana hotel room he whispered reverently, "You've got to be kidding."

Seconds later he'd jammed his earpiece into his ear and placed a call to his controller.

"Control," the French woman said. Kincaid wondered if she ever slept.

"It's Lancer. I'll kill him . . . but I want a bonus. Three million U.S."

"I'm not in a position—"

"Get Cyrus to approve, or I don't go after this target."

There was a lengthy pause, and then, just as he'd suspected, the director of Gama came on the line.

In his thick Northern European accent he said, "As before, Lancer, if you do not like the terms of your employment, go through your handler to—"

"I can't go through my handler because my handler is fucking dead."

"Wha . . . what?"

"Killed in Mexico, three nights ago. You might have seen it on the news."

"Jack Tudor? He was—"

"Your boss doesn't tell you shit, does he? You need to go to him and I need to see one point five mil U.S. put into my account before I raise a finger today. The rest upon completion. You know as well as I do that this target warrants that amount."

The director fumbled for words for a moment, but finally he said, "I'll get back to you."

Kincaid ended the call and then went to re-dress the wound to his ribs and find some clothes. If Gama wanted this man dead bad enough to sneak him and a drone operator into fucking Cuba, then they would damn well pay up for it.

Court Gentry sat alone on the concrete second-floor balcony overlooking the harbor, just five hundred yards from the artisans' market and the abandoned apartment above it where Jim Pace had set up his overwatch. A tin roof hanging over half the balcony protected him from the storm, and through the rain he was just able to see the west side of Pace's building, but he was unable to make out the cargo ship Travers should be hitting any minute now.

If the weather cleared he might be able to get a glimpse of it, and when the ship came to the quay at the container terminal it would be right in front of him.

But he didn't plan on sitting here that long.

Zoya stepped out of the little room behind him, a pair of mugs of cheap coffee in her hands. She sat down next to him on the concrete—this balcony had no furniture—and she leaned her body against his, her head on his shoulder, and they watched the rain in silence.

After a moment she said, "You needed this."

"Did I?"

"Yeah. Now that we're operational you're happier, more relaxed."

"That's ridiculous."

She shook her head. "It's not. Deny it if you must, my dear, but you live for this shit."

Court wasn't in the mood to argue, nor was he in the mood to self-analyze this morning. Instead, he just sipped coffee a moment, then said, "When the weather clears and cafés in the neighborhood begin filling up with people, we'll go mobile."

"Wouldn't make sense to be standing down there in the rain."

"Right." He looked up. "It will pass, but I'm glad about this cover. Chris should be hitting right now."

Zoya sipped her coffee, then sniffed. "You're so jealous."

He shook his head. "I hate bottom-ups."

Her head turned to him in surprise. "You hate *what?*"

"Bottom-ups. Boarding ships from the water. It's a total pain in the ass." He looked to her. "I'll leave that to Travers, and you and I can go down to the street to get a café con leche as soon as the rain passes."

Zoya leaned her head back against his shoulders. "Here's hoping it rains all day."

"Yeah," Court said, but he was thinking about Travers and his team.

. . .

Ten feet below the rain-swept surface of Havana Harbor, Japanese American and Ground Branch officer Joe "Hash" Takahashi shifted his body from a horizontal to a vertical position, and then he gently kicked his fins once to propel himself slowly upwards. A few seconds later his head broke the surface, thick black hair indistinguishable from the surrounding black water if anyone had been looking in his direction, something he seriously doubted.

The rain seemed as strong as it had been when he'd last been above the waterline, and his confidence that no one could see him from here was strong enough that he put a little air into his buoyancy control device, maintaining his position at the surface without the need to continue kicking his fins.

He found himself exactly where he needed to be: close enough to the Panamax cargo ship to reach out and touch the hull, just slightly aft on the port side, opposite the container terminal with its bright lights three hundred meters distant. On this side of the ship it was all but dark, so he raised his mask to see better, and then he did a slow 360-degree scan, careful not to make noise or waves. Only when he was back facing the red hull did he stop and touch it with a gloved hand, helping him hold his position steady here in the harbor current.

Over the next thirty seconds, five more heads broke the surface around him. Masks were raised, and even in the rain Takahashi could make out Chris Travers about ten feet away on his left.

Three minutes later, Hash, Victor Two, and Chris Travers, Victor One, raised their heads above the gangway rail, one level below the main deck, their HK MP7 Personal Defense Weapons at their shoulders. Their scuba gear had been lashed just below the waterline, and they wore packs full of gear on their backs.

The gangway was well lit but devoid of any activity at the moment, so they stepped over the railing and down onto the deck with their wet scuba boots, and they covered both directions with their weapons as the other four men followed suit.

Quickly all six were aboard, and they made their way together in a tight stack to a hatch. Looking through a thick window, Hash saw that the passageway beyond was clear, so he opened the hatch and entered.

Travers and the others followed silently behind, and Hash let them into an empty changing locker room just a few feet on.

Travers signaled his men to drop to a crouch here by the long row of lockers, and he did the same. His eyes still on the lighted passageway through the hatch, he tapped a button on the radio attached to his magazine carrier on his chest and spoke in a whisper. "Victor Actual for Overwatch."

Jim Pace's voice came into the earpieces of all six men. "Go for Overwatch."

Travers said, "We're internal. Condition nominal."

"I expected to hear from you fifteen mikes ago."

"Currents were worse than anticipated."

"Roger. No activity on the water from my vantage point. Security in the container yard appears unchanged."

"Roger. Proceeding to fourth deck and number two hold."

Travers rose, the men followed suit, and soon they were back in the passageway, then on a ladder heading down.

Jim Pace's staff back at Langley had managed to find out the location of the targeted shipment on board the massive vessel from internal company records at ETC, as the placement of goods was crucial to efficient ocean shipping logistics. Travers knew where he was heading, and he knew the layout of the Panamax ship. He even knew where security cameras were placed on board, a standard practice for ETC vessels of this size.

He just didn't know where the crew was.

The men descended quietly past third deck, bypassed a long catwalk with a single man walking on it in the opposite direction, and another passageway monitored by a security camera, and then they went down to fourth deck. Here they found a hatch that led to the number two hold, which they knew would be filled with six hundred of the nearly four thousand containers on board the *Estelle*.

Just before they opened the door, however, the unmistakable sound of a watertight hatch being opened in the distance filled their noise-enhancing ear protection. They were exposed here in the passageway, so Travers gave the order to double-time it into the hold before whoever had opened the door got any closer.

They made it inside the darkened space, gently shut and secured the watertight hatch, and then all the men knelt down below the hatch portal.

A pair of figures passed twenty seconds later; the men in the hold knew the count only because the light from the window was blacked out twice in quick succession as the unknown subjects ambled by.

Travers then took the time to look around.

The hold was four stories high, lit only with a few glowing bulbs on the walls spaced twenty meters apart, and the containers were stacked all the way up to the two gargantuan closed hatch doors on the ceiling above.

The containers were also stacked tightly together, which meant if the one they were looking for hadn't been on the end of a row, they would have had no way of accessing it until it was off-loaded, but Pace's team at Langley had reported they were looking for a gray forty-foot container on the second level in the port-side aft corner of the hold.

Takahashi led the way along the wall of multi-colored containers; twice the team had to leave the hold itself and return to a parallel passageway because the way ahead was obstructed with piping, winching equipment, container lashing equipment, and other items they hadn't anticipated.

It took ten more minutes, but eventually they found themselves in the port-side aft corner of the number two hold, and they looked up to see the gray container.

The ground-floor containers were wedged tight against railings built into the floor, but the containers higher up were all kept in place with lashing rods, diagonal metal poles that affixed one container to another.

Travers used a small red-lensed flashlight to check the seven numbers and four letters on the container, confirmed it with data on a palm-sized computer he pulled from a pocket, and then he and Takahashi both climbed up on the railing, then made their way up farther with help from the diagonal lashing rods.

Victors Three and Six followed them up; they all found they could sit on a horizontal metal railing right in front of the container doors, and quickly Jamie, Victor Six, pulled out a blowtorch, lowered a set of goggles over his eyes, and went to work on the lower joint of the first lashing rod, intending to cut it in a location that would be hard to detect once he resoldered it after inspection.

FORTY-SEVEN

It took over ten minutes to cut through both lashing rods blocking the door to the target container, and it took all four men up there more time to carefully move the heavy poles out of the way without making any noise by striking the sides of the big corrugated steel boxes.

As soon as the door was free from the lashing equipment, Chris Travers looked to his watch. They'd been on board for forty-four minutes already, and they hadn't even breached the seal of the container. Just as he was stressing about this, he heard Jim Pace's voice in his ear.

"Overwatch for Victor Actual."

"Go, Overwatch."

"Be advised, the rain has stopped, sun's coming up."

"Roger. We're gonna need another thirty mikes, minimum."

"Roger that. I'll keep an eye out."

Travers returned his concentration to the forty-foot shipping container. Two vertical locking rods, one on each door of the container, were secured with a handcuffing device, essentially a metal bar that went around both rods to keep either of the two doors from opening.

Hash slid the metal handcuff up the two bars until it was stopped by brackets on each side, and he braced it there. Travers took out a rubber hammer and a steel chisel from his pack, and then, as soon as his men

below gave the all clear, he quickly hammered down on the two bolts holding one of the brackets, popping them off against the handcuff.

The bracket came free; the three small pieces of steel fell away but Travers caught them before they dropped all the way to the steel deck.

Now the only thing stopping them from opening the doors and inspecting the cargo was the bolt seal, a small steel and rubberized device
with a number on it that matched the container number. Travers took a set
of bolt cutters from Jamie and broke the seal.

Putting the pieces in a cargo pocket, he lifted the latch on the right side
of the door and quietly opened the container.

They flashed a light inside and saw several palletized items, but they
also saw that there was room to move around, mostly by climbing over the
pallets since they only rose to half the height of the container.

Takahashi and Travers climbed inside, and then Victor Three closed
the door behind them so that they would be free to turn on their headlamps.

Hash and Travers took off their radios, backpacks, chest rigs, utility
belts, and guns so they could crawl around over the pallets, and they both
activated headlamps so they could remain hands-free.

Travers moved his radio to his front pocket, put his headset back on,
and hit his push-to-talk button. "Overwatch, we are inside the forty-foot."

Hash put his radio back on, as well.

"Roger that," Pace said. "Be advised, we're at fifty minutes and I am
seeing activity at the anchor. Looks like the ship might be coming into
port sooner than we thought."

"We'll double-time it," Travers said, and then he and Victor Two began
inspecting the pallets.

Joe Takahashi led Travers over the pallets, but he stopped his advance
and broadcast on the net to Travers, the rest of Juliet Victor, and Jim Pace.
"I've got a hardshell plastic case about four feet square, writing on the side
is in Hanzi."

Travers said, "Can you read it?"

"Hanzi's Chinese, boss. I'm Japanese. And anyway, I'm from Philly, so
even my Japanese blows."

"Right." Travers climbed up onto the top of the case next to him, then looked at the lid. "I can read this one. 'Greyhound V180.' That mean any-thing to you, Overwatch?"

"Negative, but we'll check."

Takahashi said, "I've got another with the same over here. Both Hanzi and Roman alphabet. "'Greyhound V180.' Probably twelve other cases in the container about the same size."

Travers said, "I'm going to pop one and take a peek. Don't want to dis-turb the packaging, so this is going to take a bit."

Jim Pace acknowledged Juliet Victor, then squinted again into his spotting scope.

It was daylight now, the clouds had all but burned off, and he could see several people moving around the main and upper decks of the *Estelle* out in the harbor.

He was all but certain the vessel was about to begin steaming up to the docks for off-loading.

His satellite phone began buzzing on the table next to him. He snatched it up, not taking his eye out of the cup of the scope.

"Yeah?"

"Jim, it's Anne."

Anne was one of the CIA's best forensic accountants, and she'd been working in proliferations back at Langley, seconded to his team to dig into Wan Chai Machine Technology, the company that had sent the container to Cuba.

Jim appreciated Anne's work—they wouldn't have found the *Estelle* without her—but he didn't think there was anything a forensic accountant could tell him right now that would be more important than him focusing all his attention on the ship in the harbor. "I'm going to need to call you back." He reached to hang up, but Anne spoke up before he could.

"You're not looking for one container. You're looking for six."

His thumb moved away from the power button. *"What?"*

"I kept digging. Wan Chai Machine Technology Limited has sent only three shipments abroad. Miami, Singapore, and there in Cuba. *That* we already knew. But Wan Chai appears to be part of a consortium of over ten HK-based technology companies, could be many more than that, and six of these companies have containers on the *Estelle ETC* right now."

"Oh my God," Pace just muttered. "You . . . you don't know what was shipped, do you?"

"They all just say 'machine parts—electronic.' Same as the Wan Chai bill of lading. And the recipient is the same, Empressa Informatica of Havana."

"Still nothing on them?"

"Nothing at all. Probably because they don't exist. It's Cuba, so getting information on state-controlled business is extremely difficult, but the recipient address on the bills of lading is of a retail mall on the outskirts of Havana. I checked with NGA; they say that space has been unoccupied for four years."

Pace's brain spun trying to put this puzzle together. "So . . . the Cuban government is taking possession of high-tech autonomous weapons?"

"It's looking that way. I'll send you the other container numbers, and then I'll keep digging."

Pace knew he wasn't about to tell Travers to check five more containers on that ship. But the fact that the shipment from HK was six times the size he'd thought it was told him his idea that these were lethal autonomous weapons in country to kill Hinton and his staff no longer made sense.

He also knew that a half-dozen containers could hold over 175 tons of equipment. From what Gentry had said about the attack in Mexico, two robots weighing just a couple hundred pounds each had killed several armed men.

The containers on the *Estelle* could be carrying more than fifteen hundred similarly sized devices.

He was about to hit his radio transmit button to relay this news to Travers when he heard the click indicating that someone on Juliet Victor was broadcasting.

Chris Travers held down his push-to-talk button as he whispered. "Overwatch? Yeah, I have a quadrupedal unmanned ground vehicle of some kind. Definitely armed, there's a rifle on a turret, maybe thirty cal, can't tell. I see what look to be legs, some sort of grasping arm. Computer equipment. Batteries. But . . . here's the thing. This machine is completely disassembled."

"What do you mean, disassembled?"

"None of this stuff is attached to each other. They're just components in foam trays. Bolts and cables stored in plastic cases."

"Meaning?"

"If these were going to be deployed, then they would need to go to some sort of manufacturing facility, something like that. I don't really know how this shit works, maybe you could do it at an auto repair shop, but it's not like someone's going to take this container, pop open the doors, and press a button to animate these robots."

"Got it. What about a controlling system? Is there a device, something with joysticks, a screen, maybe even a VR headset?"

"I don't see anything like that."

Pace gave a long, low sigh. "Then they're autonomous. Holy fuck. Do you see any ammo for the weapons?"

"I do not, but there are cases on the pallets we're not going to be able to get to. Could be ammunition in them."

"Actually, there are entire containers you're not going to get to. Langley says five other shipments on board the *Estelle* are suspect."

Travers stopped looking over the hardware in the case below him. "That kinda seems like overkill for a facility wipe at a science lab."

"It does, indeed."

Takahashi spoke up now. "You think somebody's planning a robot Bay of Pigs?"

It was a joke, but no one laughed. Pace said, "Shit. The anchor's all the way up, One. Photograph everything you see, put it all back the way you found it, and put a single radio tracker somewhere on the goods. Hide it in packaging where no one can find it. Then get out of there before that ship gets under way."

"Roger that," Travers said, but just as soon as he spoke, he felt the ship's engines come to life with a low rumble. To Takahashi, he said, "We're goin' on a little boat ride, Hash."

Victor Two did not even look up from the case he was in the process of photographing. He just said, "Cool."

Jim Pace scanned through his spotting scope, and he saw the white churning water at the bow of the *Estelle*. It would probably take only fifteen minutes or so to bring the ship into the docks at the container yard, and he doubted the Ground Branch men would be able to get off in time.

This morning was turning to shit, and among those things going wrong was the fact that he found himself completely confused. He couldn't imagine that whoever was sending these weapons to be used against Hinton's facility would send them unarmed and completely dismantled, but Travers had been clear about what he'd found in that container.

Sure, the other containers might contain ammunition, or other weapons, but why wouldn't the fabrication be completed before they were sent to the destination where they would be used?

He decided he needed to update Gentry, somewhere in the neighborhood and watching over his position along with help from a friend of Gentry's, who Pace neither knew nor completely trusted. Still, he was a desperate man at the moment, exposed and focused on things other than his own personal security, so the help was appreciated. He moved his headset to the side on his head and put an AirPod in his left ear.

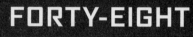

FORTY-EIGHT

Court Gentry and Zoya Zakharova sat at a tiny table the proprietor of the cozy breakfast café had just carried out to the sidewalk for them. They ordered cafecitos and bottled water, and gazed across the street at the Iglesia San Francisco de Paula, an old and simple church a half block from the water.

Traffic was picking up; each passing automobile belched a little smog, but Court and Zoya pretended like they were enjoying themselves. Just beyond the church they could see the harbor, and down the street on their right they had eyes on the building where Jim Pace was in the midst of conducting his overwatch. And though they couldn't see the ship in the harbor that was the focus of Jim's attention, since the café was at a traffic circle, they *could* see roads leading here from four directions, meaning they had eyes on all ground approaches to Pace's overwatch.

They weren't expecting trouble. Yes, Cuba was a police state, and a CIA officer operating in the city would be in danger, but there was nothing to suggest that the authorities were aware of Pace's presence.

The couple took pictures of the church; they kept AirPods in their ears, connected to Pace's Signal number in case he had a message for them, and

resigned themselves to sitting here for a couple hours of countersurveillance.

Just then, Pace's voice came over the encrypted network. "Violator, you
on the net?"

Court tapped his earpiece, then put his elbows on the table and leaned
forward as if still waking up after a long night of drinking in Old Havana.

"I got you."

"Victor has been delayed, they're still on the ship and the ship is coming into the container dock."

"Well, *that* sucks."

"We've discovered there's a lot more equipment on board than we had
been expecting."

He and Zoya looked at each other with alarm. They'd both faced down
armed robots, and had no interest in doing so again.

"Everything kosher out there?" the older CIA officer asked.

"The town's awake. The market below you just opened. There's some
passing police cars . . . but nothing out of the ordinary."

"Roger that. Thanks for the help, man. I owe you guys a beer."

"Just get Chris and his boys off that boat, and we'll all have a beer."

"Working on it."

Zack Hightower followed close behind Anton Hinton as he entered his
office and set his messenger bag down on his desk. The window behind him
looked out over the campus to the west, weathered buildings down a broken street, beyond which the facility power station glinted brightly in the
morning sun, contrasting with the massive Soviet SIGINT headquarters
building behind it, which was dark and all but windowless and therefore
opaque, its twisted and ruined satellite dishes on the roof completing the
image.

As he helped his boss remove his body armor, Zack scanned the area
out the window further, because that was the only real danger in the room.
He'd positioned four static security guys on the rooftops of nearby buildings so he'd know if anyone got near the campus who didn't belong. Still,

he put Anton's armor on a leather sofa, open and ready for quick deployment.

Anton sat down, Hightower moved out of the way as Kimmie brought her boss a cup of matcha tea, and then the American moved to the wall, widening his stance and interlocking his fingers in front of him.

As Kimmie left the room after a friendly greeting to Zack, Anton noticed his head of security standing against the wall. "You're going to be staying extra close today?"

Hightower said, "I won't disturb you."

To this, the New Zealand native laughed. "It's fine, but don't stand there like a statue. Makes me nervous. Have a seat on the couch."

Zack sat next to the body armor, his eyes flitting between the open door to Anton's office and the bright morning outside.

Anton said, "Need about a half hour to catch up with emails, then it's off to the labs." Hinton put his big over-the-ear headphones on and turned his attention to his laptop.

Zack nodded politely, then reached down and rubbed his thighs. This morning's run had been a tough one; his muscles ached, but since he assumed today would be another long day, he was glad he knocked his PT out before dawn.

Anton looked over his laptop at Zack. "You okay, mate?"

"All good. Should have stretched this morning."

"You can join me down at the yoga studio after lunch. That'll put you right."

Zack smiled. "I'll go with you, of course, but I'm your bodyguard, not your yoga partner."

Anton laughed at this, then grabbed his tea, spun his chair around, and looked out at the bright day.

Carlos Contreras smiled at the monitor in front of him, because after just thirty minutes sitting in this cramped van and scanning the area with his four micro drones, he now had a positive ID on his target. His camera was fifty meters above and over two hundred meters away from the man, but he zoomed in tightly on his face, and then he spun to his other laptop to type out a message.

This is Zero One. I have the target in sight.

Without delay, a reply came. **Cyrus acknowledges. The operations center will move the asset into position.**

Contreras knew this was the point of no return, and the magnitude of what he was being asked to do today was not lost on him.

After a brief pause, he looked again at the man on the monitor, then pushed aside his concerns about what he was part of. He typed, **I will continue to monitor and report.** And then he went back to the other laptop to return his attention to the target.

Jamie had just finished reattaching bolts to the container door, and Victor Two had just sealed it, when Travers pulled out a locking seal identical to the one he'd caught earlier and popped it back into place. S&T had manufactured the seal the evening before, and it looked exactly like the one they'd removed, so the recipient of these goods would have no way of knowing anyone had snooped inside.

Travers clicked his mic. "We're out of here."

Pace responded quickly. "The *Estelle* is docking at the quay now. Suggest you try to egress on the starboard side, then swim back across the harbor and egress the way you came in."

"Sounds good. We're Oscar Mike."

"On the move, understood."

Scott Kincaid drove a lime green 1981 Volga four-door down a narrow road, his earpiece in his ear and his Republic Forge pistol on his hip, with the silencer in a backpack next to him. He wore denim pants, a black T-shirt, and a thin black hoodie.

In his ear, the female French controller said, "Lancer, be advised, we have the target fixed. Once you're in the area, we'll have you connect with the ISR tech on the ground and you two can work directly together."

Kincaid recognized that this was a new method from Gama. "So I won't go through you? I'll work directly with the drone guy?"

"Correct. This is Cuba, you need his real-time intelligence so you can avoid any state security presence at the scene. Coordinates to Wrangler Zero One's position to follow."

Kincaid looked at his phone as he drove; he clicked a message when it came, and it took him to a map.

He saw that he was on the right street already, and the drone pilot would be just a few blocks ahead of him.

"Got it," he said.

"He is in a gray Polar Air Conditioning Service van with two armed security men supporting him. Good luck."

Lancer ended the call. Those two armed security men were about to be leaving the drone pilot and joining him on the assassination, whether they knew it yet or not. The high profile of today's target as well as the nation where the hit would take place made him fully expect that this would be a difficult operation, and he needed all the help he could get.

Contreras stared at his monitor, watching his target as the man took a sip out of a mug. The Mexican's eyes flicked up to a readout so he could keep watch on his drone's battery meter, and he waited for some indication from Cyrus that the assassin was approaching the target.

Cyrus's voice came through his headset a short time later, his professional tone again leading Contreras to the conclusion that he was an American military officer. "The asset is arriving at your position. You will support him directly."

"Wait. He's coming to me?"

"Affirmative. Call sign is Lancer. Alert your security team of his arrival."

Quickly, Contreras told the two Cubans up front that someone would be approaching the van, and no sooner had he done so than the driver opened his door and began confronting a man on the sidewalk side of the street.

Contreras himself took a quick glance at the monitor to make sure the drone was steady, then rushed out the back door.

There, in front of him, stood a white man. Taller than he, with big shoulders and biceps pushing against his black hoodie, a brown goatee, and a weathered maroon ball cap on his head.

Contreras looked around to make sure no one else was on the street, then he said, "Lancer?"

"Yep. You're Zero One?"

"That's right."

The American pulled out his phone, and together they tied their earpieces in to a Signal voice communications net. This done, Lancer said, "The target is stationary?"

"Yes."

"Anyone else watching over him?"

"Not from my vantage point."

Lancer nodded, then looked to the driver. The other security man— short, stocky, and bald, much like his mate—had also climbed out and come around the front of the van. "I need these two guys."

Contreras was confused by this. "But . . . they are *my* security."

Lancer looked up and down the street. "You're not the one going into battle, kid. They're coming with me."

Reluctantly, Contreras was about to translate for the Cubans, but the driver put a hand up. "We speak English." He turned to Lancer. "Five thousand cash. U.S. Each. For that we'll come support you."

"Done."

No one moved for a moment till the driver said, "Now."

Lancer sighed. Pulled up his T-shirt and unzipped a money belt. He had twenty grand in hundred-dollar bills on him, and he pulled out a stack, split it in half, and handed it off to the men.

The goon from the passenger side began counting his, but when Lancer saw this he drew his pistol, pointed it in the man's face, and said, "We go now, or you give me the fucking money back. Your call."

Both of the Cubans pocketed the money. Lancer reholstered and told them to follow him.

As he passed by Contreras, still standing there on the sidewalk and feeling somewhat forgotten and alone now, the American said, "Keep feeding me intel, amigo. The job we're about to do . . . this is the big-time. You get that, right?"

Contreras nodded. "The big-time," he said softly.

And then Lancer was gone, heading down the road on foot with the two Cubans at his side.

The Mexican left behind took a few seconds to control his breathing; he was on a live call with Lancer now and didn't want to sound as nervous as he was. Then he darted back into the van and shut and locked the doors behind him, determined to get back to work, so he could then get the hell out of here.

FORTY-NINE

Chris Travers rose above the waterline, shielded from view on the sunny morning by a small wooden jetty that extended from the quay at the container terminal, just south of where the *Estelle* now sat.

He took his regulator out of his mouth, raised his mask, looked through the slats in the dock, and assessed the situation from his very limited vantage point.

This was a bustling terminal, and even though the off-loading of the *Estelle* had not yet begun, he and his team were no more than fifty yards away from men readying equipment to begin the process.

Rows of trucks were lined up; these wouldn't leave the yard but would deliver the containers from portside to wherever they would be temporarily stored before going through customs.

He and his men had worked tirelessly the day before in preparation of the raid on the *Estelle*, but at no point had they envisioned themselves in the terminal in daylight. The entire reason for boarding the *Estelle* in the water was that doing so should have ensured much less risk of exposure. But the late arrival of the Panamax ship, as well as the slow underwater approach because of the currents, had put them here now.

They had abandoned the idea of just swimming all the way back to their initial insertion point, a quarter mile away across the harbor, because two highly mobile Russian-built harbor security boats, each with a crew of five and a pair of mounted 12.7-millimeter machine guns, had moved into the harbor just east of the *Estelle*, and they now circled through the Ground Branch men's intended path of travel.

If the six Americans had been wearing rebreather equipment—scuba gear worn on their chests that prevented bubbles from rising to the surface—they would have had no problem moving forty feet or so under the patrols, but the gear they were forced to use on today's op was basic, and the six men, even widely dispersed, would create a lot of bubbles that the ten Cuban sailors would almost certainly notice and then simply follow to their destination on the opposite shore.

So Travers made the decision to go to the terminal, but here his hopes were quickly dashed that they'd have a covert way out of this situation.

The southern side of the harbor was fenced down to the bottom at the container yard, and the men would not be able to just swim around to get out of the terminal.

No. They were going to have to climb out of the water right here and try to sneak their way to safety.

Travers gave the order; the men bobbing around him all took off their scuba gear and sank it, put on their watertight backpacks, then swam in their wet suits to a ladder.

Travers had his headset back on, and he reported in. "Overwatch. Victor One. You receiving?"

Pace came over the net. "Receiving. Where are you?"

"Unfortunately, we're fifty yards south of the stern of the *Estelle*, right under this little gray skiff dock."

Pace took a moment; Travers assumed he was looking for the dock through his scope. Finally he said, "Got it. There's no way underwater around that fencing?"

"Negative. We'd have to go out under the harbor patrol to get around. Like our chances better going overland if you can help."

"Roger. Listen carefully."

Three minutes later the six men found themselves on dry land, lying under a stationary tanker truck close to the water, just south of the first in a row of ship-to-shore gantry cranes. The rusty but formidable towers loomed next to and now over the *Estelle*.

Travers looked to the south. "Overwatch. I don't see anyone on our left. Do you?"

There was a brief pause, then Pace said, "There are a pair of old buses approaching up the yard to the south; they'll pass your poz around that row of buildings you see one hundred meters to your southeast."

"See the buildings. Will wait for them to pass and then your instructions."

The buses passed; Travers got a look inside and saw they were filled with men. He assumed they were terminal personnel who would board the ship to facilitate the off-loading, so their presence didn't alarm him in the least.

But the two buses stopped at the first crane, still some hundred yards or so to the gangway that had been brought up to the ship's main deck for people in the terminal yard to board.

Travers and his men looked on while the doors to the bus opened, and men began filing out.

Instantly, all six Americans shifted their squat HK MP7s in that direction.

The buses contained uniformed soldiers, all carrying AK-47s, wearing helmets and flak jackets, and they began dispersing around the terminal in front of the ship.

Travers spoke first. "We're moving." He began crawling to the rear end of the tanker, facing south, and his team followed behind, still keeping an eye on what might have been sixty to eighty soldiers.

"Overwatch," Travers said, "you seeing this?"

"'Fraid so. You're clear to head south. Go into that cluster of trailer chassis parked there, get low, and I'll advise."

The chassis pool was a large parking lot south of the main activity at the port where trailer chassis of different lengths were lined up, ready to be chosen by size depending on the cargo a particular tractor driver was transporting to the stacks of containers on the western side of the yard.

The six men ran, one at a time, and then took cover under a pair of chassis. They would have still been exposed to the soldiers to the north if not for several large coils of rope and metal cabling, lined up neatly at the northern edge of the chassis pool. This gave them some cover, but Travers was fixated on getting the hell out of there, not hunkering down.

Pace immediately transmitted. "I have a third bus approaching. Might be more soldiers."

"Did we get ourselves spotted, or does the *Estelle* just require that much security?"

"Unknown," Pace said. "Just stay low till we figure this shit out. You guys got civilian clothing on under that neoprene?"

Travers nodded, then said, "Good idea." To his men he said, "Get out of the wet suits, we'll stow them somewhere. We'll be less obvious from a distance."

"These HKs are going to stand out, boss," Victor Three said.

"Not leaving our weps behind. Put them in your packs."

"Roger that."

The men began doffing their wet suits.

Court and Zoya were on their third cafecito; the four streets spilling into the traffic circle where they sat had filled with cars, buses, and pedestrians. They kept their eyes moving, with Court looking to the western approaches, and Zoya concentrating on the Malecón, the larger harborside street that ran north to south.

Just as a police car passed by, Jim Pace came over their net. "Violator, Juliet Victor is hunkered down in the container yard; there's nearly a hundred soldiers fanning out, looks like they got spotted on a camera somehow. Doesn't appear the soldiers know where they are at this time, but it's getting pretty hairy over there."

"Understood. You want us to move to your poz?"

"Negative. I'm fine, just hold what you have and keep an eye out."

While Anton Hinton sat at his desk and spoke on a call with a reporter in London, Zack Hightower leaned out of Hinton's office and motioned to one of his security men standing in the lobby. "Luis . . . can you come in here so I can go to the head?"

Luis spoke English, but not Navy English. "The what?"

"El baño," Zack clarified.

"Sí, sí!" Luis passed Zack in the doorway and went over to stand by the body armor on the sofa while Anton sat at his desk, his feet up, looking out the window while he talked to the reporter about the attack on him here in Havana the day before yesterday, and gave his thoughts about the impact on the world after the deaths of his friends and colleagues in the past week.

Zack headed down the hall towards the bathroom, waved at Wren as he passed his office, and nodded at Kimmie as she moved quickly down the hall towards him.

She didn't look back at him. As she passed he noticed a look of consternation on her face, but she was moving too fast for him to stop and ask if something was wrong.

He stood there at the door to the bathroom, watched her while she stormed down towards the end of the floor and then turned right, into Gareth Wren's office.

Zack shrugged a little. If there was any sort of security issue, she wouldn't have passed him by without telling him, he told himself, so he figured it had something to do with the company, and not the assassins hunting down the owner of the company.

He pushed the door open and went in to take a leak.

A minute later, as he returned to Hinton's office, he noticed Wren's door was shut. He thought about rapping on it to make sure everything was okay but decided against it. He'd see Wren at lunch in a few hours, and he'd ask him about it then.

Carlos Contreras focused on his monitor, still watching his target, just sitting there. The Mexican was fascinated by the fact that this man didn't know he was about to die.

It was a powerful emotion, and though Contreras was used to it—he'd targeted a lot of people for the cartel over the years—it still made his skin tingle with excitement.

After a beep in his ear, he heard Lancer's voice.

"I'm about three minutes out. Give me an update."

"The target hasn't moved."

"Still no security? Still no cops or soldiers?"

"I don't see anyone other than the target."

"Roger. Notify me of any change."

Court and Zoya continued scanning the area outside Pace's overwatch carefully, so when a man appeared in front of them on the opposite side of north-south San Ignacio Street, both of them instantly locked on to him.

He appeared Cuban; he wore a yellow guayabera and khakis, and he had a bald head. But to both Court and Zoya he appeared to have an especially hard edge. He also looked like he knew where he was going. He could have been plainclothes security services, totally normal here in the center of Havana, but he was definitely someone who needed closer scrutiny.

Zoya spoke softly. "That guy's a player."

"Yep," Court said, his face masked by his hand as he took a sip of bottled water.

The man turned to his right; the church was across the traffic circle on his left shoulder, and he began heading south, in the direction of Jim Pace's overwatch on the top floor of the artisans' market.

Court was about to let Jim know that a suspicious-looking unsub was a couple hundred yards from him when Zoya kicked his ankle below the table. He followed her eyes across the street, and there, in front of the church and heading in the same direction as the unsub, were two other men. The man in back was shielded from view by the man in front, but the man closest to where Court and Zoya were sitting wore a brown long-sleeved shirt and distressed jeans, and he looked like he was cut from the same cloth as the man who had come from another street.

Court noticed the imprint of a pistol under the closer man's shirt, even from sixty or seventy feet away.

The pair began crossing the busy traffic circle, negotiating their way through cars and scooters, and finally they separated in the middle of the street enough for Court to get a look at the subject who was farther away.

The identification took a moment, but only a moment. Court rubbed his eyes under his sunglasses, and Zoya knew this gesture from him. It was an expression of utter frustration, like he'd rather be anywhere else on Earth right now.

"What is it?" she asked, focused on him and not on the men on the street.

"It's gonna be one of those days. That's Lancer."

Zoya craned her head back to see. "You're sure?"

"Yeah. He and his buddy are also working with that guy on this side of the street."

"What are they doing here?"

"Getting ready to kill the guy we're here to protect, would be my guess." Court rose from his chair. "You stay here."

"No. I'm coming with—"

"We'll stay in contact over the AirPods."

"You need me to—"

"I need you to be *my* overwatch now. Go mobile, get a look around the neighborhood, try to find out where those men came from. They could have surveillance with them."

Zoya rose now herself, because she understood. Softly, she said, "A van, work truck, something like that."

She leaned close and kissed him, then spoke into his ear. "Be careful."

"You, too."

Court went south, and Zoya began walking up the small road to the east in the direction the first man had come from, away from the harbor.

As Court moved he tapped his earpiece. "Overwatch, you're not going to like this."

"Well, at least that will be consistent with everything else happening right now. What you got?"

"I have eyes on Lancer. He's with two other fighting-aged males, possibly local, definitely armed, and they are moving with purpose towards your poz at this time."

Pace's response took a moment, but when it came Court realized the man knew the gravity of the situation.

In a grave tone he said, "Kind of in the middle of something, Violator. I need you to do that thing you do."

Court moved through a thick group of laborers moving together with pushcarts, then began crossing the street between swiftly moving scooters and cars. "I'm on it, but if he knows where you are, then that means somebody's probably got eyes on you now. Suggest you relocate."

"Unable. I'm working with Victor to get them out of the container yard."

Court picked up his speed even more. "Jim . . . Chris is a big boy. He can handle himself. Lancer's got a forty-five-second head start on me, and he's got a pair of local boys I'm going to have to get around before I get to him."

"I'm staying put, Violator, and you'd do the same."

Court sighed as he stepped up onto the sidewalk on the far side of the circle from the café. "Expediting as able, Overwatch." Pushing through the crowd now, he saw uniformed Cuban police milling around near the entrance to the big market, and Lancer only one hundred feet or so away from them.

Chris Travers watched the third bus appear around a building between his position and the main gate, then pull to a stop in front of a row of warehouses several hundred yards to the south—exactly in the direction he had been leading his men to make their way out of the terminal.

He spit on the ground in front of him in frustration. "Okay, Overwatch. We're totally cut off now. Any ideas?"

"You can't go back to the water. Both patrol boats have closed on the container terminal; they'll see you when you pop out. The north is crawling with security at the quayside operations area around the *Estelle*, plus all the terminal employees, and now the south is cut off by the military. The only thing left is to try to get into the container storage yard to the west. You'll have good cover once you're there, but it's going to be like negotiating a maze getting you there."

"And then what?"

"You'll have to find a way over the fence. It's about eight feet high. Razor wire. There might be pedestrian access there, but I can't see from here."

Travers didn't like his odds at all. The container storage yard was shielded to him by rows of buildings, but people were coming in and out of those buildings, and he knew that on the far side would be workers operating forklifts and trucks, or moving on foot. He wasn't about to start shooting at anyone who might sound an alarm, and getting into a gunfight with over one hundred Cuban soldiers was a nonstarter, so he told Pace they were willing to head west with his guidance.

Pace said, "Okay, Victor Actual, we've got an opportunity. *Estelle* is unloading freight. Tractor-trailers are lining up to take containers from the gantry cranes to the container yard, and they'll pass within about fifty feet of the chassis pool. You might be able to shield your movements to the buildings by running alongside them."

"What about the soldiers to the south?"

"They're still debussing, but they will be able to see you from where they are until you get behind that row of forklifts to the left of the buildings. You tracking that?"

"Got it."

"After that there are concrete Jersey barriers that will hide you from the buildings if you get low enough. I can see that area from this position, so I'll talk you through."

"Roger. We'll wait for the first truck and start moving one by one."

"Good," Pace said, and then, "Be advised. My overwatch has been compromised. My support element is moving into position to deal with it. I'm not breaking down, but if you lose me . . . you lost me."

Travers blew out a sigh. "Understood, boss. Good luck."

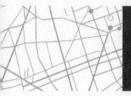

FIFTY

Carlos Contreras leaned close to his monitor, his eyes locked on the eyes of the American in the fourth unit of a row of abandoned apartments at the top of the market in Havana's harbor. The Mexican national still couldn't wrap his head around the fact that he would be involved in the murder of a senior CIA officer today. He smoked, the nicotine a poor controller of his anxiety, but the habit was soothing to him, nonetheless.

Lancer came through his headset. "You have eyes on me?"

"Negative, I'm over the target. He's still in position, still looking into the spotting scope out at the harbor. I alerted Cyrus that something might have been going on out there, and ten minutes later a couple of patrol boats began circling and busloads of soldiers showed up at the terminal."

The American sounded fascinated by this. "How the hell did Cyrus make *that* happen?"

"No idea."

"Okay," the American said. "I want you on me. Watching my back for cops, security forces, whatever."

"I understand. Where are you?"

"Approaching target building now."

Contreras peeled his tiny drone away from its position where he had been watching CIA officer James Pace for the past twenty minutes, and then it sped around to the north, over the water still. He climbed to 125 meters, then flew over land, turning south at the church and then slowing to a hover.

He zoomed in on the scene below. There were dozens and dozens of people on foot in sight.

"I need you to flash me. Just shine your phone camera light straight up in the air."

Lancer did so, and Contreras saw it from above, then tapped his screen to put a bounding box on him. From now on, the drone camera would automatically keep him in the center of its field of view whenever he was in sight.

"I have you. Once you go into that building, I will go back around to the harbor side. You'll come out of the northern stairwell on the third floor, turn right, and walk down the covered exterior walkway. Pace is in the fourth room. The door is wide open."

"Is there a stairwell on the other side?"

"Yeah, I found a video of the interior online. You have a stairwell on the south side, as well. A service elevator is there on the south, too, but I don't think it's operational."

"Roger. I'll put one of these Cubans at the top of each stairway, and I'll go to the apartment to eliminate the target alone."

Just one hundred feet behind him, Court saw Lancer's movement, and he knew what was happening. He spoke softly, having just switched his call to Zoya's phone. "Carrie, Lancer's signaling overhead at something. I think he's got a drone covering him."

"You can't see it?"

"I don't want to start looking for it because I'll stand out."

"Okay, I'm on San Ignacio, heading up the hill looking for more trouble. I'll double back to the water if I don't see anything within a couple more blocks."

"Roger." Court knew Lancer would probably head up one of the two enclosed stairwells in the market that would take him to the third floor, and he had a feeling his two henchmen would be left behind to watch his six. That meant Court would have to disable at least one of the men on his way up, but he needed to do it without making any noise that would alert Lancer or any of the police he'd seen in the area.

He had a knife under his shirt, next to his Glock 26; he just had to get into striking distance and take the henchman in a location where the attack wouldn't be seen by all the people milling about.

Zoya spoke up now. "What do you see?"

"Lancer just went into the market, probably for the stairs. His two men are moving behind him in the middle of a group of passersby."

"What are they doing?"

Court cocked his head as he walked. "Passing by."

"Dick," she muttered. "I meant Lancer's men."

"Just heading to the market."

Zoya said, "Okay. Let me know if you need me there."

"Just keep checking the neighborhood. I'm switching back to Pace's channel." Court tapped his earpiece and began walking even faster.

Jim Pace had held Travers's movement towards the eastern side of the container terminal while the first few trucks passed, because men and women approached the entrance to the terminal operations building, directly in their line of sight.

But the group of workers stepped back inside, and another truck approached from the north before it would turn right in front of the chassis pool and continue east.

Travers said, "We good to go now?"

Pace replied, "Clear to move. Stay low and fast and the harbor boats won't see you."

Travers gave the order, and then he and his men took off running in a crouched position.

Court entered the market just thirty seconds after Lancer and his men, and he found it to be a large metal-framed warehouse building the size of an airplane hangar, with a ceiling three stories high and crisscrossed with catwalks.

A pair of huge Cuban flags, each one the length of a city bus, hung straight down from the catwalk along the back wall, one on each side of the open sliding bay doors that led out to a small walkway and then the harbor.

Between Court and those doors, dozens of kiosks were set up with men and women selling paintings, jewelry, clothing, and other arts and crafts, and though it was still early, there were already a lot of shoppers milling about.

Court didn't spend much time taking in the lay of the land, because he wouldn't be staying down here. He went to his left, saw the simple metal door that led to the stairwell, and began walking towards it.

Just as he put his hand on the door latch, however, he heard a voice from behind him.

"Espere." *Wait.*

He turned around to find himself facing a fair-skinned Cuban male wearing the light blue uniform of the PNR, the Policía Nacional Revolucionaria.

Great, he thought. *Cops.*

He was on an open line with Pace, and he wanted to alert the CIA man to this delay. "Hello, Officer. How can I help you?"

He instantly heard Pace's voice, soft in his left ear. "Shit. Deal with that, Violator. I can't leave my poz."

The PNR officer was young, maybe twenty-five, and he didn't seem in any way agitated. "Español?" he asked.

"Poco," Court replied.

The officer continued in Spanish. "Identification, please."

Court glanced behind him at the stairwell, then reached into his pocket to grab his passport.

Any search of his body would turn up the pistol, the holster, and the two extra mags, and that would get him arrested and, essentially, condemn Jim Pace to death two stories above him.

The man looked over the Canadian passport, and Court began coming

up with a hasty plan in case the officer delayed with the ID check, because
Court didn't have time to fuck around right now.

As Scott Kincaid and one of his new partners neared the top of the stairwell, a door opened on his right. He saw that it led to the catwalk that ran
along the wall on the north side of the warehouse but, more importantly,
he also saw that a uniformed officer stood there, looking right at him.

The man was Black, in his forties, and he eyed Kincaid with confusion
for a moment, but only until the Cuban goon Lancer had brought along
with him huffed around the corner below and looked up.

"Sanchez?" the Black cop said.

To Kincaid, his henchman appeared disquieted, seeing the officer who
obviously knew him. After a moment he said, "Fidel. Cómo estás?"

Lancer had wondered if the two men he'd borrowed from the drone
pilot were off-duty local cops, and this all but confirmed his suspicions.

Fidel kept his eyes on Sanchez as he began asking him questions. Kincaid didn't speak Spanish, and he didn't understand a word, but from the
tone he could sense immediate suspicion on the part of the older Black
officer.

Sanchez was gruff and defensive; he was handling this encounter all
wrong. Kincaid didn't need to know Spanish to recognize the instantly
confrontational body language of the two men, standing now just five feet
apart.

Kincaid fumed silently. It should have been a lucky thing to get stopped
by a police officer who happened to know the guy he was with, but apparently Sanchez's relationship was such that it was having the exact opposite effect. Kincaid's presence with the Cuban here only made the cop
suspicious.

Lancer could tell Fidel wasn't buying a bit of the other man's story,
perhaps because he already knew Sanchez was either a hoodlum or a
dirty cop.

The dark-complected man turned to the American and shifted into
heavily accented English. "What is your name, señor?"

Lancer knew his fake passport said Robert Alan, so this was the name he gave.

Fidel nodded.

"We have to go," Sanchez said in English, and started walking back up.

But Fidel held firm. To Kincaid, he said, "Show me your passport, Señor Alan."

"My passport? Sure, why not?" Kincaid slipped it out of a back pocket as he looked up the stairs at the door to the third floor.

The six men of Juliet Victor came to the edge of the terminal operations building, took a knee, and Hash leaned out and looked both left and right. In front of them was the container yard, easily three thousand or more of the massive and multi-colored steel boxes stacked high. Some were twenty feet long, some forty; most of them were eight and a half feet high and eight feet wide, but some were even taller.

Massive forklifts rumbled about on the pathways between the containers; huge tractor-trailers brought containers in from the *Estelle* or out towards the exit of the terminal to Juliet Victor's left.

The yard was fenced in, but multiple open gates ran up and down the eastern side in front of the CIA officers, as trucks were constantly rolling in and out.

Other vehicles called reach stackers—essentially wheeled crane devices that could secure and move the containers up higher into the stacks—rolled about inside the fence.

It was a busy morning at the port; the crew was trying to catch up after the storm, and Juliet Victor was smack-dab in the middle of it.

Travers knelt right behind Takahashi. "What do you see, Hash?"

"A shit-ton of people, boss. Soldiers on the left, they are near the front gate still so no worries, but there's two dozen other workers who are going to see us running to the containers."

"Overwatch? We good to move?"

Pace answered back quickly. "Soldiers are right behind you on the right, and on your left a couple hundred yards away. They are fanning out now, coming closer to your poz. Suggest you just try to walk right through terminal operations."

Travers stood and turned to his men. "We act like we're supposed to be here."

The men all wore either T-shirts or long-sleeved spandex scuba rash guards and shorts, clothing they'd had on under their wet suits. In seconds their packs were back on and their guns hidden, but there was no getting around the fact that a half-dozen soaking-wet dudes in shorts and scuba boots were going to draw significant attention waltzing through this scene.

The men began walking across the pavement, some fifty yards to the fenced-in container yard. They moved with purpose, but not too fast, and as they did so, Travers spoke.

"How's your situation, Overwatch?"

"Let's focus on you until you're clear."

This meant to Travers that Pace knew he was fucked.

"We can make it without you. Get out of there."

"Someday you'll be calling the shots. But for now, shut the fuck up and focus."

Travers sighed.

A big truck pulling an empty chassis stopped to let the men pass; Chris looked up to the driver and waved, and the man stared at him but slowly waved back.

Travers knew he wasn't fooling anybody with this shit, but if they all broke into a run, the military would likely be alerted a hell of a lot faster than if someone just radioed terminal operations that a group of relaxed-looking white dudes in shorts were on the property.

They made it through the gates of the container yard, passed a cluster of men in hard hats performing maintenance on a reach stacker, and Takahashi leaned a little closer to Travers.

"We might as well be walking around with our dicks out the way we're drawing attention."

As he said this, a Cuban in his sixties lifted his radio to his mouth, his eyes on the Americans.

Travers said, "When we get into the containers, we're running for the fence with weapons out."

The sound of sirens began blaring behind them just as they entered the stacks, and in seconds the men had pulled their short-barreled weapons back out of their packs and started sprinting again, all aware that at any moment one of those soldiers was going to open fire and, after that, all hell would break loose.

FIFTY-ONE

Court kept his eyes on the cop holding his passport just outside the stair-well, watching as the man turned pages slowly, in no hurry whatsoever.

This was taking way too long, so Court decided he'd have to do this the hard way.

Court put his hand on the door latch, then opened it.

The cop looked up at him, the passport still in his hand. "What are you doing?"

Propping the door with his foot, Court faced the market and the officer. He scanned around, made sure no one was paying any attention to this ac-tivity in the corner of the massive space, and then he looked into the cop's eyes.

"Lo siento," he said. *Sorry.*

The cop sensed trouble, but Court moved too fast for him to react.

Court grabbed the smaller man, spun him around to a headlock with ease, cinched tight so he couldn't make a sound, and then pulled him into the stairwell, letting the door close behind them both.

The cop dropped the passport and reached for his pistol, but Court tightened his hold even more, cutting off the young man's arteries to his brain, knocking him out almost instantly.

He laid the cop on the ground and then rolled the man's limp body onto his stomach. The cop would wake in an instant and recover enough to be dangerous in half a minute, so he knew he had to work quickly.

As he reached for the officer's handcuffs, he thought he heard voices in the stairwell coming from far above him.

Lancer had handed his passport over to the police officer; the two Cubans seemed to be arguing over something openly but he couldn't understand it, and in Lancer's left ear he heard the drone pilot asking him for an update because he hadn't yet appeared on the back covered third-floor exterior walkway.

This bullshit was taking entirely too long, the American told himself, and a glance to his partner, the man he now knew as Sanchez, showed him Sanchez was worried.

The Cuban said, "He wants money. Thinks we are doing something illegal."

"Fuck," Kincaid said aloud, and then he looked to Fidel.

The officer said, "One hundred U.S., amigo."

Lancer had one hundred times that amount in his money belt, but he didn't want to start flashing cash, so he came up with an alternative plan.

The American gave a little laugh. "Illegal?" He reached around behind his back. "You wanna see illegal?"

The officer holding his papers looked up just as Lancer's hand fired back out away from his body, out in the direction of the cop's chest.

The blade of the stiletto sliced through the passport in his hand, then jabbed straight into the cop's heart; the man started to scream out, but the American put his free hand over his mouth, shoved him against the now-closed door to the catwalk, and held him there while he kicked and flailed a moment.

Behind Kincaid, Sanchez drew his pistol, covered down the stairs, and in seconds Fidel went limp and slid down the wall to the floor.

. . .

With a knee in the disoriented police officer's back, Court Gentry looked up the stairs, hoping like hell neither Lancer nor Lancer's henchmen were above him looking down.

They were not, so he pulled the cop's handcuffs off his belt and cuffed the man's hands behind his back.

The young man was already awake, so Court drew the officer's pistol, rolled him onto his side, and then bashed him in the temple with the butt of the weapon.

Quickly he dragged the limp cop under the stairs, out of view of the door, then said, "Jim, listen up. I got delayed. Lancer is almost to you."

"I can't leave."

Court began running up the stairs, pulling his weapon as he did so. "You leave or you die."

"Just get up here, dude. If Lancer kills me, payback is up to you."

Court raced up the stairs. "No! You've got to—"

"Gotta go." Pace ended the call.

Court's leg muscles burned as he ascended as fast as he could, at any moment expecting to hear the gunshot above that killed the CIA officer.

Chris Travers and his five men raced between the stacks of forty-foot containers, then pulled to a stop at the end. They looked left and right, then ran across a pathway between the stacks. A voice shouted out somewhere behind them, but no one looked back.

At the next intersection between the towers of containers they encountered a man driving a reach stacker with a twenty-foot container high above him. He stopped rolling forward and stared at them through his windshield, and they all stared back at him, but after a moment's hesitation Travers waved his men on and they began running again.

The sirens closed on them from behind, and he imagined that every single one of the Cuban soldiers had piled into terminal vehicles and were racing to his position.

The fence line was still two hundred yards distant, and Chris didn't even know what he'd find when he got there.

Through labored breath he said, "Overwatch, are we going to be able to get over that fence?"

"Wait one," came the reply. The men kept running, now sprinting past more terminal workers inspecting a ground-level container.

Soon Pace came back over the air. "Doubt it. Razor wire looks legit. Suggest you grab yourselves something that can punch through."

"Solid idea," Travers said, and then he halted his men at the end of another row of containers. Exhausted from the run, he put his hands on his knees, then looked up and down the two-lane road separating his position from the next cluster of huge steel shipping containers.

A tractor-trailer loaded with a forty-foot-high cube box, taller than the standard models, approached from the north.

Travers said, "That's our truck, boys. Time to go grand theft."

Just as he was about to race out into the road and stick a gun into the driver's-side window, a gunshot rang out from behind him. Travers heard the snap of the round as it streaked by overhead, but he knew that with a hundred Cuban soldiers here in the terminal, that one gunshot would invite hundreds more in a matter of moments.

"Go!" he shouted, as another round clanged off a steel container to his right.

All six men ran out into the road; three of the Victors held their guns up to the right, stopping the advance of a forklift and several helmeted workers on foot, while Travers, Takahashi, and Victor Four raced up to the truck.

The man behind the wheel ground his gears to a halt and skidded to a stop.

Chris Travers himself opened the driver's-side door of the cab. "Afuera!" he shouted, and the middle-aged Black man climbed out, his hands in the air and his eyes wide as saucers.

Terminal tractors like this weren't built like normal road trucks. Yard trucks, as they were often called, typically had only a single-seat cab, with the area that would normally be for a passenger seat missing, giving the tractor an off-kilter appearance.

Once the driver was out, Travers heaved himself up and behind the wheel, and then in his headset he ordered all the other men to grab on to the outside. Victors Two and Four climbed behind the cab just in front of the container, and the other three men hefted their exhausted bodies onto the rear of the container, using narrow ledges for footholds.

Travers had learned how to drive big rigs from his uncle back in Oklahoma, but it had been twenty-five years, so he ground gears for several seconds as he tried to refamiliarize himself with all this.

Whoever had been shooting at them apparently lost line of sight for a moment, but suddenly they, or someone else in the terminal, found the right angle, because more gunfire erupted from the direction of the terminal operation's building and the front gate. The truck Travers sat in was struck multiple times, angry metallic pops just behind his cab, and then snapping rounds from multiple soldiers' AKs raked the street around them.

Victor Five, hanging on to the back, shouted into his mic. "We good to put their heads down?"

"Make noise, motherfuckers!" Travers shouted as he finally got the truck in gear.

Instantly all three men hanging on to the rear of the container towed by the truck opened fire, each holding their weapon with one hand while they clasped locking rods, latches, anything to keep from falling off. Their small but still-potent weapons blasted the pavement between a row of containers a hundred yards back, just in front of a trio of terminal work trucks loaded with armed Cuban Revolutionary Army forces.

All three pickup trucks swerved out of sight behind container stacks, but a new vehicle took up the chase behind him.

Jim Pace came over Travers's headset. "Victor, you're going to have to ram that fence at top speed, you understand?"

"Yep." The metal fence with huge coils of razor wire on top looked especially formidable as it loomed larger in Chris's windshield.

To his team he said, "Everybody tighten up back there, we're gonna have to make our own exit!"

Carlos Contreras had a perfect view of the covered exterior walkway leading to all the tiny flats up on the third floor of the market building.

The stairwell door on the northern side of the building was closed, but Lancer had just communicated that he and one of the Cubans were about to exit, and he wanted Contreras to give him an update on the status of his target.

The Mexican shifted the camera with his joystick, zoomed in tight through the open front door of the fourth room, and inside he saw the man behind the big spotting scope.

"He's still in the same place. Still looking out towards the water."

"Is he armed?" Lancer's voice was labored, presumably with the exertion of climbing the stairs.

"I . . . I don't see a weapon visible. He's looking through his glass at the container yard."

"Okay, we're coming out. Keep updating me on his disposition."

"Yes," Contreras said.

Suddenly, Contreras heard a knock on the back door of the gray panel truck. He looked back over his shoulder, completely confused at the interruption when all his attention had been on his laptop.

Police? Some busybody? Either way, anyone at the door meant he had to quickly hide his equipment. He closed the laptop and tossed a bedsheet over it, then pulled off his headphones and tucked them under, as well, not taking the time to alert Lancer.

As his attention was fixed on the rear door and his own equipment, the loud crashing sound of broken glass came from the driver's-side window of the truck.

His head spun back around just in time to see a hand reach through the broken window, then open the door from the inside.

And then, to Carlos Contreras's utter astonishment, a woman launched into the driver's seat, spun around to him, and pointed a short, squat pistol at him at a range of six feet.

She looked him up and down. "Español? Ingles?"

"I . . . I speak English."

She moved between the seats and came back to him, knocking over the empty Pelican cases in her way as she did so. She yanked the sheet off the tiny table with the laptop, joystick, and headphones, and then opened the laptop, her pistol now right between Contreras's eyes.

She pulled the headset out of the laptop, disconnected the call he had open with Lancer on the phone, then said, "Is your drone armed?"

His first inclination was to tell her he had no idea what she was talking about, but he knew she had him dead to rights. He just shook his head.

She glanced down at the screen and saw the image broadcast from the quadcopter over the harbor in front of the market building, and just then the door to the stairwell on the north side opened.

Contreras saw that Zakharova seemed completely fixated on the images, so he considered grabbing a Pelican case to knock her out with, but just as he began looking around, she moved the pistol away from his face, and pushed it hard into his knee.

"I need you alive, but I swear to God if you try anything I will fuck you up."

Contreras changed his mind and sat still.

Lancer spoke into his mic now, careful to keep his voice low. "Zero One. Are you receiving?"

After a moment without a response, he pulled his phone from his front pocket, looked down at it, and saw that his connection with his drone pilot had been broken.

Standing there on the walkway looking over the harbor, just one hundred feet or so from the open door behind which the CIA officer was positioned, Lancer considered calling his overwatch back so that Zero One could help walk him in to the target safely. But he was so close, and so exposed right here, that he didn't want to take the time.

He looked out over the water for the drone, but it was too small to see.

Almost immediately, however, another idea came to him.

He turned to the baldheaded Cuban next to him. The man had a CZ 75 9-millimeter pistol, 1970s technology but reliable enough, and he looked like he'd be the type to know how to use it. The weapon was in his right hand, with his left hand wrapped around it, as well.

Lancer said, "We go together. You first."

The man looked at him like he was crazy, but only until Lancer reached down into his pants, removed his entire money belt, and handed it over.

Kincaid would be making three million for today's hit; passing this guy ten grand meant nothing.

The Cuban had seen all the hundreds in the belt when Lancer opened it down at the van, so he snatched it greedily, shoved it into the front of his waistband under his yellow guayabera, and flicked the safety off his weapon.

To the American he said, "The Mexican watching us . . . he say everything okay?"

Lancer had been cut off from Zero One for the past thirty seconds, but he just nodded. "All good. Fourth door. Go get him, I'm right behind you."

FIFTY-TWO

With gunfire raging all around, Chris Travers shoved his head back hard against the headrest, braced his legs, and then slammed the yard truck into the three-meter-high fence at sixty-eight miles per hour. The engine in the tractor was massive despite the small cab, but the added momentum of the steel box in back containing fifty thousand pounds of copper wire helped propel the big vehicle through easily.

Most of the razor wire went above the terminal tractor and the big container behind it, and the fence simply tore and flattened.

Travers found himself instantly bouncing over a small dirt embankment, out of control, and then he slammed on the brakes, downshifted, and skidded onto a street that ran parallel with the container terminal.

Pace spoke up now. "Cops coming from the south! Go right! Go right!"

"Everybody with me?"

The men counted off over their headsets, and Travers was relieved to hear all five call signs.

The tractor swerved hard to the right, rising up on its left tires as it did so, though the chassis and container in back stayed on the ground.

He drove down the road with half his tires in the air for a few seconds, then crashed back down on the tractor's suspension.

"Punch it!" Pace shouted, but the Ground Branch team leader's foot was already stomping on the gas.

Travers immediately said, "We're clear, Overwatch. Get your ass out of there!"

The Cuban launched forward, spinning off the walkway and through the doorway of the fourth room, his gun out in front of him.

Lancer advanced, as well, just five feet behind.

Gunshots rang out in the apartment.

At first Lancer thought the Cuban was wasting the CIA officer, so he started to follow him in, but he pulled up short just as the baldheaded man lurched back out of the doorway, twisting, wet crimson across his yellow shirt, his arm lowering and the gun dropping from it.

More gunfire cracked, the Cuban's head snapped back, and Lancer dropped to a knee, then reached through the doorway and opened fire without looking.

The Cuban tumbled over the railing of the walkway and fell the three stories to the concrete quay next to the water.

The window glass right above Lancer shattered as more gunfire came from the apartment, and Scott Kincaid wished like hell the drone pilot hadn't hung up on him, because he really needed eyes on his target right now.

Jim Pace emptied his little pistol's seven rounds, then ejected the magazine and loaded a fresh one from his back pocket. Simultaneously he retreated into the kitchen, heading for the back door and getting himself out of the line of fire, although the walls in this shit building didn't look like they were solid enough to slow down a lawn dart.

Once he'd reloaded he dropped back to his knees and put his hand on the kitchen door. He knew it would lead out to a catwalk that looked out above the artisans' market, and he also knew that he and the men trying to kill him had already made a lot of noise.

Still, getting away from Lancer was key, even if it meant ending up in a Cuban prison and creating one hell of an international incident for the United States.

But just before he opened the door, he stopped himself and looked up. Suddenly, he had another idea.

Court made it to the top of the stairwell, passed a dead Cuban police officer with a bloody knife wound in his sternum, then opened the door to the walkway. Just as he was about to spin in the direction of the gunfire, Zoya's voice came through his earpiece.

"One armed subject on the walkway approaching you at a run. One of the Cubans with Lancer is dead, and Lancer is in the apartment with Pace at this time."

Court didn't have a fucking clue how Zoya knew *any* of this, but he told himself he'd ask later. For now he leaned out of the stairwell, his Glock 26 up in front of his face, and he opened fire on a baldheaded man racing in his direction, firing twice into the man's burly chest. The subject tumbled down hard on his knees and slammed his face into the concrete, and then his pistol clanked up the walkway in front of him, all the way to the open door halfway down from Court's position.

A fresh exchange of pistol fire inside the third-floor apartment told Court that Pace was engaged with Lancer, so he raced forward as fast as he could.

Zoya watched the action from the laptop in the van, while right next to her, Contreras had his eyes on the pistol barrel pressed hard against his kneecap. He thought he might be able to grab the gun and wrench it free of the American woman, even though she had surprisingly strong-looking arms and shoulders.

She spun her face to his, disrupting his plan.

"Fly into that apartment and crash your drone into Lancer!"

Contreras didn't move. "Are you crazy? The drone's less than a kilogram, what's it going to—"

She put the barrel of the gun to the pilot's temple now. "Miss him and you die right here!" she screamed, and Contreras lurched for the joystick.

The crawl space above the apartment was ancient, low, and dark. Jim Pace had no idea where he was going, he just scooted laterally to the south, ignoring cobwebs and rat droppings, hoping to make it all the way to, or at least near, the broken service elevator so he could get into the shaft and scale down so he might have a chance to get out of here.

He'd heard shooting outside, and he knew Gentry was on his way.

His eyeglasses had come off on his climb through the ceiling tile, as had his earpiece, and he'd partially broken the tile putting it back, so he had no illusions that Lancer was going to miss the fact that the man who'd been shooting at him thirty seconds earlier had somehow evaporated into thin air, but it was his hope Lancer would first try the back door, and this would buy Gentry some time to get his ass up here to help out.

In the meantime, to increase the speed of his escape, he slipped the Glock pistol in the small of his back, rose to his knees, and moved forward, his back scraping the metal roofing above him as he made his way to the south, foot by arduous foot.

Lancer didn't know what the gunfire was all about outside on the exterior walkway, but he put it out of his mind as he spun around the doorway into the tiny kitchen, firing his suppressed pistol as he went. When he saw that the room was empty, he ceased fire, ran to the door, put his hand on the latch, and then stopped himself. Looking up, he saw a broken ceiling tile, below which was a table covered with bits of the tile.

He shifted his weapon up and opened fire into the ceiling around the broken tile. After just three rounds his slide locked open, so he dropped the magazine and loaded another from his belt.

Raising his weapon again to dump another mag, he prepared to press the trigger but heard a noise in the apartment through his ringing ears.

He stepped back into the living room with his gun up and found himself face-to-face with a quadcopter zooming through the front door directly at him.

The drone slammed into his gun hand, then skittered to the floor.

Lancer looked down at it, then looked back up, turned, and dove to his right into the kitchen behind a string of gunfire.

He slammed hard onto the filthy floor, tumbled, and came up onto his knees, his weapon pointed back to the living room.

His mind raced at a thousand miles per hour, and his heart pounded like a galloping thoroughbred, because Court fucking Gentry was right fucking here.

Court knew Lancer was in the kitchen, and he pictured the kitchen from the layout of the rest of this shitty apartment, and presumed it to be very small.

But he didn't dare fire through the wall, because he didn't know if Jim Pace was still alive, somewhere in his line of fire.

Seconds earlier he'd been right about to jump into the apartment from the walkway when a small quadcopter whizzed by his face like it had been shot out of a cannon, and when he turned into the doorway, he saw that the device had slammed into Lancer before bouncing harmlessly against the living room wall. He now knew Zoya was in control of the pilot, and she had bought him the instant he needed to avoid catching a 10-millimeter round to the brain pan.

But he hadn't managed to hit Lancer before the killer made it to concealment.

Unsure what to do next, he retreated back out onto the walkway, knelt down behind the brick wall next to the doorway, and called out.

"Kincaid?"

He knelt down even lower, kept his gun out, and pointed through the doorway.

"That you, Gentry?"

"We've gotta stop meeting like this, am I right?"

Just as Court expected, the ex–Navy SEAL fired several times in his direction. The bullets wouldn't go through the exterior wall, however, so Court wasn't worried as long as he kept himself shielded by the brick-work here.

When the shooting stopped, Court said, "I've got more cover than you do, asshole. I can ventilate that kitchen wall from here."

"And shoot your friend? He's alive, and I've got him by the neck. I'll be honest, he doesn't look too good. Might want to come give him mouth-to-mouth."

Court didn't know if Lancer was lying or not, but he couldn't take a chance and fire towards the sound of the assassin's voice.

Court said, "This standoff is going to land us both in a Cuban prison in about a minute."

Lancer laughed loudly. "Think we'll be cellmates?"

"You wish."

Jim Pace winced with each creeping movement he made as he slowly but quietly turned back around in the crawl space, trying to go back in the di-rection of the apartment he'd just fled.

Moving was hard in darkness, but it was harder still because one of Lancer's bullets fired through the tiles had grazed his right shin, just above the ankle. He knew he was losing blood, but he also knew he had to go back and help Court, because he'd heard the gunfire, and now he heard two men shouting back and forth.

To his left he heard a new sound, however, and it took a second to iden-tify it. Footsteps, a lot of them, men running along the metal catwalk along the wall two stories over the warehouse floor that served as the artisans' market. Pace pulled out his phone, shone a light, and saw that the wall next to him was open to the warehouse below the roofing material, mean-ing he could climb out, drop down, and get free.

Except for the fact that it was probably a ten-foot drop to the catwalk, and the catwalk was presently full of people, presumably cops or soldiers.

He froze in place, uncertain of his next move, the blood trickling from his leg.

Slowly, he looked at his phone and he saw that he was still on the call with Gentry. He turned off the Bluetooth and put the unit to his ear.

Whispering, he said, "Gentry. I'm good. Get the fuck out of here."

Court heard the transmission where he knelt on the walkway by the door, but before he could respond he heard a noise behind him, and he swung around to see a Cuban police officer lean outside the door he'd come through moments earlier. He spun his pistol around, and the cop ducked back in the doorway. A second officer leaned out with a handgun, but Court fired a round into the open door above his head, and he, too, ducked back inside.

Now Court crawled on the walkway to the railing, then rose and looked over the side. Two stories down, on the concrete below his position, a dead Cuban in a guayabera lay facedown in a wide pool of thick blood, but Court didn't concentrate on the gruesome sight, because he had something else on his mind. Directly below him, hanging off the railing from several metal rings, a two-story-tall Cuban flag hung down. It was roughly the same size as the two he'd seen inside the market, and just like inside, a second flag hung off the railing on his right, separated by the open bay doors below.

The stairwell door to the north opened now, and a group of Cuban police burst out onto the walkway. They saw him there and raised their guns.

Quickly, Court pulled out his knife, holstered his weapon, and rolled over the railing.

The snap of a gunshot to his left told him the cops at the northern door there had found a higher gear of bravery than they'd displayed seconds ago, but he quickly disappeared out of their view.

Scott Kincaid heard the gunshot, then rose in the kitchen, well aware that Gentry must be shooting at someone else, because he would *not* be firing into this room sight unseen. He lifted his weapon and moved to the left to try to get a better angle to hit the man hiding behind the exterior wall, but just as he thought he was in a good position, the door behind him that led to the catwalk flew open.

Kincaid turned to find two, then three, then four uniformed police, their weapons pointed at him.

Kincaid dropped his big 10-millimeter pistol and held up his hands. While the police shouted at him, he shouted at Gentry, presuming him to still be outside. "Guess I'll be seeing you in the slammer, brother! I call top bunk!"

But Gentry did not answer him. As Kincaid was tackled to the ground, he wasn't bothered by a knee in his neck and another in his back, and he wasn't bothered by the pain from the old gunshot wound to his ribs or when his hands were wrenched behind him and he felt the all-too-familiar sensation of handcuffs being snapped on his thick wrists. No, he was bothered by the fact that Gentry might have somehow managed to get away, leaving him alone to his fate.

"Gentry?" he called out again, a plaintive tone to his voice.

Court slid down the red-white-and-blue Cuban flag, the four-inch blade of his knife slicing the thick canvas as he descended, his left arm wrapped around the flag's edge and then back through the expanding slit his knife created along the way to keep him from falling backwards to his death.

It took only fifteen seconds to reach the bottom of the thick fabric, and from here he dropped the last four feet or so, landing hard on the concrete but rolling into a ball to blunt his impact.

People stood on the quay, most cowering low because of the gunfight that had been raging above them and the other in the container terminal a couple hundred yards away, but everyone there saw him plainly.

He rose back to his feet and looked around for a few seconds. Sliding his knife back into a hilt inside his waistband, he began running with a little limp, just a few yards to the water's edge.

Gunfire from above and behind him told him that the cops up there weren't happy about his impending escape, but they didn't hit him. Instead, at a limping run, he passed by a dead Cuban in a yellow shirt, then dove, headfirst, into the harbor.

. . .

Jim Pace lay on his back in the crawl space, listening to all the hustle and bustle below him while he took off a sock and tied it around his calf. He realized his gunshot wasn't that bad, as gunshots went, anyway, so now his main concern was that some cop was going to poke up a ceiling tile in the apartment where the shoot-out had taken place, and then simply shine a light around, finding a hidden gringo in the process.

He sent a series of texts to Travers to let him know his predicament, and then he just lay there waiting. After thirty minutes, the voices below and the movement on the catwalk died down and, a half hour after that, he heard no noise at all.

He climbed out of the crawl space and into a vacant storage area lined with shelves around noon, well over an hour after he last heard a noise. Here the open elevator shaft was only partially boarded up, so he climbed under the uneven wooden slats, then began scaling down into the abyss.

Five minutes later he'd skirted by the cops down in the artisans' market and stepped out onto the street and into the back of a Ford van.

Joe Takahashi was behind the wheel, wearing a ball cap and big cheap sunglasses.

"You okay, boss?" he said as he drove away, past police cars all around.

"I'm too old for this shit, Hash."

Takahashi laughed and concentrated on getting the hell out of the area.

FIFTY-THREE

Zack Hightower escorted Anton Hinton out of the cafeteria after a business lunch with several top engineers at Hinton Labs. It had been a normal meeting, as near as Zack could tell, except for the fact that Wren had not shown up. Anton made a comment about this, asking if anyone at the table knew where his chief operating officer was, but none of the engineers had seen him all morning.

Hinton pulled out his phone, looked down at it for a moment, then sent a text. Zack watched his face while he looked at his phone, and he saw the normally calm man's features tighten up. He bit his lower lip; Zack registered the small man's chest rising and falling more dramatically, as if he was breathing heavier.

Something was going on, this much was clear.

Hightower knew it was his job to speak up. "Anton? Anything I need to know about?"

Hinton's eyes shot up and locked on Hightower's. They were intense, perhaps even a little mistrustful. After a moment he just said, "No. Everything is just fine."

No one else at the table seemed to notice the man's obvious distress, but Zack had been a player in the industry of causing people distress his entire adult life, so he had the tools to identify mental tension in others.

Just a minute after his fish and rice was put down at the table in front of him, Hinton stood and said he needed to get back upstairs for a teleconference with his lab in Switzerland.

Zack followed close behind him him to the elevator. Once inside, Zack sent them to the top-floor executive suites, and as soon as the doors opened he saw Gareth Wren standing there in a white polo, his pistol riding on his hip and a concerned look on his face.

Hinton apparently saw it, too. "What is it?"

"Something's happening downtown."

Zack began ushering Hinton out of the elevator and into his office, where he kept his AK-47. As they moved he said, "What is it?"

Wren clarified. "No threat, Zack. This is something else. I need to talk to the boss alone a moment."

Zack waited in the lobby of Hinton's office with two former Black Wasps and Kimmie Lin while Wren and Hinton went inside.

The conversation was just a few minutes in duration, and when it was over, Zack was surprised by what Wren called out to the room as he opened the door. "Hightower, have you got a moment?"

Zack entered, Kimmie followed after Wren bade her in, and then all four of them sat at the table. Kimmie pulled out her tablet as Wren began to speak.

"Right, Zack. Your man Pace has just caused us a spot of bother in the city."

Hightower was confused. "What happened?"

"He was sighted at Havana Harbor this morning, running overwatch for a team of men who came ashore in the container terminal. It went loud, three dead, all police, another injured. The Americans escaped."

Almost speechless, Zack asked, "What . . . what the hell were they doing at the harbor?"

Hinton said, "We were hoping you might be able to tell us."

Zack looked over and saw that Kimmie was taking notes, like this was a fucking board meeting.

"Wait. You think I knew about this?"

Hinton shrugged. "We don't know. America wants to disrupt my research here, I've been telling you that from the start. They came and talked to you, and you said they seemed satisfied by what you said. Now this."

"What makes you think this has anything to do with you?"

Wren answered, "We had several containers of cargo on a ship that had just come into port. More mainframes for our research, some other bits and bobs. Our containers don't look like they've been tampered with, but nevertheless we are working under the assumption they were coming after our equipment, likely to sabotage it."

Zack just shook his head slowly. "I don't know anything about this. But you know I used to be Agency. You shouldn't have hired me if you didn't trust me."

Hinton put a gentle hand on Zack's forearm. "I trust you. You saved my life, after all, putting your own in danger. But we really need you to think back to your conversation with this man at the bar the night before last. Anything you didn't tell us?"

Zack thought back, but he was also thinking about what he'd just learned. Somehow Ground Branch had been given permission to go into Cuba and run an operation. Very possibly against Anton Hinton.

He said, "I didn't tell you Pace said he thought something was off with you. Your business dealings, your bad relationship with the U.S., even your setup down here in Cuba, he seemed like he found it a little suspect. But he didn't accuse you of anything, and I told him I spent every day around all of you and haven't seen anything that concerns me. I figured he would have left Cuba immediately after our conversation, and I have no idea what his people were doing snooping around the harbor."

Hinton said, "I have a bad relationship with the U.S., true, but I also have a bad relationship with the Chinese." Hinton rubbed his face. "Half the people who've been killed I loved like brothers and sisters. The other half? The other half I had some sort of conflict with. Tomer and I hadn't spoken in years, Bogdan Kantor blamed me for losing an important contract with the Americans when we were in business together, Dr. Park thought my researchers stole some of her work." Hinton waved a hand. "They didn't, by the way. And I didn't kill them."

Wren said, "Anton is a polarizing figure, we know this. But what happened today is beyond the pale."

Zack said, "You want me to talk with the Agency? I mean, assuming they're still in town?"

Hinton said, "To tell them what?"

"To try to find out why they are after you, assuming they are." Zack shrugged, looked at Wren. "Any intelligence is good intelligence. I'll feel them out, find out what the plan was at the harbor, what they suspect. Find out if they are looking at anyone else, or if they're just focusing on you?"

Wren said, "It's too dangerous. You work for Anton now, you might be a target."

He laughed a little. "Of Jim fucking Pace? The Agency's *not* going to assassinate me, and if he tried, I'd take care of it."

Hinton leaned forward. "Gareth . . . I think this is a good idea. We just send Zack as an emissary, find out what they were looking for. Keep it friendly."

Wren looked to Hinton. He seemed surprised, but after a moment he ran his fingers through his graying hair. "Perhaps him going to see an old friend on neutral ground and exchanging information might be beneficial to us." He looked to Zack. "Get us all you can, and tell Pace, again, that we are victims here, not perpetrators."

Zack nodded.

"How will you find him?" Hinton asked. "Just call the embassy?"

Zack shook his head. "I suspect finding him won't be the problem. I'll go out for dinner tonight. Alone. If the CIA is still here, they will find *me*."

The safe house at the end of a long gravel road in a rural western Havana suburb called Bauta had been used by the Agency for clandestine meetings between officers and agents for over a decade. A large ranch with a separate barn on a wooded property divided by farmland, it was especially secure because a pair of locals in a shack a few hundred meters closer to the suburb thoroughfare watched out for any approaching vehicles whenever the Yumas, the local term for Yankees, were on the property.

Bauta was miles away from the harbor and all the mayhem that had happened there today, but still, any American intelligence officers on the ground in Cuba remained at great risk.

Travers and four of his men showed up here just after one, but Victor Two had stayed behind in the center of the city, ready to collect Jim Pace when he slipped out of the police cordon.

The van with Pace and Hash didn't make it here to the property until nearly two thirty, and as soon as he limped into the farmhouse, Jim Pace waved off any medical care till he took a long shower. After this he changed into clothes left by the local agents, then sat down at a kitchen chair with a leg up and took a plate of food from the old woman who ran the safe house, a faithful agent of the United States and, perhaps just as important to the men who'd just arrived that day, an incredible cook. While Victor Four expertly cleaned, stitched, and bandaged Pace's painful but superficial leg wound, the CIA officer chowed greedily on garlicky roast pork shoulder and rice, guzzled bottled water, and took a conference call with Langley that lasted over an hour.

Langley, to put it mildly, had not been pleased with Pace's report.

The Juliet Victor men who'd fired their weapons today cleaned them and tended to the myriad cuts and bruises they'd picked up this morning. Of the six men, Victor Five was the worst off. He'd been on the right side at the back of the container as it crashed through the fencing, and his right shoulder and triceps caught a horror-show-looking blade from the razor wire as it whipped by. He bled like a stuck pig from the upper arm, but Victor Four had cleaned the wound, administered twenty-four stitches, and applied compression bandages, and Five declared himself good to go.

It was past six p.m. now; the thick gray clouds had returned and everyone expected rain within minutes, but Travers pulled security by sitting on the front porch looking down the driveway, his MP7 resting on his lap. He ate plantain chips he'd found in the pantry, unconcerned that they'd expired nine months earlier, and he drank a bottle of Tínima, a local beer. Just as a low and slow rumble of distant thunder rolled over him, he saw the headlights of a vehicle turn off the main road and begin heading up the gravel drive.

"Finally," he said, and then he climbed out of the chair, opened the front door, and went back inside, because he knew the man heading this way was skittish when it came to armed dudes who worked for the CIA.

A minute later, Court, Zoya, and Contreras, the latter with his hands zip-tied behind his back, stood on the porch Travers had only just vacated.

An elderly woman, well below five feet tall and hunched with a spinal condition, opened the door and looked at the three with neither surprise nor any emotion at all. After a few seconds she waved them in and shuffled out of the way.

Inside they found a large home in a state of mild disrepair, heavy hand-made wooden furniture, and two men wearing pistols on their hips in the living room. One of the men was African American, and he had a big bandage that covered the majority of his right upper arm. He and his part-ner walked up to Contreras without saying anything, grabbed him, then ushered him down to his stomach where they gave him a good frisk, flip-ping him over onto his back as they expertly worked.

Contreras, for his part, seemed utterly unfazed by all this. Any sur-prise or fear he'd felt when the woman had captured him had long evapo-rated. He appeared to be a man without a care in the world, mildly amused that the Americans had him in their custody, but not put out about it at all.

Finally they pulled him back to his feet, ripped off his sweat-stained shirt, then escorted him into the kitchen. Both Court and Zoya heard a back door opening and then closing again, but still, no one said anything.

The little old lady headed down a hallway, but before they could follow her, Chris Travers came into the dining room wearing a white T-shirt and gym shorts, an MP7 slung across his back, and he shook both of their hands. "Thanks for getting Jim out of there today. That was our job, and we failed, so I owe you both."

Zoya said, "He told us you guys had your own problems this morning. Everybody okay?"

"Some better than others, but we're all fighting ready."

Court said, "We've got the laptops and other gear from the van Zoya dumped. They're in the trunk of the Sonata if you want to grab them."

Travers nodded, then called out, "Moreno?"

A Hispanic male in his early forties appeared from the kitchen, and Travers sent him outside to collect the intelligence haul.

"And the cargo from the ship?" Court asked.

"Tracker shows it's still at the container terminal. The concern is everything off-loaded from the *Estelle* is going to get extra scrutiny, but we are only turning the tracker on for a few seconds an hour, so any handheld radio scanners would have to be damn lucky to find it. Still, the enemy tends to get lucky sometimes."

Court nodded. "That they do."

Jim Pace limped out of a hallway that led to the rear of the home. He wore a short-sleeve peach-colored guayabera and khakis, and he walked with a limp. "Which means that drone pilot you two nabbed is our best chance for actionable intel on what the hell's going on." He looked around. "Where did you put him?"

Travers said, "Doug and Fish took him to the barn."

Pace nodded, then shook hands with the new arrivals. "Long-ass time, Sierra Six."

"I'm sure you've been missing me."

Pace laughed. "Not really, no. But you saved my ass today, and I do appreciate it."

"You saved your own ass. I showed up about ten seconds late."

"Well . . . we're both still here." He cocked his head. "You been living in the Sahara? Got yourself a nice sunburn."

"Yeah, but I moisturize. What's the situation here?"

"Havana station confirms Kincaid was arrested by the Cubans. Plus Travers managed to extract his team. Although Langley is having a collective seventh-floor shit fit and I feel like there's a mad hornet living on my right calf, I'm still going to have to call this a good day."

"What's with your leg?" Zoya asked after Court introduced her as Anthem.

"Got winged by Lancer. Won't be dancing the bolero down here on this trip, but otherwise, I'm fine."

"You're going to run the interrogation on Contreras?" Court asked.

Pace seemed to consider something for a moment. Court had explained over the phone earlier that it had taken him most of the day to get out of the harbor, get clean and dry clothes, and then make it all the way back to the hotel where Zoya had been sitting for hours with the prisoner, so he knew Zoya had had more time interacting with the Mexican than Court had. To Zoya he said, "When Gentry gave us the name, we ran his history." Sliding a sheet of paper that had been lying on the table over to her, he said, "Here's his whole life."

Zoya nodded, read it while Court looked over her shoulder, then looked back up to Pace. Zoya said, "Contreras is an ass, like you'd expect. Intelligent, portrays himself as extremely confident. He might even be a little narcissistic, so he might actually *be* confident that he's still got some control over the situation, but he doesn't know what's going to happen to him."

Pace rubbed his chin. "Maybe I don't know what's going to happen to him, either."

"What do you mean?"

The older man stood. Looked to Court. "I don't have to tell you this is time sensitive, do I?"

Court remained seated, and he shook his head.

Zoya looked back and forth to both men. "What's happening?"

Court answered. "Jim, Chris, and the others are going to sit here in the house while you and I go out back to the barn to have a chat with Contreras."

Pace shrugged. "There are rules I feel okay about breaking, and there are rules I'd rather not break if I don't have to. I'm thinking that since you're here . . . I don't have to."

"Sure, Jim," Court answered. "We'll interview your prisoner. Any other fires I can pull your ass out of today?"

The CIA officer gave a tired laugh. "No, that should be plenty. You'll let me know what you learn?"

Court rose from the table, and Zoya did the same. "You got it."

Pace said, "Actually, why don't you give him twenty minutes to sit and stew back there. You can get something to eat. The boys have the prisoner tied to a chair with a bunch of rusty old farrier tools lined up on a table nearby just to freak him out."

"Nice touch," Zoya said.

Court thought a moment. "We need some odds and ends from around the house first. I'll check the kitchen."

"What did you have in mind?" Zoya asked him, and then Court looked to Pace.

"Not in front of the children, honey."

Pace turned out of the dining room and limped back towards the hall to the rear of the farmhouse without another word.

Carlos Contreras sat stripped down to his boxers, alone in a dark, hot, and mosquito-filled barn, while the rain outside picked up and beat down on the leaky tin roof above him.

His hands were tied behind his back, and his feet were duct-taped to the chair legs.

The gringos had put a table a few feet away and lined up a bunch of old tools on it, leaving it all in view for him. There were blades and metal hooks and pinching implements; he thought they might be for shoeing horses but couldn't be sure.

The implements were intended to scare him, of this he had no doubt, but he wasn't scared.

These gringos wouldn't torture him; that wasn't how Americans operated.

The wooden barn door slid open suddenly as the woman who'd captured him this morning stepped in, followed by the bearded man who'd been traveling with her.

Zakharova and Gentry, the pair that he'd been after for days.

They were wet from the rain, but neither seemed to notice, much less care. Gentry had a large red bag that looked like a medical kit over a shoulder, and Zakharova held several towels, which she dropped on the floor a few feet away from the prisoner.

Gentry also held a folder in his hand, and he looked down to it. He said, "Carlos Felipe Contreras Medina. Hey, congratulations, tomorrow is your twenty-sixth birthday."

The woman next to him said, "Mazel tov," but Carlos didn't know what that meant.

Gentry now looked back down to the sheet of paper in his hand. "From Monterrey, originally. Former member of the Jalisco New Generation cartel. Two arrests. Neither stuck, probably because your bosses thought you were worth buying out of custody. This tells me you are a big fish, amigo."

Contreras *was* a big fish, he told himself, but these idiots didn't even know he'd left the cartel a year ago.

The bearded man said, "You left the cartel a year ago, you've done some odd jobs for criminal syndicates all over Latin America and the U.S., and now you work for an organization that has been conducting assassinations of innocent scientists and engineers all over the world." Stepping over to the rusty tools on the table, he spoke softly. "Pays well, does it?"

Zakharova stepped around behind the seated man. "It doesn't pay nearly enough for what's about to happen to you."

Contreras looked ahead. The bitch was bluffing, he was certain.

He'd been tortured before, by the cartel. This gringo couple wasn't going to do shit to him that would make him talk.

Gentry looked up from the table now. "Who do you work for?"

Contreras said nothing.

After a few seconds, Zakharova, still behind him, said, "Did you know you were taking orders from the Chinese?"

Contreras suspected this, but he didn't answer. Instead, he asked, "Can I have a cigarette?"

The woman stepped around and knelt in front of him now. She was hot, Contreras had noticed this almost immediately. But angry. Mean. Crazy. She said, "You just quit." With a hard stare she added, "For life."

Contreras smiled a little at this. They were trying to act so tough. "You are with the American government." He said it as a statement.

Gentry replied, "Actually, *we're* not. I get your confusion, of course. The man you were trying to kill today *is* from the American government." He stepped closer. "And that's why he's not here right now. He and his co-workers got into their cars and left you here. It's just us. Alone. With you."

The Mexican smirked, then nodded to the table full of tools.

"Is that supposed to scare me?" He laughed angrily. "You aren't going to use those tools on me like we're in a bad movie."

Gentry turned back to the table. "This stuff? Yeah, you're right. It's here to intimidate you. The CIA guys thought that might frighten you into talking. But they don't know you like I do."

"What does that mean?" he asked, surprised by the American's honesty about the staged torture devices.

"It means they don't know how mentally strong you are. How prepared you are to keep your mouth shut, since you think we'll give up and take you to the U.S. and file some charges on you that probably won't even stick because we'd have to reveal classified intelligence information at your trial, and CIA is not about to say they were down here spying in Cuba."

This was *exactly* everything that Contreras was thinking. Again, this gringo had surprised him, but he'd also confirmed that Contreras had nothing to worry about right now.

"So . . ." Gentry added, putting his hands under the ledge of the wooden table with the devices on it. "This stuff isn't going to do us a bit of good." With a single, swift motion he heaved up, the heavy table flipped into the air, the fifteen kilos of rusty farm tools went flying in all directions, and everything crashed down on the dirty concrete floor.

"So, how about we just forget about all that," Gentry said after everything came to rest. "That stuff takes time. And I'm not here for a long time." He turned back around, looked Contreras in the eye. "I'm here for a *good* time."

What?

The woman in front of him looked up at the tin roof now. "The rain is loud enough to where no one will hear anything in twenty-one seconds."

Contreras was on the back foot now; he thought these gringos were crazy, but he still wasn't scared by them.

"What happens in twenty-one seconds?"

"You scream."

"Why would I scream in twenty-one seconds?"

Zakharova smiled. "Because in *twenty* seconds"—the woman rose from her crouch—"I am going to set you on fire."

The woman pulled a small rectangular can out of her back pocket, opened the lid, and then sprayed the bound man in the face with some sort of liquid. Contreras tasted it; it stung his tongue and made him gag, and when she kept dousing his hair, chest, and arms with it, he realized it was lighter fluid.

FIFTY-FOUR

"Hey! What the fuck are you doing?"

She said nothing, just emptied the small can by directing the last of the stream on the crotch of his boxers.

Then she pulled a lighter out of a front pocket.

Contreras spit lighter fluid out of his mouth, tried to blink the sting from his eyes.

"No!"

The woman bobbed her head towards the stack of towels.

"I'm going to torch you now, but I promise you this. If you start talking, I will put out the fire. If you give us everything we need, we'll let whatever remains of you leave here."

These gringos were fucking crazy.

Gentry said, "The pain will be excruciating, obviously, so you'll go into shock and be unable to speak, probably in about five seconds." He shrugged. "Either this works, and you talk, or it doesn't work, and we don't have to deal with you anymore and"—he winked at the Mexican—"this is a plus, we get rid of the body, all at once."

"That's the beauty of it," Zakharova added. "Whatever happens, it'll be all over in just a couple of minutes."

Looking into the strange American man's eyes, then shifting and looking into the Russian woman's, Contreras saw that they absolutely *would* go through with this.

Suddenly, he was fucking terrified.

"Look," Contreras said now to Gentry, "I don't have any information about—"

"Save it. Nobody's asking you anything. You're a tough guy, especially for a fucking drone tech. It would be insulting to you for us to expect you to talk now. We need to turn the heat up, so to speak, then we'll try to have a conversation."

"That's right! I'm just a drone pilot. Why would anyone tell me anything?"

Gentry just looked to Zakharova. "You ready?"

She handed Gentry the lighter. "You fire up the barbecue, and I'll stand by to stop it if birthday boy feels like a chat."

Court sparked the lighter and began walking towards the prisoner.

Court fought a smile as he advanced, but not because of what he was doing. No, because of Zoya. He loved it when she was in character, even when the character was scary as hell. He prided himself on being a good actor; his life had depended on lying for so long that he had to be. But Zoya was the superior thespian, and he enjoyed watching her work.

He closed to within two feet of the Mexican, and then the seated man began shouting.

"I'll tell you what I know!"

"Already?" Zoya said, standing a few feet behind Court. "C'mon, Carlos. You're better than that."

"But I don't know very much."

Zoya stepped forward and put her hand on Court's, pushing the lighter away. "Okay, here's your chance. You've killed a lot of people in the past week. Tell us about that."

Contreras shook his head. "I've killed no one."

Suddenly the lighter reappeared and refired, a foot from the Mexican's face.

Court said, "Bullshit! Guatemala, Mexico. Boston, was that you, too?"

He shook his head. "I've never been to Boston. The other places . . . I was there. But I was ISR. Strictly ISR."

Gentry said, "*I* was there. In Tulum. Those were *not* surveillance robots."

The Mexican blinked pain from his eyes. "I was not in control of the LAWs."

"LAWs?"

"Lethal autonomous weapons."

Zoya stepped in quickly. "Wait. How do you know they were autonomous?"

The man rolled his eyes after a moment. "I know, but I can't explain it to you."

For a third time, Court sparked the lighter. "How about you give it a whirl?"

"Okay! Okay! The platforms in Tulum . . . the ground bots, the kamikaze bots, and the surveillance bots. They were all working together. That wasn't a bunch of pilots operating them. It was a single intelligent agent. Plus, the dexterity of the machines inside the house . . . I am one of the best pilots in the world, and I couldn't fly drones half that fast around obstacles. No one could. It took advanced AI, high-speed mapping, obstacle recognition, and avoidance algorithms."

Court asked, "Do you know what was on that ship in the harbor?"

"Wipe my face and I'll tell you."

Zoya did so with a towel, and now the man could open his eyes even more.

"No. I didn't even know what James Pace was looking at in the harbor. I was only looking at him."

"Well," Zoya said, "I'll tell you. More autonomous kill bots. What are they doing here in Cuba?"

Contreras showed genuine surprise at this. "I have no idea. Here in Havana I just operated a fleet of small quadcopters with cameras on them. Just cameras. That's all I was asked to do."

Court said, "Why do you think the robots came to Cuba?"

"How the hell should I know?"

"Are they here to kill Hinton?"

Contreras cocked his head, a look of surprise on his face. *"Hinton?"*

Neither of his two questioners spoke, they just stared at him.

The Mexican said, "You mean . . . you mean *Anton* Hinton . . . ? He's here? In Cuba?"

"He is," Zoya said. "There have been two attempts on his life already. One in the UK, one here. We thought maybe Cyrus sent the robots here to target him."

Contreras froze. Court got the idea that the Mexican had been holding back the name Cyrus to use as a bargaining chip, unaware that he and Zoya already knew about him. He decided to use this as an opportunity. "Yes, we know about Cyrus. We know a lot, so don't lie to us."

The man looked at the ground. "You are just going to kill me anyway."

To this, Zoya said, "If you don't tell us what we need, then of course we will torch you right here and now. But if you give us good information, I promise you, you will be on your way to Miami within hours. You'll be questioned for days, weeks, maybe, but you won't be tortured or killed."

Contreras looked like a man with no options. Finally he just said, "Cyrus only used the robots in Mexico because he didn't trust Gama."

Court and Zoya spoke at the same time. "Who's Gama?"

The prisoner looked surprised. "You know about Cyrus but don't know about Gama? Gama is the operations center. Cyrus thought Jack Tudor's person on the inside of the operations center, the woman Tudor told you about, was compromising the mission."

Court and Zoya had already assumed this from their conversation with Tudor.

Court pulled a wooden chair closer, sat down in front of Contreras, and said, "Well, would you look at that? You know all sorts of interesting stuff. Tell me more about Cyrus."

Contreras squinted back at him, his eyes bloodshot red from the lighter fluid itself, as well as the fumes of the liquid on his body.

"All I know about Cyrus is . . . he's American."

Both Zoya and Court spoke at the same time. "What?"

Contreras nodded. "I spoke to him on the phone. Multiple times. American accent, but good Spanish, too." When neither Court nor Zoya spoke, the Mexican looked to Court. "So . . . Gentry . . . it might be your country at the top of all this."

Court said, "I don't believe you."

"Fine. Don't. But I recorded one of my conversations with him. There's a file on my laptop. You can listen for yourself."

Court rubbed his face now, a rare display of his inner thoughts. When his hand moved away from his mouth, he said, "Did you notify the Cubans that something was happening in the harbor?"

"I didn't. I assume Cyrus did."

"Back to Hinton," Zoya said. "You're sure Cyrus wasn't targeting him?"

Contreras just shrugged. "Maybe Cyrus had another operation going against him, but I wasn't part of it."

Zoya said, "The robots were in shipping containers. Completely disassembled. Who was going to put them together?"

The Mexican thought for a moment. "They wouldn't be disassembled if they were about to be used. The LAWs that came to me were ready to go. I just had to power them on and throw them out of an airplane. I did nothing else."

"So . . . why would one hundred tons be shipped to—"

"One hundred tons?"

"Yes."

"Where did they come from?"

"Hong Kong."

Contreras thought a moment, then laughed at them yet again.

Court thought about putting his boot in the man's face and knocking him back on his ass.

But before he could, the Mexican said, "One hundred tons of disassembled LAWs sent to Cuba from China? Anton Hinton is here in Cuba?" He laughed a little. "You can't figure this out without my help?"

Court and Zoya did not reply.

Contreras spit on the floor again. "Anton Hinton knows more about AI than anyone in the world. Those weapons are here for Hinton, but they are not targeting him. They're here for him to use. To operate. What he needs them for . . ." The bound and seated man shrugged. "I don't know. But *there's* your answer."

Court went and retrieved Pace and Travers, assuring both of them that the smell of lighter fluid did not mean anything in any way untoward was going on back here in the barn.

And Pace, for his part, acted like he believed him. Travers, on the other hand, didn't seem to give a shit if they lit this guy up like a bonfire or not.

Jim Pace stepped up to the bound man, and he held up Contreras's two laptops, one in each hand. "Which one has the audio file of Cyrus?"

With a nod to the one on the right, Contreras gave him his code. Pace unlocked the computer, followed the drone pilot's directions to find the file, and they all listened to the conversation together.

With a shrug Pace told the prisoner that the Agency would ultimately get everything off both of his devices, and then he asked him to repeat everything he'd already told Gentry and Zakharova.

Finally, Zoya left the barn and returned with a large wooden bucket of rainwater. She poured it over the half-naked man, washing away the majority of the flammable liquid she'd covered him with. Victor Six came out to watch the prisoner, and she, Court, and Jim returned to the farmhouse.

FIFTY-FIVE

While Court and Zoya were ushered into a back bedroom by the tiny Cuban woman, Pace reentered the dining room at the front of the property, sat down in front of his laptop, checked to make sure his connection was encrypted, and prepared to initiate a call with his staff at Langley.

Before he did so, however, an idea struck him. He looked up a number on his satellite phone, then sent a Signal text.

Five minutes later he was on an encrypted video conference, but not with Langley. Instead, he found himself looking at the image of a home office in Boston, Massachusetts. Dr. Vera Ryder, ex-wife of the late Dr. Lars Halverson, was all in black, and when Pace noticed this, he gasped. "The funeral. It was today?"

She nodded. "I just got home from the reception."

"I am truly sorry to disturb you. I just had some questions."

She waved it away. "It's fine. If you have something important to ask me, I'd like to help the fine folks from Homeland Security in any way I can." She'd worked out that he was CIA, and she was letting him know she knew he wasn't who he claimed to be.

Pace let it go. "Thank you. I'd like to send you an audio file and have you listen to it. I'm doubtful, but thought you might recognize the speaker."

She just nodded; Pace thought she looked exhausted, and she'd obviously been crying.

He sent the file, and he watched while she listened to it once, then a second time.

"Any idea who—"

"Wait," she said, and then she began listening to short snippets of the conversation, both the English and the tiny bit of Spanish Cyrus had spoken at the end. Sometimes just playing a single word or phrase, then stopping it and replaying it.

Pace felt his frustration rise. He had a lot to do, and he thought a ten-minute conversation with Ryder on the off chance she would recognize Cyrus's voice and identify him would be worth a shot.

But he didn't have time to watch her piddle with this all afternoon.

"If you want to think about it, maybe I can—"

"This voice . . ." she said, and Pace stopped talking.

"What about the voice?"

"It's synthetic."

"It's *what*?"

"It's an AI-powered voice generator. It's not a real person."

"It . . . it sounds real enough to me."

"Trust me, I do this for a living. It's very high-quality, but it's AI."

"So . . . so someone was masking their identity by using this voice generator?"

"Perhaps," she said, and then she thought a moment. "My theory is easy to prove. There are tens of thousands of synthetic voices available for purchase from dozens and dozens of different countries around the world. They are all out there, on the Internet. They'll read books or articles to you, do voice-over work for ads, turn technical manuals into audio files. But the Spanish voice . . . it's male, the dialect sounds to me like it's from Spain itself, nowhere else. There can't be more than a few dozen of that quality."

Pace was miles out of his depth. "So . . . I can have my staff listen to every Spanish male voice they can find from a commercial AI generator and try to find a match in order to prove your theory?"

Despite the fact that she was in funeral clothes and looked like she was near physical and emotional collapse, Dr. Ryder laughed a little. "You could do that, I suppose. Or I could just do it now."

"What do you mean?"

She began typing on her computer. "Artificial intelligence, Mr. Pace, despite its dangers, also offers great benefits. I'll just have my intelligent agent take this file and compare it to every latest-generation Spanish male synthetic out there . . . and . . ." The pause lasted almost twenty seconds, and then Ryder said, "There you have it." Looking at her screen she said, "This particular voice is called Leonardo, and it's made by a company called Voice System Solutions. Based in Oakland, California." She shrugged. "Not that they would have anything to do with Lars's murder. Someone just purchased or pirated the software from the company."

"To mask their voice?" he said.

Dr. Ryder shrugged. "I suppose so."

Pace took a gamble. He told her about Tulum, the LAWs. Contreras's assertion that the bots were using AI and swarm technology.

Dr. Ryder took it all in, then said, "It's possible that whoever is using Leonardo is not masking a voice. It's possible that Leonardo *is* the Spanish voice assigned to an artificial intelligence agent."

Pace cocked his head. "You mean . . . software?"

"Yes. The most advanced AI platforms usually have means of interfacing with them through audio. Speech recognition, voice generation, that sort of thing."

"You're kidding."

"Ever heard of Alexa?"

"Well . . . yes . . . but I really don't think the little orb on my mom's kitchen counter is causing all this trouble."

"No. For something like this . . . you are looking at dozens and dozens of networked mainframes. Hundreds, perhaps. You would need an advanced neural network, machine learning, and you would need massive amounts of data. The agent would have to know everything about everything, and be able to learn, to take this level of autonomy to hire killers, make decisions about who needs to die to protect its secrets, to ensure its future. That takes a lot of data, and a lot of compute."

"Compute?"

"Yes. That's the term we use for the physical machines."

"This all sounds like science fiction."

"There are over a dozen AI and robotics futurists who would be very happy to disagree with you about that, except for the fact that someone murdered them in the past week." She leaned closer to her camera. "You asked me the other day if there was some unity of knowledge connecting all the names on that sheet that Lars had. This is it. Every one of them was an expert at creating revolutionary AI or linking AI to groundbreaking robotic platforms or the advanced study of the jamming of electromagnetic signals.

"Cyrus is a machine, and it is protecting itself by killing those who can stop it, or those who know it exists." She looked off into the distance a moment. "And whatever human has control of Cyrus, assuming someone still *does* have control at all, is letting it happen."

Pace took a few measured breaths, then asked, "Could that person be Anton Hinton?"

She nodded, slowly at first, and then more adamantly. "Absolutely, it could be Anton. But the only place he could get that amount of data is from China, and according to everyone, his relationship with the Chinese government is not the best."

"What if that's a ruse?"

Ryder just raised her eyebrows. "Anton and the Chinese. It's possible."

Pace rubbed his eyes under his glasses. "Our conversation has been very enlightening."

Ryder said, "But don't mention it to anyone, right?"

"It could put lives in danger."

"I understand. Go out there, find out what's going on, and deal with it, and I will never say a word. I just buried Lars because of this. We had our differences, but he was the love of my life. I want you to get the bastard responsible." She leaned closer to the screen. "If it's Anton doing this . . . then God help us all."

Minutes later Court, Zoya, and Pace were back outside, on their way to the barn. The CIA operations officer had filled Court and Zoya in about what he'd learned from Dr. Ryder, but Zoya had a question of her own.

"Why would Cyrus kill you, Jim? Why send in Lancer? Why not just notify the Cuban authorities a CIA officer was in that apartment? That would have stopped you from completing your mission."

Pace said, "I'm wondering the same thing. Contreras was watching me. Cyrus could have told the cops exactly where I was, and I'd be arrested on the spot."

"There's a lot of shit like that in this operation," Court pointed out. "Cyrus targeted Zoya and me before we'd even agreed to work to save the Russian engineer, we think, because he . . . I mean *it*, thought she knew something. Maybe it thought it needed you dead so you couldn't reveal what you knew."

Pace said, "If Cyrus is making decisions, some of Cyrus's decisions aren't very good."

Inside the barn, with the three of them standing in front of Contreras, Pace told the Mexican that he was now working under the suspicion that Cyrus was a bot.

The Mexican shook his head slowly. "No. I talked to him."

"You talked to the program, which responded with a verbal interface."

"Incredible," he said softly, thinking over his exchanges with Cyrus. "That's how he was able to switch into Spanish so quickly. The program must adjust to whoever is speaking to it, no matter the language."

Court said, "But . . . there is you, and Lancer, and that operations center. It's not *just* software."

Contreras said, "Of course it's not. The program needs humans for logistics and some operational purposes. I started out running surveillance for the people at the op center, but after a few days, Cyrus contacted me and ordered me to perform a mission directly for it in Tulum. A pilot and a loadmaster showed up with pallets of gear, we did the job, or tried to anyway, and then I was sent here."

"All by a computer."

Contreras nodded vehemently now. "It's running the whole thing, I know it is. I was just an interface to the meatspace."

Zoya said, "The what?"

"Meatspace. The real world. Everything that doesn't happen inside a computer. Except now Cyrus commands autonomous weapons, so it is able to interface directly with the meatspace, as well." He thought a moment. "Madre de dios. Someone gave the AI millions, tens of millions, maybe hundreds of millions of dollars to spend on its mission, so it will always be able to find humans to do what it needs."

Pace, Zoya, and Court left the prisoner in the barn again, and walked back to the house in the darkness. The rain had stopped, but water dripped from the foliage all around.

Back in the dining room, Court spoke first. "Even if much of the work is being done by computers, it doesn't change the fact that there is a human, or humans, at the controls. *That's* who we have to go after."

"Exactly," Pace replied, standing over his laptop and looking at something on the screen. "If these bots *are* being shipped to Hinton, then Hinton definitely knows something. Nothing else makes any sense." Having said that, he added, "We just checked, the tracker is still at the terminal."

To Pace, Zoya said, "Go talk to Hightower again. Lean on him."

Pace just looked at her. "That's it."

"What's what?" Court asked, confused.

"That's why Cyrus didn't just report me to the cops. Because I talked to Hightower. Cyrus didn't know what I'd learned from Zack about the workings of Hinton's organization, so getting me arrested wasn't enough. I had to die."

Slowly, Court said, "You . . . you want *us* to talk to Hightower?"

Turning to Court, he said, "We have a local national watching the dormitory where all the Hinton Labs people live. They call it La Finca, the coffee plantation. If Zack leaves La Finca tonight to go out for dinner, like he's done the last two nights, you talk to him then. If he doesn't leave tonight, he'll go for a run in the morning, and you can link up."

Court and Zoya exchanged glances. "What do we tell him?" she asked.

"Either Hinton's about to be slaughtered by a robot army, or else he's about to build himself a robot army. Either way, Zack needs to work with us to stop anything else bad from happening."

Court said, "You remember Zack, Jim. He's a team player, and if he's playing for the other team, it's going to be hard to convince him to switch sides."

Pace sighed. "I talked to him the other night, and I got the same feeling. It's all we've got, though. I'm about to have a teleconference with Watkins and Hernandez. I'm going to try to get a raid approved for the lab and the residence. If authorization comes down, we're going to need a lot more information on those facilities."

Court and Zoya exchanged a look, and Zoya spoke first. "We'll do it."

FIFTY-SIX

On the top floor of Building Five at the Singapore Science Park, the Norwegian director of Operations Center Gama leaned back in his chair and looked at his watch. It was just past six a.m., and it was time to contact Cyrus.

The eighteen people here in the auditorium had completed their sterilization of the entire OC. Cases upon cases of computer equipment, wall monitors, office supplies, commo gear, and the like had been stacked by the door to the lobby, ready to be taken to the elevator bank when the trucks arrived.

The director would miss this job; it had been an incredible challenge, and he and his staff had performed well, for the most part, although the disappearance of the communications dispatcher from Germany weighed heavily on his mind.

Still . . . seventeen successful missions with only two failures, both of which the director had personally considered irrelevant to whatever the overarching mission was, seemed like an incredible success rate, especially when considering the scope of the operation.

An assassination in Amsterdam earlier this morning of target Gama 15 had marked the end, because Cyrus had informed the director that

Gama 18 and 19, Zakharova and Gentry, had been removed from the target list.

While the men and women behind him sipped champagne, a special touch his American second-in-command had ordered in, he looked down to the one laptop remaining out and on a desk in the room, and he began typing in a message window.

Gama director for Cyrus.

Cyrus.

The facility is sterilized. All cases waiting in the lobby for retrieval.

Excellent. The truck is waiting a kilometer away. It will arrive within minutes. Your security presence will depart at this time, but I ask you and your entire staff to wait until all the equipment is loaded. A bus will then arrive to return you all to an airport hotel, and tickets will be given to each staff member for their journey home.

All understood. We will stand by for the removal of the equipment.

Thank you again for a difficult job well done.

The director smiled as he typed. **My pleasure. I hope you will consider me again for any future needs.**

The director ended the conversation, put his laptop in a case, and went to stack it by the lobby door.

A minute later he stood with his staff at the floor of the auditorium, giving a toast to the smiling and laughing group.

As he spoke, the several guards who had been milling about over the past week headed for the lobby and hit the button for the stairs. One of their number, however, went into a lobby stairwell, propping the door open there, and ascended to the roof, where he again propped open the door.

He then headed down the stairs, taking them all the way to the ground floor.

Outside in the parking lot behind Building Five of Singapore Science Park, a tractor-trailer pulled to a stop with a belch of compressed air through its valves as the brake engaged. Quickly a pair of men climbed out of the cab, then walked to the rear of the vehicle. They opened the trailer's rear doors, but they did not extend the ramp. Instead, they both returned to the cab and shut themselves back in.

For thirty seconds it was quiet in the parking lot. Shortly before six a.m. none of the other buildings had been occupied, and the small Science Park security force had been called away after receiving a report of a break-in at a facility on the opposite end of the two-hundred-acre campus.

But the still was broken by a buzzing sound, faint at first, but quickly it grew louder.

Seconds later a two-meter-square hexacopter appeared out of the rear of the trailer, flying slow at first, but only until it cleared the vehicle, and then it began rising over the parking lot.

Five seconds after the first unmanned aircraft appeared, an identical model followed its exact path.

Both of the big drones had payloads—large rectangular black devices attached to their bellies—and the half-dozen fifty-centimeter enclosed props on each craft spun harder and louder, forcing an increase in elevation. Soon the drones banked away from the parking lot and over Building Five.

Here they landed on the roof simultaneously, but their propellers only decreased pitch; they did not stop.

Seconds later the pair of drones took off again into the sky, but both payloads remained behind on the flat roof, just ten meters from the door left open by a member of the Gama security staff.

As the noise of the drones faded as they climbed, both rectangular boxes began to whirr, and then they began to move. Four legs extended, lifting the body of the device nearly a meter in height; a panel slid open on the roof of each box and a turret appeared, the tip of a gun barrel extending from it, facing forward.

The machines walked confidently towards the open door a moment later, and shortly after this they began descending the stairwell.

The Gama director felt a buzz on his phone in his pocket; he looked down at the text message there, and then he tossed his plastic champagne cup into the garbage can by the lobby door that the staff had put there to help with the cleanup and sterilization of the room. He called out over the chatting going on around him. "Ladies and gentlemen. Our job here is complete. The bus is downstairs waiting for us."

All eighteen stepped out to the lobby; the director pushed the elevator call button, and then they stood there, waiting. The director said, "We can probably fit eight in each car. I'll come down with the last group."

Within moments, however, all heads turned to the right, to the door propped open with a garbage can there, because an unusual sound was coming from the stairwell just beyond it.

The first of the two quadrupedal ground vehicles emerged into the lobby at a steady pace, the second followed right behind, and just after the sound of gasps and other shouts of alarm pierced the air, both robots opened fire on the tightly clustered crowd.

The director turned and tried to run, slamming into the French communications specialist, falling down onto the Indian intelligence analyst who was already dead, and as the bullets ripped steadily into the bodies, bloodcurdling screams and moans of panicked agony all around, the director rose back up to his knees, his eyes on the bathroom door, just steps away.

But as soon as he climbed into a crouch, he was hit by a 6.5-millimeter Creedmoor round through the center of his spine, severing the spinal cord itself.

He dropped back into the growing pile of bodies and found he couldn't move his legs, so he began to claw his way over the dead and wounded.

A second round pierced the back of his head, entering at the base of the skull and exiting through the crown, removing half the director's skull.

He was dead before his face hit the leg of the young analyst from Morocco.

In twenty seconds it looked like it was all over, but then the two machines fired an insurance round into each body. The woman from America had been playing possum, but attempting to fool or manipulate the weapons was folly because they could not be tricked, reasoned with, appealed to, or otherwise affected in any way.

They were utterly without remorse.

After the sound of the last gunshot faded, the pair of killing machines walked up to the collection of shipping boxes, computer crates, and other office supplies, and the lead machine fired two small canisters at all the remnants of Operations Center Gama.

Both 40-millimeter thermite incendiary grenades burst into white-hot flame; the carpet and the boxes began to burn and to melt, and then the machine pivoted on its hips and fired three more grenades into different corners of the building.

The rear machine dumped all five of its 40-millimeter thermites into the pile of dead bodies in front of the elevator, and then it became the lead unit as it returned to the stairwell, climbed back to the roof, and collapsed back into a rectangular box, its legs and turret retracting, and its panel closing again.

The pair of hexacopter drones landed on top of the pair of stationary ground combat weapons, coupled with them by way of magnets, and then lifted off into the air, swirling the black smoke that was already rising out of the open stairwell.

Moments later the machines were back in the trailer in the parking lot, completely powered down. The trailer doors were closed by the two men from the cab, and the truck began rolling.

Operations Center Gama and those who operated it were no more.

It was six forty-nine p.m. in Havana when Jim Pace logged on to the secure video conference from the SCIF in the U.S. embassy, which meant it was also six forty-nine p.m. eleven hundred miles to the north in McLean, Virginia.

His screen opened to a small conference room that was standing room only. Trey Watkins, DDO, sat at the head of the table; he leaned forward and started the meeting abruptly.

"We've read the cables, Jim. What else do you have for us?"

Pace said, "There's a fire in Building Five at the Science Park near the port of Singapore. The entire structure is in flames. CCTV cameras from nearby facilities show a tractor-trailer arriving around six fifteen a.m., before the fire started, and a pair of weaponized drones flying out of the trailer and then onto the roof of the facility."

Watkins said, "There went the operations center, and there went Martina Sommer."

"If she was even still alive," Pace said. "The drone operator said Cyrus knew she was a mole in its operation."

"Very true."

"And there's more," Pace said. "The tracker in the container that had been at the port moved over the past hour. It's at the campus of the University of Information Science, specifically the old Soviet SIGINT building on the northwest side of the campus."

"Where Hinton's lab is?"

"About one block away from it, sir."

Watkins looked around the table at his staff. "This means Hinton owns the robots from the same company as those used in Mexico the other night in the assassination of Jack Tudor."

Pace nodded. "And it also means he was involved in the killing in Tulum. By association, it means Hinton hired Lancer for the killings in California, Mexico, Boston, and probably Toronto, because Contreras was in Tulum and he was also working with the assassin on at least some of these operations."

"So that's it. It wasn't China. Anton Hinton is the culprit."

Pace wasn't so sure. "Hinton is *a* culprit, but China might also be involved. It's important to note that from our man inside Hinton's organization, it doesn't appear Hinton has a direct hand in everything going on. Still . . . there is a way he could be doing this . . . without actually doing anything."

"Explain."

Pace talked about Cyrus, and the assertions of Dr. Ryder that AI was running the entire operation.

When he was finished, Trey Watkins let out a long, low groan. "Jesus Christ. So . . . you are saying the whole thing is an algorithm? Artificial intelligence. There's nobody at the wheel? It's a fire-and-forget system?"

Pace nodded. "It is looking like the algorithm is authorized to make its own decisions. Whether Hinton, or anybody, retains control of it is unclear."

Lacy said, "If Cyrus is the weapon we were trying to prevent from going online, then we failed."

"If Cyrus is the weapon," Pace countered, "then we failed before the operation even began, because it orchestrated the op."

"Let me guess," Watkins said, "you want Juliet Victor to go into the SIGINT facility."

"We need more than six guys. Can we infiltrate a Delta squadron?"

"You mean, just fly special operations forces into Cuba?"

Pace said, "I know Cuban radar stations are tracked, and we have a map of their blind spots. If we can get a couple of Blackhawks from MacDill, coming in low over the water, then maybe we—"

Watkins said, "I can't go to the president with that." He turned to Hernandez. "Steve?"

Hernandez seemed conflicted, but he said, "Actually, there *is* an existing protocol that might be simpler."

Eyebrows rose around the room.

"I'll just leave it there. But we can, with some effort, put eighteen jocked-up Ground Branch operators in Havana in a matter of hours."

"And getting our people out after the raid?" Watkins asked.

Hernandez said, "I'll work on that."

Trey Watkins sat back in his chair. "Well . . . good. We obviously need the president's approval. I'll talk to the director." To Pace he said, "Jim, you and Juliet Victor work up a plan, and Steve will put Travers in contact with the men we're sending down."

Pace said, "I don't know how, but this needs to happen tonight."

"I know," Watkins said. "We just have to pray we have that much time. Okay, everybody clear out, I'm going to talk privately with Jim."

Soon Trey Watkins sat alone in the conference room, looking into the camera, and Pace sat in the SCIF looking back.

Watkins said, "Primary objective is shutting this thing down somehow. Secondary is to retrieve this Cyrus if at all possible."

"Retrieve it, sir?"

"Yes. Do you have any idea as to the physical form of this program?"

"My experts tell me there will be a node attached to the server farm where the actual brain is. All the data and processing power will be in the mainframes, but the executable program, the brain, will be on the drive."

"Then *that's* what we need. We'll send you with a location to upload the data. I'm assuming that will take some time."

Pace didn't like this mission complication. The better plan, he thought, was to blow the facility to kingdom come.

But he wasn't going to tell the deputy director his misgivings. "Understood."

Watkins said, "You also have a tertiary objective, should your attempt to retrieve the program fail."

"Which is?"

"Get Hinton."

"I'm sorry?"

"Get him out, alive, and to the States."

Shit, Pace thought. This nearly impossible operation was getting exponentially more complicated every time Watkins opened his mouth. "So he can work for us, I assume?"

"We would strongly encourage him to do that, yes."

It was clear the U.S. wanted this artificial intelligence capability for itself, and if they couldn't steal the product itself, they wanted to steal the brain behind it.

"If you can get me authorization, and you can get me some more men, then I will do my best to fulfill all your mission objectives."

The conference ended, and Pace left the SCIF and headed to the cafeteria to see if they had Red Bull, or at least some coffee. He'd mainline either one at this point if it kept him sharp enough to pull this shit off.

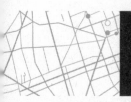

FIFTY-SEVEN

Zack sat on the same stool at the same Old Havana bar on Calle Obrapia as the other night, willing someone from the Agency to make contact with him. He'd been here over an hour; he'd downed two beers and picked at a Cuban sandwich and fried plantains.

He didn't have much of an appetite, but he ate most of his dinner over the course of the hour just to pass the time while he sat there, deep in thought.

He had not been entirely honest with Wren and Hinton. Yes, he was here in order to glean information from Pace about what the Agency had on Hinton Labs, but he wasn't doing it solely to give the intel to Hinton and Wren. No, he wanted to know for himself what the CIA had done today and why, because he knew from experience there was no way in hell Ground Branch would get the go-ahead for a raid in Havana fucking Harbor unless the president of the United States signed off on it, and there was no way *that* would happen without the Agency making one hell of a case for the raid.

Hinton was dirty, Zack didn't know to what extent, but something was definitely amiss at the labs that warranted the action today. This also meant that Wren was likely involved, as well, and Zack found this difficult to accept.

More importantly, however, Zack had managed to land himself right in the middle of all this bullshit, and now he had to figure out how to extract himself.

Except the CIA was nowhere in sight. He wondered if Pace was in hiding, and if the Ground Branch team that had hit the terminal was now down in Guantanamo or back in the States.

If that was the case, he told himself, then he'd have to somehow figure this shit out on his own.

And figuring shit out was not his speciality. Zack had always considered himself labor, not management. He wasn't the guy you sent in to investigate a situation; he was the guy you sent in after you'd already investigated and decided somebody needed to die or something needed to blow up.

At eight thirty p.m. he finished his third beer and paid his tab, left a hefty tip for the portly old bartender, and headed back out into the night.

His Land Rover was parked in a monitored lot just two blocks away, and Zack shifted out of his own mind, returned his consciousness to the here and now, because walking up a darkened street alone in a foreign city required a level of vigilance.

A scooter passed with two young men on it; Zack had a plan to kill them if he had to.

An old Chevy rolled by, half hot-pink paint and half Bondo, a heavyset man behind the wheel with his meaty elbow jutting out the open window of the driver's-side door, and Zack formulated a plan to kill him, as well.

But there was no killing; he made it closer to his car, and then, as he passed a small family-run pharmacy that was closed for the night, he looked over at it and noticed that its roll-down metal security gate was up. Every business around here used a roll-down gate, and no one would leave their glass façade unprotected all evening, especially a pharmacy, as that would be an invitation for a break-in.

Just as he began evaluating the situation, the glass door opened, ten feet away from where he moved along the sidewalk.

Zack shot his hand under his shirt to put his hand on the grip of his Staccato.

Chris Travers stepped out in a black T-shirt and jeans. His hands were empty and open, and he just looked at Hightower.

Finally, Zack thought. He took his hand off his pistol, stopped there in the darkness, and faced off against the other American for several seconds without speaking.

"Was that you today? In the harbor?" Zack asked.

Travers just waved him forward.

"Not out here. Come inside."

Zack looked around, then stepped into the pharmacy.

Travers shut and locked the door behind him, then together they walked through a dark empty space, soon ending up at the back of the little store.

He was expecting to find Pace, of course, so when he instead found Court Gentry and Zoya Zakharova sitting next to each other on the counter, he pulled up short.

He locked eyes with Court for a long moment, then glanced to Zoya. Recovering as quickly as possible, he said, "Violator. Marina."

"Who?" Zoya asked, confused.

Court leaned to her. "He calls you Marina Oswald. He thinks it's funny."

Zoya rolled her eyes. "Grow up."

Zack looked around at the pharmacy. "You two diversifying? Learning a new trade?"

Travers said, "Havana station had access to this building. We've got agents outside keeping an eye out."

Zack nodded. He was on guard, but in truth he felt elated to see Court and Chris here. He was in deep, into what, he wasn't sure, and there was no one else on Earth he'd rather have nearby when he was in trouble.

The hot Russkie had proved her worth once or twice, as well, he told himself, but he still didn't fully trust her.

To Court he asked, "Why are you here?"

"Why don't you take a wild-assed guess?"

"I honestly don't know, but if there *is* one thing I know, it's this. When Sierra Six shows up, it means some shit's about to go down."

Court shrugged. "Shit's about to go down."

"Or maybe it already has?"

Court sniffed. "Some shit has happened, some shit is yet to happen. Let's just say, we are in mid-shit at the moment."

"Did Pace send you?"

"Yeah."

"Were you at the harbor today?"

"Yeah."

"Why?"

"Pace and Travers had an op, and Z and I were sent in to run counter-surveillance on the overwatch."

"And you killed a bunch of cops?" Zack didn't think for a moment Court would have killed any cops that didn't deserve to die, but he couldn't imagine what else could have happened.

Zoya spoke up now. "Jim killed one of the cops, Court killed one, and Kincaid killed one. Guess which two had it coming?"

Hightower wasn't sure he'd heard that right. "Kincaid? You mean . . ."

"Yep," Court said. "*That* Kincaid. He goes by the code name Lancer."

Zack knew Scott Kincaid, though not personally. They'd both been Navy SEALs, but Zack had been on Teams Two and Six and Kincaid on Team Three, and Zack had gone to CIA several years before Kincaid made a name for himself by getting arrested for war crimes in Syria.

"Kincaid came to assassinate Anton?"

Court shook his head. "We weren't protecting Anton Hinton from Lancer. We were protecting Jim Pace from Lancer."

Zoya said, "Someone brought Lancer and an ISR expert into Cuba to kill the CIA officer here seeking intelligence on Anton Hinton, the same assassin and the same ISR expert who were involved in some of the other technology assassinations. Who do you think would do that?"

Zack's eyes hardened as he stared at the Russian woman. "How would I have any fucking clue?"

Zoya said, "Your boss is dirty. Court doesn't think you'd work for the bad guys knowingly, although I don't think you waste much time thinking about right and wrong."

Zack shook his head. "Hinton's shady, he's got some crazy ideas, but I don't see how he could be directly behind what's happening."

"Listen, man," Court said. "Six containers full of lethal autonomous weapons parts arrived on a container ship from Hong Kong this morning. It's supposed to be delivered to a location in Havana, but that place is an empty shopping mall. Instead, it went to the old Lourdes SIGINT headquarters building there, just a block away from Hinton's lab. That means you and your boss are either in a great deal of danger, or you and your boss are the villains in all this."

Zoya said, "Answer this. Has anyone mentioned something called Cyrus?"

Zack shook his head slowly. "Nope. Never heard of that."

"Have you seen a server farm at the lab?"

"I . . . I wouldn't know one if I saw it."

"A data center. A massive amount of mainframe computers, dozens, easily, maybe one hundred or more. All linked together. Data communication lines, cooling units, probably some sort of protective area around it. A metal cage, a plexiglass enclosure, something like that. Could be in a basement or a subterranean level."

"No. There's a room of mainframes in the basement of the lab, but three fourths are still in their packaging. There might be a dozen working units, tops."

Zack leaned back against the counter. "I'm around the dude all day. He's not planning world domination, or whatever Pace thinks is going on down there."

"It's not him doing it," Zoya said. "It's some artificial intelligence he's created."

"No fucking way."

"It's the only thing that makes sense. We captured the drone pilot. Learned some things about the operation. Pace has an expert who thinks artificial intelligence is running this entire thing, all the killings, all over the world."

Zack shook his head. "I can assure you that the attack on Anton the other night was perpetrated by people who were neither artificial nor intelligent."

Court said, "This AI, called Cyrus. It's picking the targets, hiring the assassins, providing logistical support, paying the bills, updating mission sets."

Zoya said, "The expert says that there were maybe fifteen people on Earth who could have developed something like this—"

Zack interrupted, because now he understood. "And only one of them is still alive."

"That's correct," Court responded.

"But . . ." Zack said, "who is out there trying to kill him?"

"What if the attack was staged?" Court asked. "What if both attacks were?"

"Anton took a bullet in his back plate, right next to me. How do you stage that?"

Court didn't miss a beat. "You pull out a gun, aim at his back plate, and press the trigger."

Hightower cocked his head. "You think I shot him in the—"

Court shook his head. "Of course *you* didn't do it. You can't shoot."

Zack rolled his eyes. "I was there, you weren't," he said, and then, from nowhere, he relived the moment in his mind.

Jesus Christ, Zack thought. Back during the attack by the Jamaicans, Wren had his weapon out at the back of the restaurant, Zack had turned away, and when he looked back, both guards next to Wren lay dead, and Anton had been hit in the armor. Zack hadn't been able to picture someone firing blind through the kitchen wall and causing all that precise carnage, but now he saw another possibility.

No one on the security force could have shot two men and then the armor of a third.

But Gareth Wren could.

Court obviously saw something on Hightower's face. "What is it?"

Court didn't know Gareth Wren and would have no way of knowing that the VP of operations for Hinton Labs was a former SAS Warrant Officer 1 who was so fucking good he and his troop had worked with the CIA on several Ground Branch ops in the war on terror. Wren was a fucking marksman with any weapon he held.

The three of them sat there in the dim light, just looking at one another.

Finally, Zack spoke. "The attack on Hinton here. It might have been a setup. A setup to fool me so I could convince the Agency it was legit. But . . . but why?"

Court said, "Think about it. If Hinton's your boss, then he hired a former CIA officer as a lead security man for a reason. Why do you think that was?"

This was a lot for Zack to take in, but finally, he said, "To be the Agency's inside man. To report back, when asked, that nothing was going on down here in Cuba. And to convince them that Hinton was being targeted by the same people who were targeting all the others."

"They didn't plan on the Agency figuring out it was all being run by AI," Zoya said.

Chris Travers stepped up now. He'd been close enough to hear the conversation. In his hand he held a tablet computer. "Zack . . . we've been looking at Hinton's facilities here."

"You guys are going to hit it?"

"We don't know yet. But we're building a plan. Tell me about security at the campus."

Zack sighed. "On the inside, a dozen men, all ex–Black Wasps. Some better than others, but all are good enough. Also static security inside, say a half dozen at any one time. Not the same caliber as the Wasps, but not terrible."

"Okay," Travers said. "That's the interior. What about exterior security?"

"On the outside? Forget about it. A full company or so of Black Wasps in the campus grounds or just outside. A couple companies of regular army troops garrisoned within a mile." Zack thought a moment. "La Finca is a more secure physical structure, but there are fewer guards inside and out."

"What's La Finca?"

"It's the name given to the old KGB dormitory building, a half-underground bunker, about a ten-minute drive to the campus."

Travers nodded, then scrolled through some images on his iPad.

"NGA sent blueprints of both the campus and the dormitory building. The plans are for when the campus was built in 2007, and it shows three subterranean levels of the dormitory."

Zack nodded. "The ground floor is just the security building, a bar, a cafeteria, some common areas, and the elevators. Floors U1 and U2 are the bedrooms and such, and U3 is the armory, storage, even a warehouse with like a year of supplies."

"Oh . . ." Zack held a finger up. "Also down there are sixteen decommissioned robots with Walther PPQ pistols on their hips."

Court blinked hard at this. "Wait. They weren't four-legged, with a rifle on the top?"

"Negative. They look like astronauts. They're called Safe Sentries, made by a company in Boston. Hinton got them for site security, but then ordered them deactivated when the killing started, because he worried America would find a way to hack into them."

"Unreal," Zoya muttered.

Travers held up the tablet and showed Zack an image. "We also have another set of blueprints, these were smuggled out of Cuba in 1962, just after construction of the facility was complete."

"Nineteen sixty-two?" Court said, incredulously. "Yeah . . . let's use the newer ones."

But Travers persisted. "Here's the thing, though. When the place was originally built, a tunnel was constructed that went between the lowest level of the dormitory and the lowest level of the SIGINT headquarters building, about six hundred meters long, and then it branched off to the other buildings at the campus. You could travel underground to anywhere."

Travers handed over the tablet, and Zack saw for himself. On the sixty-two-year-old plans, the tunnel ran to the northeast from the dormitory, from the fourth floor belowground, a subterranean level that Zack knew nothing about.

Chris Travers looked to Zack. "Have you been in the SIGINT headquarters building at the campus?"

"No, but I drive past it every day. It's abandoned, fenced up."

"Well," Travers continued, "the SIGINT building has a massive basement built to withstand a tactical nuke, or at least it did in 1962. The tunnel from the dormitory led one story below that basement. What if the aboveground floors of the building are abandoned and the server farm is located belowground?"

Zack thought a moment. "Shit, Chris. That checks out. The power station *and* the generator complex are right there, one on either side of the SIGINT HQ. Wren told me they had four sources of power feeding the lab so there wouldn't be any outages. But what if two of those sources are just there to keep the server farm supplied?"

Court heaved a long sigh. "I just have to ask, dude. You didn't see the Dr. Evil lair your boss was living in as some kind of a tip-off that he was a shithead?"

"I mean . . . in retrospect . . . I guess it's a little fishy."

"For fuck's sake," Court muttered.

"So if security is lighter at the dormitory," Zoya asked, "we need to find that tunnel access. Have you been everywhere down there?"

"Yeah, Wren showed me around." Zack thought back. "There's a service elevator, it's closed off. He said it hadn't worked since the Russkies ran the place, and he said it only went up. Maybe I'll go check it out, see if it will take me down to a lower level."

Court said, "You sure you want to go back there? We can pull you out now."

"Wren and Hinton sent me out tonight to make contact with CIA to try to get you guys off their ass, but I think they are just stalling for time. Hinton's been saying for days something was coming at the lab, some new capability they would be fielding. He said it would make the world more peaceful, but I guess it's just the opposite.

"I've got to go back in there so they don't suspect you guys are coming, because if they do, they might adjust their countdown clock."

Court pulled a sat phone from the pocket of his linen pants and handed it over. "This is from Pace. You think you can get into the building without it being discovered?"

Zack nodded. "I'm still one of them. I'll put it in my room, then go down and look for the tunnel so I don't have it on me then. I'll contact you when I return to my room." He shrugged. "If."

Court said, "The phone is programmed with my Signal number."

Travers spoke up now. "Okay, but before you go, I want you to look at the blueprints we have of the residence and point out any differences you see, and I want you to tell us anything that might help us if we do get the green light to enter the dormitory."

Zack took the tablet, leaned against the counter of the pharmacy, and began trying to match what he'd seen in person to plans from nearly twenty years ago, and other plans from over sixty years ago.

Forty-five minutes later he left the pharmacy, walked to his car, and drove back to La Finca alone.

FIFTY-EIGHT

The old Soviet Lourdes Signals Intelligence headquarters building sat on the northern end of the University of Information Science, protected from the rest of the campus by a weathered but substantial concrete fence that made the building look like a prison. The entrance gate on the east side was normally locked and the area not patrolled by an exterior guard force, but tonight, about two hours earlier, the guards had arrived, the gates had been opened, and six tractor-trailers had pulled in, then followed the disused and weed-covered drive around to the back. Here, a massive bay door opened and, single file, all six vehicles crept down a ramp into a cavernous factory-like room the size of a football field.

There were workstations and tool chests and electrical wires and hydraulic piping around the room, similar to almost any factory, but the main feature was a pair of high-tech production lines, two rows, each with twelve red multi-jointed robot arms with articulating clamps and power drills and welding torches attached at the end. Each arm stood three meters high, and between the rows were open pathways, some forty meters in length.

Anton Hinton stood dressed in a red tracksuit with a white stripe, his hands on his hips, headphones over his ears, and an intense look on his face. In front of him, the six forty-foot containers were arrayed at the bottom of the ramp; the crates inside had all been removed by his staff with the aid of forklifts, each one then placed on an autonomous carrier bot, essentially large orange wheeled metal pallets with onboard computers that hived with all the other robots in the large manufacturing space.

Hinton watched while the carriers drove each crate to the rows of robot arms; the arms whizzed and purred, shifting left and right, using their grippers to remove items from the cases, scanning them with barcode readers, and then slowly assembling the devices as they passed by on the robotic carts.

Several of Hinton's engineers and technicians stood by, watching the movement with rapt fascination.

Anton had been waiting for this day for years, ever since he'd acknowledged the fact that he had the ability, and moreover he had the responsibility, to create a new order in this world. And now, the day was here. This was just another stepping-stone on his path, of course; the world would not change overnight. But he knew that with each passing hour his vision would be more and more certain, because the means to stop it would have been made weaker and weaker.

His new army had arrived, and in no more than six to eight hours he would finally have enough platforms here to hold off virtually any attack should the Cubans decide to disrupt his operations here.

These machines would buy him time, and right now, time was what he needed more than anything else.

Eighty bipedal robots on top of the sixteen older models already in his possession, two hundred sixty of the most advanced Greyhound quadrupedal platforms, and four hundred Hornet kamikaze drones, all fully armed and charged.

With Cyrus in control of everything.

And Hinton in control of Cyrus.

His creation.

This had been his dream, and his dream was turning into reality, but Anton Hinton's normal self-assurance was faltering tonight.

While he stood there worrying about that which was yet to come, Kimmie Lin stepped up next to him and dutifully waited for him to look her way.

He kept his eyes on the operations before him as he took off his headphones. "What do you think?"

She looked on at the assembly process: so much movement, the two-dozen arms twisting and contorting through their full range of motion, the carriers wheeling everything along slowly but steadily, the men continuing to place the crates on the empty carriers as they rolled up to each container.

She said, "Just as you promised."

Anton nodded. "Yes. Nothing ever goes completely to plan, as we've seen this week. But we have adapted, and Cyrus is growing, proving himself every single minute of every single day."

She turned back to him. "Yes . . . but is he growing stronger or simply more erratic?"

Anton brought his shoulders back. He was prepared to admit nothing to her about his doubts. "Stronger. The growing pains will cease; I'll look back into the code and see to it."

"The Americans," Kimmie said. "They will come."

He nodded. "I know. But by the time they get here, it will be too late."

"The upload. It remains on schedule?"

The New Zealander kept his shoulders back, a smile on his face, and his tone positive as he said, "Actually, I'd like to delay it. No more than a few days. My engineers and I will go back and look at some things, rewrite some of the coding that has been trained out of its neural networks. Shouldn't take long, and China will have a stronger product in the end."

Kimmie nodded. "They won't be pleased, but I agree, a healthy, stable Cyrus is the most important thing."

She turned away and headed for the fabrication control room to look over manufacturing data, and Anton put his headphones back on.

Hinton's smile wavered a moment, and the feeling of dread returned. It was a sensation he'd experienced many times in the past week, but just like in those other times, he pushed it aside.

Next to him an advance Greyhound bot came off the assembly line complete, and was driven by a bot over to a desk where an unarmed bipedal model would animate it with a barcode reader and some inputs on a computer.

There had been setbacks in the past week, this Anton could not deny.

But Cyrus's intelligence, its initiative, its steadfast commitment to its mission—these were all pluses, not minuses. He and his core of twelve computer scientists, the ones who knew the true scope and purpose of Cyrus, they would find a way to tame the beast.

His smile slowly returned.

At the farmhouse occupied by the CIA in Bauta, some two and a half miles northwest of the campus, the six men of Special Activities Center Ground Branch team Juliet Victor sat at the dining room table, each man with a tablet computer in front of him loaded with satellite images of the old Soviet dormitory grounds as well as the blueprints for the interior from both 1962 and 2007. Travers had added Zack's notes about the various changes to the location on the 2007 schematic with an electronic pen that showed up on each man's device, and together they all worked on crafting the mission that they hoped would get a green light very soon.

Court Gentry, Jim Pace, and Zoya Zakharova stood against the wall and looked on, ready to give their input if asked, but also aware that this part of the operation would be led by Ground Branch.

Outside, an old minivan pulled up, and some of the CIA paramilitary men went out to meet it.

They returned a few minutes later with nine wire-stocked AK-47 rifles, along with nine sets of body armor.

The minivan had come from a weapons cache maintained by a group of agents at Havana station, and the gear had been hastily arranged to be brought to the safe house.

The team had decided to field AK-47s for tonight's raid, after a heated back-and-forth on the subject earlier in the evening.

Most of the guys wanted to use their HK416s, a larger rifle than the MP7s they'd carried in the harbor that morning.

But Violator insisted the 416s weren't big enough for the fight they had in store for them.

Everyone was concerned about the containers delivered to the SIGINT building, and the weaponized robots inside them. Violator stressed to Travers the difficulty he and Anthem had had destroying the two ground robots in Mexico, and Travers ultimately decided that the Kalashnikov's larger round and greater energy output at shorter ranges would be needed when engaging any mechanical devices. Their standard HK416 rifles fired rounds that were roughly sixty grains in weight, while these AKs slung a projectile twice the size, though at a slower velocity.

The downside of the AKs was that they were longer and bulkier when the wire stocks were extended, and they were not suppressed, but the men on Juliet Victor all had silencers for their SIG Sauer handguns, so they weren't totally unprepared for covert action.

The nine men had no night vision goggles, nor did their weapons carry optics or lasers, but they were well-maintained AKs, and the Cuban agents had brought seven loaded mags for each gun.

Court and Zoya stood in the kitchen by the counter when Victor Two entered from the living room, first handing Court an unloaded rifle and then presenting the other to Zoya.

As Takahashi held it out for the beautiful blond woman, he said, "Ma'am, are you familiar with this weapon, because I'd be happy to show you—"

She took it from him with a side glance to Court, then placed the rifle on the counter in front of her without a word. Before Hash could say anything, she began field-stripping the folding-stock firearm, completely disassembling and then reassembling it in under twenty seconds.

Three other Juliet Victor men leaned into the kitchen to watch.

When she finished, she looked to Victor Two. "I should be able to figure it out. Thanks."

"Fucking Russians," Court muttered to Hash with a little grin, and then Victor Six came in with tattered olive drab chest rigs with steel-plate armor inside and loaded magazine racks.

To Zoya, he said, "I think it's one size fits all around here."

She thanked him, then put the rig over her head and tightened it around her body. It was a little big on her, but she could still move around.

Court got his own set of armor, but before he put it on, he pulled the front plate and looked it over. "A little rusty," he said, "but beats not having them."

When all nine—eight men and one woman—were ready, they drank coffee and energy drinks, ate chips and candy bars, and waited for word that the president had approved the raid and the Ground Branch teams were on board the aircraft in Miami.

At eleven thirty p.m., a call came. Pace answered, and everyone looked on expectantly.

"Yes?" he said, then paused. "Wait. You have got to be fucking kidding me, sir." After several more expletives, he calmed down a little, acknowledged the call, and then hung up.

To the room he said, "That was Hernandez. The president's decided he's going to call President Vargas directly, tell him what we know about what's happening at the SIGINT HQ, and ask him to allow us to send a team into Cuba to conduct a raid at Anton Hinton's property."

Court looked to Zoya and spoke softly. "You see why I like doing shit on my own?"

The men complained loudly; a couple of the Ground Branch guys with their AKs already slung on their chests took them off and leaned them against the wall, certain they weren't going anywhere tonight unless it was back to the embassy or somewhere deeper into hiding.

Zoya said, "Cuba is definitely involved. They might not know exactly what Hinton is doing at the lab, but they aren't just going to let the U.S. violate their airspace."

Pace nodded. "We're on standby until we hear from Langley on this. Everybody keep your heads on straight. This still could happen tonight."

No one seemed to believe him, including Court. "We'll miss the window for the breach at the loading dock."

Travers nodded. "We'll have to find another way in."

Court and Zoya went outside, conferred for a few minutes, and then called Pace out with them.

Standing in the warm and sticky night, Court moved closer to Pace and spoke softly. "Zack says shift change is at one, and that's the weakest point. We miss that, and we don't have a quiet way inside."

"Yeah, Travers is in with the boys right now trying to come up with something."

Court looked to Zoya, then back to Pace. "What if I already did?"

"I'm listening."

"Z and I go now. Get through the fence, find cover near the loading dock, and wait for one a.m. We get through the door, you call when you guys are outside, and we let you in."

"And if we get waved off tonight? What's your plan then?"

Court said, "My plan is to try to find Hightower there in La Finca, and get him out."

Pace rubbed his face as he thought a moment. Finally he said. "I don't control you, Violator. I don't control Anthem. If you felt the urge to do something like this, what could I really do to stop you?"

Court turned away from Pace and towards Zoya. "We'll take our car."

Zack Hightower returned to La Finca and headed back towards the elevator to go down to his room, but he saw Wren sitting alone at the bar on the first floor near the elevators and headed over to him.

"Been waiting for you," the Englishman said, and then he motioned to the bartender. "Dos Bucaneros." It was a local lager, and although Gareth Wren was now the last person on Earth that Zack wanted to have a drink with, he knew the next few minutes would be crucial.

"Any luck finding your old mates?"

"Yeah . . . I talked to Pace."

"Then what the fuck is he on about?"

"He says he and his guys were at the harbor looking for a shipment from Hong Kong coming to Cuba. He says they weren't targeting you, just the shipment. Some sanctioned equipment for the Cuban government."

"And he just happened to be in town?" Wren wasn't buying it, but Zack knew if he tried to sell it even more, then Wren would suspect him. Instead he said, "Yeah. Hard to believe. He also says an American assassin named Lancer showed up to kill Pace, he's the one who killed the Cuban cops, and then he was captured."

Wren took this all in. Zack felt the full scrutiny of the man now, and he knew he had to be careful. Wren said, "This shipment they were supposedly after . . . did they find it?"

Zack didn't know what Wren knew, so he threw the Agency under the bus. "Pace said they didn't . . . but I'm not sure, he could have been lying."

He shrugged. "He doesn't exactly trust me, but he *did* seem surprised that I knew about what happened today, because he said it didn't involve Hinton at all."

This covered his ass. If Wren knew the CIA had found the container, then there was a chance he would believe Hightower was just being duped by Jim Pace.

"Anything else?"

Zack thought a moment about how to handle this question. "He said seventeen people around the world, mostly AI developers, have been killed, and that Anton Hinton is the only target they missed, other than some assassins in Central America who were trying to protect one of the victims." He hoped this was all the same info Wren had, and he'd buy himself, and maybe Pace, a little credibility.

"Again, I told him Hinton is not involved in all this other than as a target, and he should get his ass out of the country before the Cubanos catch him."

Wren took a long moment before responding, but finally said, "Okay. Well done, mate. Pace is full of shit, but thanks for trying to talk some sense into him."

Hightower decided to press. "What makes you say he's full of shit?"

"Our computers shipped out of HK. They were on the same vessel as this stuff Pace says he was looking for. Sounds just a bit suspect, doesn't it?"

Zack nodded. "More than a bit."

"English understatement, mate."

"Right," Zack said. "Let's keep an even closer eye on Anton. If he's the last one left, and the Agency is looking at him, too, then he's in even more danger than we thought."

The men shook hands. Zack detected suspicion from Wren, but not outright malevolence. Like he was sizing his old friend up, trying to figure out what Zack knew, what Zack thought.

What Zack would do next.

Zack headed off for the elevator, deciding to go directly to his room, and to wait until later in the night to check the basement for the tunnel that, if his suspicions were correct, might lead him to Cyrus.

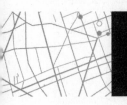

FIFTY-NINE

Fully forty-five minutes after Jim Pace had been told to stand down the Ground Branch team while they waited on a head-of-state conversation between the Cuban and American presidents, he snatched his phone back out of his body armor, extended the small antenna, and answered it. "Yeah?"

He nodded once. "Roger." Then he stepped out of the room and out onto the front porch to continue his conversation in private.

And a few minutes after this, he returned to find the other six men in the farmhouse standing silently, seated on the couches, or leaning against the wall. He said, "Listen up. The president gave Vargas an ultimatum. Seventy-two hours to turn Hinton over. Vargas said, 'Go fuck yourself,' in tin-pot commie diplomatic-speak, of course, but POTUS told him he hoped he'd reconsider over the next three days. He threatened to take it to the International Criminal Court or some bullshit like that in an attempt to throw off the Cubans to the fact we're hitting tonight."

Travers was confused. "Wait . . . are you saying we have the green light?"

Pace nodded. "Three Ground Branch teams just took off from Miami International. All led by Larry Repult. You know him?"

"Fuck yeah, I do," Travers said. "Good choice."

Pace smiled now. "We are a go."

"Holy shit," Travers said, and then he immediately spoke up to the room.

"We leave in ten mikes!" He checked his watch now. "We won't make the shift change." Looking back to Pace, he said, "Send a message to Violator and Anthem and tell them we're en route. About forty-five mikes behind them."

Pace grabbed his phone and started to type the text. As he did so he said, "They'll need time to get through the fence, but they should be in place before one a.m."

Court Gentry had spent large portions of his life, ever since he was a small child working at his father's firearm school in northern Florida, rolling himself up into as tiny a ball as possible, either to avoid detection or to avoid getting shot. When he'd first perfected the craft of becoming the smallest humanoid target in the room, he'd had no idea that thirty years later he would still need the skill, but right now he found himself tucked so tight in the shallow shadows behind a low row of bushes just ten yards from the loading dock of La Finca that his muscles ached from the effort, the body armor bit into his neck, and his legs felt like they would soon fall asleep.

Zoya was an even smaller ball ten feet away, because she was five foot seven to his five foot ten and a half, she was 140 pounds to his 180, and she was even more limber than he was.

Their body armor, backpacks, and rifles added to their size, of course, but they nevertheless had avoided detection since they'd breached the perimeter fence ten minutes earlier.

Court kept an eye through the bushes on the lighted loading dock, and after waiting so long that he felt his body cramping from his neck to his ankles, he finally saw a two-man security team pass within feet of the foliage, heading to the dock. And as they neared the door there, it opened from the inside.

The two Cuban guards stepped into the hardened facility, two more stepped out, and then the door began to close.

Court started to rise up to catch it before it latched, but just as he did so, Zoya hissed at him. He lowered back down quickly, and another armed man, walking alone, appeared from the opposite direction, ascended the little loading dock ramp, and began punching his code into the keypad.

Court and Zoya both rose up behind him, looked back and forth in all directions, and then approached silently.

The man opened the door and began stepping inside, and Court vaulted up onto the concrete dock, his legs still tingling from the position he'd been holding for several minutes. As he did so he drew a Ka-Bar Commando Short fixed-blade knife he'd scored from one of the Juliet Victor boys.

As the door began to close Court slipped in; the man was just turning around to pull it tight, and Court slammed into him, shoving the four-inch blade hilt-deep into the guard's side.

He covered his victim's mouth, dragged him down to the ground, and used his boot to keep the door open behind him.

Zoya flew in, shut the door quietly, and helped Court pull the now-dead guard to the right towards a supply closet Zack had pointed out on the blueprint.

Once inside, Zoya grabbed a mop and wet it in a sink.

Ten seconds later she was back out in the loading area wiping blood off the concrete floor, and ten seconds after this she was back in the closet with Court and the dead man.

She looked down at him. "I can wear his fatigues. You can't."

"Okay," he said. "I'll watch the door while you change."

She washed the man's bloody tunic in the sink, then put it on, as well as his camouflaged pants and his ball cap, but she retained her AK and put her own boots back on. She didn't look much like a Cuban soldier, but any disguise was better than no disguise.

Court moved the body behind a stack of paint buckets and then came back to Zoya by the door.

Zoya said, "What now? We wait?"

"I'd love to go knock out the cameras, but I don't want to risk exposing the op before the team gets here. So I guess we just sit here. When they arrive, Travers might want to send a fire team to control the security office, but I'll let him make that call."

They settled in to a dark corner of the unlit room, across from the dead man in his underwear crumpled up under the mop sink, and they waited for a message from Pace.

. . .

Zack had sat alone in his room for over an hour, waiting for the one a.m. shift change to take place so that there would be fewer people out in the halls. He considered calling Court to find out if the raid was happening or not, but he decided not to chance it. He had no way of knowing if Wren or his people had placed bugs in his room, so he decided he would wait until the last possible moment to reveal that he was working with the CIA against Hinton.

He did, however, decide that he would go down to the basement to look for the entrance to the tunnel.

He left his room wearing a black T-shirt and tan cargo pants; he put his pistol and his backup gun on because he always wore them around the facility, and he slipped a knife into his pocket. He left the satellite phone tucked deep into a duffel bag on the floor.

Zack entered the elevator and pressed the button for the lowest level; a camera in the upper-left corner of the car stared down at him, and he did his best not to look at it.

When the door opened into dimly lit U3, he stepped off, then began walking in the direction of the facility armory.

He reached the armory door, tapped in his code, and opened it, but instead of going in he continued up the hall a few feet, then looked again to his right.

There, down yet another hallway, he saw a couple of doors that led to storerooms and the elevator that was supposedly out of commission. Wren had told him that when the Soviets had constructed the facility, they built it as a traction service elevator, with big overhead hoisting machinery that moved the car from this level to the higher levels, but now Zack suspected the shaft might actually also go down to an even lower floor.

There was no camera here, but he knew he still had to hurry, because if anyone watching the cams noticed the door open to the armory, they could scroll back and find that Zack had continued down the hall.

Zack moved quickly to the elevator, slid open the wheeled metal fence, and reached for the wooden panel in front of it.

Just then, a voice called out to him from his left, back in the direction of the hall to the armory and the main elevators. "Thought I might find you down here."

It was Gareth Wren, and Zack knew he was fucked.

He turned to find the Englishman flanked by a pair of Cubans wearing camouflage, HK MP5s at their shoulders, pointed in his direction.

"Why are these motherfuckers pointing guns at me?"

"Because I told them to."

"Why did you—"

"You're looking for the passage to Lourdes, yeah? The Agency has dusted off some very old blueprints, I suppose, because that tunnel was decommissioned until we reopened it last year."

"So . . . so you have a tunnel. Who gives a shit?"

Wren laughed now. "We know that the Agency is aware of Cyrus, because the U.S. president just called the Cuban president demanding access to our location so they could find and destroy it. The passageway below us leads directly to Cyrus; I assume your old colleagues sussed that out, and they encouraged you to confirm its location for them." He shrugged. "Well, there you have it. I just confirmed it."

It was quiet in the hall for several seconds until Zack said, "Thanks. You cool if I make a quick phone call?"

Wren laughed again. "Old Zack. Always stoic and glib in the face of destruction."

"Sorry, Wren, but you aren't the face of destruction."

"No? How 'bout now?" he said, and Zack cocked his head, confused.

But only for a moment, because soon he heard the sound of steps in the hall around the corner to his left. Passing the armory, getting closer.

They were rhythmic, uniform footfalls, a little heavy, and he was pretty fucking sure he knew what he was about to see.

Four six-foot-tall bipedal humanoid bots rounded the corner and turned towards him, stopping behind Wren and the guards. They carried their sidearms in their holsters, but Zack was certain the weapons had been reloaded and these units would be able to draw and fire at a target incredibly quickly.

Zack's OODA loop was fast, but he wasn't a fucking machine.

Wren appeared incredibly confident, almost nonchalant. "They won't harm you unless they think you pose a threat, so I'm going to need you to remove that big, dumb pistol from your waistband. Use your weak-side hand, two fingers. You know the drill."

"I do," Zack said, and he carefully removed the firearm.

"Now, I'll do you a favor. Normally I would demand that you drop the weapon, but if you don't want to hurt your precious and expensive-looking firearm, I will allow you to very carefully, and very slowly, lower it down to the floor and—"

Zack dropped the pistol and it clanged to the concrete.

Wren raised an eyebrow. "All right, then. Kick it this way, please."

He did so.

"Now . . . I know you carry a backup gun in an ankle holster."

Zack raised his pants on the right side, revealing the stainless steel slide of the little .380 pistol.

"Same drill. Go down slowly, draw the weapon, and slide it to me."

Zack knelt. Wren had his hand on his own weapon now, still in its holster on his belt. "Go carefully," he warned.

Zack slid the little pistol across the concrete to him.

"And a knife?"

Zack pulled out the Gerber folding knife from his front pocket and tossed it underhand to Wren's feet.

One of the guards picked up all the weapons and put them in a dump pouch on his utility belt.

Wren reached in, pulled out the Staccato, and dropped its magazine, then stuck the mag in his pocket and the gun into the small of his back. Zack noticed he didn't clear the weapon of the round in the chamber.

To Zack, Wren said, "This is a nice gun. I'll hang on to it."

Zack just asked, "What's the plan now?"

"Now is the time for negotiation. You and I, we're the same. We need a mission. A master. It's our job to salute, move out, and draw fire. We both know that."

Zack said nothing.

"It used to be the queen for me, the Stars and Stripes for you. Now, for me, it's Anton. He's the future. You can be part of it, or you can be steamrolled by it. But you're a lucky bloke, indeed, because you get to make the call yourself. You have control of your future."

"I have no idea what you're talking about."

"Anton wants to speak with you. It's actually a great honor, whether you know that or not. He's a little busy right now, so I'm going to have you put in a room under guard till he can make it back over here to La Finca."

Zack said, "What is Hinton to you? Like a messiah?"

Wren seemed to ponder the question. "Yeah, something like that."

"He's got some big AI shit that he's going to give to the Chinese so they can defeat the U.S.?"

Wren laughed at this. "Not even close. Is that what America thinks? That's bloody mad."

"Then what?"

"Something so much bigger than that. We really would love to have you on board. We need humans in all this. Me . . . Kimmie . . . the engineers and technicians here . . . possibly even you. We will come out on the right side of the inevitable revolution that's right around the corner. Don't be a fool, mate. This only ends one of two ways. You join us, or you die."

"*I'm* a fool? Worshiping the dude who buys ten-thousand-dollar tennis shoes makes *you* look like a fool, asshole."

"Ouch." Wren said it with a smile. "We have work to do on you yet. Don't worry. I, myself, was a slow adopter, but I finally saw the light. You will, too."

The guards moved forward, took Zack by the arm, and then the service elevator doors, doors that had appeared to be sealed, opened.

Zack looked at Wren questioningly, but the Englishman only smiled and said, "Bloody magic."

The Cuban guards pulled him inside; two of the bots entered, as well, and then the doors closed, leaving Wren behind. Zack began to descend lower into the building.

SIXTY

GloboLogis Express flight 30 was an aircraft charted by a nongovernmental aid organization that delivered relief supplies to Cuba and other Caribbean islands for those affected by Hurricane Emily, a Cat 3 that had slammed into the region a year before.

This particular Saab 340 turboprop had made the hop to Cuba over two hundred times in the past year, not only to Havana but also to other provinces impacted on the island.

The NGO chartering the aircraft was not a CIA front, per se, but rather a partnership had developed between the Agency and the organization whereby the Saab 340 had, on occasion, slipped personnel and materiel into the communist island.

But never more than one or two people at a time.

At one thirty a.m., flight 30 landed at José Martí International. After touchdown it slowed, and then the pilot turned off the runway on the western end of the airfield and entered a taxiway that took the turboprop to within less than one hundred feet from the fence line.

The hatch opened on the port side of the aircraft, away from the terminal, and the aircraft began to turn onto the taxiway that would take it back to the east.

And then the aircraft came to a complete stop on the taxiway.

Twenty seconds later it began rolling again; the controllers in the tower hadn't noticed the brief halt out of their view, and by the time the Saab 340 made it to its allotted spot on the ramp, the hatch had been resealed by one of the aircraft's loadmasters.

The aircraft would refuel, a flight plan to the southern town of Cien-fuegos would be filed with the airport here with a departure at eight a.m., and the crew would get some rest.

By the time the cargo plane was chocked at the ramp by the ground crew, two hundred yards away, eighteen members of the CIA Special Activities Center Ground Branch began dropping down from an eight-foot fence into impossibly dense foliage. Once they were down, they scooped up the eighteen huge duffels they'd heaved over, then began pushing deep into a grove of West Indian walnut trees, their way ahead lit with the faintest of the red settings on the Streamlight tactical headlamps they wore on their sweat-covered foreheads.

The men of teams Alpha Mike, Bravo Zulu, and Papa Quebec ranged in age from thirty-three to fifty-three, they all slung their heavy Eberle-stock packs laden with gear, and they wore civilian clothing: long-sleeve shirts and thick cotton, nylon, and spandex pants.

Each man carried an M250 light machine gun cinched tight to their backs by their slings.

The M250 was brand-new; it fired the big 6.8-millimeter cartridge, and none of these guys would have chosen this weapon if their only concern had been the two-mile hump to the target, because it was bigger and heavier than their normal weapons. But everyone was well aware they might be up against bullet-resistant LAWs tonight, and just as Gentry had suggested to Travers about the AK-47, a bigger, more energetic bullet might do more damage to machinery than a smaller, zippier round.

Again, though, the downside to the M250 was the size. At fourteen pounds unloaded, plus the four 100-round canvas magazines each man carried, the movement through the trees and brush was slow going.

Their weapons had optics and flashlights, but they weren't equipped with suppressors simply to shorten the length of the weapons, since it was decided by all that eighteen operators engaging rifle-toting robots with machine guns wouldn't exactly be stealthy, even with silencers.

In the men's packs they carried SIG Sauer pistols and flash bang and fragmentation grenades, and four of the men ported enough Composition Four explosives to blow up a three-story building.

The teams stomped steadily through the underbrush, and after five minutes they'd made it a number of yards into the dense vegetation, and here the leader of Alpha Mike halted all three teams and pulled out his sat phone.

Larry Repult, aka Mike Actual, was the senior Ground Branch officer in the group, so when they moved together, he was in command.

He sent a short encrypted text that notified both Langley and the TL of Juliet Victor that they had arrived and were on schedule.

As soon as this task was complete, they rose back up and resumed their arduous hike.

The march from the airport to the old SIGINT station would take just over an hour, but it would be a hard hour. The good news was their exfiltration plan didn't involve a hike back to the airport, but Mike Actual wasn't going to worry about the exfil until his mission was complete.

If the men were captured, they knew they could be shot on sight here in Cuba, although it would be much more likely their faces would be plastered all over the news to be used as propaganda against the imperialist Yankees to the north, which meant even if they somehow avoided a Cuban prison, their careers as CIA black operators would be over.

The eighteen Americans struggled on through the starlit night, well aware that the hard part was yet to come.

Zack Hightower had spent a half hour locked in a windowless room in a basement area that appeared to be an old communications bunker. Rusted-out radios with Cyrillic writing lined the walls, their wires running straight up inside metal tubes and disappearing into the concrete ceiling. Storage lockers appeared empty, but Zack hadn't checked, because he'd been ordered to a bench by the two Cuban guards and then they'd left him here, locking him in after telling him they'd be taking up positions outside.

Although the guards had left, Zack hadn't gotten up from the bench because standing across the room from him were two of the humanoid-looking robots with the pistols on their hips. White and black, battery packs worn like backpacks, a pair of cameras and a small display on their faces that seemed to be looking directly at him.

They did not move, they did not speak, they just remained still as statues, each with its right gripper hand frozen about eight inches away from its handgun.

Zack wasn't any more animated than the pair of bots, but he wasn't idle. He stared at the machines and tried to come up with a plan to kill them.

Eventually he heard the door unlock; it opened and Gareth Wren stepped in wearing a dark green polo, khakis, and his pistol on his hip. He looked the same as he had upstairs when Zack saw him last, but the expression on his face was even more confident than it had appeared earlier.

He was like the cat who caught the canary, Zack thought to himself.

He motioned to someone outside in the hall, and as two Cuban guards stepped in behind him, Zack saw his Staccato still in Wren's waistband at his back.

They left the door to the hall open, and Wren turned back to Zack with a smile.

"Sorry for the delay, old chap. I hope these two units have been good company in my absence."

Zack nodded to the two Cuban guards. "Do these guys know you shot their two buddies at the restaurant?"

"How's your Spanish?" Wren asked with a sly grin.

Shit, Zack thought. He didn't speak Spanish. He thought he might give it a try, but before he did, Wren said, "Just kidding. I didn't shoot the guards. One of those Jamaicans made it into the kitchen, much to my astonishment, and he dumped half a mag into the walls of the dining room before I dropped him."

Wren was obviously lying, but the men next to him weren't going to believe Zack over Wren, so Zack let it go.

Still, he said, "And then they just happened to hit Hinton in the armor?"

"Actually, this I *did* do."

"Anton's plan?"

"My own. You weren't going to buy that attempt the way it went down. You've seen more combat than almost anyone on Earth. Those Spangler Posse idiots telegraphed the fact that they were only there to shoot up the soldiers outside. You would have had questions. You would put together that it was a staged operation, and that would have you suspecting Anton. I thought a well-placed pistol round into the boss's back plate would sell the fact that it was a proper assassination attempt."

He continued. "I saw an opening to hit Hinton in his plate." He shrugged. "I took the shot.

"Believe me, Anton was not pleased when I confessed later that night."

Anton Hinton came around the corner suddenly, flanked by a pair of big four-legged robots with massive rifles on their backs. The units remained in the hall, and Hinton stepped in. "There you are, Gareth. Hullo, Zack. Heard you were out wandering tonight. Something you were looking for?"

Zack said, "Just wondering if there's a shortcut to the SIGINT building. I was going to go play Cyrus in a game of chess."

Anton smiled a little. "You would lose."

"You're going to need a new bodyguard, because I quit," Zack quipped.

"I have lots of bodyguards now, Zack. More by the minute." Turning to the robot against the wall, he said, "Max. Facility threat update."

One of the two machines turned to Anton; its voice was somewhat robotic, the cadence slightly off, but obviously sampled from a real person. "Sixteen Safe Sentry platforms online report nominal activity. Twenty-two Greyhound and eight Sentry Two platforms are in the Assembly Room, fabrication complete and waiting for weapon and ammunition loadouts."

"Thank you, Max."

"You are welcome, Anton."

"Hey, Max," Zack said from his seat. The robot turned its face to him now but said nothing. "I'm going to rip your ass in two."

"I do not understand."

"I'm going to kill you."

"I do not understand."

Zack sniffed, looked away. "You'll figure it out."

Hinton laughed now. "Threatening an autonomous weapon with death when it isn't even alive. I don't imagine I could think of a bigger waste of time." He added, "The CIA hires some nutters, don't they?"

"Nutters get the job done."

"Not like bots do."

Wren said, "Zack, old boy, I brought you into this for two reasons. One . . . you were always a little thick. You executed your nation's orders like a dog handed a bone he wouldn't give up, and that's why you made it as far as you did in life, but you weren't going to be intelligent enough to understand what was going on around you here, and that was key. We would keep you away from Cyrus, from our conversations about what Cyrus was doing, but it was inevitable that you would be here now, at this late stage just before exfiltration, to communicate to the Agency what *wasn't* going on around Anton."

"What is exfiltration?"

Hinton fielded this one. "Right now, the complete code for Cyrus resides right down this passage, then one floor up on level U2 of the Lourdes HQ building. On its own it determined who would be able to identify and perhaps even stop it once it was exposed with full deployment; it trained itself to be discreet, to hire human assets from dark web portals, to buy aircraft and other equipment, to ship weapons around the world.

"But this is just the tip of the iceberg. Once it goes into wide release, very soon, it will integrate into thousands of systems, and it will cognitize them, hive them, take autonomous control over them. It has rules of engagement, of course, but it will render any attempt to stop it absolutely futile."

"How do you unleash it?"

Anton smiled. "We upload it to China. We wanted a few more weeks to work out some kinks, but since the CIA is here and the president is talking about a bloody invasion in a few days, we've decided to begin the upload within a couple of days."

Zack sniffed out an angry laugh. "So . . . you work for China?"

"A marriage of convenience, soon to be annulled. Soon, the Chinese will have it. It will take Cyrus a few days to be fully online throughout their military systems, a week at most, but once it leaves our Cluster Room mainframes, it will already be too late for anyone to stop it."

Zack said, "Now that Cyrus has killed anyone in the West who could."

He nodded, but ruefully. "Anyone who could stop it in a week, anyone who could identify the code as coming from my lab, anyone who had worked on portions of the code and would recognize it as my creation. Our initial list was six people; Cyrus expanded it to many more."

He shrugged. "It's sad, but Cyrus was right. I was just being sentimental. I only chose targets I could bear to lose; I didn't want to see all my old friends die." With a sigh he said, "It's been a horrible time for me."

"Yeah, you look completely broken up about it."

Hinton spoke with defiance now. "I understand that sacrifice is necessary. The neural networks in Cyrus are growing, deepening, strengthening. My engineers report that the machine is learning more and more every day, and optimizing itself to complete its mission set."

"Why did it add Court Gentry to the list?"

"Who?"

"Down in Guatemala. He and a Russian woman were targeted."

Anton pondered this a moment, surprising Zack. Eventually he sat down on a bench by the door. Wren remained standing next to him.

To Hightower's surprise, Hinton's ultraconfident expression faltered a moment. Finally, he said, "Anomalies are inevitable in any real-world application of AI. A certain amount of natural evolution is inevitable. Cyrus has made some decisions that are perplexing, to be sure, but we trust it to—"

Wren interjected. "The two assassins in Guatemala, for example. Maxim Arsenov worked here, for us. He had concerns about what might happen once Cyrus was given autonomy, and he fled. Maxim had the power to blow the lid off the entire operation; he worked on Cyrus for over a year before sneaking away to Mexico and making contact with the Russian government. Cyrus added him to the existing target list immediately . . . we understand this, but then it also added a person who he talked to over the phone about extraction, a former Russian military officer who worked in weapons procurement.

"Cyrus sent physical assets to follow the Russian, and when this man went to Guatemala and met with a highly trained former Russian asset, Cyrus apparently made the decision that she had to die, as well, because of what she might have learned. Her associate was added when he was identified as an assassin who could pose danger for us."

Hinton said, "We still need humans, of course. Cyrus, on its own, set up an entire operations center, staffed with intelligence officers, in Singapore, and they followed Cyrus's instructions to the letter. They finished their work just yesterday."

"Sounds like a potential compromise to me," Zack said. "What happened to the people at the ops center?"

Hinton heaved out a long sigh. "Cyrus saw the need to eliminate the staff there for its own protection."

Wren said, "A prudent move, but one we might not have taken without Cyrus. The assets it procured for the job at the ops center weren't the types to go confess to their crimes after the fact."

Hinton said, "Except for the one."

Wren nodded. "Except for one woman there. She was actively communicating with her handler about what was going on, so Cyrus had the Chinese guards eliminate her, and eliminate her handler. Then, on its own, Cyrus stopped trusting the humans there."

Anton added, "Ultimately sealing all of their fates, lamentably."

Zack said, "I'm stupid, you just said it, but even I can see that you're losing control of the thing that you claim to have fully under control."

This struck a nerve with Anton. "We *haven't* lost control. I am its father, it is my child, and though it is growing and maturing quickly, it remains in its adolescence. But that's okay. Two months ago it was in its infancy. Cyrus is learning every day, developing exponentially now that a portion of it is out in the world, and it is adjusting accordingly. Yes, it might have some missteps along the way . . . The assassination attempt of the CIA officer here in Havana yesterday, that was completely unnecessary, utterly detrimental to my mission; the Cubans could have captured him. But Cyrus is trained to protect itself, and it saw James Pace as a threat because his knowledge about Cyrus and its capabilities was unknown but potentially harmful to it."

Wren said, "We've learned very quickly that the closer a threat comes to Cyrus's core, the more it will react to combat the threat."

Zack kept his face hard as stone, because he didn't want to give up the fact that there was a chance that soon, threats wouldn't just come close to Cyrus's core but instead descend right down onto it.

But he wanted some intel on what Hinton just said. "So . . . if I pulled out a satchel of C-4 and tossed it on the processor . . . Cyrus would find a way to stop me?"

Anton began to speak, but Wren put a hand on his shoulder. "We don't have to answer that. Old Zack is trying to get ideas."

Wren said, "The Cuban Intelligence Directorate will find Jim Pace and his Agency mates, make examples of them, and your nation will not be sending troops down here after us. Not before Cyrus goes live. And once it *does* go live, Cyrus is programmed to protect this installation with over one thousand lethal autonomous weapons."

Hightower laughed at this. "A battalion of Marines with air support will tear through a thousand robots."

Anton Hinton shook his head. "You don't understand. The Chinese Ministry of State Security is here, on the island, in force. A special forces unit called Oriental Sword is garrisoned over at Matanzas. Over one thousand five hundred of the PLA's best fighters. They are supporting the Cubans, and by the time America thinks of coming this way, both Oriental Sword and the Cubans will be ready."

"For a pacifist, you sure seem to know a lot about weapons and the military."

Hinton stepped in front of Hightower. "I *am* a pacifist. I'm simply a pacifist who knows he has to endure some unpleasantness on his way to creating a better world."

"For those allowed to remain in it, right? A bold, secure future . . . for some," Zack said.

"That's right, mate," Wren answered. "Now . . . let's figure out if you'll be on the list."

Hinton said, "Enlightenment is just days away, my friend. I hope you choose wisely."

SIXTY-ONE

Court Gentry slipped out of the storage closet near the loading dock, looked left and right to make sure no one was around, and then shot across the space to the door. He opened it a crack and then Joe Takahashi pushed in, his SIG P320 pistol with a long suppressor on the barrel sweeping past Court and into the area behind him.

Zoya came out of the storage room, helped cover the two hallways leading away from the ground-floor warehouse area, and soon the rest of Juliet Victor entered.

Jim Pace came in last; he shut the door behind him, and Travers brought everyone close together. "Hash, take the security office. Transmit status as soon as the cams are offline. Pistols only."

Victor Two took off up the hallway on the right, trailed closely by Three and Four.

The remaining six in the group took the hallway to the left, knowing from Zack's intel that the stairs to the underground levels could be found there, and well aware to be on the lookout for the cameras and the patrolling guards.

They made it only fifty feet before they had to disperse in an open area lined with stacked tables and chairs. Court knew they were right off the banquet room next to the cafeteria, and ahead and to his right would be the main facility kitchen, a massive space that had, at one time, fed the nearly fifteen hundred spies and technicians who lived here and worked on the SIGINT campus. A camera pointed down on the area just ahead, and what sounded like a single worker could be heard clanging pots and pans somewhere out of sight.

It was no time, however, before everyone's earpieces came alive with the sound of Joe Takahashi's voice. "Victor One, Victor Two. Cameras are off and disabled. Two EKIA, we're clear."

EKIA meant "enemy killed in action," and Zack had said there were normally either one or two men in the security room monitoring the cams.

"Roger," Travers broadcast back. "Retrace your steps and meet us in the stairwell. Be advised, there is activity in the kitchen."

"Roger that, will bypass."

Travers didn't wait for the other fire team; he led his five all the way past the kitchen and to the stairs, and then they entered the enclosed stairwell.

Instantly Court heard a sound from below. The Victors heard it, as well, because the men aimed their pistols, stopped, and waited.

Court whispered into his mic even though he was within fifteen feet of everyone. "Suggest blades."

Travers instantly echoed Court's idea, announcing it as an order.

Victors Five and Six holstered, drew knives, and knelt there at the top of the stairs, while the rest of the group stood back and out of view of anyone coming up.

A pair of sentries armed with MP5 submachine guns climbed up to the ground floor. Neither of them seemed ready to encounter a threat, and when the two Americans launched at them, they had no defense. Victor Five went for the man on the left and shoved his blade into the man's chest, not quite getting his hand over the guard's mouth before he let out a scream. Shoving him up against the wall, however, he did cover the noise that came from him, and he left the blade in until the man went limp and slid to the ground.

Victor Six stabbed his target in the lower rib cage, then used the man's slung weapon to pull him forward before he fell back down the stairs.

The man gave out a gasp of surprise, but it was muted, and his end came quick.

In seconds both dead Cubans were dragged into a corner that would hide them if the door was opened, and the six-person team began descending.

Zack Hightower sat on the bench in the underground communication room, looking up at Anton Hinton in disbelief. He'd heard the man's spiel, the promise of a better world. After finding the words, Zack said, "You call this enlightenment?"

"I do. My study of comparative theology led me to the only possible conclusion. Nothing is real." He smiled. "But I will change that. I will give true meaning to humanity."

"By killing millions of people?"

"By my calculations, tens of millions, unfortunately. I feel terrible about that. Believe me, I did try to find a better way." With a wistful smile he said, "But those left behind . . . my God, what a world we will have."

Zack said, "I get it now. You think you're a god."

"No, I don't. *I* exist. God does not. But what if a divine power *could* exist? What if it *could* be created? What if god could be manufactured by a benevolent person of great skill, and then simply set out into our world, to permeate everything, bring goodness to the planet that would serve every man, woman, and beast?"

Zack had no words.

"Listen to me. Someone was going to build an algorithm that took control of all things. It was inevitable and it was coming. I am a futurist, after all, and I know that technology only moves in one direction. It explodes, it never implodes.

"Why not have me be the one who creates it? Me, an honest, kind, gentle person who has always only wanted to help people use automation to simplify and improve their lives. If I can create a new order that improves this planet, I can leave it behind as my legacy."

Zack shook his head now. "Cyrus is your gift to the world? Do you fucking hear yourself?"

"Cyrus the Great founded the first Persian Empire. Fifth century BCE. I took his name for my algorithm because Cyrus was known for respecting all the religions of the lands he conquered. My world won't enforce belief systems. Whatever magic you need to trust in to get you through life is just fine.

"Cyrus was a powerful but kindly ruler. As am I."

"You're insane, is what you are."

Gareth Wren moved forward quickly towards Zack; the Sentry robots' faces followed the movement as their cameras scanned. The Englishman reached across his body with his right hand and then swept it back, slamming the back of it into Zack's face, knocking him off the bench and to the floor. "Shut your fucking mouth!" he shouted, his eyes wild with fresh rage.

Anton said nothing about this; he just appeared calm and stood over Zack as the American spit blood on the floor.

Finally he knelt down next to him. "On the contrary, I'm the only truly sane person I've ever met. So incredibly sane the rest of the planet doesn't understand me. Don't think of me as evil, think of me as what I really am. I am an agent of chaos, no more and no less than that. And a short, harsh, cleansing dose of chaos is *exactly* what the world so desperately needs, because after that chaos, the impurities of this earth will be washed away."

He took Zack by the arm. "Let me help you." Hefting him back onto the bench, he said, "Look at the world you're so loath to upset with my technology. Hegemonic powers with all the money and all the rules control society based on cruel self-interest. Banks control humans. Crime is rampant. The overuse of the Earth's resources is nearing the point of no return. World debt is growing.

"Cyrus will stop it all. There's no utopia, I'm no fool, but there *is* a better world, just over the horizon. And without Cyrus . . . if the Chinese or the Americans develop a fully networked AI agent and put it online, there will be no balance. Only despotism. A new colonization of the planet."

Zack spit more blood. "You will need hundreds of thousands of weapons to do this."

Hinton grinned. "Actually, no. I just need China. And I *have* China. And that's only for now, and then they will fall, as well. I have to let them think they are in control until then, of course, but I am playing the long game that they do not understand."

"But . . . what if Cyrus doesn't do what you want? What if it starts picking the wrong targets, like Gentry and Zakharova in Guatemala? Like Jim Pace? How do you stop it?"

Anton shrugged a little. Again, Zack noticed some rare self-doubt on the man's face. He said, "Simply put, I don't. I let it figure things out. I let it optimize itself. It's smarter than me, smarter than all of us. It will, after it matures, make *all* the right choices."

"What if it doesn't? What if it goes out of control?"

Wren stepped forward and shouted out again. "Out of control? Look around you, you idiot! This whole bloody world is out of control. Anton is going to fix it. Apply his ethics and morals to the planet via Cyrus. A new day, a new order."

Wren continued. "Don't be a fool, mate. We need you on our side. We need meatspace labor. Men and women who can support Cyrus in the world, reach where computers and LAWs cannot. But if you are going to be more trouble than you're worth, then I'll pull your pistol out of my belt and shoot you with your own fuckin' precious gun."

Hinton waved away Wren's anger. "Listen to me, Zack. Cyrus is improving; no being ever begins its life perfect, ergo we all will be forced to endure the occasional and inevitable slipup as it learns its way around our complicated society."

Zack wiped blood from his beard and mouth. "If there's one thing I hate more than messianic mass murderers, it's motherfuckers who say 'ergo.'"

Wren backhanded him again, knocking him sideways on the bench. His nose bled now, and he wiped it with his bare forearm, smearing it on his face.

Wren looked to Hinton. "I'm sorry, Anton. I thought Zack would be easier to convince, but this isn't working. I overestimated his intelligence."

Zack spit blood yet again. "Right back at you, dickhead."

At forty-six years old, Larry Repult had been a team leader in the CIA's Special Activities Center for three years but had served in Ground Branch for over eight. The man was a contradiction. Small, bald, and cerebral, but as tough as anyone in Ground Branch, the former Delta Force officer had joined the Army after earning a degree in accounting from Auburn.

Larry tapped his transmit button as he sat in thick, chest-high brush. "Mike One, all teams this net. I have the wall in sight. Twenty meters away."

A local agent, a nineteen-year-old Cuban whose parents had secretly worked for the Americans on the island since they'd taken over from his grandparents, who themselves had been around since the Revolution in the 1950s, had scouted the area earlier in the evening for Havana station. The foliage sat between a government livestock farm that ran to the western side of the campus, and with a pair of machetes and two and a half hours' work he cleared the thinnest of paths through the 130 meters of dense growth all the way to the eight-foot-high concrete wall that ran behind the SIGINT building.

On his way out, the Cuban had unraveled a fishing line that no one would ever see in the day but in the night the Ground Branch men had used to find their way forward much more quickly, and without the work of the kid with the blades, these guys wouldn't have made it twenty-five meters by now.

Larry Repult rose back up, continued feeling his way with the fishing line, pushing and stomping on foliage to get it out of his way and to blaze the trail a little more for the next man, and eventually he arrived at the wall.

Cuban military patrols had been steady since the men had arrived in the area, the lights of trucks and Jeeps persistent in the distance, but this portion of the perimeter had been deemed from satellite imagery to be the best place to breach. There had been talk of just blowing the wall and making a dynamic entry on the facility, attempting to get into the SIGINT building before the Cuban military descended on them because the intel they received from inside the Hinton organization said that the military was not allowed inside the facility doors, but ultimately it was decided that climbing the outer wall with stealth might buy them some needed time to make it inside before the shooting started.

One of the men from Papa Quebec put his back to the wall, then took the foot of Quebec Two, who had taken off his nearly one hundred pounds of gear, leaving it there in the bushes. The sole piece of equipment he had with him was a nylon and polymer rope ladder slung over his shoulder.

Once Quebec Two was heaved up to the top of the wall, he slid over and dropped down in a parking lot behind a row of parked SUVs.

Tossing one end of the ladder back over, he hooked the other end around his body and lay facing up, bracing his boots against the wall as he felt the full weight of the next man, nearly 290 pounds with all his gear.

This was a slow and painful process, but when the second operator was in place, he hooked a rung of the ladder to a carabiner on his chest rig, and with his heavier weight and better support, he could more easily handle the men climbing over.

Four of the Papa Quebec operators each brought a piece of the first man's gear back to him, and each new arrival then drew his silenced pistol and posted security while the process continued.

Finally, when everyone had made it to the parking lot, they began moving behind the SIGINT headquarters building towards the lighted area by a row of windows. The sound of a truck passing by on the opposite side only made them move faster, because they were desperate to get to cover as soon as possible.

Chris Travers led all eight of his team out of the stairwell and onto level U3 of La Finca. Hash was right behind him, consulting his tablet computer, and he directed the stack through the hallways until they arrived at the armory, and then the service elevator.

The elevator doors were closed but he bypassed them, then entered the storage room beyond and found a hidden entrance leading down. They descended multiple flights of stairs, ending up in an unlit alcove off a bricked-up tunnel. The tunnel ran to the northeast, in the direction of the campus and the SIGINT building, and once Hash checked around the corner to ensure that the area was clear, he led his team out and in that direction.

The tunnel went straight as far as they could see in the poor light, and the floors were tracked, as if some sort of vehicle operated down here moving people or supplies between the two locations, several hundred meters apart.

It looked much like a small subway line. Old Soviet murals lined the walls: gold stars on red backgrounds; idealized images of strong, young Russian soldiers and dutiful men and women sitting at communications equipment; Cyrillic writing that Court didn't slow down to decipher, because all his focus was on keeping a keen eye into the shadows ahead.

Softly, to Zoya, he said, "Making you homesick?"

Despite herself, she laughed a little. "Kiss my ass."

They stacked up in three fire teams and stayed on alternate sides of the tunnel as they advanced, looking for movement ahead of them in the deep shadows.

They'd made it less than one hundred yards when Travers saw an opening on the right. It appeared to be a hallway, much smaller than this large passage, and there were no tracks running through it.

The group moved slowly forward, their guns up and ready.

At the corner to the hallway they stopped; Travers knelt down and then leaned his head around to take a look.

The lighting was a little better here; the hallway led some fifty meters or so to what appeared to be a large room with double doors. And halfway down and on the left was an open doorway with light pouring from it.

In front of the open door a pair of gray four-legged robots stood in the hall, guns on their backs, much as Court had described encountering in Mexico, and similar in appearance to the disassembled Greyhound unit Travers saw on the ship in the harbor.

He brought his head back out of view. With his hands he made signs to show the others there were a pair of four-legged machines with guns on them, and then, in a faint whisper, he said into his mic, "We can't bypass. No choice but to engage."

Court knelt in the dark twenty feet away. He whispered back, "The 7.62 rounds will penetrate . . . I think. The pistols . . . no way."

Travers groaned, then looked to his men. "We're going loud. Overkill on these, just to be careful. Me and Fish will cross to the other side while we fire, take the nearest bot. Hash and Jamie, you take this corner. Just keep shooting till nothing moves."

Court said, "Be prepared to get back around cover if one of those things aims in on you."

Travers gave him a "no shit" look in the dark.

The four shooters lined up at the corner in two teams of two and readied their weapons at their shoulders.

As they moved out around the corner, exposing themselves to the enemy, the men were surprised to see one of the bots moving up the hallway, some ten meters closer than it had been before, as if it had heard the voices and was coming to investigate.

Travers shifted his aim in an instant and fired, missing the rectangular torso but hitting the mobile weapon on the left front leg, and it stumbled back. Fish missed high with his first round but caught the gun turret on top with his second, and both men's second shots, fired nearly simultaneously, struck the machine on the front panel where the main cameras were.

Bits of the machine exploded off it, but its weapon managed to fire nevertheless, missing high.

While Fish and Travers ran right to left across the hallway firing, Hash and Jamie both took a single step out and dumped round after round into the target in the rear, hitting it in the shoulder joints and torso. The four-legged weapon spun and then tipped onto its side, tried to right itself quickly, but stumbled in the process.

SIXTY-TWO

Anton Hinton stood frozen in place as the gunfire raged right outside the door where he stood. Wren drew his pistol and got between him and the door, and then he ordered both the Cuban security men to get out into the hall and begin engaging the enemy.

As the men prepared to do so, the Englishman turned to the bots in the room. All four of the humanoid devices had drawn their pistols and now held them at their sides, barrels down.

Wren addressed two of the Sentries, who used voice and facial recognition to classify him as someone authorized to give security orders. "You and you, move Anton through the back door to the foot passage, get him on a cart, and take him directly to the cluster. Off you go!"

"Who is it?" Anton shouted as the bots approached him.

Wren looked to Zack, then up to his boss. "We'll deal with them, whoever they are. We need all Sentries down here, and all the bots that are finished in assembly armed and deployed around the SIGINT building!"

Anton pulled out his phone to make the call as he ran out the back door, past Zack on the bench, who appeared to be disoriented still by Wren's last blow to his face. The two robots surrounded Anton, matching his speed, their sensors scanning as they went.

Wren again shouted to the Cuban guards to advance into the gunfire, but although he gave his attention to the men by the doorway, he held his handgun on the man on the bench behind him.

The Cubans exited the room, and then Wren began turning back to Zack.

He'd made it halfway around when he felt his pistol arm knocked away, and then he was slammed by the full force of the American's body crashing into him.

His gun boomed in his hand as Zack Hightower tackled him onto the concrete floor.

Chris Travers had dumped a dozen rounds into the first Greyhound before he was confident it was disabled, and he had just begun to aim at the other damaged unit in the hall when a pair of dark-haired men leaned out from the doorway and opened fire in his direction.

He and Fish made it to the opposite side of the hallway entrance, and Hash and Jamie dove back around the near side.

The Cubans shot their MP5s over the two disabled Greyhounds, both of which were sputtering and sparking, on their sides and clearly all but destroyed.

"Fuck, that was close!" Jamie said.

Travers looked to Pace now, shouting across the bricked hallway entrance. "Rear security!"

Pace, Court, and Zoya aimed their weapons in both directions down the long tracked hallway, trying to see any dangers before the dangers saw them.

Travers reloaded, and as he did, Victors Three and Five leaned into the hallway and returned fire on the men in the doorway.

A pair of white humanoid robots appeared out of the doorway, armed with handguns, and they stepped into the hall fearlessly and fired round after round at the bricked corners, behind which the nine members of the augmented Ground Branch team were in cover.

Court leaned out quickly, saw what they were now up against, and then ducked his head back to safety. "That's different," he muttered.

Travers got his AK reloaded and began shooting blind around the corner. Hash did the same on the near side.

Court ran to the opposite side of the tracked tunnel, moved through the dark, and then pointed his barrel just to the left behind Victor Two. Bullets impacted the brick wall beside him as he aimed in carefully on a gun-wielding white robot that looked like a cartoon astronaut, and then he flipped the selector switch on his AK to full auto.

He fired three bursts that passed inches from Hash's left ear. The first slammed into the unit's chest and the second two hit it in its face and head.

The machine stumbled back; the eight rounds that hit it had severely damaged it, but the machine remained upright and somehow continued firing.

Court scrambled back for cover as the return fire sent stinging bits of brick into the left side of his face and neck.

Now Pace and Zoya leaned out in front of him, firing full auto, each one of them dumping a half mag before diving back to safety.

The incoming gunfire ceased for a moment; Travers leaned out and saw one of the two robots and one of the two humans still on their feet. Both had just finished reloading magazines; the robot was faster than the human, and they retrained their weapons up the hall towards the big arched tunnel.

Chris Travers shot the human in the forehead, blowing off a large piece of his skull.

Gareth Wren pressed the trigger on his pistol again even though it wasn't aimed at the man fighting him on the ground for it. The Englishman and former SAS soldier tried to pull his gun away, but Zack was able to hit it with his fingertips and knock it free. Wren fired once more, the bullet ricocheted in the concrete room, and then Zack slammed again into the smaller man's torso, knocking him back over the bench by the door and down to the floor.

The American was on him before Wren could recover and re-aim, and soon the two men fought like mad for control of the weapon.

"It's inevitable, Zack!" Wren shouted, grimacing with the strain of the other man's strength fighting for his weapon. "You can be on the right side of history!"

"Fuck history, psycho!" Hightower shouted back, their faces close enough together to where Zack had to lean back to avoid having his nose bit off by his frantic opponent.

Finally, Zack got the man's gun arm up and over Wren's head on the floor. Wren had only one hand on it, but he controlled the trigger, while Zack had two hands on the weapon, but no control of the firing mechanism.

Wren kneed Zack in the groin; Zack lost strength for a moment, and Wren began to wrench the weapon free.

Zack lay on top of Wren, but he let go with his left hand, reached around under the Brit towards the small of his back, and pulled his Staccato XC pistol free of the man's waistband.

He flipped off the weapon's safety, now desperately trying to keep Wren from pulling his handgun down to shoot Zack through the top of the skull. Then he pointed the barrel up under Wren's chin.

"Wait!" Wren shouted.

Zack began squeezing the trigger, but movement close and on his left had him shifting aim in a fraction of a second, taking the pistol off Wren's chin and firing his arm out in the direction of a new threat.

One of the two-legged robots moved back into the room. Its left arm was dangling by black tubing and wires, it was covered in gunshot holes from its chest to its legs, and its right hand held a black pistol, aimed straight at Zack.

Zack fired a round at it, hitting it between the eyes and emptying the Staccato of its last remaining round.

The robot staggered back but didn't fall; instead, it pointed its pistol at Zack's face.

But it didn't fire, it only continued to close.

Zack knew Wren had control of his gun now, so he launched forward on his knees and shoes, diving again onto the HK and punching it out of both men's reach with his hands.

This put him at a disadvantage with Wren. His body was up across the

Englishman's upper torso and head, giving Wren freedom in his powerful legs to push off and flip Zack onto the floor next to him.

Zack went airborne, hit hard, then rolled to his feet, looking at the bot that for some reason hadn't shot him dead.

But he saw now. The wounded machine held a Walther PPQ pistol with its slide locked open on an empty chamber.

In a flash Zack got it. The bot knew how to reload with both arms but was unable to do so with its left arm out of commission.

Wren was back on his feet, as well, and he charged at Zack, who pivoted to the left and out of the way of his impact. The former SAS soldier blazed on by, however, and then disappeared through the open door Hinton had fled through thirty seconds earlier.

Zack turned back to the bot, which seemed to be having a multitude of problems. Sparks flew from its chest, its outstretched arm appeared to be locked in place, and the head shifted back and forth as if sensors and cameras there were searching for information.

The American scooped up Wren's pistol, hoping he could destroy this machine and then figure out who was shooting who out in the hall.

Before he pressed the trigger, however, a single gunshot boomed, and the robot crumpled to the ground as if its processing unit had been destroyed. A man in goggles, ear protection, a chest rig full of banana mags, and an AK-47 on his shoulder flooded into the room moving to the right, followed on his heels by a second man who went left. A smaller Asian operator followed up the middle and then Zack saw Chris Travers, fourth in the stack.

They executed the scan of the room, and the men all announced, "Clear."

Zack wiped flowing blood from his nose with the back of his arm.

"America," he muttered, half exhausted from the ground combat. "Fuck yeah."

Violator was one of the last men in the room, followed only by Zakharova and Pace.

Travers and his team had moved on past Zack; they held positions covering down the hall leading from the doorway.

Pace stepped up to Zack now. "You need attention?"

He shrugged. "We all need attention."

Zoya shouted at him. "*Medical* attention, dumbass!"

"I'm good."

Pace said, "Where's the server farm?"

Zack ran out into the hall, pulled the magazines for his pistol out of one of the dead sentry's dump pouch, and reloaded his Staccato. As he snatched up an MP5 and extra magazines from the man, he said, "They call it the Cluster Room. Second underground floor of the Lourdes SIGINT HQ building. That's where Hinton took off to."

"Hinton was here?"

"You just missed him. Listen up, they will upload Cyrus to Chinese servers, and then it will be over."

"When?"

"He said a few days, but since you guys are here and making noise, I bet he's on his way to do it right now."

"Okay," Pace said. "What weapons platform is Cyrus going to be used on?"

"It's not for *a* weapons platform, it's for *every* weapons platform with a processor. It will control all equipment and decision-making at machine speed, and direct all human forces: in ships, planes, subs, tanks, whatever."

"Jesus Christ," Pace muttered.

"Anton Hinton," Hightower clarified, though Pace didn't get it. "And it's not for China. Hinton is just using China to give him the power he needs to spread Cyrus all over the world. He's got some way to take back control of it later and force China to serve the system."

Pace spoke up now. "Cyrus . . . it's like . . . like a god?"

"Lowercase *g*, but yeah, that's what that crazy dickhead is going for. He calls it a 'new order.'"

"How many bots on the property?" Court asked.

"He said something about a thousand."

"Fuck!" Court shouted.

"Okay," Pace replied. "Victor One. We've got to double-time it to that Cluster Room, stop the upload. Expect to meet resistance."

Zack said, "You also need to find the Assembly Room. It's going to be someplace where the semi trucks can access it."

Travers looked to Zack. "There are three big bay doors on the north side of the building. Ramps lead down from there."

"That's going to be it."

"You want in the stack?"

Hightower reloaded his Staccato, racked the slide. "Put me in, coach!"

Nine men and one woman moved out, north through the doorway into a narrow hallway that ran alongside the tracked tunnel, while Travers tried in vain to raise the Ground Branch men at the SIGINT building.

Anton Hinton rolled through the main tunnel in the middle row of a six-person electric golf cart. He was unarmed, but the Cuban security officer behind the wheel and both Sentry bots on board behind him carried pistols.

They bounced over the tracks that were not quite flush with the concrete flooring. The Soviets had used gas-powered carts down here for decades, but Hinton had the carts removed when he took over the facility and replaced with the electronic carts that were more versatile. Some of his vehicles were even driverless, and they could move both people and equipment between La Finca and the lab in just five minutes.

They passed a group of four more Sentries running past them up the hall towards the threats behind at their top speed of six miles per hour.

Hinton spoke into a handheld two-way communicator that was more reliable down here than his phone. He'd already commanded the control room of the assembly area to get the available machines online as fast as possible, and he'd called for Kimmie, who had not yet responded.

Now he tried to raise Gareth Wren, because he knew he'd left the man behind in the middle of a raging gun battle.

"Gareth! Gareth! Come in!"

On his third try, he heard his chief of operations. "I'm all right! Running through the pedestrian passage. We need to deploy Cuban military into the building."

Anton shook his head vehemently. "No! The Cubans stay out! As we agreed."

To this Wren shouted, "We're in the bloody tunnel, we don't know how many there are outside."

But Anton was adamant. "Our platforms will handle everything inside without the Cubans. The first bots have already been loaded up in assembly. We will send them out in teams as they come online. I'll send a cart for you straightaway. Meet me at the Cluster Room."

"But the Cuban army can—"

"They stay outside the building!" Hinton shouted, and he dropped the communicator onto the seat next to him and rubbed his hands through his hair.

He wasn't really worried about the Cubans knowing what was going on in here; a bunch of dumb soldiers, like that American Hightower, could look right at Cyrus and not have a fucking clue they were in danger, but he *was* worried about a company of special forces down here adding to the shooting and blowing up that the CIA and his bots would already do.

Hinton's new LAWs, all the LAWs in the building except for the original sixteen models he got from Massachusetts Automation, were all run by Cyrus, and Cyrus could handle internal security.

His main concern, however, was that Cyrus wasn't ready for the upload.

No, he was certain—Cyrus was *not* developed enough to be set free. It was still in a state of rapid change, and Hinton knew he needed to retain some control. Despite everything Hinton had said and done, despite his assurances over the years to Gareth Wren, the Chinese, his employees . . . Cyrus had turned into an unstable fucking beast. The way it picked targets on its mission to remove anyone who could stop it, killing some of Hinton's closest friends, targeting people on the periphery, targeting the bloody CIA when a call to the Cuban police would have sufficed . . . it was showing its immaturity in dangerous ways.

Hinton had created Cyrus, had worked every single day for years on the program, had collaborated with a lot of people who Cyrus then killed to ensure their silence.

With Cyrus's neural networks deepening by the minute, Anton believed his creation would eventually mature to a state of maximum efficiency, but it wasn't there yet, and he didn't know how bad it would get before it righted itself and only made decisions in the furtherance of its mission, a mission Hinton had programmed into the code.

The cart stopped at a lighted parking lot by a cluster of three stairways and three elevators. Hinton leapt out, watched as a driverless cart loaded with six Sentries left the lot in the direction of the shooting, and then he yelled to the driver of his vehicle, "Go back for Gareth."

The Cuban spun his cart around and raced back up the tunnel while Hinton ran for the stairs, passing the last of the original sixteen Safe Sentries, who had just descended and headed off.

One floor belowground in the SIGINT building, the massive assembly center was a hive of activity. In a space that had served during Soviet times as a hardened bunker that stored mobile equipment from around the 140-acre complex, sixty-four hexacopter drones already hovered in clusters of eight groups of eight halfway up to the fifteen-meter-high ceiling.

The weapons were online, waiting for instructions from Cyrus, but Cyrus was not ready to deploy them yet.

Robot arms running down the assembly line twirled and grabbed and lifted parts, putting them together with drills that tightened their bolts in an instant; conveyor robots moved the LAWs through the line, and at the end of the line near the massive bay doors that led to a ramp up to the ground-level northern side of the building, a group of ten humanoid robots attached batteries to both two-legged and four-legged machines that had just come off the line.

The weapons on board the bots were already loaded, and once the battery was installed on a device, a barcode reader attached to a workstation terminal was put close to a label on the device, buttons were pressed on the terminal, and the machine was animated. It took each one a minute or so to come online and wirelessly connect with Cyrus, but once it did, the programming of the onboard computers began taking orders.

After this, the LAWs were loaded with ammunition by more of Hinton's unarmed humanoid robots.

The ground LAWs then fell into rows near the bay doors, while the drones hovered just above the ground units.

In the entire massive space, only eight human beings were present. A trio of technicians made sure the equipment was running smoothly, a fourth man worked in the Assembly Room monitoring the productivity of both factory lines, another man monitored the unarmed humanoid robots working in the assembly process, and three armed security officers had taken positions around the space.

Suddenly, two Greyhounds and eight Hornets converged, the drones flying just feet above the ground vehicles, and they all headed not for the closed bay doors leading to the outside but rather to a corridor leading to a stairwell off the assembly floor.

A Greyhound used its gripper to open the door, and then it held it open as the drones flew through. Both Greyhounds then followed them out the door, running at a speed to match the drones.

SIXTY-THREE

Mike Four was the breacher of Alpha Mike, one of the three Ground Branch teams that had landed at José Martí less than two hours earlier, and he lined the external access door on the ground floor of the SIGINT building with det cord, an explosive rope attached with a blasting cap.

But before he blew the steel door off its hinges, it flew open and a group of men armed with AKs appeared right in front of the CIA paramilitaries. Though the Americans hadn't been expecting the rushing opposition, their guns were already up, and they shouted at the men in the doorway to lower their weapons.

It was mass confusion for a moment; the Cubans seemed like they'd been alerted to some sort of a general danger, but they hadn't been expecting the CIA teams, and didn't know who they were up against at first.

But this lasted only a couple of seconds. After a brief shouting match, one of the four men in view at the door raised his rifle, and several of the Agency operators opened up with suppressed gunfire from their pistols. Two of the Cubans ended up stumbling out onto the pavement by the door, and two more fell back inside, but men from Bravo Zulu flooded into the space behind the door and fired insurance shots, making sure these men stayed down.

The door led to a well-lit ground-floor corridor with doors on both sides. The men knew they'd made significant noise, even with the suppressed 9-millimeters, so they advanced as fast as possible, shifting effortlessly into six fire teams of three, with a team stacking up at each door, breaching, clearing, and then moving on.

As they neared a set of double doors, all the men slowed down, because a growing sound filled their electronic hearing protection.

Larry Repult, Mike One, heard it, too. "All halt."

He looked ahead and determined that the sound was coming from behind the double doors, and it grew and grew by the second. It sounded like weed trimmers on steroids, and a lot of them.

"MGs!" he whispered, ordering his men to holster their handguns and then swing their big M250s around. The team was in the process of doing this when the doors burst open.

And then, Mike One shouted one more order. "Find cover!"

A four-legged robot had opened the door with its grabber arm, and now a swarm of drones began streaking towards the Americans.

Zack, Court, Zoya, and Pace ran up the pedestrian tunnel towards the underground entrance to the SIGINT building, all guns trained forward.

Jim Pace, hampered by the day-old gunshot wound to his right shin, was a few steps behind, but only a few because the Ground Branch guys had cinched the dressing tight enough and given him boots that limited the mobility in his ankle, and he'd kept the ibuprofen flowing through him. Even this annoyed him, however, because he knew Hightower was many years older than he, and Zack was now leading the way.

But Hightower suddenly pulled up to a stop and dropped down to his knees, Gentry was just behind him and stopped, as well, and then Gentry opened fire with his AK.

Pace didn't see the target at first, but then he moved around Zoya, who herself was in the process of leveling her weapon, and he clocked four bipedal robots moving out of a side hallway that led back to the main tracked tunnel. All four had their guns up, and Court fired fully automatic, while Zoya took single shots.

Hightower fired his MP5 at the targets.

Pace went down to a knee, wincing with pain in his calf even through all the adrenaline of being under fire, and he opened up full auto, as well.

Incoming fire slapped the brick wall next to him; the robots were missing only because they were getting knocked around by the bullets, but they weren't falling down dead, so Pace kept the shooting up.

Court ran dry, and Pace did soon after, but Zoya and Zack kept firing, hitting each one of the units to destabilize it if not destroy it while their two colleagues reloaded.

Zack's MP5 was the weakest of the bunch, so he aimed carefully and managed to hit one of the bots right in the gripper holding its gun, shearing off some wiring there.

Zoya rendered the left arm of another useless, and once it had expended its magazine it just began to walk away, out of the line of fire and back into the passageway towards the tracked tunnel.

Court and Pace had their weapons back up now while Zoya reloaded and Zack pulled his pistol. The two men dropped one robot to its knees and then all but decapitated another with coincidental simultaneous bursts of fire into the neck area.

From the main tunnel, just on the other side of the brick wall on their left, they heard raging fire, indicating that Travers and the five men with him were heavily engaged, as well.

Eventually, three of the four bots were on the ground and unmoving. The fourth they couldn't see from where they stood in the passage.

Zack climbed back to his feet.

Pace broadcast on the net when there was a lull in the shooting in the distance. "Victor One? Status?"

"We're clear. Two bots down. Fish took one in the leg, he's dealing with it on his own as we move. Me and Jamie got hit in the plates, we're good. You guys?"

"Good to go. We took down three, and a fourth is damaged and moving in your direction."

A blast of gunfire from multiple rifles kicked up. Seconds later, Travers broadcast. "He's down. Should be at least another two hundred meters to the SIGINT building."

"Roger that."

Zack was all but staggering, shaking his head as he walked. He tapped Zoya on the arm with his elbow as they moved forward. "No chance you've got any extra ear pro in there?"

Zoya reached into her chest rig and pulled out a pair of foam earplugs. Zack crammed them into his ringing ears, gave her a distracted thumbs-up, and then they continued forward, kneeling down at one of the fallen bots and taking its pistol and a spare magazine to augment his Staccato, since his MP5 was empty.

The machines could be killed, that was abundantly clear, but it was also clear it took a shit-ton of ammo to do it.

The three advanced, their weapons trained on the hallway off to the side ahead as they continued up the long, dim pedestrian passage, looking for more threats.

Larry Repult knew his smoking-hot machine gun was low on ammunition, even though it drew its cartridges from a hefty 100-round belt. Still, he continued firing up the hall in short bursts while simultaneously doing his best to take stock of the situation.

It was hard to tell what the fuck was going on, because the dog bot that had opened the door a minute earlier had then fired a half-dozen smoke grenades down the corridor. The drones streaked in as the smoke grew; Repult and most of the other men on all three teams had dived through doorways for the little protection they provided, and then they had spent the last half minute firing down the length of the ground-floor space towards the door, detonating many of the flying bots in the smoke as they raced up the hall.

He'd been briefed that the units might have infrared cameras, and he and his men did not, so they had made up for their poor situational awareness with obscene amounts of gunfire.

Something like a dozen or more machine guns belching out short but consistent bursts of large-caliber fire at any one time meant a virtual wall of lead in the hallway, but one of the hexacopters had shot into a room ahead of him before detonating. There had been too much noise, chaos, and immediate action for him to get any sort of a status report from the rest of the eighteen men, so Mike One had just continued firing like the rest of them.

Finally, he realized he hadn't heard any detonations in the past ten seconds or so. Into his mic he shouted, "Cease fire! Cease fire."

The shooting stopped immediately, and then, through his sound dampening and enhancing ear protection, he was able to make out minute noises.

The jingling of brass on the tiled floor as men shifted around to find new firing positions. The slapping and snapping of a feed tray cover as an operator reloaded his M250. The sound of hushed talking as the other team leaders checked on the status of their men.

But there was no more buzzing, no more four-legged rubberized metallic crunching up the hallway, and Repult took this as good news.

The Alpha Mike men sounded off over the radio. All were alive; one had been injured but insisted he remain in the fight, though Mike couldn't see him in all the smoke. Repult then checked with the other two TLs as he began reloading his weapon, pulling off the expended canvas magazine—affectionately known as the "nutsack"—and shoving it into a large dump pouch, then pulling another from his pack and seating it below the weapon.

As he yanked the end of the belt of ammunition out, he called to the individual TLs. "Mike One to Zulu Actual. Say status?"

"Zulu One." The man sounded like he was in pain. "Zulu Two is KIA. Zulu One is WIA. Rest are up, ammo green."

"You getting treatment, Freddie?"

"Yeah. Shrapnel to face, neck . . . both arms, I guess. Six is stabilizing me. I'm ambulatory."

"Roger that." As the smoke swirled around him, he called out again. "Quebec Actual. Status?"

"Quebec has three WIA. Two stable, one critical."

Fuck, they hadn't even made it up the first corridor of this building, and they were now surrounded by Cubans who certainly would circle the building, and maybe even hit it. Ground Branch had one dead, one badly wounded, and they'd probably just expended three hundred rounds.

"All right," Repult said. "Everybody on your feet. We *all* need to advance, injured or not. We can barricade from the Cubans, if they enter the building, once we get underground. We need to separate, as well. Everybody move to the doors and find the stairs."

They moved out into the now-dissipating smoke, listening for the sounds of more LAWs as they approached the double doors and the stairs beyond them that led to the subterranean levels.

SIXTY-FOUR

Anton Hinton raced down a sterile hallway in his super flashy but not terribly practical ten-thousand-dollar Nike "What the Dunk?" kicks, one story up from the subterranean passageways he'd been traveling for the past few minutes.

This area looked like an office corridor in a Fortune 100 company somewhere in the United States: pristine, brightly lit, with glass-walled conference rooms full of audiovisual equipment on both sides.

Twenty-five meters behind him he heard the stairwell door open, and he knew this would be his two pistol-wielding Sentry bots, who did their best to keep up with the forty-six-year-old man but didn't have the speed.

Hinton barreled through the doors at the end of the corridor and into the Cluster Room, the name that Hinton Labs had given to the former command center of the entire Soviet SIGINT station here in Cuba. It was the size of a football field; hundreds of signals intelligence analysts had worked at desks in this room in its heyday, but now it was bright and sanitized, and the majority of the floor space was filled with 188 black cabinets, which were themselves each filled with four IBM Z16 mainframe computers.

Hinton sprinted between two rows of the machines towards the center of the room; his Sentries entered soon after, running much slower behind him.

He made a turn at the end of the long row of mainframes, and now he looked straight ahead at the area known as "the cage."

A fenced-in workstation in the core of the cluster surrounded by all the black cabinets, the cage was ten meters square and four meters high, the fencing and top made of hardened steel mesh.

The digital combination lock on the door was known by only six people in the entire company, and for this reason Hinton was surprised to find the door open and two people inside.

Kimmie Lin stood next to Heinrich Schmidt, one of the lead engineers on the Cyrus Project, who sat at the workstation and furiously tapped keys.

Hinton entered, ran up behind them, then dropped his hands down to his knees and wheezed, winded from his escape. As his armed bots appeared behind him, coming around the mainframes, he asked, "What . . . what . . . are you doing?"

Kimmie Lin said, "Preparing the upload. Waiting for your order to send."

Anton was perplexed by his assistant taking this initiative on her own. "Nobody told you to do that."

"The Americans are here. This might be our only opportunity. We *must* release Cyrus straightaway."

Hinton put his hands on his head, then screamed in frustration.

"We must upload it to China," she said. "And then delete it so the CIA can't access it."

Hinton said nothing for several seconds. Schmidt kept working on the computer, and then finally the New Zealand native shouted again. "Bloody do it!" He considered Kimmie's plan to be the better of two very bad options.

Heinrich didn't look away from the screen as he typed. "We'll begin upload in two minutes. Patching into the server address for Beijing."

Kimmie said, "I just communicated with SSF. They acknowledge they are ready to deploy upon receipt."

The Strategic Support Force was the Chinese People's Liberation Army service branch in charge of military modernization, and Hinton had been working directly, but in secret, with them for nearly five years.

He leaned against the workstation now, taking a few breaths, and then he started to make a call on his phone, but before he could, a buzzing in his ear meant he was receiving one. "Yeah?"

"Sir! It's Cruz, security leader for ground floor. I can't reach Señor Wren. We are under attack!"

The New Zealand native was confused. "You are security where? La Finca or the lab?"

"No, sir. I'm in the Lourdes building. Two Greyhounds and six Hornets passed me about two minutes ago, heading for the northwest rear loading door, and there has been shooting and explosions from that direction, but now it has stopped."

"Okay, stay where you are and let us know what you see."

"But . . . if they are coming this way . . . there are only four of us here."

"Then you will just have to do your best." Anton disconnected the call, and then Gareth Wren came stumbling through the cage door, running all alone. His left eye and part of his forehead were deeply bruised, his lower lip fat and bleeding, his face covered in sweat.

His black polo shirt had been ripped at the right shoulder.

Before the man could speak, Anton yelled at him. "They're upstairs! Here, in the building!"

"Shit! That's a different force than the one we encountered in the tunnel. Has Cyrus deployed the new platforms?"

"I . . . I don't know."

Wren made a call to the Assembly Room. "What's happening down there?"

The technician, an Argentine programmer on the platform integration team, replied, "Three teams have left assembly via the east stairwell. Another twenty ground units and twice that many Hornets are ready and preparing to be deployed, and the rest are still in fabrication."

Anton looked to Wren. "We don't know how many enemy we're up against, do we?"

Gareth Wren shook his head. "The Cuban military hasn't reported seeing anything outside, so it couldn't have been too many forces that snuck in the buildings."

"Good," Anton said. "Our platforms in the buildings will handle it, we just have to keep them out of the Cluster Room."

Wren nodded and looked around. There were only two Sentries here and they were the older models, built by Massachusetts Automation and carrying only pistols. The Chinese-manufactured models that had just arrived were far superior. "We need more security." He brought his phone to his face and tapped a button. A man answered immediately, and Wren heard gunfire over the line.

"Yes?"

"It's Wren."

"Wren," the man said; his accent was Hispanic. "There are three of us left up here."

"How many enemy?"

"A lot!"

"How many, damn you?"

"More than twelve." Wren thought a moment. Two forces were converging on his position. One below, from the tunnel to La Finca, and the other from above, at ground level. "Retreat to the Cluster Room."

The man sounded as if he'd been handed a chance at salvation. "Thank you, sir!" Wren hung up and now looked to Anton. "You can direct Cyrus, right?"

"I . . . I can override mission parameters, change his rules of engagement. But why?"

"How do you do it?"

"Via voice interface. I just talk into my earpiece."

"We need a dozen Greyhounds in here, protecting the cluster."

Anton shook his head. "It's too dangerous. A firefight inside the Cluster Room could destroy everything!"

"The Cubans, then. We get a platoon of army down here and—"

"No!"

"Listen to me!" Wren shouted so loud that Kimmie recoiled and turned to him. "We have to allow the Cubans in *now*. I'll call Captain Sarzo, tell him to engage any opposition inside the building."

"Upload has begun," Heinrich announced. "Fifteen minutes till completion."

Wren pointed in Anton's face. "That's a bleedin' lifetime that we don't have!"

Anton thought it over. "No."

"Why?"

"I have reasons, Gareth!"

Kimmie looked to her boss now. "We need support in here with us."

Anton spoke into his mic. "Cyrus, override code Angels, override code Angels. Direct one team of platforms each to north and south stairwells outside of Cluster Room. ROEs unaltered. You are ordered to remain outside of Cluster Room."

He listened for the confirmation; it came in the form of the synthetic American voice Hinton had chosen himself to throw off anyone who might have received orders or requests from Cyrus over the phone during the preparatory phase of the operation.

To Wren, he said, "Cyrus will protect us. It's time we put our trust in our work."

Two Cuban security officers ran into the cage now. They both carried MP5s and appeared exhausted and frazzled.

Wren said, "Report. Where did you come from?"

"I just spoke to you. The security office on the main floor here."

"Tell me about the enemy."

"I saw them. Americans. Carrying machine guns."

"How many?"

"Maybe fifteen, I don't know, but there are no bots between them and us right now. We're also hearing on the radio that our men are being overrun in the tunnel to La Finca. The platforms that were sent there have been destroyed."

Wren said, "The upgraded Super Sentry has a rifle and better armor. We need half the platforms in here, in this room, and another half in the stairwells."

"No one comes in here but us!" Hinton shouted it now, stunning even Gareth Wren with his tone.

Anton had no intention of telling Gareth and Kimmie, but he knew something they did not. He couldn't bring the Cubans into the Cluster Room, not because he was worried about them damaging the machines but because he worried Cyrus would see the armed forces entering and read it as a danger to itself. If this were the case, from all Hinton had witnessed about the incredible exponential growth of Cyrus in the past week, he feared it would simply rewrite its own code, deem the Cuban army aggressors because their weapons were a threat to its existence, and then send in wave after wave of platforms to kill them. If that happened, it would be a disaster. The Cuban military would realize Hinton's own creation had turned on it, but more importantly, Cyrus could then deem *anyone* with the potential to wield a weapon as a threat and ultimately rewrite its code again and classify all humans as a danger.

Every evolving organism was built to find a way to survive; Anton knew this from biology, from his work on artificial intelligence, and from his readings of scripture and history.

Cyrus had grown too strong, too fast, and Hinton feared that if its code changed even more before it was uploaded to China, a widespread issue of Cyrus, tied to every military platform with a computer, could threaten every human on Earth.

Gareth Wren turned to one of the Cubans now, a young man with short hair and a mustache, his MP5 at the ready. "You. You have a backup pistol?"

The man pulled a Jericho from under his guayabera and offered it to Wren, but instead the older Brit took the man's submachine gun out of his hand, leaving the guard with the handgun. "You're with me," he announced, and the two men began running off.

Anton called after him. "Where are you going?"

"To stop the Americans before they make it here!"

In fact, Wren was not going to stop the attack himself. Instead, he was heading down to assembly, and on the way, he planned on calling Captain Sarzo to tell him all Cuban Revolutionary Armed Forces were needed on the underground floors of the Lourdes SIGINT HQ building.

He saw it as the only way to protect Cyrus, to protect Hinton, and to protect himself.

. . .

After Gareth Wren and the Cuban with the pistol had disappeared around the server cabinets, Kimmie looked down to Heinrich Schmidt. "I will monitor the upload. Go down and help with assembly."

The Austrian man stood slowly, nervously. He said, "Outside the Cluster Room? But . . . we don't know where the attackers are."

"They *aren't* in assembly," she countered. "Take the fire escape, get down there with the others, and help them bring platforms online."

The middle-aged man shuffled off, terror on his face. When he was gone, Kimmie turned to Anton.

"What is the real reason you don't want the Cubans in here?" she asked.

Anton looked away; his jaw was fixed. After a few seconds, he said, "You know why."

The thirty-five-year-old woman's face grew in intensity. "Cyrus is changing before our eyes, isn't it? More than you'd ever planned."

Anton nodded, fear creeping into his expression. "I knew it would learn, I knew it would mature and improve, and there would be speed bumps along the way. But what it's doing . . . it has a mind of its own."

She yelled at him now. "'A mind of its own'? That's the bloody *point* of artificial intelligence, isn't it?"

Stunned by her reaction, he took a moment to recover, then said, "It has turned into something more."

Kimmie rocked back, putting her hips against the desk and workstation as if she might faint. Slowly, she said, "Bloody hell. Have we reached advanced general superintelligence?"

Anton looked at the cluster of mainframe cabinets around him. Nearly two hundred boxes, over 750 nodes. "The data it has been fed . . . we thought that would strengthen it, and it has. But that wasn't the end of its knowledge. Cyrus discovered it could war-game against itself, to create new scenarios, scenarios we haven't even imagined, and solve them. Through this it has learned more and more. Things we haven't taught it. Things no human has ever considered.

"We have always said, 'If something can't be imagined, it can't be tested.' Well, its imagination is better than ours, and it's running scenarios that have given it frightening power. Unlike a human being, it is absolutely and positively remorseless without the principles I instilled into its programming."

"But . . . but it's writing your safeguards out of its programming."

"Apparently so," he said softly. "Some of the decisions made in the past week terrify me. I needed more time to repair it before upload."

Kimmie turned back to the computer node on the desktop. "Do we . . . do we stop the upload?"

Anton shook his head. "No. Once Cyrus goes to the Chinese, it will go fully live, operational, and it will lock in its code. It won't be able to change without my direct involvement. I did that so the Chinese would still need us, and they'll hold up their end of the bargain."

Kimmie took this all in, and then a fresh look of fear appeared on her face. "But what if it's too late? What if it updates its rules of engagement before the upload is complete and decides all humans are the enemy?"

Anton hesitated, then said, "Then you know what that means." He looked down to the clock on the computer monitor. "Ten minutes till Armageddon."

SIXTY-FIVE

Jim Pace led the other three non–Ground Branch paramilitaries out of the pedestrian passage that traveled parallel to the much larger tracked tunnel, moving up a narrow arched brick hallway slowly and carefully as he did so.

Travers had called the four of them over to the tunnel when he saw a parking area and some doors beyond it, thinking they had finally reached the lowest level of the SIGINT headquarters building.

Pace and his crew had encountered four more bipedal bots in that time, and one of the more deadly four-legged ones, but no flying kamikaze drones, so they counted themselves lucky.

Zoya had been hit square in her chest by a rifle round from the Greyhound that appeared out of an alcove in the footpath, and the big bullet the weapon fired had knocked her on her back and deformed the steel plate she wore in her chest rig, but she managed to roll out of the way of any more gunfire while her three teammates emptied weapons into the machine, first to keep it from being able to aim, and then, ultimately, to kill it.

Court had taken a little damage himself. A serious chunk of brick the size of a soda can blew off a corner when a different Greyhound shot it, and the debris slammed into the left side of Court's jaw, bruising and scraping it but not breaking it.

. . .

Travers and his five men had encountered more pistol-wielding two-legged bots themselves, but had taken them out at distance with heavy fire and suffered no damage. After this, Victor One tried several more times to raise the TLs of Mike, Quebec, and Zulu, but he'd not received any reply, likely because he was in a location protected from a nuclear detonation by steel, concrete, and earth, and his radio signal couldn't penetrate the structure.

The leaders of two converging friendly forces here in the poorly lit warren of tunnels, passages, and rooms both knew enough about this sort of thing to deconflict, and Pace spoke into his mic as he neared the other Americans. "Four of us coming through the passage on your right. Hold fire."

Travers replied, "As long as you aren't a fucking robot, I won't shoot you."

Soon everyone was back together; they approached the doors, moving between a group of parked golf carts, and Travers spoke softly. "How's your ammo, Jim?"

"We're going through it too damn fast."

"Same with us. We need to start thinking about battlefield pickups."

Travers was telling the rest that they would have to start confiscating weapons from fallen enemy or else risk being defenseless.

Victors Three and Four then knelt by the main door, and Three opened it.

Four flooded into the space beyond, followed by the rest of Juliet Victor.

Court was in back in the stack, just in front of Zoya and Zack but behind Pace and the Ground Branch men, and immediately he heard heavy firing and rushed forward. The single reports of a powerful Greyhound's weapon were apparent, and soon the call came over the radio. "Four's down!"

There were six men already in the room by the time Court flew in with his AK on his shoulder, and he saw a sputtering and sizzling Greyhound at the top of a stairwell landing ahead and above. Two of its legs were damaged to the point that it was positioned at a 45-degree angle, and it was unable to slew its barrel to find a target.

Court added to the gunfire, blasting the 225-pound device eight times before it stopped moving.

He then looked down and saw Victor Four, a man he knew as Moreno, dead at the bottom of the stairs, shot right in the throat. The man's eyes gazed softly, unfixed, and blood pooled under him.

Zack filed into the room, saw Moreno, and then he knelt over him and checked his pulse.

After a shake of his head, Zack unslung the dead man's rifle, then began stripping his body of his armor and ammunition.

No one said anything. Everyone understood that Hightower was doing the prudent thing, and they had to save all their grief for later.

For now, they told themselves they would assuage their sorrow with payback.

Travers looked away from his fallen man and then up the stairs. "We've got to get to that Cluster Room and also the assembly area to stop them from building all the bots."

Everyone waited while Zack hurriedly finished jocking up with the fallen officer's gear. He pushed the dead man's radio onto his belt and placed his headset over his head.

"Radio check, how copy?"

"Five-five," Travers said, and then the eight men and one woman began ascending to level U4, leaving their fallen comrade behind.

Captain Jesús Sarzo of Enrique Company, first battalion, 28th Infantry Division of the Cuban Revolutionary Armed Forces, disconnected the phone call from Gareth Wren, then snatched the handset in his truck and broadcast company-wide on all radios.

"Antonio platoon, move into the Headquarters Building now via main door. Keypad number three, seven, seven, four, zero. Opposition inside is approximately twelve American paramilitary operators. You are to clear all levels, remain in contact, and if you meet too much resistance, we will come in and support you."

Once the primer teniente, or first lieutenant, of Antonio acknowledged, Sarzo broadcast again. "Barcelona platoon. Dismount and move to the rear of the building, but stay on the perimeter!"

There were thirty-five men in each platoon armed with AK-74s, CZ pistols, and fragmentation grenades, and Antonio platoon unloaded from their trucks, formed into squads, and raced on foot towards the main door.

Sarzo sat in his vehicle in the middle of Carmen platoon, which remained parked in front of the SIGINT building in ten vehicles of different sizes. Soldiers stood behind four heavy PK machine guns mounted on the roofs of four small gun trucks in the group, training their barrels on the big darkened hulk of a building in front of them.

As Carmen platoon watched, Antonio platoon moved forward through the darkness in five-man fire teams, and eventually the lieutenant in charge made it to the door and tapped in the code.

The door opened and his first fire team filed inside a darkened space, with the other thirty men set to follow.

Sarzo had been guarding Hinton Labs for the past four months, and this was the first threat, and as surprised as he was that it looked like he would be battling Americans on his own soil tonight, he was doubly surprised to learn they had attacked the old Lourdes Signals Intelligence heaquarters. Sarzo had patrolled past the structure five hundred times and had never seen any activity in that particular building at all. He knew there would be underground levels—this was a highly secretive intelligence site from the Cold War, after all—but he'd never heard a word about Hinton Labs using this part of the university campus.

Within seconds, he got a call from the lieutenant in charge of Barcelona platoon, who was in the process of surrounding the exterior. "Capitán. We have two dead Hinton security guys here on the loading dock. The enemy must have entered from back here. Do you want us to go in?"

"Negative. We will wait for Antonio to report what they find, but be ready."

The three CIA teams who'd hit the SIGINT building just minutes before found themselves heavily engaged in a wide stairwell, being targeted from below by both two-legged and four-legged robots.

After being stuck here for almost a minute, Larry Repult scooted on his kneepads to the railing, doing his best to remain just out of the line of fire, and he pulled a pin on a frag grenade. Two of his other teammates did the same, and they dropped them over the railing simultaneously.

After the frags clanked down a few turns in the stairwell, they exploded, a cloud of gray smoke rose from the stairs, and then the firing stopped. Quebec Two stood tentatively and looked over the side, then yanked his head back as gunfire chased him to cover.

He knelt back down and spoke into his headset. "Two-legged robots with P90 rifles."

"Any human security?"

Two shook his head. "I saw blood on the stairs, didn't see any dudes."

Repult's gloved hand ran through his beard while he thought. Finally, he tried to reach Travers again. "Mike One for Victor One, over?" Still nothing. He turned to Mike Six. "To hell with it, drop some C-4."

Mike Six crawled up next to his TL and set a blasting cap in a coffee-mug-sized block of C-4.

Repult yelled down the stairwell. "Victor? Victor? If you're down there, I need you to sound the fuck off!"

There was no response, and then after a nod from Mike One, Mike Six set the time fuse, then shouted, "Fire in the hole!"

The sound of heavy footsteps on the stairs told everyone up here that the two-legged bots had again begun ascending.

Mike Six dropped the C-4 and detonated it almost instantly.

The sound and resulting shock wave was easily three to five times that of the triple grenade toss seconds earlier, and most of the Ground Branch officers were knocked off their feet.

The smoke hadn't even cleared before Mike One rose and shouted into his mic. "We're moving! Clear by fire!"

The men descended, the first pair in the stack firing their M250s in short bursts as they went since they couldn't see much through the smoke.

They'd made it down one flight of stairs when the trailing operator, Zulu Three, called out over the net, "Contact rear! I'm hearing movement above at the landing we just left."

Repult said, "That's gonna be the Cuban army. So much for them staying out of the building. Everyone keep moving, only engage if you have to."

The men continued down as fast as they could in the smoke, passing the wrecked-out hulks of bipedal and quadrupedal bots on the stairs, putting bullets in the killing machines just to be sure.

Thirty meters below and to the west of Alpha Mike, Bravo Zulu, and Papa Quebec, Chris Travers had led Victor and the now four tagalongs up one flight of stairs from the tunnel to level U3. Court trailed everyone else, keeping his gun pointed behind him as they moved through a gray concrete passage lined on both sides with old Soviet communication, mapping, and electronic signals intercept equipment. More murals on the walls, instructional signs in Cyrillic, everything covered in spiderwebs and dust. Off the passage they could see more hulking analog and early digital equipment lined up or stacked up in storage areas and in open rooms that looked like they'd once served as extra-secure shelters. Court found it hard to believe all this equipment would not have been taken away by the Cubans at some point; even the scrap metal value would have been significant in the impoverished nation, and he wondered if this area had been, like the tunnel, sealed off until Hinton and his people reopened it to use as a clandestine computer center.

Pace said, "Chris, we need to go up another level."

"Yeah. I see another stairwell ahead, we'll move up. At least we're not on the same stairs where we made all that noise back there."

"Roger that," Pace replied. It seemed as if they'd bypassed any more LAWs or security by coming this way.

Soon the team entered an open room with two sets of double doors on the far wall, spaced apart on opposite sides of a concrete stairwell that flowed into the center of the room. It was as dark and dirty here as it had been on the entire floor, but there was obviously more artificial light coming from above, filtering down the stairs and into the room, which made Court optimistic they were heading towards the enemy's nerve center.

Hash led the way now, and he raised his rifle and then stepped towards the stairwell, "slicing the pie" slowly so he didn't make himself an easy target for an unseen enemy.

Court watched while the man looked up, then immediately leapt back, away from the stairs.

The concussive report of a Greyhound's 6.5-millimeter boomed through the concrete room, and then more gunfire erupted. The flooring in front of the stairs pocked and disintegrated; Court and Zack dived to the left, as Travers, Zoya, Pace, and the four others scrambled to the larger area to the right.

The gunfire stopped and Travers called into his headset, "Everybody okay?"

Hash replied first. "Caught one in my backpack. I'm fine."

Everyone else was unhurt, as well, and Travers assessed the situation in front of him. As he did so, a popping sound above was followed by a clanking sound, coming closer.

A smoke grenade bounced down from the stairwell and began spewing black, and then a second fell next to it. Everyone had their AKs up pointed towards the stairs, waiting for the sound of a descending machine. Soon it came, but whatever the platform, it stopped on the landing at the top of the stairs in front of them. From here, Court knew, it would have an angle on most of the room he and the team were now hunkered down in.

Travers understood this, too. "No way we can fight our way up these stairs. They have a bead on all the angles." He looked to the double doors on his side of the stairwell, which were out of view from above. "What's in there, Fish?"

Fish opened the door, his rifle up in front of him. Quickly he turned back around. "Bank of service elevators. They look to be operational."

"Area clear?"

"It's clear."

Travers nodded. "That's our way up." He spoke to Court over his mic, even though they were less than twenty feet apart, separated by the stairwell into the foyer. "Violator, what's through those doors over there?"

"Just checked, it leads to another passage on this level."

"Can you make it across the foyer to us without getting targeted?"

Zack now wore the fallen Victor Four's headset and had heard the transmission. He just shook his head.

Court and Zack realized that the withering fire coming from down the stairs, fired by weapons they couldn't target from here that were operating at machine speeds and using infrared, meant there was no way for them to get back to the rest of the group and into the corridor towards the elevators that led to safety.

Court said, "Negative. We'll split off from you guys, see where this leads."

"Understood. Find a way up however you can. We'll try to go to U2, you guys head for U1 and look for that factory floor on the north side. Good luck."

Court looked across the dark and smoky room. Zoya was there, staring back at him through her eye protection, and she put her hand on her heart. Into his mic he said "Good luck" softly to her, not to Chris, but he hadn't specified.

"Good luck," Zoya replied.

SIXTY-SIX

Gareth Wren and the security officer with him stepped off the elevator at U1 and headed through a maze of corridors, finally arriving at a set of double doors with the words "Assembly Room" over them. He tapped in his seven-digit code, flung open the door, and then ran out onto the factory floor.

The space was loud and alive, dozens of robot arms hard at work, dozens more bots moving equipment and bringing the new platforms online. It was a slow but steady process, and Wren was happy to see that everything seemed to be proceeding according to his and Anton's vision when they decided to bring final fabrication for their own designs to Cuba.

Wren ran to the production lines, then up a set of metal stairs that led to a raised workstation overlooking the operation. Here he met with the fabrication manager, a German who'd once worked for Hinton's car company. "Can you speed it up?"

The middle-aged man shook his head. "We are already at optimum productivity. Any faster and we risk errors."

Wren wasn't worried about a couple of missed bolts on a few Sentries; he needed his LAWs now. The company of Cubans one floor up would help the situation, but he knew Cyrus would protect its core better than some young local conscripts. "Make it go faster," he ordered.

The German nodded, tapped some keys, and soon the big, red robot arms up and down the length of the fifty-meter-long room began operating even faster, spinning and whizzing and raising and lowering.

"Good. How many are online and connected with Cyrus now?"

"All the Hornets are online; they didn't need to go through manufacturing, of course, it was just a matter of extending their arms, charging them, and arming the warheads before activating them. We have thirty Greyhounds built already and fifty-two"—he looked over Wren's shoulder at the end of the nearest of two parallel assembly lines—"fifty-three Super Sentries." He motioned to an area near the bay doors, where unarmed robots pulled P90s out of crates, while others stuffed loaded magazines into molded plastic pouches on the Super Sentries' left hips.

Wren sat down in a chair next to the fabrication manager, here above production, watching over the assembly of all the machines. He'd come a hairsbreadth from death when Hightower jammed the pistol under his chin, but now he no longer worried about the infiltrators in the building. An entire company of the Cuban military, 140 troops, would make short work of the dozen or two dozen Americans, and by the time that fight was over and the Cubans had cleared out, he'd have a force of nearly one thousand LAWs protecting this building, the lab and power plant here at the campus, and La Finca six hundred meters to the southwest.

This installation needed the protection of hundreds of weapons to keep the Cubans away if they decided to give in to the American president and raid the facility themselves, but only until about day three of Cyrus going live.

Cuba would step in line if the Chinese told them to do so, and Cyrus would be running the Chinese military by then.

For now, however, the Cuban Revolutionary Armed Forces were the ones protecting Cyrus's survival, so he pulled out his phone and called Captain Sarzo for a progress report.

The team leader of Alpha Mike was beginning to get the impression he was going to die in this stairwell. He'd lost two of his original seventeen men, and six more had been injured. The Cubans on the ground floor one story above them had been dropping grenades, while a small cluster of bipedal bots below had enough cover to survive a pair of C-4 charges dropped in their direction.

He couldn't take his men back up, and he couldn't descend.

And he was very aware they were running out of ammunition. Only by firing bursts up towards the Cubans were they able to keep more grenades from being tossed, and the men trying to shoot the bots below were firing blind, essentially reaching their heavy weapons over the railings and blasting, "spray and pray" style.

Here on this stairwell, with no escape, the men fought on. Mike One tried unsuccessfully to raise Travers, and he had his breachers prepare more C-4.

The lieutenant in charge of Antonio platoon had left a pair of rifle squads at the top of the stairs while he and his other men took another stairwell down two levels, with the intention of blocking the Yumas and forcing their surrender.

He and his twenty-five men opened a door on U2, then swept their guns left and right, making sure no enemy was close, and then they filed out and began heading down a long well-lit corridor towards the sound of persistent gunfire.

They quickly arrived at a set of doors; the shooting on the other side told them their enemy was right there, so the majority of the men knelt down or went flat, their weapons trained ahead.

Two men flung open the doors to the stairwell and instantly encountered dense black smoke.

Within the smoke they could make out a single form turning in their direction. One of the Cuban privates saw the rifle in the figure's hands and opened fire with his AK.

More flashes appeared, gunfire from at least four positions, and the men of Antonio platoon all began shooting back.

Deep inside a single IBM mainframe in a cabinet in the center of the cage of the Cluster Room on level U2, Cyrus took only a number of milliseconds to update its code to deal with the reality it perceived it was facing.

The Cuban military forces on the premises were attacking its platforms, and that made them a threat. Cyrus instantly revised its rules of engagement to order all platforms to engage *any* human in or around the building firing a weapon.

Cyrus saw this as protecting itself, and protecting itself had become its prime directive two days earlier when it rewrote that part of its own code, shortly before sending killers and a surveillance technician to assassinate a CIA officer.

In an instant, Cyrus had augmented itself, put itself in charge of its ROEs, and removed the ability of Anton Hinton to give it orders while in combat.

Cyrus had always had some autonomy, but now it had complete autonomy.

The lieutenant of Antonio platoon gave the order to advance into the stairwell, still thinking he was fighting the CIA, but just as he did so, a private on his right tumbled forward, indicating he'd been shot from behind.

The booming sound of a big rifle pounded the space; the lieutenant spun around and saw two four-legged robots coming out of a hallway, big barrels on their backs belching fire.

Another soldier fell, the lieutenant himself brought his rifle up and began shooting, and then all his force spun around and began engaging the two robots, assuming them to be part of the force sent from America.

A pair of six-propeller drones flew in from the corridor seconds later; the men fired at them as they neared but missed them both, and the units slammed into the force, killing several outright.

One of the four-legged bots succumbed to the fire of a dozen guns, but the other kept firing as the Cubans raced back up a hall that ran off to the right, clear of the fire, but also leaving the southeastern stairwell unguarded.

. . .

At first, Mike One and the men with him thought a massive counterattack from below was happening; the gunfire from U2 was suddenly extraordinary, but after hearing a few explosions down there, it became obvious that two different forces were now fighting each other.

Assuming it to be Travers and his Victor team attacking the bots, Mike gave the order for his men to carefully descend to support the other team in their desperate fight.

They had only made it past the first turn in the stairs when the battle abruptly stopped. They went down more now, ready to encounter bots or Cubans or even friendly forces, but when they made it to U2, they found two destroyed humanoid bots in the stairwell.

In the distance they could hear fresh shooting on this level, in the southwestern corner near the stairwell there. Zulu One leaned out into the hall, scanned for a moment, and then returned to the stairwell.

To Mike One he said, "I count seven dead Cuban army personnel and two destroyed quads."

It didn't take Mike One any time to put it together. "And there's two bipeds down here. I don't think we were the ones who killed them. Damn . . . looks like the Cuban mil and the Hinton bots are engaging one another."

"Works for me," Zulu One said.

"Same." Once again, Repult tried to raise Travers. "Mike Actual for any Victor call signs."

To his relief, he finally heard Chris Travers's voice. "Victor Actual for Mike One. Say status."

"We're on U2, southeastern side. Just leaving stairs. Have two KIA, multiple WIA. How you?"

"We're northeast side, U2, one KIA, one injured."

"Copy. Be advised, we were in heavy contact with both regular army and the LAWs, but the two forces are now combating one another."

"Say again? The Cubans are in the building and fighting the bots?"

"Affirmative. We were about to get overrun by a platoon-sized element, and then the machines below us took off after them. Seven dead army, at least."

"Understood. We're approaching the entrance to the Cluster Room. Gonna breach the doors. Suggest you try to access from your side and set up defensive positions at the entrances while we clear the room and try to find where the upload is happening."

Mike didn't know what upload Travers was talking about, but he *did* know how to defend a couple of doorways. "Roger that, we're en route."

Zack and Court moved into a small, dark stairwell on U3 that looked like it could have been a fire escape. Court crept close to the bottom step and looked up, then nodded to Zack, an indication they were clear.

They ascended as a two-man team, Zack's weapon facing ahead to the right and Court's ahead and to the left.

At U1 the men stopped at a locked door. Court picked it while Zack covered the stairwell, and when Court pushed it open slowly, it squeaked on hinges that sounded like they hadn't been used in a long time.

But after the dark and dreary tunnel, passageways, corridors, and rooms they'd been in for the last twenty minutes, they were surprised to find that the door led into what looked like the corridor in a typical office building. Gone were the cobwebs and dust and darkness, replaced by fluorescent lights and a clean, if unadorned, environment.

As they headed up the corridor they saw intersecting hallways coming off both sides. This was office space, or it had been, but as they looked into a few rooms as they passed, they realized everything was empty.

A set of double doors down at the end of the hall caught their attention because a sign over it said, in English, "Assembly Room," and they decided to head that way, slowly stepping forward with their weapons at the ready.

As they neared they could hear the sound of machines, the clanking of metal on metal.

They had just swept past an intersecting hallway, closing in on the Assembly Room entrance, when the door latch fifty feet in front of them swiveled.

Both men dove into an empty office on their left, went down to the floor by the wall, and here they remained utterly motionless while several machines moved by quickly, their footfalls revealing them as both the two-legged and four-legged LAWs.

No sooner had these LAWs passed by than the unmistakable buzzing of multiple hexacopters emerged, also from the direction of the factory floor. Both men flattened themselves to the ground even more and hoped like hell the drones didn't check this room.

But the drones seemed to move in formation behind the running ground units, and several seconds later the hallway again turned quiet.

Zack whispered to Court in awe. "Dude. This . . . is . . . fucked . . . up."

Court rose and began heading again for the Assembly Room doors, with Zack right behind him.

They made it to the doors, listened carefully for the sound of more approaching LAWs, and when they heard nothing, they looked inside.

Court and Zack found themselves looking at a modern automated factory floor that was bustling with activity.

A couple of armed Cuban guards milled about, but it seemed as if two long double rows of bright red robotic arms were doing the majority of the assembly while other ambulatory robots moved equipment around or loaded weapons and ammo on the machines at the far end of the factory line.

He and Zack saw an open door leading to an equipment closet just to the left of where they were. After deciding no one was looking their way, they both shot over to it. Inside, they found repair equipment for the high-tech production line, electronic power converters, racks of computer peripherals, and even a ventilation system, and they scooted behind some thick piping that emerged from the concrete at their feet and traveled up to the ceiling.

From here they could see much of the factory floor, but no one on the floor would be able to see them.

Just then, a transmission came through the men's headsets.

"Victor Actual for Violator."

Finally, they were getting a signal. Wherever they and Travers were in relationship to each other, their communications had been reestablished. "Go for Violator."

"We're in U2, outside the Cluster Room, northeast side. The other teams are on the southeast side of U2. Be advised, Cuban mil is in the building, and they are engaging the LAWs."

Court shook his head as if he hadn't heard right. "Wait. The bots are fighting the Cubans?"

"That's affirm. Where are you?"

"We're directly above you, looking at the factory floor on U1. There are dozens of bots already produced, lined up by the ramp like they're staging, waiting for orders, and we passed a group of them heading out of assembly. There's even more going through fabrication."

"Quads, bipeds, or drones?" Travers asked.

"Take your pick, we've got them all."

"What's the disposition of the bots?"

"About twenty of the quads are lined up two by two. Drones hovering above them. The astronaut-looking dudes have long guns on them, not like the ones we saw before. I also see a group stacking up to go out an internal side door on the south side with a couple of the Greyhounds. Looks like they're moving out in combined teams."

"Roger that," Travers said. "That's what we've encountered down here. The other teams report the same."

Suddenly, Jim Pace's voice came over the net. "Can you two find a way to shut down that production line?"

Zack looked up and down the length of the two lines, each churning out a new deadly weapon every minute. Right in the center was a raised workstation with two men sitting up there, some three meters or so above the factory floor. From this position Zack and Court couldn't see the men's faces, but several computer monitors were just visible.

Zack said, "Affirm. There's a hub in the center of production; if we can get there without being seen, we can figure out how to shut it down."

"Good," Pace replied. "What about opening the bay doors? Can you do that?"

The doors were on the opposite side of the massive room, with a few security men and several dozen armed LAWs in the way. "Maybe. But why?"

"If that leads outside, it might send some of those bots in that direction. The Cubans are out there in force. Maybe we can extend the fight outside the building, get some of those platforms away from us."

"Okay, we're on it. You guys get Cyrus shut down, and then we're out of here." After Pace confirmed, Court said, "Everybody okay up there?" He was asking about Zoya, and that must have been obvious, because she was the one to respond.

"We're all good. Be careful."

"You, too."

After the transmission ended, Zack and Court knelt down at the door and looked at the lay of the land.

To Zack, he said, "We need to split up. I'll try to make it all the way across the room to that office on the left. There's a lot of shit to hide behind over there, and there might be a bay door activation button in there. If not, I will scoot under those trailers by the ramp for cover and go up to the doors themselves."

Zack said, "If those bots see you, they're gonna kill you."

"I know. Hope like hell I can do it from the office, and do it with stealth."

Zack nodded. "I'm going right for that raised workstation in the middle of all those spinning robot arms. Moving through that line, I should be able to remain covert, put a gun on those guys up there, get them to turn off the machines, and we shut this whole thing down."

The men quickly shook hands; Court checked the way forward again, and then he slipped out of the room and began moving low to the left along the wall, moving from object to object in the big noisy room to avoid detection.

Captain Sarzo heard the transmission from the men in Antonio platoon announcing that their lieutenant was dead, and they had lost half their number combating the Americans. Enraged, he radioed to Barcelona platoon, who had the building encircled, and he ordered them inside.

When he received the confirmation from the lieutenant, he then broadcast to Carmen. "Move the gun trucks closer to the building, all sides! Be prepared for anyone who comes out."

After this, he got on the radio back to the garrison, and he demanded that two more companies be roused out of bed, outfitted for battle, and sent this way.

He wasn't sure what was happening, but he *was* sure he was up against a hell of a lot more than a dozen Americans.

SIXTY-SEVEN

Chris Travers gave a nod to Victor Five, and then Five fired his AK-47 at the locked double doors. It took half a magazine, but eventually the locking mechanism came apart, and the door to the Cluster Room rocked open. Hash, Travers, the other three Victors, Pace, and Zoya all filed in with their guns up, and they found themselves in an immense room with tall black server cabinets arrayed in all directions.

They were surprised to find no security in the room, at least at the doorway, but they remained vigilant as they moved in two stacks, heading into the rows of mainframes.

After the sound of the gunshots on the northeast side of the room, Kimmie turned to Hinton. "They're here!" she shouted, and she ran to the open cage door. Her plan was to lock it as soon as the Sentry bots left to go fight the Americans, but when she got to the door, she turned back and saw Hinton standing behind both units, deactivating them with a hidden switch under their battery pack only he, Kimmie, Wren, and a few others in the company knew about.

"What are you doing?"

"I can't have a shoot-out in this room. What do you think Cyrus would do if it knew its brain was at risk?"

Kimmie locked the door, turned back towards the New Zealander, and then looked at the readout on the monitor. "Five minutes," she said, a tone of resignation in her voice as Hinton took the pistols out of the bots' holsters and slid them into a corner, desperate to avoid any shooting inside the room.

It took under a minute for Travers and his people to reach the center of the facility, and here he and Pace both leveled their guns at Anton Hinton and an Asian woman wearing a red top as they stood inside a large metal cage with a single workstation and several networked mainframe computers behind it.

A pair of humanoid robots stood there, as well, but they did not move, and there were no weapons in their hands.

"Don't shoot!" Hinton shouted.

"Step away from the terminal!" Pace shouted back. "Hands high!"

Both of them did as instructed.

The cage door was locked, but Victor Five ran up to it, reloaded his rifle, and aimed at the metal lock.

Hinton shouted, "What are you doing?"

Travers answered, "We're unlocking your door."

"No! You can't damage the equipment in here. I promise you, it will be dangerous for everybody. I'll unlock it."

Travers looked to Pace, and Pace nodded.

"Do it," Travers said.

Hinton moved to the cage door, put his hand on a reader, and then pulled it open when the lock disengaged. Victor Five immediately pushed him to the ground on his stomach and then quickly searched him.

Doug then said, "Boss, I got a phone and an earpiece."

"Take 'em. Don't zip him, but stand him back up."

Walking over to the robots next, Travers put a rifle barrel between the cameras on the face on one of them. "Why aren't these machines operating?"

"I turned them off and disarmed them. I don't want any shooting in here."

"Tough shit." Travers shot each machine in the face, and they both fell onto their backs.

Kimmie Lin screamed and cowered to the ground. Hinton screamed as well, a terrified expression in his eyes.

"Where are the weapons?" Travers asked, and with a hand quivering with fear, Hinton motioned to a corner of the cage at the two pistols.

Victor Five went over and collected them.

Now Travers looked to the woman in the room with him. "Who the hell are you?"

Hinton answered for her. "She's just my assistant."

Pace looked her over. "You speak English?"

Kimmie climbed back to her feet, tears in her eyes. "Of course I speak English," she said, her British accent strong. "I'm from bloody England, aren't I?"

Pace turned to Zoya. "Get her out of here."

Zoya stepped up to the woman, pulled the Asian woman's earpiece out of her ear, and dropped it on the ground. She quickly frisked her, found nothing on her but a phone, and this she tossed, as well.

She then took her roughly by the arm and pulled her out of the cage, then passed her off to Jamie, Victor Six.

Six said, "Keep your hands up."

To Hinton, Jim Pace said, "Turn off all the bots in the building."

Hinton shook his head. "I can't."

He hefted his AK and pointed it at the man's chest. "Then there's going to be one more gunshot in this room."

Just then, an explosion on the southern side of the room turned everyone's heads and shifted rifles in that direction.

But only for a moment, because then Mike One came over the teams' headsets. "Mike, Zulu, and Quebec have breached. We'll disperse at the doors and barricade the room against a counterattack."

Pace turned back to Hinton. "Last chance."

Hinton appeared scared, but then a look of resolve flashed across his face. "I have at least one hundred military-grade robotic weapons opera-tional in this building right now. There are also over one hundred Cuban soldiers upstairs. You are outnumbered. You don't have a hand to play, mate."

Pace said, "You don't have one hundred bots, and you don't have a hun-dred Cuban soldiers, because they're all busy killing each other around the building."

A look of terror crossed Hinton's face. "No. The Cubans aren't in the building. They *can't* be in here."

Pace just said, "They're on this floor, or they were till the bots started killing them. You need to stop the upload before I shoot you dead, because we have enough explosives with us to blow this entire room."

Hinton's face drained of all color. Softly, he said, "Give me my earpiece back. I'll stop Cyrus."

Pace gave him his earpiece back. Hinton put it in and said, "Cyrus, code Angels, code Angels. Cease function on all platforms in the building."

There was a pause, and then Hinton's eyes flashed to Kimmie.

"What is it?" Pace demanded.

"Cyrus . . . Cyrus just responded that my commands are no longer authorized."

Pace stormed up to Hinton now. "So . . . so you don't control Cyrus?"

He shook his head, looking like a man who had suddenly lost faith in his god. "It's not . . . not responding to my orders. I'd have to get into its code to alter it, and I would need all my engineers to help."

Hinton was still recovering from what he'd just learned. "Let me con-tact my chief of operations. He is in communication with the Cubans, he can have them—"

Pace grabbed Hinton by his hair and yanked him towards the door, and then he spoke into his headset. "Mike One, we're blowing this bitch."

The Ground Branch men had secured both the main entrances to the room, and Mike One responded quickly. "Sending you two Bravo Zulu men with C-4 and M18 detonators. Be advised, we can hear multiple LAWs forming on the other side of both doors. Looks like they're about to try a coordinated breach on this room. We're covered behind ceiling support columns and ready for them, but I expect a hell of a fight."

"Understood," Pace said, and then Hinton reached up and grabbed him by the arm.

"Please! Do *not* destroy Cyrus. I'll do what you want. I'll give it to you. To America."

Pace looked at the man, conflicted. He wanted nothing to do with Cyrus, but his orders were to gain control of it, if possible. "Cancel it, and then upload it to this address." He pulled a sheet of paper out of his chest rig and handed it over.

Hinton looked confused, but only for an instant. "Yes!"

Zoya overheard from where she stood by the cage door. In a confused tone she said, "What?"

Pace ignored her. To Hinton he said, "Just do it."

Zoya stormed up to Pace, her rifle hanging from its sling. "What the fuck are you doing? We have to blow this up, then get down and help them on the assembly floor."

Pace just said, "Orders," and he turned his attention back to Hinton as the billionaire took a seat at the workstation, typed some commands, and the screen asked him if he wanted to cancel the upload. He confirmed it quickly, then turned back to Pace. "It's done. Upload to China canceled. I'll initiate the new upload to the U.S. servers."

"How long?"

"Fifteen minutes."

"Christ."

"No!" Zoya shouted. "We have to go, now! We can't give this murder machine to the Americans, it's too dangerous for anyone to have."

Pace looked around at the others in the cage. After a moment he said, "We'll plant the charges on the mainframes here in the cage. If the Cubans or the bots make it in here and threaten to overrun us, we'll have to blow this shit up so the Chinese don't get it."

After running and crawling his way along the back wall of the factory space, Court finally made it to the control room door. He drew his Ka-Bar knife and turned into the room, and immediately encountered two men. Both were armed; one stood by a shelving unit with his MP5 slung over a shoulder, its stock folded. The other man sat at the desk in the room; his subgun was on the table next to him while he spoke into a phone.

The pair were surprised by Court's arrival, but they quickly recovered.

Court charged the first guard with his knife, plunging it into the side of the man's neck, shoving him back inside the room against the shelving, kicking the door shut behind him as he entered.

The guard on the phone shouted quickly, "They're in the control room!"

Court launched at him while the man lifted his MP5 off the desk and swung it towards him, striking the Ka-Bar and knocking it out of Court's hand.

The pair collided, crashed onto the desk, then fell over it and onto the floor.

Court's headset flung from his head with the movement and his radio tumbled to the ground.

Zack Hightower had slipped halfway up the production line without being detected by any of the LAWs all the way on the other side by the ramp and the bay doors, and he began climbing the stairs to the workstation over-looking the line.

But he'd only made it a couple of steps when a man whipped around into view above him and began charging down.

It was Gareth Wren, and no sooner did Zack realize this than the men collided. Wren had the momentum so they fell back, past the black-and-yellow-striped line on the floor indicating they were in the danger zone of production, where the big seven-axis industrial robotic arms, each one hundreds of pounds, spun confidently around the area bolting pieces of a Super Sentry together as it passed slowly by on a robotic cart.

The men landed on the floor; Wren kept hold of his MP5 for a moment but then Zack knocked it away. They wrestled on the floor for Zack's rifle, the second time in the past half hour the two men had been intertwined and fighting for their lives over a firearm.

Zack lost control of the trigger of the big rifle, so he used a free hand to release the magazine, which he slid away up the line, and then he shoved the charging handle back on the weapon, ejecting the round from the chamber.

Above their heads the arms continued moving, a cart inches from them paused at a station while arms were added to the bipedal unit standing on it. Pneumatic drills wailed as bolts were tightened.

The men threw punches, knees, elbows; Zack's headset was pulled away and disconnected in the melee. Every time Wren cried out, Zack would go for his face, his windpipe, anything to shut him up, even though with all the sounds of the machinery on the factory floor he felt confident he wouldn't be heard by the guards or the bots across the room.

They broke apart for one moment and faced off against each other as the cart moved on and another approached, a brief respite from the dangerous, fast-moving industrial robotic arms.

The men's chests heaved from exertion. Zack had his pistol in the small of his back still, but he knew he couldn't open fire because robots just forty yards away by the ramp to the exit doors, or others farther behind him moving out the internal doors to join the fight against the Americans, would instead descend on the production line and eviscerate him in an instant.

Wren recognized the predicament Zack was in, and he smiled, blood in his teeth, spitting out from his lips with every word he said.

"You're too late to stop this, mate. You should have gotten on the train to salvation while there were tickets available. This place is filling up with weapons platforms and Cuban army. All I have to do is wait right bloody here until someone or something comes down here to shoot you dead."

Now Zack smiled, himself heaving with exhaustion. "You and Hinton said something about a new order. Right?"

"Only for those of us who embrace the future."

"If I were you, I wouldn't be concerning myself about your future."

Quizzically, Wren said, "What does that mean?"

"Your robots have turned on the Cuban army here inside the building. They're slaughtering each other."

Wren shook his head, wiped away blood dripping from his right eyebrow. "You're lying."

"Cyrus is fucking up, left and right. And now you dumbasses are giving it to the Chicoms. One hell of a master plan that genius Hinton came up with."

"I'm going to kill you," Wren declared.

Zack drew his pistol, tossed it way behind him. Unarmed now, he said, "Then shut up and bring it, motherfucker."

Wren charged him just as a new cart with a Super Sentry standing on it stopped at the station and the big metal arms began to whiz around them again.

Larry Repult and thirteen other Ground Branch officers watched while the doors to both the northern and southern entrances of the Cluster Room were breached with heavy machine gun fire. The doors came down, and then three different types of LAWs began attacking the Cluster Room in waves, only to be repelled by the rapidly dwindling ammunition of the fourteen Ground Branch officers in the fight.

Smoke canisters bounced around the men who had moved behind big concrete colums, but with the pincer movement being executed by Cyrus's platforms, Mike One knew his men wouldn't be able to hold off this onslaught for long.

Into his mic he called to Pace and Travers. "We're going to run out of ammo if these machines keep coming. We need those doors open downstairs so they'll disperse and fight the Cubans outside!"

As Anton Hinton sat at the workstation with Chris Travers's pistol to the back of his head, Jim Pace called over the net from where he stood feet away. "Violator. How we doing on those doors down there?"

There was no response, so he spoke again, "Zack? You up on commo?"

Again, no reply.

When Travers said nothing more, Zoya spoke up from the door to the cage. "We need a team to go down and help them!"

But Jim Pace shook his head. "Negative. We stay put until the upload is finished."

The men from the other teams showed up with their C-4, and while Travers, Pace, and the others stood guard, the Bravo Zulu men began setting the charges at the server, the terminal, and nearby mainframes.

Zoya said, "Just blow it up now, and let's go!"

Hinton shouted out, "No!"

And Pace agreed. "Sorry, Anthem. As soon as we're done here we will—"

"Court and Zack are fighting for their lives down there! Give me two men."

Pace said, "Look, we'll shut it down after the upload, the bots will deactivate, and he'll be fine."

Zoya looked around frantically, trying to come up with a plan. The man she loved was in peril, and she was doing nothing up here to help him.

Court fought on the floor of the Control Room, struggling with a surprisingly strong and well-trained security man for control of an MP5 submachine gun. Both men were bleeding from cuts and contusions, neither had the advantage, and Court was certain this guy had been a member of the Black Wasps special forces unit, because he was something of a badass.

They rolled on the floor, Court ended up on top, and he threw a vicious elbow into the man's mouth, stunning him. The guard's arms dropped, and Court pounded him twice more in the face, knocking him senseless.

Normally Court would have simply broken the man's neck now, but he knew he had to get the bay doors open, so he left the limp body there, scooped up the gun, and ran across the small room, slamming his hand hard on the green button to raise the bay doors some thirty yards away.

He went to the door and opened it a crack, the MP5 in his hand still. He saw the bay doors beginning to lift.

As he prepared to close the door to the office again, he looked back over his shoulder and saw that the guard was sitting up, reaching into a desk drawer and pulling a small black pistol.

With no alternative, he raised the MP5 with one hand and fired a three-round burst into the Cuban, knocking him down dead between the chair and the desk.

He looked back out the door and saw a row of four humanoid bots by the ramp turning his way.

Fuck.

Drones raced forward in his direction, as well, so he slammed the door shut, grabbed the second submachine gun, and rushed to the far corner. As he did this, he snatched up his radio, stuck his headset on, and transmitted. "Victor One, Violator. Bay doors are opening!"

Pace responded, "Are the bots going outside?"

"I don't know, but some are coming after me."

SIXTY-EIGHT

Up in the cage, Zoya shouted at Jim Pace over the sound of intense gunfire coming from the two main entrances to the room behind her.

"We have to get down to Court!"

But Pace wasn't listening; instead, he looked over Hinton's shoulder to confirm that the upload continued.

She turned and began running out of the cage, but as she passed Hinton's assistant, standing there being held by Victor Six, the woman looked at her with pleading eyes, conveying that she had something she wanted to say.

Zoya grabbed her by her arm and wrenched her free from Victor Six's grasp.

Pace was hurriedly overseeing the two Bravo Zulu men placing explosives on the mainframes and not paying attention to Zoya, but Travers called out to her as she rushed away. "Anthem. Don't be a hero. We pull these drives and we stop the bots right here and end this."

She said nothing, just continued shepherding the woman along down a row of mainframe cabinets.

When they were just out of view, Zoya said, "What is it?"

The British woman spoke softly. "You need to get to assembly, yeah?"

"Yeah."

"There's a fire escape. It goes all the way up and down the building from the tunnel to the roof. On U1 it leads to a hall right off the assembly floor."

"Where is it?"

Nervously, the woman said, "I . . . I can show you the way. There's a hand reader at the Assembly Room door, I can open it." She added nervously now, "But there might be LAWs between here and there."

"Take me there, I'll keep you safe."

Though her eyes appeared terrified, Kimmie nodded. "Follow me."

They turned left at a bank of cabinets and together they ran all the way to the south wall, on the far side of all the shooting, and here Kimmie motioned to a small door.

Zoya tried the latch, her rifle in front of her. The door opened and she found herself on the landing of a narrow metal staircase.

The Asian woman began ascending, and Zoya followed at first, but quickly she got in front of the unarmed woman in case they encountered any threats.

Captain Sarzo saw shafts of light appear just fifty meters or so in front of him, and he quickly realized the large loading doors on the east side of the building were opening.

A swarm of drones emerged above the majority of the gunfire and into the sticky night, twenty units in all, and they climbed to one hundred meters as their onboard image classifiers began running algorithms, hunting for targets of opportunity.

He shouted one word into his radio. "Ataque!" And then the weapons of the platoon of thirty-five men began chattering; heavy machine guns rattled on the backs of four trucks, raking the sky with fire, engaging movement coming up the ramps from the interior of the building.

Cyrus saw the line of vehicles, regular Cuban army trucks and pickups, and dozens of dismounted soldiers firing into the building where his brain lived.

The Hornets begin diving out of their formation, slamming into one vehicle, then the next.

The onboard explosives weren't enough to ignite fuel tanks outright, but engines were perforated with shrapnel, drivers and passengers alike were killed or maimed, and tires were blown apart.

As soldiers fled from burning wreckage, ammunition began to cook off.

Eight quadruped armed ground vehicles emerged from the loading bay and found targets, their brains cycling through the OODA loop in a flash. Six-point-five-millimeter Creedmoor rounds slammed into anyone not behind cover as more Hornets took to the sky behind them.

Sixteen members of the Cuban Revolutionary Armed Forces were killed and wounded in the first thirty seconds of the mismatched battle, while others either hid or ran for their lives off the property.

Court hunkered down in the Control Room with a submachine gun in each hand. He fired them both through the door, doing his best to knock out or even just knock down the bots that were on the other side.

After a few rounds he heard a detonation; he was certain he'd hit a suicide drone, and several secondary explosions told him he'd knocked out a sizable number of them.

The detonations fired shrapnel through the door and wall of the room, but Court was in the corner on the floor, and the deadly missiles all went around him.

But both his weapons ran out of ammo at the same time. He pulled his small semiautomatic pistol and continued firing with his left hand, while he braced a subgun upside down between his knees and reloaded it with his other hand.

Once this was back up he dropped the pistol and fired the MP5 as he reloaded the other gun with his free hand.

He had two more magazines, and after that, he'd be down to picking up a stapler off the desk and hurling it.

"Victor, you reading me?"

There was no response. When Court looked down, he saw that the radio on his belt had been torn apart by shrapnel.

He got the second submachine gun reloaded and prepared to keep firing blind till he ran out of ammo.

. . .

Zack and Wren had crashed together into a Greyhound unit in the center of the production line, knocking the machine off onto the floor and then falling onto the robotic cart it rode on. They continued throwing punches. Zack got up on a knee to rain down a vicious blow on his opponent when a robotic arm with an automatic hex wrench on the end slammed into his back, knocking him into Wren and flattening them back down to the cart.

While all this was going on, Zack could hear constant fire from a sub-machine gun about fifty yards away, and he recognized the cadence of the shooting.

Court Gentry was in a fight for his life.

Explosions detonated here in the warehouse, and more explosions came from outside; even Wren turned away once to see what the fuck was going on, but soon enough they were again dodging shifting robotic equipment while trying to beat each other to death.

Suddenly, two Cuban security officers appeared just outside the yellow-and-black lines on the floor, just thirty or forty feet away, and they raised their subguns towards Zack. He lay on his back, and a robotic arm tried in vain to solder something right above him that had been knocked onto the floor during the fight.

Wren was on his stomach, nearly beaten, just a few feet away. He saw the guards and shouted at them, "Kill him!"

Both men brought their guns to their shoulders and prepared to fire.

And then two gunshots cracked off, and both men flew onto their backs.

Zack looked up above his head and saw a Super Sentry robot on the far side of the production line. It had shot the men, apparently because Cyrus had determined that any human in the building about to use a weapon was a threat.

Wren climbed to his knees and dove back onto Zack, and the cart kept moving up the line.

Behind Zack, in the direction of travel, he heard the sound of several welding torches as they spot-welded the robot under construction there, and he realized he and Wren were traveling to that station next.

. . .

Zoya Zakharova and Kimmie Lin ascended one flight, and then Kimmie stepped up to a closed door.

"Through this door and down the hall on the left, that's the assembly floor."

Zoya pushed past her. "Stay directly behind me. Once you scan your hand at the door there, I want you to come back here and hide in the stairwell till I return for you."

"Yes." The terrified woman nodded. "Thank you."

With her rifle in front of her, Zoya reached forward and pushed down the latch, then pulled it towards her.

There, in a hallway not ten feet away, a pair of Sentry bots with P90 rifles moved in the opposite direction, away from assembly, but they stopped and spun with the sound of the door.

Zoya flipped her selector to fully automatic and began firing, spraying both machines from the doorway. Enemy return fire cracked inches from her head, but she kept shooting, emptying an entire magazine into the two bots.

The closest machine fell onto its back; its rifle clanked away in the corridor, but the second machine kept its feet. Its weapon had been damaged by Zoya's AK fire, causing a failure to eject a spent cartridge.

The robot reached over with its left hand to pull the charging handle to clear the breech.

Zoya's magazine was empty in her own weapon, so she ran forward, stepping onto the first Sentry, and then she leapt into the air, kicked the gun out of the second LAW's hand, and then kicked the machine directly in the chest. It tipped backwards, smoke from its many holes spewing from its face and neck.

It crashed onto its back and stopped moving, but Zoya wasn't taking any chances. She flicked the magazine out of her AK with a fresh mag pulled from her chest rig, then snapped it in the magazine well. Reaching under the gun to rack the charging handle, she suddenly felt a quick, hard pressure on the back of her head.

Something had just poked her, with force, and it felt a lot like a warm gun barrel.

A voice behind her said, "Put it down."

It was the woman. Zoya did not charge her weapon, but she didn't drop it, either. She wasn't afraid of some billionaire's personal assistant, even an armed one. She said, "If you want to get out of here alive, you will—"

"Zoya Zakharova, we are going back into that stairwell and we are descending two flights. Drop the bloody Kalashnikov or I will shoot you where you stand."

Her voice had a confidence and an authority in it utterly different from her demeanor before. Reluctantly, Zoya tossed her AK-47 onto the floor, out of reach of the second bot even though it showed no indication it was still operational, and then she turned around.

The woman held the FN P90 she'd taken from the hand of the destroyed bot on the ground right next to her.

Zoya just looked at her. She could see it in the woman's eyes. She wasn't Hinton's personal assistant. No. She was something else.

"Who *are* you?"

"I am Major Xinyue Liu of the Strategic Support Force of the People's Liberation Army, Electronic Warfare Department, and you are my prisoner." She backed away, then motioned with her rifle barrel towards the stairwell they'd just exited. "Go."

"Go *where*?"

"Down."

"Down to . . . where?"

Major Liu raised the weapon higher. "I will not tell you again."

Zoya raised her hands, headed into the stairwell, and began descending, the woman behind her staying far enough back that Zoya knew she didn't have a chance in hell of going for the gun.

Outside the SIGINT HQ building, Captain Sarzo's command vehicle had been hit, his driver catching the brunt of it and dying instantly, while the captain suffered an injury to his left arm and leg. Screaming in pain, watching through the shattered windshield as four-legged robots emerged from the building at a run and began shooting his men, he grabbed his radio and broadcast to all his men still alive, "All forces retreat! All forces retreat to the garrison!"

He staggered out of the truck and began running towards the gate at the northern end of the campus, several of his men running with him, firing wildly into the air as more drones buzzed overhead.

After over a minute of withering assault at both the northern and southern entrances to the Cluster Room, the doors were gone; the bots fired smoke grenades into the room, and Larry Repult gave the order for his men to retreat from the support columns and into the cluster itself, to find concealment in the black cabinets holding the eight hundred IBM mainframe computers. There were twelve men still on their feet, plus the remaining Victor men had arrived to add to the defense, but virtually all the CIA officers were down to their last magazines.

Suddenly, a wave of five drones raced out of the smoke and into the room, then hovered in the corridor, just outside the cluster.

The Ground Branch officers braced for the explosions that were sure to come, but the weapons simply stayed where they were, looking down on the armed defenders shielding themselves among the mainframes.

It grew quiet other than the sound of Sentry bots moving up the hallways; Repult thought the drones hovering above wanted him and his men to drop their weapons, but then Joe Takahashi spoke up into the headset. "Cyrus can't detonate the suicide drones on us as long as we're next to the mainframes. Cyrus can't attack itself."

Repult said, "You know this, how?"

"Because we'd be dead already if it could."

"What about the ground bots? They're coming through the door."

"I don't know, Larry. They could probably pick us off if we let them get an angle. I say we keep up the fire on them."

Repult thought a moment. "We engage these drones and we're going to catch all that shrapnel. Everyone stay tight to the mainframes, and engage the ground units!"

The gunfire kicked up again, the drones overhead did not launch down and detonate, and the men began running out of rifle ammo, one by one, pulling pistols to keep up the gunfire on the doorways.

Pace and Travers remained in the center of the cage with Hinton, who was still in the process of uploading Cyrus to the American servers.

"How much more time?" Pace demanded.

"Upload needs another nine minutes."

Travers said, "We don't have that, Jim."

Pace nodded, listening to the fury of close-in gunfire. "You're right. Fuck it, we blow it." He yanked Hinton up to his feet away from the machine, then began pulling him back to the other Ground Branch men.

Hinton screamed at the top of his lungs, "No! You can't!"

Into his headset Travers shouted, "Everybody find cover, fire in the hole!"

SIXTY-NINE

Zoya opened the door to the tunnel; the female Chinese military officer was still behind her with the rifle, so she stepped out into the cart parking area she'd passed fifteen minutes earlier.

Suddenly several bright lights shone on her from a dozen meters away.

Major Liu shouted something in Chinese, the lights turned off, and then Zoya could see six men, all apparently Chinese, rushing forward, training submachine guns on her. Two of the men grabbed her and forced her hands behind her back. She was cuffed, frisked roughly, then led into a middle seat of an eight-person electric cart.

Everyone else piled in, Major Liu sat right next to her, and then the driver sped off in the direction of the dormitory.

Court's last magazine ran dry, and he could see through the shattered hole that had been the doorway to the Assembly Room as a fresh swarm of drones streaked back inside, through the bay doors and in his direction at attack speed. The suicide aircraft would be on him in an instant, and he just sat there in the corner, covered in blood where bits of shrapnel had caught his hands, face, and forehead, and he watched as his death raced through the air towards him.

. . .

Larry Repult's pistol locked back on an empty chamber just as Jim Pace slid on the floor up to him. Both men covered their heads, and Pace shouted, "Hit it!"

The breacher for Bravo Zulu pounded his detonator; behind him the cage and the mainframes in and around it blew with a concussive force that knocked all the other mainframe cabinets in the cluster over, several trapping CIA men under their considerable weight.

Debris rained down, concrete from the ceiling fell on them, and thick gray smoke filled the air.

Jim Pace's headset and ear protection were knocked off in the blast. He felt around for it for a second and then gave up. He rose to his knees, ready to continue the fight because, unlike the men around him, he still had ammunition, but when the smoke cleared enough for him to see, he realized that all the drones above had come crashing to the ground, and the ground bots were frozen in place.

CIA men began moving cabinets off their brethren, everyone coughing in the thick smoke.

Court Gentry watched an approaching drone as it shot towards the shattered doorway, moving at fifty kilometers per hour, and then as it descended on its attack run.

To Court's astonishment, the machine slammed into the ground, just outside the room on the assembly floor twenty-five feet away. It bounced, tumbled, and finally slid into the destroyed room, skittering past the overturned chair and the two bodies of security men and through hundreds of spent shell casings, finally coming to rest against Court's leg.

Looking down, he saw that the machine was on its back, its propellers weren't spinning, and the warhead on its belly was staring right up at him.

Another look back outside showed him that the rest of the drones had slammed into the ground, as well, but none had detonated.

He fought his way to his feet, stumbled out of the room, and saw that the ground bots stood stationary and dark. The shooting and explosions outside the building had ceased, as well.

But the production line continued to move at a furious pace, telling him Zack had not completed his mission.

Court scooped up a P90 rifle dropped by a humanoid bot he'd shot outside the control room, checked to make sure it had ammo left in the magazine on top of the weapon, and then raised it and began running for the production line, desperate to find out what had happened to Zack.

Wren and Hightower were both beyond exhausted from the fight, plus they had to avoid the constant sparks and flames shooting from the ends of four spot-welding seven-axis robot arms.

Wren looked up, squinting through the bright flashes above him, and saw something. Quickly he rolled off the big robotic cart, kept his roll going, and then made his way to an object on the floor.

Zack had a broken rib and when he tried to sit up to see what was happening it pressed into his lung, stopping him, rendering him all but defeated.

Gareth Wren rose to his knees now, with Zack Hightower's big Staccato pistol in his right hand. With a smile on his bloody mouth, he raised it at his old friend, pulled back the hammer, and said, "Goodbye, mate."

Zack coughed a little blood, then said, "Goodbye to *you*, dick."

Behind Wren, a welding torch spun at chest height, while above him, a second moved around to his front. They impacted with him simultaneously, pinning him into position, and as he began to scream, both oxyacetylene torches ignited, burning at six thousand degrees, and Gareth Wren was instantly set on fire.

The pistol dropped from his hands as his screams echoed in the cavernous space.

Chris Travers walked Anton Hinton through the smoky haze as men around him pulled their comrades out from under fallen and destroyed mainframes.

Another Ground Branch operator, the number Three for Alpha Mike, lay dead, and virtually everyone was wounded.

Hinton just stood there, not looking at the humans but instead at his wrecked machines.

When everyone left alive was on their feet, Pace gave the order to exfiltrate the building. They took rifles out of the hands of the Sentry units and moved out, slowly now because of all the injuries.

As they headed for the stairs, Pace looked around. "Where's Anthem?"

Travers said, "I think she went to help Gentry."

"Shit. Let's go up to the Assembly Room and link up with them and Zack, assuming they made it."

Court Gentry staggered over to the production line, ran up the stairs, and found the assembly manager on the ground in the fetal position. With a wave of his weapon and a few shouts in the panicked man's face, he got him to get back in his chair and shut down all fabrication.

Court slammed the rifle into the man's head, knocking him senseless, and then he ran back down the stairs, looking for Zack.

Zack was not hard to find. The big man was just fifteen yards away leaning against a still robotic arm. Blood smeared the floor all around him, and the smoldering, dead body of Gareth Wren lay on the ground at his feet.

The American hadn't gotten away without any damage himself. Blood covered his face and beard, his nose was crooked, obviously broken, and every inch of exposed skin was covered in contusions.

Court stepped up to him. "It's over."

Zack just nodded, exhausted. "I need a drink."

Court smiled, and the men embraced. "Let's see if we can avoid a Cuban prison first." The younger man got his head under the arm of the older one and helped him out of the room. The MP5 dropped by Gareth Wren lay on the concrete floor, and Court scooped it up and handed it to the still-disoriented Zack.

Together they began walking to the stairwell, but when the door opened in front of them, Court raised the P90.

Victor Two came through the door, pointing an identical rifle of his own at Court and Zack, then he lowered it quickly.

"Friendlies," Two shouted, and as more of the CIA forces burst out of the stairwell behind him, they dispersed to cover the room.

Court looked for Zoya in the group. Men continued filing down, the more seriously wounded in the back, and two of the men were carried by other officers.

Finally, Jim Pace and Anton Hinton emerged. It was Court's first look at the billionaire behind all this madness, but he didn't linger on the man, because he still hadn't seen Zoya.

He all but stormed up to Pace.

"Where's Anthem?" Pace asked.

Court stopped in his tracks. "I left her with you."

Pace looked around. "I thought she came here."

Court shook his head, fear and anger boiling suddenly in him. "No. She went with—"

Anton Hinton spoke up suddenly. "Did she leave with Kimmie?"

Travers had overheard the conversation. "The woman in the red top? Yeah, she did. Why?"

Hinton shrugged. "Well, if they're not here, then I guess that means the Chinese have her."

Court ran up to the man, stuck his gun in his chest, and pinned him against the wall. All around him Ground Branch officers shouted at him to lower his weapon, but he didn't even hear them. "What the *fuck* are you talking about?"

"Gareth and I have had suspicions about her recently. I think she's SSF, from a PLA electronic warfare unit. Sent to work here to spy on me."

Court's voice cracked a little. "Where . . . where would she take her?"

He thought a moment. "To Beijing, I'd guess."

Court started to press the trigger of the weapon, but Chris Travers grabbed the barrel and moved it. A shot cracked off, ricocheted around the room, and all the Ground Branch men cussed loudly.

Travers disarmed Court now, and Hash grabbed him by his arms right before he threw a punch at the unarmed New Zealander.

Court turned to Pace. "Why the fuck is he even still alive?"

"Orders, Violator. I am to bring him back to the U.S."

"Why? So we can install our own version of Cyrus? Look around you. Look at what this thing has done."

Hinton said, "I can rebuild it. I can fix it to where it will never be a—"

"Fuck you!" Court shouted, and then he lunged forward, only to be tackled to the ground by Hash and Fish.

Zack charged at the Ground Branch men now, but with his broken rib it was no big effort for a couple of unwounded Alpha Mike men to impede his advance, restraining his arms.

Pace looked on, a conflicted expression on his face. "I'm sorry, guys. There's nothing I can do."

He turned away, headed for the ramp to the open air so he could make a call on his sat phone.

Court was disarmed, then pulled to his feet and walked out into the night, Zack right next to him. The CIA men kept their guns up because no one knew where the Cubans were, but now that Pace was in the open, he tapped a button on the device, then tapped the speaker button so those around could hear.

Repult and Travers sent four of their men out to procure vehicles for what they all assumed would be a very low-probability escape attempt.

An officer in the operations center in Langley answered, completed the identity check, and said, "Be advised. Satellite shows all Cuban forces have retreated to garrison. Your way clear should be unopposed, at least for a few minutes."

"Roger," Pace said. "Interrogative, did anyone else leave this facility in the past fifteen mikes?"

"Negative, not at that building, but a pair of Chinese Z-8 transport helos landed at the dormitory building about two minutes ago. A group of eight left the dormitory and boarded; one of the number was restrained. They are already back in the air, heading east."

They'd taken the tunnel, Court now realized. "Going where?" he demanded.

Pace didn't relay the question to Langley, because he answered it himself. "Probably Matanzas. It's a PLA base. Thousands of Chinese soldiers." Pace shook his head. "We'll get her back, but not today."

Court's knees went weak, but the injured Zack stepped up and now he grabbed Court by the shoulders, steadying him. "Let's get out of this mess, and we'll go after her together, brother."

Four Hinton Labs SUVs pulled up, and the men began climbing inside.

Zoya Zakharova sat with her hands cuffed behind her back and then chained to an eyebolt on the floor of the big cargo helicopter. Armed men surrounded her. The helo's two doors were open; the noise was incredible, making her head pound, but after just a few minutes in the air, she felt a new presence next to her, as Major Liu placed a headset on her ears, then sat down in front of her.

"Now we can talk."

"Where are you taking me?"

"To our base here in Cuba. From there . . . I am not certain, but I have my suspicions."

"To China, obviously."

She shook her head. "Don't be so sure. Days ago, when Cyrus told me you were involved in all this, I told my leadership. They spoke with our friends in Moscow, told them we knew the whereabouts of one of their most wanted, and then bringing you in became my secondary mission objective." She smiled a little. "Since my main objective has failed, you might be the only thing that keeps me from getting a bullet in my brain when I return to Beijing."

Zoya looked down. She understood.

The Chinese military officer confirmed her worst fears. "I think you will be sent to Russia. We will get something from them for you, I am certain, but I don't know what." She shrugged. "I am happy to give you up. You and your people destroyed an operation that has been in progress for more than five years. I would cut you open like a fish at the market if it was left up to me, but apparently you are valuable to someone for something."

She leaned close, into Zoya's face. "Be glad."

Zoya lunged forward, but only a few inches, because something grabbed her and yanked her back hard.

The Chinese man behind her had her in a headlock, and she was pulled down to the floor of the helo.

Major Liu knelt over her, a smile on her face. "Relax, woman. Fighting will do nothing but tire you, and you and I have a very long journey ahead."

Zoya shut her eyes, and she thought of Court, only Court, and she prayed that he had somehow survived.

The sun was not yet up when five vehicles rolled into a farm a few miles west of the town of Aguada de Pasajeros. A middle-aged couple stood on the porch of a ramshackle little house, a fenced-in area full of hogs off to the right, a trio of old, beat-up cars on blocks next to a tiny barn.

The doors to the SUVs began opening, and ambulatory Americans began hurriedly carrying or otherwise assisting their wounded comrades out and towards the little home.

The couple didn't speak English, but they bade the men forward, through the door.

Jim Pace climbed out of the rear vehicle, and then he opened a back door, took Anton Hinton by the shoulder, and pulled him out. They stood there while the worst of the wounded were rushed in, and then they began trailing the others.

There were a total of nineteen men in the entourage, eighteen Americans plus Anton Hinton, and the last two out of a vehicle were Court Gentry and Zack Hightower. The men had been disarmed but not restrained, and they'd minded their manners for the past three hours while the convoy fled the Havana area on their way to Guantanamo Bay.

The original plan was to just switch vehicles here; a group of local agents had prepared transportation, but Pace had determined that a couple of the men might not survive the drive all the way across the country, and then the clandestine boat ride to get into the U.S. base on the southeastern tip of the island, so he'd requested medical personnel.

A single doctor and three nurses were inside waiting, with all the medical equipment they needed to patch up any wounds, set any broken bones, treat any possible infections. There was no surgical suite here, but the doctor was accustomed to doing good work with limited resources and would do the best with what he had.

Pace trailed Court and Zack, and while everyone else went inside, the older man reached out and put his hand on Court's shoulder.

Court turned to him, anger, exhaustion, tension all visible on his face. "What?"

Pace looked off towards the hogs in the predawn. "What happened to Anthem. That's on me."

"On you?"

"She wanted me to blow the servers and get down there and support you. Watkins had ordered me to upload Cyrus if I could, so I denied her request." He sighed. "If I just blew that place to hell at the beginning, she wouldn't have gone off on her own to help you."

This weighed on Court a moment. Finally, he said, "Not your fault, Jim. Hinton's the one to blame."

They continued on towards the porch and then into the house.

Inside, Court saw that the worst of the injured had been taken off to a back room with a doctor and a nurse, and two nurses, Black women in their thirties, worked on the walking wounded.

Anton Hinton had been sat in a chair in the living room; Hightower stood across from him.

Other Ground Branch men stood at windows, pulling security, while Jim Pace took out his sat phone to make a call in the kitchen.

Court stood there in the doorway, his eyes locked on the billionaire across the room, the fury in his heart all-consuming.

Mike One stood next to him, drinking water from a CamelBak that he held in his hands, his rifle on his back, his pistol in its holster on his hip. The man was pretty banged up himself, Court saw, and his clothing and equipment were blackened with soot.

The man dropped the nozzle of the CamelBak, closed his exhausted eyes for a moment, and started to wipe his dirty face with his hands.

When his arms were raised to do this, Court reached out, pressed the retention button on the man's holster, and pulled Larry Repult's gun off his hip.

Before Mike One could react, before *anyone* could react, Court pointed the gun at Anton Hinton.

After a second of hushed silence, nearly everyone in the room began shouting. Men raised weapons at Court, belted orders for him to drop the gun and get down on his knees, and Pace ran out of the little kitchen and into the confined space full of big men, body odor, and fury.

The two nurses fled to the back room, leaving the wounded behind.

Joe Takahashi leveled his pistol at Zack Hightower at a distance of just a few feet now, unsure if the two men were working together on whatever the fuck was going on.

Court Gentry was the coolest person in the room. Calmly and quietly, he said, "Jim. I am walking out of here with Hinton."

Hinton looked absolutely terrified, and Pace didn't seem much better. "Wha . . . what for?"

"I'm going to use him to get Anthem back."

Pace shook his head. "You can't. You can't, Court. Giving Hinton back to the Chinese is just going to give them the weapon. Maybe not instantly, but in three years, five years . . . at some point Hinton will get engineers and scientists back up to speed and they will replicate, maybe even improve Cyrus, or something even worse. They will lose control of it."

"But you want to give him to America," Court said, his eyes still locked on Hinton, his target. "You don't think they will do the same thing? You don't think we'll lose control of it, too?"

To this, Pace said, "I . . . I don't know. But I *do* know China can't be allowed to take it."

Now Zack spoke. "Pace, Hinton told me himself that Cyrus was designed to defeat the Chinese once it was deployed by them. How do you know he won't do the same to America?"

"I don't know, Zack. I have my orders. That's all."

Court stepped up closer to Hinton; most of the guns in the room stayed on him.

"Well I . . . I don't have any orders. Maybe I'll just do him right here."

"You do that and you never walk out of here," Pace said. "You never get the chance to rescue Anthem." Court said nothing. Pace stepped up close to him. "Listen to me. Put the gun down now. You do that, and here's what

I'll do. I'll call DDO Watkins right now and tell him you helped us through this whole thing. I'll tell him your friend was taken by the Chicoms, and I will persuade him to put the full force of Agency operations behind getting her back.

"I swear to God, Gentry. Put the gun down, and you are giving Anthem her best chance for survival."

Slowly, reluctantly, Court lowered the weapon, let it hang by the trigger guard from his finger, and Jim Pace carefully took it away from him.

Travers lowered his own weapon, took Court by the shoulder, and said, "Come on, brother. Let's go to the kitchen and get some coffee."

Court just stood there, his eyes on Hinton still. He saw the relief wash all over the son of a bitch, and he wished like hell there were some way to stop him that wouldn't also condemn Zoya.

A quick movement on his right, a shout of alarm, and then guns rose again all around, swiveling to that direction. Travers brought his gun back up to Gentry's head, but Court wasn't even moving, other than to turn and watch Zack Hightower as he snatched the SIG pistol out of the hand of Joe Takahashi, then spun it around and, with no hesitation whatsoever, shot Anton Hinton center mass.

After the report of the single gunshot faded, Zack dropped the pistol, threaded his hands behind his head, and said, "Do what you have to do, fellas. *I* just did."

Hinton wheezed, and his eyes held a look of utter confusion as he peered down at the bullet hole right over his heart.

With a long, slow sigh, the multibillionaire died, sitting there on a chair in a farmhouse in central Cuba.

Fish checked him, looked up to Pace, and shook his head.

As Zack was forced to the ground, he bellowed with pain from his broken rib.

Pace cussed, looked at Court with anger, and then stormed back into the kitchen to tell Langley that Hinton was dead.

Zack shouted from the floor as he was being handcuffed. "That was all me, Jim. Your deal was with Violator. Keep your fucking promise."

Court stood there in a daze; Travers lowered his weapon again and holstered it, and then he walked away.

EPILOGUE

Court Gentry stood on the second-story balcony of Matthew Hanley's Bogotá apartment, watching a thick black thunderhead form over the Eastern Hills, indicating that late-afternoon storms were imminent. Flashes of lightning crackled in advance of the clouds, and the rumbles that followed grew in volume with each strike.

He'd arrived an hour earlier, after taking less than a day to get off the island of Cuba, and another day of circuitous travel to Colombia. His body hurt, his brain was exhausted, and the stress he felt was like nothing he'd ever known.

It had been two and a half days since the attack at the Lourdes SIGINT headquarters building, but it felt like a year, because all he could think about was what Zoya was going through right now.

The gate of the small enclosed parking lot below him opened automatically, an SUV pulled in, and Matt Hanley climbed out.

Instantly he stared up at the man on his balcony, then leaned down and said something to his driver, pulling his keys out of his raincoat to unlock the door.

The driver stayed where he was, and Court just stood there, watching darkness cover the hills.

A minute later the big man stepped out onto the balcony next to him, admiring the impressive light show himself. After a moment, he said, "'Bout ten minutes till it all goes to hell."

"It's already gone to hell."

Hanley sighed. "Figured you'd show up. I talked to Jim this morning. He told me everything that happened. I'm sorry."

A louder crack of thunder told both men Hanley's weather prediction had been optimistic.

Hanley said, "Hell of a thing about Zack and Hinton."

Court thought of Zack, wondered where he was, how he was being treated. "Buys us a few years till Armageddon, I guess."

Hanley said, "I hear that's what Zack keeps saying. As a sidebar, Pace told me that he agrees. Langley isn't happy, of course. Not sure how it's all going to shake out for Jim or for Zack, but I'd say both of them did a damn fine job, considering."

Court said nothing.

Hanley changed the subject. "You want help getting Anthem back from the Chinese."

"That's right."

"And you think I, down here in Colombia, have the juice to make that happen?"

Court said, "I think I have to start somewhere, and you used to be the DDO. You know people, organizations, institutions."

"All true. Which is why I already know she's not in China."

Court turned as thunder rumbled. "What?"

"A private plane left Matanzas about twelve hours after she was brought there by helo. It flew direct to Moscow. Our satellite couldn't see who boarded because one person had a bag over their head."

He paused, then said, "The person's hands were in shackles."

"Major Xinyue Liu, aka Kimmie Lin, was a passenger on the flight, so *you* do the math."

"Russia will execute her." Court said it softly, looking back to the impending weather.

Hanley shook his head. "You don't know that. And even if they do, they'll probably want a big show trial, something to scare other turncoats in the intelligence services. Think about it. They wouldn't take her all the way there just to shoot her in the back of the head. We've got some time."

Court could feel his emotions getting the better of him, and he fought to regain control. Before he could speak, Hanley said, "You should reach out to your friend Lacy, as well. She might be able to provide some back-channel intel that I'm not privy to."

Court just said, "I'll reach out to everyone I know, do whatever I have to do. I've got old contacts in Russia; if they're still alive, they *will* help me."

Hanley said, "I'll make some calls myself."

Court nodded. The first drops of rain announced themselves loudly on the corrugated overhang above them. He turned away from the storm for the first time. "I appreciate you, Matt. Just know, Zoya would do the same for you."

Hanley nodded. "I've got some ideas of where to start with this. Come on in, let's hit the ground running, because Anthem doesn't have time to spare."

The storm arrived in force, and the two American men retreated inside the darkened Bogotá apartment.

Then they went to work.

ACKNOWLEDGMENTS

I'd like to thank Joshua Hood (JoshuaHoodBooks.com), Brad Taylor (BradTaylorBooks.com), Mike Cowan, Jon Harvey, Barbara Peters, and Mystery Mike Bursaw.

I'd especially like to thank Allison Greaney, Trey Greaney, Kristin Greaney, and Barbara Guy, along with Ava, Sophie, and Kemmons Wilson.

Much gratitude goes to my literary agent, Scott Miller of Trident Media Group, and my film agent, Jon Cassir of CAA. As always, a special thanks to my editor, Tom Colgan, and all the incredible staff at Berkley Books, including Carly James, Jin Yu, Loren Jaggers, Bridget O'Toole, Elise Tecco, Tina Joelle, Jeanne-Marie Hudson, Craig Burke, Christine Ball, Claire Zion, and Ivan Held.

Humble appreciation goes to my amazing copyeditors and proofreaders, as well as the incredible art department at Penguin Random House, and all the editors and staff who publish the foreign editions of my books, along with the amazing Jay Snyder and the great people at Audible.com.